Will Colhoun was born in Ireland and educated at Portora Royal and Cookstown High School before studying Speech and Drama at Stranmillis College, Belfast.   Subsequently he completed an M. A. at Edge Hill College, and later was awarded a Doctorate in Creative Writing at Lancaster University.

Some of his poetry was included in *Trio Poetry*, published by Blackstaff Press.

His working career was spent teaching English in schools in Ireland and England, and he now divides his time between writing, walking and managing his gardens and woodland.

A Price to Pay

To Jacquie, Laura, Glenda and Naomi with love.

My wife Jacquie, for her constant love, support and encouragement. Without her invaluable assistance this book would not have materialized.

My daughters, Laura, Glenda and Naomi for being the people they are.

PREFACE

I'm Irish. Irish and Freud of it. The sport with the punferals goes, as they say, with the territory; an expression of the split personality, comedy/tragedy identity shisis and birthmark of the sentient whose lot includes Ulster and Protestantism.

At the heels of the hunt I'm one of many: an Irishman from the North who immigrated to England. I babbled in verse, and then committed myself to writing a novel, despite possessing scant knowledge of the literature of my homeland. Joyce, Beckett, Wilde, Sterne and Swift aside, I was ignorant of the creative history of the novel written by men and women from my country of origin. Like me they would have to have worked in English as I have no grasp of the mother tongue.

That aside I determined to check out the opposition, come up with some facts about their fiction. The fiction not the factotum; anyone can look up biographical detail, so I would give it sparse attention. I would stick to their stories, select key passages and compile a slender book of evidence. Maybe I could come up with some insights into their motivations, what had driven them to commit their times on paper.   I might even pick up a few hints along the way.

Who knows…?

As for that novel, in my head there's a tangled mesh-mess of story but I'm in no mood for unravelling it yet and besides I can't decide whether the I/Me, I/She should be a first, a third or even a second (whoever that is) person.   No rush, I'll sit on it for a bit and keep myself in suspense.   I mean, the more I think about it the more I understand the word is my oyster.   Omniscient is what I am.   As for you Dear Reader, I envy your lot, I really do – you'll get two for the price of one; not a bad deal!   And you can read them in any order or not at all as your mood moves you.   I wish I had that kind of freedom!

Anyway while we ponder, instead of paring our fingernails, what about a bit of that Lit/ Crit/Crib to upset your appetite?

DEAN SWIFT TO OSCAR WILDE

FROM IRELAND: THE

NOVEL

WRITTEN IN ENGLISH

J. Carson

Contents

PART ONE: THE

EIGHTEENTH CENTURY

ONE

In 1169 the Norman-French rulers of England turned their
attention to Ireland and landed a force in Wexford.   This event
marked the onset of a political struggle between the two countries
that in one way or another has continued until the present day.
The struggle in Ireland for emancipation from England, was fought
out in literary as well as in political terms.   Within their texts Irish
writers resisted English literary expression and attempted to forge
separate artistic identities.   For many novelists, the page became
the battleground and there defiance was mounted against the
crushing power of the English realist model.   The middle march
was largely an English accomplishment; writers from Ireland
wanted to strut their own stuff.

In our times, theories proposing links between nationality
and cultural expression tend to be viewed with suspicion.   Today
emergent states are more likely to merge and national
idiosyncrasies become subsumed.   Now the dominant view sees
nationalism as a base form of tribalism and so passé; the prime
signifier of a people's enlightenment rests in their willingness to

cast off what are seen as the chains of nationality and embrace their neighbours.   No island is an island any more.

However this high-minded view continues to be challenged by sporadic and sometimes enduring outbursts of national feeling. The potency of nationalism cannot be underestimated and it is nowhere more compelling than in a region where it has been aggressively displaced.   From around 1170 the island of Ireland was subjected to first Norman then later English conquest.   The English colonial occupancy was crowned in 1541 when Henry V111 appropriated the title 'King of Ireland'.   A title does not necessarily bequeath entitlement and in the minds of the indigenous populace nationalist fervor became if anything more embedded.

Ireland was by then Christian and Catholic (due chiefly to the missionary work of Patrick in the fifth century).   Unable to overpower the island militarily, during the sixteenth and seventeenth centuries experiments in plantation were conducted as a way to embed English civilization and the Protestant religion in strategic areas of the country.   Such settlements proved financially viable in that they could be employed to reward English soldiers at little cost to the crown and the new landowners were pressed to pay back revenue to England. The placing of loyal English and Scottish Protestant settlers in Ireland as counters to the hostile Celtic/Catholic population was viewed as a win-win solution. The irony was that these ostensibly civilizing planters existing henceforth in a state of physical and mental siege came to forge a new frontier nationality which, as it came to age, proved just as resistant to English manipulation.

In ancient Ireland the poet or *file* was not only held in high regard, but also feared. In a warrior orientated society, reputation was valued highly and so the *file's* words had significant weight in that they might not only praise but could also damage the warrior's prestige. Care was therefore taken not to offend them. The story goes that Guaire, a feared king of Connacht in the seventh century, slighted a *file* who responded by going on hunger strike at the king's palace. Even though king Guaire personally offered him food and begged him to eat, the *file* Seanchan chose to die. The hunger strike, that powerful political weapon in Ireland, has respectable literary antecedents.

The *file* was integrated into the machinery of government in that he was charged with keeping a record of laws. One the one hand a civil servant coping with bureaucratic restrictions and on the other a free thinking artist and creator of wild and fantastic tales, the bygone Gaelic bard provided a behavioural model for writers from Ireland down through the ages. All participated in the telling of lies with style while paradoxically conveying the impression that the fabrication was not fictional but fact. That is the craft of storytelling. Ireland was a place where the novel, once invented, would surely find a home.

Triumphalist Protestantism reached its defining moment at the defeat of the Catholic King James 11 and his army by the forces led by William of Orange at the Battle of the Boyne in 1690. The foundation of the Ascendancy, with the consequent economic and educational penalization of Catholics in Ireland dates from that time. The Catholic religion of the mass of the population was treated as inferior, while the Protestant Established church of Ireland conferred a source of privilege through the establishment of a Protestant elite.   Out of all this there emerged that Janus-like category of persons who inhabited Catholic Ireland but were of Protestant English or Scottish descent: the Anglo Irish.   It was this ruling class that produced the early novelists from Ireland.

So there you are.   By now you could be forgiven for thinking that like a Protestant on a horse I've galloped through the bog lands of early Irish history at a rollicking rate and not given a shamrock about the sensibilities trampled on along the way.   Not true. Believe me when I say that I have reined in any tendency to ride roughshod.   I know the terrain is treacherous so have proceeded with extreme care.   Yet it's certain I will have offended some. You run a gauntlet when you write about Ireland - especially if you have a name like mine...

Any road this seems as good a time as any to take a breather and try to kick-start that fiction I mentioned earlier.

A START

ONE

In some film it was John Wayne, I think, acting the part of somebody tough, as he invariably did, who drawled ("said" didn't seem fitting for Wayne, so, as you will have noticed, I used the more descriptive "drawled") that to apologize was a sign of weakness. Incidentally that second time I called Wayne by his surname, something I would never have dreamed of doing if I had ever been talking to him in person. Writers can get away with that kind of thing and call all kinds of important people by their second name only: Swift, Sterne, Wilde, Joyce (that's a second name by the way), Beckett... You can even do it with women though I can't ward off a slight *frisson* (that's written that special way as it is French. I could have used an English word but writers do that kind of thing and don't have to apologize. That would be a sign of weakness) when I go: Austen, Edgeworth, Bronte, Eliot...in case you didn't know the latter's first name was George but she's still a woman. (That's a literary conundrum. I think.) Mind you, as they say in literary parlance, the context would have made that clear.   (I nearly fell into the trap of writing "literary circles" but that would have been a cliché and writers avoid those like the plague.   That last bit's a cliché, but I left it in deliberately, because then I could make a literary joke.   I think. The wider space there was a comic effect that made the joke even funnier.   I think.)   I bet you're glad that's over (at this point what you're going through is a spasm of comic relief).

What about the brackets or parenthesis as the literary critics (they're like food critics, only more vicious and writers do their best not to offend them, which probably is a sign of weakness) call them?   Am I seasoning my textual mix (that's a metaphor and writers use those to make their prose more lofty) with too much spicy verbiage (that's an example of an extended metaphor; think of a ladder that can be made longer and longer so that it can reach up to the ceiling and then into the loft if the customer wishes). Critics call that an image.

Back to those parenthesis.   I confess I looked up parenthesis in my dictionary.   (l looked up "dictionary" in my dictionary or I might have spelled it with an "ery".   I have trouble with my erys and arys).   I have my dictionery (well it's not mine,

its Collins really) with me at all times and always consult it when

in doubt.   As you will have noticed I did not follow my own

advice there and was guilty of a flagrant miss-spelling.   No

apology; I did it deliberately in a crack at another literary joke.

I used to use my Thesaurus (well really it's more accurate to

call it Roget's) till I realized it's too much like a literary condom

(that's a simile; I bet you saw that one coming).   I mean, it stops

you being in touch with the real thing.   I mean your own words,

the ones inside you, the writer.   They need to be allowed to spill.

Stain the page with spontaneous ejaculations is the best advice I

can offer to embryonic young authors.*

I hope that last paragraph wasn't too long.   I might go back

over it later and tighten it all up.   Writers do that a lot.   They

read over again and again and cleanse the pages of all those

spontaneous ejaculations.   It's by far the worst part of the job, the

bit I hate most of all.   All that drafting and re-drafting, worrying

about whether you used the best possible word in the best possible

place, about whether you were concise enough.   I mean I read somewhere that it's what you leave out that counts most. Maybe

I should have left it **all** out, not started in the first place. Perhaps

the whole enterprise is a mistake.

Writers are like that - very nervous about their calling,

always doubting. Take me for instance. I mean I just started

and then went on. What you see before your eyes I shot straight

down on the page. Don't get me wrong, I mean I did think of you

and tried my best to pleasure you but to be honest (and I would

like us to have that kind of relationship - one where I can tell it as

it is) my private satisfaction was paramount. And is that so

terrible? I mean if I don't like it what would be the point? I

hope it's good for you, I thrust (wrong word there but I'll leave it

in; sometimes I can't stop myself) I'm stimulating you but I can

only do that when I'm pleasuring myself. Otherwise I might

begin to feel the whole thing is just a meaningless grind and I have

too much respect for you to want just that out of our relationship.

I'm sure you do too; you wouldn't have put up with me this long if

you weren't a sensitive soul.

Definitely no irony intended there by the way; not that with your intelligence I need to point that out.   No irony in that remark

either, nor in that…   Nor in that…   LOOK I'M SORRY

(writers do this to make their voice louder. Is the opposite the

case?   I mean: can you hear this?)   IF I'VE OFFENDED YOU!   I

DIDN'T MEAN TO!   I'm sorry.

    There I've apologized.   I can do no more.

*At this point I took a break and for a variety of reasons did not

return to the page for about four months.   Could you tell?

Enough said.   The font is dry.   I've typed myself into a cul-de-

sac, hit a writer's block and can go no further.   I've lost the plot

and need to sort things out before I start again.   Next time I think

I'll take a route that avoids too many comic turns; no wonder we

crashed to a standstill.   While we're waiting I think I'll steady the

old nerves with another dose of the literary stuff.

TWO

Writing of any kind is attached to other writings. The English

novel, harbinger of the novel from Ireland, was itself indebted to a

European model. Translated into English in 1612, the Spanish

Miguel De Cervantes's *Don Quixote,* describes the picaresque

progress of the eponymous hero as he encounters different persons

and becomes involved in various adventures…*Don Quixote* also

contains an element of satire aimed at the society depicted in the

novel. At the heart of the early novel in English from Ireland,

these two themes dominate: the idea of a chronological,

geographical and psychological journey; and social criticism of the

people and places the hero, or much less frequently the heroine,

encounters.

Social as well as literary forces acted to promote the

emergence of the novel in Ireland. In 1550 printed material

became possible when Humphrey Powell set up his printing press

in Dublin. Then in 1591 the University of Dublin was founded to

provide knowledge and civility which previously Irishmen had

sought at English and Scottish universities, or even those in

France, Spain or Italy. The new university in Dublin proved a haven for inspiring writers and one such student at Trinity College was Jonathan Swift. After graduating, Swift left his native land and immigrated to England, where he entered the Church. Ironically he was later posted back to Ireland, when in 1713 he was appointed Dean of St Patrick's Cathedral in Dublin.

Back in Ireland Swift missed the intellectual stimulation afforded by his companions at the Scriblerus Club: Pope (not the, but the poet), the pamphleteer John Arbuthnot and the poet and dramatist John Gay. Enforced outsider from England Swift was ever a cultural outsider in Ireland where the language, music and dancing was 'foreign' to his Anglo/Irish heritage.

Ireland grew on Swift however and he became increasingly uneasy with its colonial and cultural position vis-à-vis the 'mainland' of England. An example of his subsequent openness to Irish literary expression was his collaboration with the poet Aodh Mac Gabhran and the blind harper Turlough Carolan (there's a trio for you). Swift wrote an English rendition of Mac Gabhran's poem *Plearaca na Ruorcach* (*O'Rourke's Feast*) which

Carolan set to music.   The conclusion, a splendidly ribald finale to an Irish celebratory occasion, must surely have afforded the translator great pleasure in the rendering:

What stabs and what cuts,

What clattering of sticks,

What strokes on the guts,

What bastings and kicks,

Come down with that beam,

If cudgels are scarce,

A blow on the weam,

Or a kick in the Arse.

The free-wheeling gusto of these lines illustrates perfectly how writers from Ireland in the eighteenth century and subsequently, while mastering the discipline of the English model, resorted at intervals to an outbreak of lawlessness in their mode of telling. Such rejection of propriety was a two - fingered gesture against the literary authority exerted by the Anglo side of their Irish identity.

Gulliver's Travels (1726) And the four voyages of Captain Lemuel Gulliver are at one and the same time a soaring flight of literary imagining and a satire on four aspects of 'civilized' humankind: physical, political, intellectual and moral. By adopting the persona of his central character Swift was able to intrigue his reader about the source of the narrative voice: when is it the author, when his character? This apparent surrender of authorial voice through adopting that of his protagonist, gave the lie that is fiction a carapace of truth and became a feature of imaginative writing in English from Ireland from Swift onwards. First person narrative evolved inexorably into stream-of-consciousness and restricted point-of-view narratives that heralded the modern movement in literature.

Like its English predecessor *The Life and Strange Surprizing Adventures of Robinson Crusoe* (1719), *Gulliver's Travels* (1726) is presented to the reader as an account of a voyage at sea and the subsequent mishaps that follow. Like Crusoe, Gulliver narrates his tale and through the telling we are led to understand his progress from being a child and man amongst family and acquaintances, to his peculiar form of personal enlightenment where he prefers the smell and conversation of his two horses to the company of humans, including his wife and children. An example of merging between author and central character can be detected here. In a letter to his friend the English poet Alexander Pope, written in 1725, Swift had opined:

I have ever hated all Nations, Professions and Communities; and all my love is towards Individuals; for instance, I hate the tribe of Lawyers, Physicians, English, Scotch, French and the rest. But principally I hate and detest that animal called Man, though I heartily love John, Peter, Thomas, and so forth.

Gulliver is allowed to pursue his creator's maxim to a more extreme position and this pushing of human aspiration to its most logically extreme absurdity is the essence of the satire that runs throughout the novel. In it, Swift attacks humans when they surrender their individuality to the group and focusses continually on the shocking difference between what humankind professed to be and what, beneath all the layers of artifice, it really was.

While *Robinson Crusoe* was presented throughout in realistic terms, *Gulliver's Travels* contains much that is pure fantasy and unbridled soaring of imagination. For what it's worth my favourite blend of fantasy and social comment occurs during Gulliver's stay with the Lilliputians where a war kicks off because of a dispute over whether an egg should be properly addressed by breaking it at the little end (the orthodox view) or the big end (the heretic view). These disputatious Little Enders and Big Enders cleverly lampoon warring theological fighting between Catholics and Protestants in Ireland.

Gulliver is massive in size compared to the inhabitants of Lilliput and then miniscule to those in Brobdingnag; with the Houyhnhnms he appears as uncouth, while compared to the Yahoos he is refined. Through all these incongruities runs a rich, labyrinthine vein of political, psychological, social and physical innuendo that scholars are still seeking to tap. And all this rich mixture of fact and fantasy, realism and imagination, logic and absurdity set in fabulous locations like Lilliput, Brobdingnag,

Laputa, Balnibarbi, Glubbdubdrib, Luggnag and Japan is held together by a realist form of English prose that is both plain and simple.   Indeed to ensure it remained so, Swift apparently read passages to his servants to ensure clarity was being sustained.

This clear, direct style is illustrated perfectly by the novel's opening:

My father had a small estate in Nottinghamshire; I was the third of five sons.   He sent me to Emanuel College in Cambridge, at fourteen years old, where I resided three years and applied myself close to my studies…

Thereafter the most extraordinary events are recounted through language as plain and simple as that.

I would have liked Dean Swift.   And Lemuel Gulliver.   We would have got on like a ship on fire.   It's . . .

PART ONE

AS SIMPLE AS THAT

CHAPTER ONE

They married, were together for two months, and then what happened, happened.

She went back to work in the tiny office, hung up her coat, sat in her chair, opened the ledger to a new page and began entering the pounds, shillings and pence.   The simple arithmetic coaxed her through the day till on the bus home, when suddenly powerless to hold back a moment more, the tears began to spill. She removed her spectacles and wiped her eyes.   As far as she could tell no one was watching but anyway unable to stop herself she pressed her forehead to the glass then silently and with shoulders shaking, she wept.   At last her stop; a final rub at her eyes, her spectacles fumbled back in place then unto her feet, a deep breath and staring straight ahead she stumbled down the aisle. Not trusting her voice and fearful of making a show of herself she held back her customary thanks to the driver and swung unto the pavement before setting off up the hill to her house.   Their house: hers and his.

The night air was chill so not breaking her step and tucking her handbag under her arm with her free hand she pulled up the collar of her coat. Keeping up her usual short quick strides, if she met someone she recognized she would dip her head slightly then speed on. To stop and pass the time of day was not in her nature - never had been - she did little small talk or much talk of any kind for that matter and that made the last two months seem so unreal; like it was all a dream and now he was gone and the dream, their dream was gone too. Crying openly now she stumbled on up the hill and past the corner shop till at last and almost running, she veered left and into her road.

Three houses down, up the step unclasping her handbag, a fevered scrabble for her key then pop it in the lock, twist, shoulder the door open, retrieve her key then in and collapsing against it she slammed the door shut before back against it slid gratefully to the floor. She had made it and leaning back against the inside of the door she willed herself into the present, savoring the peace, soothed eventually by the hall clock's ticking till in a rush the milestones of the past two months played over and over inside her head…

That day because the sun was shining, instead of eating in the office and reading her book she walked to the park to have her sandwich and drink from her flask of tea sitting on a bench enjoying the fresh air, the open space and watching the children, the children with their mothers, playing.   In an instant all changed and she was fumbling in her handbag, knocking over her flask searching for her handkerchief as the tears fell and once again the day was ruined, she had spoiled it with her selfishness, her preoccupation with herself and her own petty problems.   The death of her parents; the trouble over the will; the terrible fall-out with her brother; ordinary families being happy and together: it was all too much!   Where was that handkerchief, she was sure it should be… Then she remembered swatting the insect on her ledger and using spittle on her handkerchief to clean the smudge on the page.   She could see it now still there on her desk.   What to do but take off her glasses, perch them on her knee and palms open cover her eyes with her fingertips while slivers of light raced across her vision and her eyeballs became sore with the pressure.

"Please I couldn't help... I was out for a walk and... I was wondering is there anything ...anyway I can help?"

That accent!

Startled her hands flew apart and she was blinking in the sunshine, unable to see, reaching for her glasses, which in her haste she had brushed off her knee, and this man was bending before her then straightening with her glasses dangling in one hand and in the other her flask.   Overcome with embarrassment she reddened in that way she could not stop and was conscious she must look a sight what with her blotchy skin and tear streaked face.   What must she look like, how could she possibly...

And then it became as right as rain.   He made it all right.

To start with he talked.   She was in too much of a state to really take notice of what he was saying but that did not seem to matter as the music was so matter of fact, so everything is going to be all right, worse things happen at sea everyone has a good old cry at some time or other especially these days what with all the uncertainty and here's your glasses and take this handkerchief there go on I don't need it only carry it out of habit and you're lucky I don't think your flask is broken and even on a day like this we can feel as if we have swallowed a cloud at times I know I do the only thing is we men aren't supposed to cry and I know there are times I wish that was not the case as it's the most natural thing in the world and I'm sure it must do you good so don't worry there's nothing to be ashamed of in shedding a few tears and do you mind me asking but were you crying over anyone in particular?

"Were you crying over anyone in particular?"

It was the query that broke the spell, that and a slight barely perceptible change of tone.

"Oh no there's no-one, I have no-one I was just... "

And then she could go nowhere with the thought, her words dried and she could not halt the blush of her embarrassment spreading again and the consciousness she was making a fool of herself when he did it again only this time as if it was the most natural thing in the world he sat on the bench beside her leaning forward elbows on knees his head tilted back looking away and not at her giving her time to find her handbag take out her compact

open it check the damage in the mirror dust on some powder and

even apply a little lipstick till all done and faced with the slope of

his back she could relax once more in the ebb and flow of his

meanderings.

I feel now's the time to tip-toe off and leave them be there in that

park on that bench in the sun.   Perhaps they'll still be there when

we return.   Then again, perhaps they will not.   Who knows?

THREE

After Swift, two profound influencers of the novel in Ireland were the English writers Samuel Richardson (1681-1761) and Henry Fielding (1704-1754). Of the two, Fielding had the greater impact, as his playful, iconoclastic approach had more resonance in Ireland than in England. There, the artful and more conventionally moral Richardson had the greater effect.

The History of Jack Connor by William Chaigneau was published in 1752. The author had been born in Ireland, then served oversees in the army and this is part of the fate of Chaigneau's eponymous hero, who in the end returns to Ireland, the country of his birth, where in a typical eighteenth century class reversal (Fielding's *Joseph Andrews* is a classic example) he is revealed as the natural son of a prosperous landowner.

The story initiates a theme subsequently popular in Irish literature: that of exile and, as in this case, the exile returned. During his picaresque adventures in England, Jack Connor experiences prejudice and intolerance. His return to Ireland and embracing his identity as a Protestant landowner has moral and political significance. Chaigneau's hero reveals sympathy for the Irish peasantry and for the descendants of 'The Wild Geese' (leaders of the Catholic army who fled abroad after defeat at the Battle of the Boyne) whom he encounters on his travels. As the son of a Protestant father and Catholic mother, Connor forges a personal identity, tolerant towards yet apart from both England and Ireland and in that sense his character can be viewed as a representation of the psyche of the Anglo- Irish class of which the author was a member.

That aside *The History of Jack Connor* speeds along in the Fieldingesque tradition of eighteenth century fiction. There is that ubiquitous theme of the English novel and drama of the period: what constitutes a good person and how can one distinguish the well-intentioned from the wicked, when humans can hide behind a cloak of hypocrisy thereby disguising their true natures and intentions? So it is that in Chapter III the parish priest visits Jack's mother and "surprised her in the act of *giving Suck*" (Author's italics.) The priest restrains her from covering the act, then:

"The sweet little fellow, said he, it looks like an Angel, I must kiss it, were it but for the sake of the Nurse."- He kept his Word; but guiding his Head a little more on one Side, he feasted his Lips (as if by accident) on these Charms his Eyes had been Witness of for half an Hour.

His Reverence recovered himself at last, and - "I ask your Pardon, good Mrs Connor, said he, for by my own Conscience I had no Harm in my Thoughts, but God forgive me! In troth I was going to t'other Side, for fear it would be jealous; tho' if I had, you know, there would be no Sin in it, neither, for what is a Breast but Flesh? And so is your hand and what Sin, my Dear, in touching a Hand?" - This Reasoning was so strong that Conviction sat on Mrs Connor's Countenance, which the good man perceiving, he very fervently transported his Kisses from one Side to the other."

Like Tom Jones or Joseph Andrews, Jack Connor struggles to preserve his Self in a world that is morally corrupt and abounding in envy, greed and hypocrisy.   His cultural pluralism and struggle to find and cling to his true self would not be out of place in the novel from Ireland in our present age.   The narrator's tone is often ironic, and employed frequently to direct satires at persons and institutions the hero encounters. Like its English equivalent, a large part of the novel's intention was to provide moral instruction; a function that persisted until the end of the nineteenth century.

CHAPTER TWO

"Pass the milk please, Mrs Noble."

His eyes were smiling and he conveyed that look of boyish concentration she so loved as he took the jug, added the milk, sprinkled sugar carefully on his porridge, stirred the mixture and began to eat slowly, pausing between each spoonful to pick up his napkin and dab at his mouth. All precise, neat and, and polite; qualities so characteristic of her – her husband. Just to watch him eating brought her warmth, calm and a rush of tenderness she had never felt before.

For till Peter - she thrilled still at her access to his Christian name- for until *Peter* blessed her with his company and then chose to be with her of all people, she had had no-one to love and no-one to care for her. Her parents were dead and her brother lived too far away and anyway he had his own family to think about and they had never been close. Not really and especially after that awful row over their parents' will. But hadn't she looked after them in their illness and dotage and anyway where else could she have lived. She dismissed the thought; for the first time in God knows how long she wanted to savor the here and now. For was she not on *her honeymoon*, a married woman, happier than she had ever been in her whole life and it had all happened so quickly that she had not even had the time to tell her brother or anyone else for that matter. It was all so - so not her. Over the last month there were times she felt she was a heroine in a movie like Bette Davis her favourite actresses who Peter had actually said she reminded him of. Perhaps she should take up smoking. No that would be a step too far but even thinking that thought was a product of the effect Peter had on her. He made her feel she could do all kinds of daring things. Why she had nearly... She blushed at the thought.

On *that* however she had stood firm and she was pleased she had remained so. Peter was glad too. He told her, said she was right to wait till their wedding night when he made it all, all so right with his gentleness and patience with her and her shyness and lack of any knowledge about, about how to make a man happy *in that way*.

"You haven't finished your porridge. I can heat it up for

you if you like." The landlady's voice shook her. Deep in thought, she hadn't heard her approach despite the fact they were the only guests in the small boarding-house Peter had found.

"No thank you, I, I…"

"Waste not, want not," and Peter reached across and stacking her plate on his took up his spoon. "It certainly is nothing to do with your cooking. My wife never eats all her porridge but if I guess right, from the, the lovely aroma coming from the kitchen she will doubtless do justice to the second course. Mmm that was great, you'll never know what you missed my dear," and spooning up the remains he smiled and handed both cleaned plates to the landlady who taking them smiled in return before padding off in (she could not help noticing) rather down at heel and threadbare slippers. That would explain why she had not heard her approach. A spot on the tablecloth caught her eye so, with the back of her hand she brushed it only to find it stayed stubbornly in place; not a crumb but a stain. Oblivious, Peter was buttering toast. He tended not to talk at mealtimes and she was glad - it gave her time to take stock, think her own thoughts.

Since meeting him the last few weeks had flown by so fast that she'd been caught up in the whole rollercoaster of it all, too exhilarated to ever want it to stop and yes, scared at times it would and she'd be thrown off and spun back into her old routine.

"There we are," and the landlady was reaching over her shoulder and placing a plate with bacon, an egg and fried bread before her, then reaching across and doing the same for her husband.

"Thank you Mrs Mullen, this is just what the doctor ordered!" exclaimed her husband rubbing his hands together and reaching for the salt.

"Thank you, thank you very much."   With a surge of warmth she felt suddenly drawn to their dowdy host who was, surely, trying only to please.

The landlady reached over, lifted the teapot and gave it a swirl.   "I'll fetch you a fresh pot of tea.   Just tuck in and enjoy yourselves.   My brother's a farmer - that's how I came by the bacon and eggs.   No worries about rationing yet.   Live for the day, that's what I say."

"And quite right too Mrs Mullen and don't you worry, everybody says that Hitler needs to be taught a lesson and he will be you mark my words, why…"

"Peter," and she stared him in his eyes and gave her head the tiniest shake, "could you pass the salt please." And after a surely imperceptible but still meaningful pause he reached for the cellar and mercifully the landlady (was she taking the hint) shuffled off with the teapot.

He was cross. She could tell and was mortified. But she was right she knew. Mrs Mullen was Catholic; her surname and that crucifix on the wall gave the game away. Being English, Peter simply could not read the signs. Across the border they said they were staying neutral but everyone knew Catholics hated the English more than the Germans. Why he had wanted to go to Bundoran for their honeymoon weekend; to cross the border and risk life and limb in the Free State.

With his accent!

She stole a glance across the table. Head down her husband was cutting up his bacon. She kept her eyes on his ruler straight hair parting till eventually he looked up and she smiled and

after only a slight pause Peter smiled too and straightaway all in

her world was as it should be. She picked up her knife and fork

determined to eat because she knew instinctively that would please

him. Cutting and pronging bacon and fried bread she dipped the

forkful in the fried egg. Deep yellow yolk oozed across the plate

and after a mouthful she found she was hungry, was actually

enjoying her food - a sensation she had not experienced in a long

while. She could have even eaten the second slice of bacon but

checked and instead positioning it between her knife and fork

maneuvered it across the table unto her husband's plate. He

looked up, raised an eyebrow, paused for a moment then bowed his

head and continued eating. In her heart of hearts she knew she

would do anything for this man, make any sacrifice because she

was honoured, grateful, and yes, privileged to be the one chosen to

be his wife in sickness and in (God grant) health as long as they

both should live.

She shivered at the thought of her greatest dread. Peter had

told her, not long after they met that he was waiting to be called up, that it could happen any week now. He wanted to do his bit

for the war effort. *Your Country Needs You* the posters screamed

and he was not going to dodge the challenge. No one would point

the finger at him - he was no shirker even if his job had protected

status and he could have legally avoided the draft. He was in the

construction industry and had been sent over from Preston to assist

on developments in road and runway making techniques. It was

all way over her head but the consequence of his patriotism

banished all considerations and she could only view the matter

selfishly. What could she do without him? How would she live

from day to day? It was too awful to even think about. He was

all she cared about in the whole world especially when (and the

memory made her smile even now) this man she loved so had gone

down on one knee on only their third meeting in the park and

asked her to marry him. It was sudden yes but the war was on

and people were seizing the moment because who knew there

might be no more moments to seize. More than anything she had

wanted to say yes there and then but it was all too much and all she

could do was shake her head, look at him and cry and cry. Then once again this love of her life, this wonderful man spoke and made all her worries dissolve. *He did not mind! He understood!* This was no world to marry and even think about bringing children into but he would be taken away soon and surely the two of them had a right to their happiness and she had no cause to worry for he had no wish to leave any wife of his alone and holding the baby and precautions could and would be taken and anyway and anyway and anyway…

He had talked on and on rubbing out worries that had never even crossed her mind but the words held no meaning for her – they were music; music for her ears and hers alone.

And looking across the table at her beloved as he mopped his plate with the heel of his toast she felt a swell of tenderness that so overcame her that it once again brought tears to her eyes so she bent, retrieved her handbag and fumbled for her handkerchief.

"Are you alright dear?   Is there anything wrong?   Can I…"

"No, no, honestly I, I'm just being silly.   It's just that I'm so happy.   It all came over me in a rush and I, I couldn't stop myself. I often cry when, when…"

Words failed her; there was nowhere she could guide this thought. She could not bring herself to say *when I am happy.* It simply would not be true because until this here and now she had never been so happy in her whole life. Flustered she felt herself redden and was on the verge of breaking down completely when the landlady's appearance saved the situation. Her husband, bless him, had not noticed the state she had worked herself into.

"Ah Mrs Mullen, that was delicious, just delicious. A cup of tea will make all right my dear," and he rubbed his hands together. "You mark my words."

As you mark mine Dear Reader. You mark mine.

FOUR

The po-faced narration of fantastic tales that are surrounded by realistic detail *and* that the narrator insists are *true* (*Gulliver's Travels!* How Swift haunts…) has always been a popular mode of telling in Irish fiction. This tackling of the task can be traced back to the Gaelic oral tradition of *seanchas*, a form of imaginative story telling that the reciter presented as authentic. In this way Thomas Amory's *The Life of John Buncle Esq.* (1756-66) opens with *A Preface by way of Dedication* addressed to *Gentlemen* in which the narrator assures the reader that his "*book…is to serve the interests of truth, liberty and religion, and to advance useful learning to the best of my abilities…*" Then, he continues: "*As to some strange things you will find in the following journal…however wonderful they appear to be, yet they are, exclusive of a few decorations and figures, (necessary in all works), strictly true.*"

Amory's central character is a devotee of Unitarianism, one who delights in religious dispute, in acquiring access to obscure learning, in appreciating the majestic beauty of nature (especially that of the English Lake District) and in acquiring a sequence of eight beautiful and reverent wives.   Above all, John Buncle is an inveterate story teller, fascinated by the history and culture of the people of Ireland and of the other regions of the world in which he travels.   Buncle's experience is delivered in the first person in an idiosyncratic, anecdotal fashion which serves to present the wildest fantasy as gospel truth.

As with predecessors like *Don Quixote* or *Gulliver's Travels*, *The Life of John Buncle Esq.* opens in the traditional picaresque mode.

On the first day of May then, early in the morning as the clock struck one, I mounted my excellent mare, and with my boy, OFin, began to journey as I had projected, on seeing how things went. I did not communicate my design to a soul, nor take my leave of anyone, but in the true spirit of adventure, abandoned my father's dwelling, and set out to try what fortune would produce in my favour. I had the world before me, and Providence my guide.

Buncle leaves Ireland and travels to England, where in the

market town of Harrogate, he encounters six men of his

acquaintance from Dublin, one of whom, Mr Gallaspy he describes

as follows:

He was the most profane swearer I have ever known: fought

everything, whored everything, and drank seven in hand; that is,

seven glasses so placed between the fingers of his right hand, that

in drinking liquor fell into the next glasses, and thereby he drank

out of the first glass seven glasses at once. This was a common

thing, I find from a book in my possession, in the reign of Charles

the Second, in the madness that followed the restoration of that

profligate and worthless prince. But this gentleman was the only

man I ever saw who could or would attempt to do it; and he made

but one gulp of whatever he drank; he did not swallow a fluid like

other people, but if it was a quart, pored it in as from pitcher to

pitcher.   When he smoaked tobacco, he always blew two pipes at

once, one at each corner of his mouth, and threw the smoak out of

his nostrils.

Such soaring and embroidery would not appear out of place on the pages of a novel by Flann O'Brien.

Then again, being silly for your Art is not an ignoble condition. Literature from England in Ireland could be viewed as yet another form of colonial imposition. In Donegal in the 1830's the British Army Engineer Corps began an ordinance survey of Ireland, mapping and re-naming place names and changing them from the Irish language into English to accord with the recent (1800) integration into the United Kingdom of Great Briton and Ireland (how that Great could grate). In some quarters this Anglicization of Irish place names was resented bitterly and viewed as a threat to Gaelic intellectual practice. In this context it is illuminating to quote from the views of Edmund Spencer (c. 1552-99), the English poet and colonial administrator who spent nearly twenty years in Ireland as an official of the government and later as one of the 'planter' settlers in Munster. Presenting the case for, no less than, the destruction of the Irish language, Spenser opined:

The wordes are the Image of the mynde, so as they proceeding from the mynde, the mynde must be needes affected with the wordes: So that the speech being Irishe, the harte must needs be Irishe, for out of the abundance of the harte the tongue speaketh.

Of course writers from Ireland who felt antagonized by English colonial strategy could always cock a snook (whatever that is) by writing in Irish, as some still do today. From this perspective, Anglo-Irish novelists in the eighteenth century could be categorized as collaborators, choosing to turn blind eyes to the aggressive displacement of their literary heritage, assimilating, rather than resisting the invader's scheming. Any resultant conscience pangs could be assuaged through involvement with antiquarian or revivalist movements or …by simply being silly.

The novelist from Ireland who writes in English has frequently been guilty of playing the fool within the text, messing around, introducing intrusive fantasy within a realist framework and attempting to shock. Such writers would demonstrate their skill at playing by the rules of English Literature, then go and commit cheeky fouls and thereby invite derision and possible censure.   Why?   Well acting the eejit in this way was partly a playing to the gallery, exploiting the stage Irishman's reputation for challenging any form of restraining authority.   In part also it was a form of literary freedom- fighting; a resistance in prose designed to stage a separate artistic identity.

To joke could help cast off the yoke!

Undoubtedly the play spirit is ubiquitous in literature from Ireland.   Perhaps it can be accounted for by a subconscious race memory dating back to tropes that emerged in ancient Gaelic literature.   Or can the spirit of play be attributed to a peculiar form of literary political consciousness?   Is the *modus operandi* of the Anglo/Irish writer a function of racial constitution or a reaction to the dichotomy arising from a dual cultural identity? Was it race remembrance or racial resolution; a bit of both; or neither?   No matter, there is no gainsaying the Anglo/Irish writer's comic inventiveness and arguably the greatest of them all was another clergyman, wit, traveler, philanderer and novelist - the incomparable Lawrence Sterne.

Had enough?   Want to leave all this speculative ruminating about a literary past that's dead and gone?   Well I'm sorry but I'm the one who makes the decisions around here.   I'll decide when we visit the Nobles again.   In the meantime be patient and I promise I'll do my best to make it all worth your while.

FIVE

It would not surely be out of order to designate Lawrence Sterne's *Tristram Shandy* as the original stream-of-consciousness text. Inventive and experimental in form the novel, like James Joyce's *Ulysses,* seeks to encompass everything by displaying the fleeting moment in all its multifarious complexity.   In this spirit, Sterne reins back the narrative at intervals to intrude one of many explanations of his craft.   In Book 1 Chapter XIV, for example:

Could a historiographer drive on his history, as a muleteer drives his mule-straight forward, for instance, from Rome to Loretto, without ever once turning his head either to the right hand or to the left,-he might venture to foretell you to an hour when he should get to his journey's end;-but the thing is, morally speaking, impossible: For, if he is a man of the least spirit, he will have fifty deviations from a straight line to make with this or that party as he goes along, which he can no ways avoid.   He will have views and prospects to himself perpetually soliciting his eye, which he can no more stop standing still to look at than he can fly; he will moreover have various

Accounts to reconcile;

Anecdotes to pick up;

Inscriptions to make out;

Stories to weave in;

Traditions to sift;

Personages to call upon;

Panegyrics to paste up at this door;

Pasquinades at that:-in short there is no end to it.

Sterne does not hold back but indulges his every impulse as, for example, when he deliberately holds back his hero's birth; includes blank, black and marbled pages and defies conventions of conventional chronology.   At the same time however he focusses with clarity and compassion on the idiosyncrasies and absurdities of human behaviour.   There is no end to his cheeky inventiveness and boy (or girl) does he love to shock.   An illustrative passage occurs in Book V Chapter XV11 where Sterne recounts his hero's accidental circumcision.   The artfully placed asterisks make a fitting accompaniment to the waggish tone.

*-The chamber-maid had left no ******* *** under the bed:*

-Cannot you not contrive, master, quoth Susannah, lifting up the

sash with one hand, as she spoke, and helping me unto the

window- seat with the other, - cannot you manage, my dear, for a

*single time to **** *** ** *** ******?*

I was five years old. – Susannah did not consider that nothing

was well hung in our family, - so slap came the sash down like

lightning upon us; - Nothing is left, - cried Susannah – nothing is

left – for me, but to run my country.-

My Uncle Toby's horse was a much kinder sanctuary; and so

Susannah fled to it.

Sterne is the eighteenth century exemplar of the writer from

Ireland as English drawing-room entertainer.   He came to London

in 1760 and was greeted with equal measures of acclaim and

disapproval.   Writers like Oscar Wilde in the nineteenth century

and Brendan Behan in the twentieth, owe much to his trail blazing.

A memorable testimony to *Tristram Shandy* is provided by the novel's closing lines:

-L--d! said my mother, what is all this story about?-

-A COCK and a BULL, said Yorick - And one of its best kind, I ever heard.

CHAPTER THREE

After breakfast they went for a walk and she explained to her husband about the crucifix, their landlady's surname, why it was so important and why, with his accent, he needed to be more careful.

"Oh, you Irish I'll…"

"Northern Irish Peter; there is a difference."

She was surprised at the firmness of her tone but felt duty bound to make her husband aware of the pitfalls and booby traps his Englishness could provoke. For her it was simply a matter of life and death. She was not, like some she knew, narrow minded or bigoted but loyalty to her Protestant faith was, until she met her husband, the most significant attachment in her life. Her father had marched on the Twelfth of July and worn his sash with pride. He had never missed an Apprentice Boys parade and had brought her up to respect the tradition while her mother told her stories about the suffering in the siege of Londonderry and was, if truth be told, more bitter about the past and suspicious of her Catholic neighbours than she, or her father, could ever be. Her brother, on the other hand, would have nothing to do with religion, the Lodge, or any sectarian marching.   Stubbornly he stood out against any involvement and that caused no end of rows with their parents. No wonder they left him little.   She slapped the back of her hand; a gesture adopted as a personal reprimand for unworthy thoughts. But there was some truth in it.   It was all very well for Peter to make light of the situation; where she was from, these things mattered.

To give him credit and to her relief her husband seemed to appreciate the depth of her feeling and take on board her concern for him and they spoke no more of the matter.

The rest of that day they held hands, walked, talked, laughed, looked at people, peeped into shop windows and in this way the day flew by.   After their evening meal, at her husband's insistence they went to a public house where he drank pints of Guinness while she, again at his behest, had two glasses of whisky and water.   Then clinging together they made their way back to the guest house where Peter pretended to fumble fitting their key into the lock then with his finger to his lips made exaggerated schussing noises as they climbed the stairs.   Undressing he continued his tom-foolery, at one point going so far as to goose-step round the bed his arm extended in a comic parody of the German foe; then stubbed his toe and so milked his hurt, hopping about grotesquely on one foot, that she laughed till she hurt and felt she would die laughing.

In their lovemaking she clasped her husband tightly, held his head and looked into his eyes with tears in her own as he moved on top of her.   Then when he groaned and finished she held him tight not minding his weight, just not wanting to let go, holding on, trying to make this time last for as long as she could.   For deep inside her lurked a nagging dread.   She was too happy and this bliss could not go on.   She did not deserve this wonderful man or the light and life he had brought.   This bliss would only be an interlude that certain as night followed day could not last; for sure, she felt, there would be a price to pay.

All too soon their honeymoon was over and they returned to her, no, no to *their* house and to married life together.   Peter had explained he did not own his own home but paid rent for council premises in Preston.   He was an only child and like her, both his

parents were dead.   The revelation thrilled her: she would be all

the family he possessed and that her home should be his was, to

her mind, fitting recompense for the purpose and fulfilment their

union brought to her life.

In the morning she would waken early to experience the

sight, sound and yes, even the smells of the man still sleeping

beside her.   So as not to wake him she would ease herself

carefully from their bed.   In the bathroom she washed, dressed,

put on her lipstick and dabbed powder and perfume on her face and

neck, again taking great care to make as little noise as possible.

Downstairs she sliced and buttered three slices of the wheaten

bread that Peter was so fond of and that he had never encountered

before.   She munched one slice herself as she made a pot of tea

and slipped on the cozy her grandmother had crocheted.   Then

she made fish or meat paste sandwiches for Peter and herself,

slicing the Pan bread her husband also loved and that again was

new to him.   Pouring herself that first and what she always

thought of as the day's best cup of tea, she filled her flask and one for Peter before lighting the gas to warm the kettle and make

another fresh pot for her husband when he came down.

Love you my darling

Now and forever

xoxo.

She left the note beside his plate, ate the last morsel of bread,

drank the dregs of her tea, rinsed, dried and put away her cup and

plate, wiped up any crumbs and spills, wriggled into her   coat,

placed the flask and sandwiches in her handbag before shouldering

it and then as silently as she could left the house.   Her husband

went to work later and also came home after she did, a routine she

grew to appreciate because the time on her own she could devote

to caring for him in the ways she loved and she felt he so truly

deserved.   Initially, it was true she did tut-tut a little when she

discovered the mess Peter left her to clean up in the kitchen and

bathroom and how he left the bed all rumpled and unmade but as

she busied herself rinsing and washing his cup and plate, wiping up the crumbs, cleaning the bathroom sink, wiping the toilet rim and the few splashes on the floor, making the bed and gathering up assorted items of clothing for the laundry basket she caught herself on.   This was the way men were.   Why her brother and father had been just the same.   Anyway nobody was perfect; not men anyway, and at the insight, she giggled and glowed.

It was her duty and trust to open up the shop.   Jenkins and Son Haberdashery had been on the High Street for over fifty years and she had worked there for nearly thirty; her first job after leaving school.   Starting as a shop assistant she found she had an aptitude for all aspects of the business and Mr Jenkins Snr had appreciated her enthusiasm, encouraged her and over the years increased her wages until eventually he made her his personal secretary and put her in charge of the accounts and handed her a set of keys.

She took great pride in her work: never any errors in her typing, all invoices checked and accounted for and the books balanced to the last half penny.   Lately however her high standards had slipped and she found herself making a few uncharacteristic errors. Why last week she spent ages searching for an unaccounted three shillings and nine pence and to her horror discovered when reading a copy of a letter that had been dispatched she had miss-spelled receipt. The find made her slap the back of her hand. Twice.

Mr Jenkins Snr had retired and the business was now the responsibility of his eldest son. She had known her new boss since he was a boy and sensed he was a little wary of her. Still she hoped he had not noticed any drop in her performance, especially since he was having difficulty appreciating her new status. On two occasions Mr Jenkins Jnr had referred to her as Miss Carson forgetting she was now Mrs Noble. He had been very apologetic but she recognized that probably like everyone else, he had never expected her to marry. Not at her age. Then again, neither had she.

Since her courtship and marriage, work was not the be-all and end-all it had been and this accounted, she was sure, for the errors. Her mind was elsewhere, thinking of James and the treats she could conjure up for their evening meal. That such preoccupations were paramount was an indication of how much her life had been transformed since their meeting at the bench in the park. The encounter had changed the whole course of her life and definitely for the better. For sure she would take greater care not to make any more silly errors but she could not and would not stop thinking and caring about the man she idolized. To her way of thinking there was no doubt; her husband came first.

"I enjoyed the sandwiches and the little note."

She smiled at his appreciation. Her husband never wrote her any such sentiments but undeterred she was determined to create one for him each day of their working week. Little things like this, she felt certain, meant a great deal. "Look after the pence and the pounds will look after themselves," was one of her grandmother's favourite sayings and in her opinion that was true not only in money matters, but in life in general. She fully appreciated her husband with his knack of always saying the right thing but deep down she did wish he would write her a little note if only just once. If he did she would keep it forever, she just knew she would and it did upset her when she discovered her notes crumpled up in the waste bin.   Then she had slapped the back of her hand.   Men were different she reasoned and in their world they had more important affairs to occupy their time.

"I know the **Xs** are kisses Mary," Peter asked, "but what about the **Os**?"

"They're hugs my love.   Don't they do across the water?"

"Maybe, I don't know, perhaps I just never came across it before.   Mind you, I never had anyone writing me love notes. That could explain it."

The sentiment stirred something inside and arms spreading she stepped forward yearning to embrace her husband and be cuddled against him but he had turned away so she checked herself and lowered her arms for regrettably the moment had slipped away.

For another month the days melted one into another as their life together settled into its domestic pattern.   For her it was the happiest and most gratifying time of her life.   Until one evening she came home from work to find her husband sitting at the kitchen table, a letter in his hand and a frown on his face. As she entered he stood up, walked over and embraced her.

"Take your coat off love and come and sit down. There's a good girl."

At the words she dropped her handbag and shopping, ran back into the hall, struggled out of her coat, hung it up, then raced back and sat opposite her husband.

"What's wrong dear?" she managed with a catch in her voice. Then, "It's your call-up papers isn't it. I knew this day was coming but..." Then the tears came and she was fumbling for her handkerchief, removing her glasses, wiping her eyes, inconsolable with grief and shock.

A chair scraped the kitchen floor; her husband stood, walked behind her and placed his hands on her shoulders. "Don't take on so Mary. It only makes things worse." He shook her. "Come on; make us both a cup of tea. No better still; where's that bottle of brandy you say you keep for emergencies? I know, it'll be in the chest of drawers in the parlor. Do stop crying. Stay here, dry your eyes and try to pull yourself together.   I'll get it.   It'll only take a second."

He left the room and after a moment she levered herself to her feet and almost blinded by tears groped her way to the bathroom and closed the door behind her.   Breathing deeply she did her best to stop sobbing and gradually her tears dried.   She set her spectacles on the sill, leaned over the washbasin and peered in the mirror at the ruins of her appearance.   Her eyes were puffy and swollen and her skin red and blotchy so she turned on the tap and splashed her face with cold water.   Then as she dabbed herself dry she remembered she had left her handbag on the kitchen table.   No lipstick and powder puff!   She could not be seen like this so on impulse she opened the bathroom door and rushed out.

In the kitchen her husband was standing at the table pouring brandy into their glasses.   As she entered he raised his head. The look on his face she would never forget.

"Good God!"

At the words she snatched her handbag and now nearly

blinded by an unstoppable flow of tears retraced her steps. In the
sanctuary of the bathroom once more she shut the door, snibbed
the lock and head in hands collapsed unto the toilet seat where she
cried herself hoarse before lapsing into a coughing and wheezing
fit that so shook her whole frame she felt sure she had done herself
permanent damage. Hawking and spluttering she stood and
taking shallow breaths bit by bit she regained some composure and
was able to wash her face and apply her make-up.

Carefully she un-snibbed the lock and crept into the hall.
The house was dark but light spilled out from the kitchen and in
the gloom she could make out the dial on the grandmother clock.
Ten to nine! Nearly three hours since… Taking a deep breath
she entered the kitchen. No James! She righted a glass on the
table and picked up the cork and brandy bottle. It was empty.
Setting it down she took the glasses to rinse and dry at the sink.
Splashing was everywhere; even on the floor and then a stench
caught the back of her throat. No, no, surely not, he could not
have vomited and left all in this state! Poor man! Treading
carefully she opened the cupboard, took out the bleach and

sprinkled it in the sink, the washboard and on the floor, then with a cloth she wiped all carefully before tossing it into the sink and running the hot water tap. Not capable of touching the sodden cloth she poked it under the water with the handle of the washing up brush then fetched her rubbish bin. Again employing the brush she maneuvered it and the dripping cloth into the bin which she placed in the yard outside the back door. She locked up then stole into the bathroom where she washed her hands over and over. Finished, she crept carefully up the stairs.

In the bedroom her husband lay, fully clothed and snoring on top of the covers on his side of the bed. As quietly as she could she undressed, pulled her nightgown over her head, knelt by the bedside and said her prayer then slid under the covers on her side.

Next morning after a sleepless night she arose and completed the breakfast ritual. As always she left him a note on the kitchen table.

Sorry about last night. I am ashamed at the way I behaved. The thought of losing you upset me so much that I lost control.

Please forgive me.   I love you now and always.

XOXO

When she came home after work the note was still there in the same place on the table.   She tidied up the mess her husband had left then busied herself with the evening meal: her surprise, a full roast dinner, his favourite, even if it was not Sunday.   So what! He deserved a treat.   Wasn't he going off to the war any day now and at the thought she had done her utmost to suppress all day, tears began to well but she fought them back.   A little brandy; that's what the doctor ordered!   She had bought a new bottle on the way home so poured herself a small tot and sat down in the warmth of the kitchen to wait for her husband's return and for things between them to be as they had been for wasn't it the best thing ever that she had a husband she loved with all her being and every day wives, mothers and sweethearts were having to go through the same torment as she felt and worse, much, much worse.   At the thought she gasped then swallowed the dregs of her brandy.   She must be strong, strong for her husband.

Another little brandy couldn't hurt.   She poured and was suddenly

overcome by a huge yawn that made her eyes water.   Too little

sleep and with the oven the kitchen was becoming cozier by the

minute.   Another sip from her glass and she set it carefully on the

table before settling herself in her chair, leaning back and closing

her eyes.

Sshh.

SIX

Sir Isaac Newton (1643-1727) had demonstrated in his writings

that there was order, law and design in creation.   In his *Principia*

(1687) and then in *Optics* (1704) he promulgated the view that

discernable rules of nature could be proven by Physics and

Mathematics.   All, Newton argued, revealed a complex and

wonderful symmetry.   In the light shed by Newtonian thinking,

harmony, cooperation and order would be the guiding principles

for proper reflection on the workings of nature.   It became the

received wisdom in the eighteenth century artistic mindset that music, painting, architecture and literature should be promoted through an ideology driven principally by moderation, reason and symmetry.   Such ideas of balance and assumptions of shared values as an indicator of 'good breeding' proved anathema to many of those of Irish birth who wrote in English so they were compelled to make a virtue of eccentricity, as this idiosyncratic stance served best to declare their separateness and afford them an opportunity to distance themselves from the English model.

For these writers a means to resist cultural colonization and prize open reason's clamp was to unleash the powers of the imagination.   This methodology had the added advantage of utilizing cultural ammunition from their own stockpile: fairy tales, legends, sagas and romances and fantastic creatures like 'the little people', giants like Finn McCool (Swift mined this vein), banshees and woodkerns, were an integral part of their and their readers' literary inheritance.   All harked back to the tradition of the *seanchas* referred to previously.   To complete their strategy first person narrative was adopted to give an illusion of veracity.   Thus there came into being a bookish Trojan horse these eighteenth century writers from Ireland propelled into the English literary tradition. In this way they could be both a part of the latter yet still maintain their separate cultural status.

Charles Johnstone (c 1719-1800) was born in Ireland and educated at Trinity College, Dublin. When extreme deafness prevented him from practicing Law he turned to writing to make his living and produced *Chrysal; or, The Adventures f a Guinea*. The narrator of Johnstone's novel is no young hero or even heroine from the Age of Reason, but a pure invention: Chrysal or the spirit of gold. While written in the style of a fantasy the novel enjoyed success and notoriety related to its claim to leak political secrets and ridicule public persons. (*Gulliver's Travels* was surely a significant influence.) In the opening chapter and before transmutation into the form of the guinea in the title, the spirit makes clear its contempt for the limiting powers of reason.

The works of nature are infinitely various, and her methods of operation inscrutable to the curiosity of that vain intruder Reason, which has of late presumed to pry into her ways, and to doubt, if not deny, the reality of all effects which her shortsighted eye

cannot trace to their causes! A presumption that has justly

shortened the line of human knowledge, and condensed the mist of

ignorance which overspreads the world.

Fantasy literature, like the later Gothic, afforded the practitioner the opportunity to construct coded comment against perceived contemporary shortcomings. Much later, writers as diverse as Flann O'Brien, Brinsley McNamara, Mervyn Wall, and James Stephens all slipped Reason's chains for a fling with Inventiveness.

During this period men are traditionally perceived as masters of mainstream fiction, and the centre of consciousness in their novels tends to be that of a young male. A popular exception from Ireland at this time that purported to express the point-of-view of a young heroine was Frances Sheridan's (1724-1766) *Memoirs of Miss Sidney Bidulph* (1761). Mother of the playwright Richard Brinsley Sheridan she was introduced to and influenced by the English writer Samuel Richardson and, in particular, by the latter's *Pamela; or Virtue Rewarded* (1740) which had become a huge success.   Like her mentor, Sheridan employs an epistolary style so enabling her central character to speak for herself in her own manner.   Like many a novel of the period the main theme is the threat posed to virtue by a corrupt world and the key issue of who is a good person is central to the action.   *Memoirs of Miss Sidney Bidulph* is also concerned with the imperative of the watching countryside in influencing the destiny of women in the eighteenth century.   In this respect, the double standard in sexual morality applied to men and women is placed under scrutiny; the character of Mr Faulkland is a precursor of Mr D'Arcy in Jane Austin's *Pride and Prejudice* (1813), and Sheridan's device of the letter as a means of dramatic denouement, also proved a popular Austen trope.

The novel's moral intentions are signaled in the, by now, obligatory introduction which, true to course, testifies to the authenticity of what is to follow.

She (Sidney Bidulph's mother) had educated her daughter, who was one of the greatest beauties of her time, in the strictest principles of virtue; from which she never deviated, through the

course of an innocent, though unhappy life... it (the memoirs) may

serve as an example, to prove that neither prudence, foresight, nor

even the best disposition that the human heart is capable of, are of

themselves sufficient to defend us against the inevitable ills that

are sometimes allotted, even to the best.

As with Samuel Richardson's *Pamela,* the presentation of virtue threatened proved irresistible; so much so that Frances Sheridan provided her readers with a further account of her heroine's travails in *Conclusions of the Memoirs of Miss Sidney Bidulph* (1767).

Readers do not have to delve deep into a Frances Sheridan novel before unearthing a soft vein of sentimentalism. The term when applied to fiction meant concerned with the emotions and an acceptance that spontaneous impulse was the ideal prompt for virtuous action. *Chrysal; or the Adventures of a Guinea* had its sentimental aspect with the Jean Jacques Rousseau - like association of American 'savage' Indian society with virtue and 'civilized' Western society with vice.   The emotional exclamation "Oh!" occurs frequently in *Memoirs of Miss Sidney Bidulph* and its sequel, invariably prefacing a release of excessive feeling.   For example, on coming across a letter from a young rival A.B. written to the man Sidney Bidulph is about to marry, our heroine exclaims:

"Oh! Mr Faulkland, I am the most unfortunate woman in the world!   Fatal have you been to me, and I am undone forever."

Writing of this nature paved the way towards melodrama but was a particular feature of fiction written in Ireland at this time.   Why?

Perhaps in one sense it is not surprising that sentimentalism had such traction; anyone privileged to endure the repertoire of an Irish tenor will surely testify to the ubiquity of the sentimental. Then again there was the ancient bardic conceit personifying Ireland as a woman to be worshipped, protected and, when occasion called, to be died for.   Irish poets in the seventeenth and eighteenth centuries frequently referred to Ireland as female: Cathleen ni Houlihan or Cait ni Dhuibhir.   At this time, Ireland as woman helped perpetuate the notion that the country was ungovernable. The notion that feeling provided pure motive for action and attachment and the Ireland as woman trope, helped to fuse the literary cult of sentimentalism with political commitment like the ennoblement of love of country. Sentimentalism and patriotism proved a fertile combination that has endured in Ireland till the present day. For the writer from Ireland penning works in English this could prove a problem; they ran the risk of being accused of not playing the patriot game. In their homeland, cutting capers within their texts or serving up extravagant fantasy could be interpreted as tactics of appeasement or avoidance; to employ their native language would have been seen as a braver and more powerful act of rebellion.

Then again, Ireland in the seventeenth century was struggling with the aftermath of what was referred to as *Cogadh a Da Ri*, which translates as The War of Two Kings (1688-1689). The protagonists in the one field were James the second, champion of the land losing and Gaelic speaking Catholic population and in the other William of Orange representative of the winning side from the Ulster Plantation - the new Protestant landowning elite in Ireland.   Divided by class, language and religion and pumped-up by bitterness on the one hand and triumphalism on the other this was a fight sparring to be fought.   The conflict began when Jacobite forces won a first round at Dromore in County Down and then flushed with success attacked significant Williamite territory at Enniskillen and Derry.   The onslaught at the latter led to fierce resistance that lasted for 105 days.   The siege of Derry (later to be Anglicized as Londonderry by the Protestant side), where the defenders endured starvation and disease, resulted in a significant victory for Protestant propaganda.

The battle of most import took place near Dublin in July 1690 (the twelfth is disputed - nothing new there) on a site where flowed the river Boyne.   The rest, as they say, is history and the aftermath can still froth up a *frisson* in Protestant and Catholic hearts and minds.   The situation was not helped when those who had supported James on the losing side were punished further by having their lands seized.   The confiscated acres were distributed by William amongst his victorious supporters.   William was free now to claim joint kingship of both Britain and Ireland. Salt was rubbed further into wounds when Penal Law legislation was introduced with the overt intention of removing power from Catholic landowners in Ireland and transferring it into the hands of the minority Protestant gentry. This was viewed as necessary to guard against further insurrection on the part of a Catholic majority deemed disloyal and treacherous. Predominantly, English was the language of the new ruling class and the Irish language and its ancient tradition of literature and poetry was censored and banned. The ensuing cultural disempowerment provided momentum for revivalist defiance relating to the Irish language which flourished in the next century. For now however Anglican Protestantism reigned supreme as a newly created Protestant landowning elite supplanted an ancient Catholic one.

What to do then when the foolery or fantasy you create as a form of cultural apartness is viewed perhaps as political appeasement? Well why not mentally obliterate the whole Anglo-Irish mish-mash and write simply for the sake of writing. The latter option is a luxury, rarely, if ever afforded to writers from a colonized land electing for whatever reason to write in the language of the invader. Was there no escape?   Mentally or physically fleeing the land of their birth and seeking to trade ideas and methods with their European fellows would help eventually. At this time the influence of sentimentalism had to be acknowledged and responded to artistically.

Henry Brooke's *The Fool of Quality; or, The History of Henry, Earl of Moreland* (1765-70) provided the first extended account of boyhood in fiction written in English.   Its author (1703-1783) was father of twenty-two children (surely a feat to be acknowledged – except that with one notable exception none survived adolescence). As a matter of interest, Charlotte the surviving daughter became a celebrated figure in Irish literary history with the publication of her *Reliques of Irish Poetry* (1789). Her father, the son of a Protestant clergyman was born in Ireland and lived also in London.   Brooke studied Law at Trinity College, Dublin but abandoned that career to embrace instead a difficult literary life as poet, dramatist and novelist.   He even found time to argue publically against laws persecuting Roman Catholics.   In

The Fool of Quality the novel's comic tone is introduced in typical breezy style:

I hate Prefaces.   I never read them, and why should I write them? They stand like Pales about a Park, I always overleap 'em, if I am told there is anything, within, worth seeing.   But, what can I do? I am likely to lead a fine life with this Performance, when People begin to quarrel with me, upon reading the first Word, of the first Page, of my Works.

Throughout *The Fool of Quality* Brooke has fun interrupting his narrative to discuss playfully the text in progress.

Friend.   How many volumes do you expect this work will contain?
Author.   Sir, a Book may be compared to the life of your Neighbour.   If it be good, it cannot last too long; if bad you cannot get rid of it too early.
Friend.   But how long, I say, do you propose to make your Story?
Author.   My good friend, the Reader may make it as short as he

pleases.

Such a passage would not be out of place in *Tristram Shandy* as Brooke, like Stearn enjoys light hearted interaction with his reader and mixing up discursive and narrative writing. Like so many novels of the period, *The Fool of Quality* is concerned with the progress of the simple hero from birth to marriage involving a series of set pieces and encounters with various persons in different places along the way. The aspect of the sentimental is easily illustrated. Take as example this meeting with a tearful male stranger.

What is your Name my Dear? said the old Gentleman. Harry Clinton, Sir. Harry Clinton! Repeated the Old Man, and started. And pray who is your Father? The Child, then looking tenderly at him, replied; I'll have you for a Father, if you please, Sir. The Stranger, then caught him up in his Arms, and passionately exclaim'd, You shall, you shall, my Darling, for the tenderest of Fathers, never to be torn asunder, till Death shall part us.

It would be difficult to imagine a chance meeting so described that would be more removed from our time. In this sense its worth bearing in mind that the novel in the eighteenth century (despite the profusion of irony and larkish iconoclasm) was conceived of as dealing with moral issues. Novels of the period were curates' eggs that boiled down to extended sermons addressing important concerns like how to be a good person leading a good life, avoiding temptation and resisting social pressure to compromise and make choices prompted by base motives. Within their pages innocence and virtue were set against corruption and vice and after much tribulation and trial the good would prevail and receive just reward. Lurking in the background and exerting a benign influence was John Bunyan (1628 – 1688) and his *Pilgrim's Progress* (1678 – 79). In this regard, John Wesley the founder of Methodism was so enamored of *The Fool of Quality* that he proposed a copy should be given out to all new Methodist churches.

All of which segues neatly towards *The Vicar of Wakefield*

(1766) of whom its author Oliver Goldsmith (circa 1728 – 1774) writes in his Advertisement:

The hero of this piece unites in himself the three greatest characters upon earth; he is a priest, a husbandman, and the father of a family.

Son of an Anglican curate, Goldsmith followed the by now familiar biographical byway of being born in Ireland and educated at Trinity College, where he studied theology and law. Neglecting his studies he failed to pursue both careers, travelled abroad and subsisted through busking (he played the flute), then apothecary's assistant and school usher before turning to hack writing for London publishers. All helped to fund a dissolute lifestyle in which his addiction to gambling left him continually in dept.

Dr Primrose, the eponymous hero of *The Vicar of Wakefield* begins the novel with a good living, a fine house and a happy marriage in the midst of a host of supporting neighbours.

Then calamitous fate, allied to a personal flaw of hubris with regard to his intellectual powers, brings him to the edge of ruin. *The Vicar of Wakefield* even contains a sermon within the sermon. Tripped up by misfortune and injustice, Primrose is in prison, where he performs good works and addresses his fellow inmates as follows:

My friends, my children, and fellow sufferers, when I reflect on the distribution of good and evil here below, I find that much has been given man to enjoy, yet still more to suffer... When I look round these gloomy walls, made to terrify, as well as to confine us; the light that only serves to shew the horrors of the place, those shackles that tyranny has imposed, or crime made necessary; when I survey the emaciated looks or hear those groans, O my friends, what a glorious exchange would heaven be for these... when I think of these things, death becomes the messenger of very glad tidings; when I think of these things, his sharpest arrow becomes the staff of my support; when I think of these things, what is there in life worth having; when I think of these things, what is there that should not be spurned away: kings in their palaces should groan for such advantages; but we humbled as we are, should yearn for them.

Like the hero of tragedy, Primrose gains moral insight through his suffering, but for him the lesson does not come too late, although it has to be conceded that the fairy- tale aspects of an improbable ending detract from the sermonic power of the vicar's pilgrimage.

CHAPTER FOUR

With a jolt she was awake. Instantly alert, she focused on the clock on the mantelpiece. Ten past eight! The chicken! In her rush she knocked back her chair and it clattered to the floor behind her as she scurried across the room and opened the oven door. Smoke billowed out so she grabbed for the drying-cloth and flapping it frantically was able eventually to survey the blackened ruin of her roast dinner. She turned off the gas and beat back the tears. "Aw well, at least nobody was hurt." Unbidden her grandmother's mantra sprang to mind and as always her load was lightened. She would let all cool down and then roasting tin and contents she would chuck in the bin and that would be the end of that. As for their tea she would fry a tin of Spam with tinned peas and potatoes. Why that was one of her husband's favourite meals so there was no harm done. "Worse things happen at sea," she said aloud and smiled. Peter should be home any minute now.

On impulse she climbed the stairs and entered their bedroom. The bed was rumpled as she expected but unusually both wardrobe doors were open. As she approached and glanced inside she saw as always her clothes hanging neatly on the left hand side. The right, where her husbands should be, was a glaring gap. Ineffectually, not trusting the evidence of her eyes, she extended her arms and waved her hands about the space, then spun and kneeling down peered under their bed.

His suitcase was gone!

Too suddenly she stood up, blood rushed to her head and she folded and fell to the floor.

After a time her senses returned. Aware of a thumping beat in her heart and an intense pain in her head she rolled over unto knees then hands before crawling to their bedside where gradually she levered herself upright. Then all the while leaning for support and seeking hand holds she made her way down the stairs and into the bathroom. A glance confirmed her worst fears.

Why had he gone without telling her? There must be a note – yes that was it. She sped back into the kitchen. There was nothing on the table or the worktops or in the cupboards or drawers but refusing to give up the search she went through the rest of the house before conceding defeat she struggled back to the kitchen,

righted the fallen chair and flopped down.   What had she done?
What had she said?   Where had he gone?   Why had he gone?
Was it her fault?   It must be so she played over their time together
and reddened the back of her hand with slaps when she recalled
occasions her behaviour could have caused offence.

At last the pain in her head became too insistent so levering
herself upright she lurched towards the bathroom where supporting
herself with one hand on the rim of the sink, with the other she
opened the cabinet and took out her bottle of aspirin.   Shakily she
tipped out two, then a third and popped them into her mouth before
replacing the bottle and closing the cabinet door.   On her passage
back to the kitchen she stopped and peered at the clock and could
simply not believe the evidence of her own eyes.   It was HALF
PAST ELEVEN.   Where had the hours gone?   She had to go to
work in the morning and it was near morning already.   Her
tummy rumbled and she felt sick and realized she had eaten
nothing and would have to make something or she would never fall
asleep and sleep she must.   A sudden bitter taste in her mouth
signaled the aspirins were dissolving so she ran the tap water, filled

a glass and drank it down.   Then she sliced bread and forced

herself to eat two slices with butter and jam and sipped a cup of tea

before one step at a time and holding the bannister tightly she

managed the painful trek up the stairs and to bed.

Each day bled into the next as the thoughts and

recriminations swirled round and round in her head.   On

weekdays she simply had to rise and make her way to work where

somehow she coped.   She counted the takings; entered figures in

the ledger; added up the columns; copied out invoices; checked

orders and telephoned customers and suppliers.   In her little office

at the back on the first floor she could toil away uninterrupted and

the distance from her fellows she had maintained throughout the

years now stood her in good stead.   Perhaps the old Mr Jenkins

she could have confided with; he was the only one who might have

shared her load, but he was gone now and there simply was no one

else she could turn to.

Weekends were the worst.

Saturdays she would lie in bed curled up, bunching the

covers in her fist and pressing it to her stomach. Of late she had begun to experience an unpleasant sensation: it was as if a trio of butterflies was fluttering about inside her tummy and the only way she could prevent their trembling was to restrict their space. Eventually she would force herself out of bed, get dressed and make some effort to tidy the house. With no appetite and lacking any energy she would be drawn back again and again to bed where in her foetal position or on her back with both hands this time pressing down on her stomach she would lie for hours at a time drifting in and out of sleep. When she could she would force herself to drink tea and eat a piece of toast. Her grandmother had always maintained that when she was "out of sorts" the best thing was mashed potato and a little butter – champ her grandmother called it – so she made some but for her it did not work as she simply could not swallow it down.

On Sundays and suppressing a growing panic she forced herself to church.

To her, attending church each Sunday was as natural as breathing. She could never dream of finding fault with her husband but his carefree attitude towards religion had disturbed her. From the outset she had determined never to try to persuade Peter to adopt her point of view. In their house they would never quarrel and certainly never about religion so after an initial inquiry when he had laughed and declined she had simply slid out of their bed of a Sunday morning and as she had always done, dressed in her best and made her own way. She would pray for him as she did each night when, before he climbed the stairs, she knelt at their bedside, made a steeple with her hands and went through the nightly ritual she had practiced since childhood.

Born and raised a Presbyterian her faith was unshakable and wrapped in its embrace she felt protected and comforted. The small plain church with its bare wooden pews was suited to her temperament. All that kneeling and crossing oneself, the statues and images, Stations of the Cross, vestments, high ceilings and ornamental architecture had, she knew deep down, nothing to do with true faith. For her, worship should be conducted in plain, unadorned surroundings with no chanting or mantras but instead an honest to God sermon and hymns, clear, fervent and tuneful which the congregation could get their lungs into.   That was the true

faith.

For her, it was as simple as that.

The music of the organ swirled around her as head down,

she scurried down the aisle and took her accustomed place at the

end of a row in the middle section of the church.   Then, her heart

beating, she glanced around and feigned a nervous smile to

acknowledge the smiles and nods of those around her.   Always

shy and nervous with people she had of late developed a rising

growth of something approaching panic in their presence but she

pushed all inside and settling her handbag at her feet concentrated

on retrieving the hymnbook from the slot at the back of the pew in

front.   A glance at the board on the other side of the pulpit

announced her favourite hymn was on offer.   She sat back in the

pew and closed her eyes.   Inside her head the organ played and

she sang the familiar words, achieving a rare and precious few

moments of peace as mentally she swooped and soared at the

hymn's behest.

Guide me, O thou great Redeemer,

Pilgrim through this barren land;

I am weak, but thou art mighty;

Hold me with thy powerful hand:

Bread of heaven, Bread of heaven,

Feed me till I want no more, Feed me…

A muffled cough followed by a whispered "excuse me" punctured her reverie and she had to rise to let a pair of late comers past her. The man lurched as he tripped on her handbag and she could tell from the set of the woman's shoulders as she stepped cautiously in front of her that she was annoyed.

The service over she spun from the pew and head down and heart beating rushed outside.   Her route home took her past the chapel and, as always, observing those who elected to make the sign of the cross she experienced that familiar sense of exclusion and distance.   Deep down she knew religion should promote togetherness in the sight of one true God but in truth, from what

she had seen and heard right from when she was a little girl,
Catholicism was anathema to her. Confessing intimate details to
a priest; bread turning into flesh and wine into blood; pilgrimages
to Lourdes; hanging crosses and holy pictures; the sprinkling of
incense and all that kneeling and genuflecting – her grandmother
had told her all about it, as had her mother. At home and at
school she had been warned about Catholic boys. How if you
made the mistake of marrying one your children would have to be
brought up as Catholics. And anyway her grandmother had told
her all they did was have babies so that one day they would
outbreed us Protestants and vote us into bed with the Free State
because their big aim in life was to have a united Ireland and
smash our union with Britain, our big neighbour across the sea
where Protestants had landed from in the first place. From her
mother's milk she had imbibed this knowledge and for the life of
her she could not fathom why people like her brother, for example
could ever question it.

In truth John had made life very difficult for the whole
family. For a start he was very clever and had won a scholarship

then point blank had refused to accept and attend the Grammar

School where their parents knew he could achieve great things.

No, John had to follow his friends, leave school early and become

a carpenter like his grandfather.   Those two were "cut from the

same cloth" her grandmother used to say, shaking her head.   Then

John had friends, "mates", he called them who were Catholic.

Why he even played Gaelic football with them on a Sunday of all

days and that caused no end of a ruckus.   In the end it was small

wonder that her father finally lost patience and threw her brother

out of house and home; all with her grandmother's blessing.   Her

mother took it to heart however and was never the same woman

from that day on.   Her health broke and soon after she took to her

bed.   When her father died, John did not even attend the funeral.

As for her, she cared for her mother - what else could she do?

What with that and having to go each day to work she never had

any time for herself and no chance ever to go out and enjoy herself

or meet any one until…

Thoughts like these spun their web, fogged up her brain and

wore her out with their repetitive intrusion.   In all the content there was no spark of ease or lightness. That had been supplied in plenty in that blissful interlude with her husband and now he was gone and without him there was nothing to care about because there was no one to care for: no one in the whole world. She was alone and every conscious moment must be spent living over and over a life that had meted out nothing but disappointment and regret. But there was her faith; that and her Presbyterian heritage. Saying her prayers and attending her church were surely something to cling to; that surely gave her life purpose and direction. There was light in her darkest hour, for sure there was light.

That was until she returned from work the Friday following, unlocked the door, removed the key, closed it and there it was on the mat beneath her feet: her worst nightmare.

A TELEGRAM.

O no, surely not...

SEVEN

In 1781 an "Irish Lady" published anonymously the epistolary *The Triumph of Prudence over Passion; or, The History of Miss Mortimer and Miss Fitzgerald.* The novel pre-empts Jane Austen with the pragmatism and balance directed towards the position of young persons in families. Here is Miss Mortimer writing to her friend and relating the matrimonial situation of a mutual acquaintance:

I cannot with any degree of patience reflect on her being sacrificed to a man with whom it was impossible she could be happy, merely because his estate and her father's were contiguous: it is astonishing to think, that such ridiculous motives can actuate rational creatures, in the most material circumstances of life: I cannot say I should have been quite so obedient as Emily was; for the child has a natural right to a negative voice, when it concerns the happiness of her life. I do not mean by that to justify all the pretty masters and misses who in direct opposition to the will of their parents, as well as to every dictate of reason and discretion, are daily performing the tragedy of, All for Love; and indeed, it usually turns out a very deep tragedy to them; for whatever they may think before marriage, they soon discover, that a competency, according to their rank in life, is absolutely necessary to matrimonial felicity...

The artfully balanced syntax and preoccupation with marriage illustrates how these writers from Ireland sought a readership in England where acceptance conferred a kudos and cosmopolitanism not possible if they remained in thrall to the provincialism associated with the Irish side of their identity. That said, even in a text as Eng. Lit. as *The Triumph of Prudence over Passion* the mold can be cracked as when the author has no qualms about issuing in the topic of politics, as her heroine is allowed to air her opinions with prejudice in, of all venues, the drawing - room and in mixed company.

The uniform conduct of the English towards this colony, (Ireland) as well as to America, justifies an opinion of them; and I dare say, a little time will show what dependence we can have on their affection, that is, provided we give them an opportunity, for no doubt they will dissemble till they are sure of carrying their point.

How some of the wise heads would laugh at a girl pretending to give an opinion in politics; it is not, I believe, a very usual subject for young ladies to correspond on; but I know you have been taught to think, the welfare of our country is of as much consequence to women as to men; and when public affairs are the general topic, to write on them is an agreeable variety, and at least as improving as intrigue or scandal, which the men generously allow us to talk of as much as we please, and indeed make no bad figure in such conversation themselves.

The Triumph of Prudence over Passion is passionate in its united pleas for freedom for Ireland and also for the condition of its women. While marriage invariably produces resolution in novels of the period centered on both male and female characters, the novel defies convention when its heroine refuses to marry her suitor, preferring instead to stay in her single state.

Despite this sliver of intellectual equality it is still the case, in general terms, that women in novels of the eighteenth century tend to abide at home where stuff happens to them. It is the male protagonists who are allowed the freedom to pack bags and set out in picaresque fashion to alter their destiny.

Three other literary genres justify consideration.

To start, the eighteenth century in Ireland produced a glimmering of the Gothic vein of fiction which later became popularized in the nineteenth century through writers as diverse as Charles Maturin, Isaac Butt, Sheridan le Fanu, Oscar Wilde and Bram Stoker. While it is generally acknowledged that Gothic fiction came into being with *The Castle of Otranto* (1764) by the English writer Horace Walpole, in Ireland it was resurrected by female writers: Elizabeth Griffith's *The History of Lady Barton* (1771); Sophia Lee's *The Recess* (1783-5) and Regina Maria Roche's (1764-1845) *The Children of the Abbey* (1796).

Born in Waterford, Roche moved to Dublin as a child and then to England in 1794 after her marriage. *The Children of the*

Abbey contains the usual trappings of the Gothic: a vulnerable heroine, a will, and dramatic deaths and of course the obligatory Big House.

Castle Carberry, to which our travelers were going, was a large gothic pile erected in the rude and distant ages, when strength, more than elegance, was deemed necessary in a building: depredations of war, as well as time, were discernable on its exterior; it stood on a rocky eminence, over-hanging the sea, and commanding a delightful prospect of the opposite coast of Scotland, on one side rose a stupendous hill, covered to the very summit with trees, and before it stretched an extensive lawn.

The historical novel (admittedly there is a crossover with the Gothic) can still be cited as being initiated by Thomas Leland (1722-1785) with his two volume romance *Longsword, Earl of Salisbury* (1762). Leland, who also wrote a popular *History of Ireland* (1773), was born in Dublin, educated at Thomas Sheridan's school and then at Trinity College where in 1763, he was appointed Professor of Oratory.   In 1748 he became a Church of Ireland clergyman.

Longsword, Earl of Salisbury is written in a straightforward, lucid and slightly pedestrian style, which is illustrated perfectly by its opening paragraph.

When Henry, the third of that name, reigned in England, Sir Randolph, a valiant knight of Cornwal, now too old to take part in the affairs and commotions of the realm, retired to the peaceful enjoyment of thofe honours and fortunes, which he had purchafed by a fieries of hardy fervices in the field.   The eve of his life was engaged in the pleafing occupation of training up two youths, his fons who were rifing faft to maturity; in teaching them the facred duties which they owed to heaven and to their country, infpiring them with a gallant love of arms, and poffeffing their minds with undaunted courage duly tempered with benevolence and humanity.

Thirdly, Jonathan Swift (who else), is surely a contender for founding the genre that is Science Fiction.   Take as an instance his description of the lode stone powers of propulsion of that memorable image of the crushing capability of colonization in *Gulliver's Travels*.

By means of this loadstone, the island is made to rise and fall, and move from one place to another. For, with respect to that part of the earth over which the monarch presides the stone is endued at one of its sides with an attractive power, and at the other with a repulsive. Upon placing the magnet erect with its attracting end towards the earth, the island descends; but when the repelling extremity points downwards, the island mounts directly upwards. When the position of the stone is oblique, the motion of the island is so too. For in this magnet the forces always act in lines parallel to its direction.

Enough. I trust you are as keen as I am to return to the travails of our heroine. Perhaps you already know because you skipped pages and caught up with her before me. In that case it's a pity you can't tell me what happened next.   I'd love to know

but, as ever, to find out I have no option but to do it the hard way.

So here goes.

CHAPTER FIVE

Her heartbeat quickened as she kneeled, picked up the telegram and sped towards the sanctuary of the kitchen where she pulled open the drawer of the table, stuffed the missive inside and shut it out of sight.   Trembling all over now she thought she must be, in what her grandmother would have described, "A state of shock". The remedy was twofold: brandy and a cup of strong tea.

When she woke the next morning she could tell all was not well.   Inside her tummy the butterflies had multiplied and their fluttering made her nauseous.   Panic swelled and she knew in the depth of her being she could not face the business of washing, dressing and going to work.   The thought of the bus, the business with the conductor, the other passengers filled her with so much dread that the ideas made her feel sick.   With a start she remembered it was Saturday and the realization provided a flood of relief that was quelled instantly and she was drowned in a black surge of despondency.   What was the use of ever again rising from this bed?   What use was she and what use the empty rituals that made up her whole life? What was she doing living still in this house – she hated it! She should have left home like her brother did instead of wasting all those years, tying herself down with misplaced duty and responsibility. What had she got to show for it all? The only person who she cared for, the only one who had really cared for her was gone, and for what? It was all so cruel, so unfair, what had she done to deserve this misery? What was there to look forward to except more of the same in the same mess she had made of her whole worthless life? Who would miss her if she was not here at all – would she miss any of it if she was not here at all? Round and round thoughts spun and churned till they drained away finally and she fell to sleep and waked and slept while inside her tummy the butterflies flitted their wings and clothed in panic she curled up and lay with the curtains closed against the light and wished she could sleep and sleep and never wake again - ever.

The lack of light filtering through the curtains signaled it was dark outside so pulling back the bedclothes she raised herself and taking great care wheeled round and sat head in hands on the edge of the bed. Her heart was thumping and her head felt light, while inside her tummy tiny hairless baby mice were scooting about and snuffling and gnawing. When eventually she managed to lean forward and rise, the bed had such magnetic force that immediately she succumbed and fell back in its embrace. This would not do so with a wrench she was on her feet again and making her way to the bathroom.

Dressed and ready and her bed still beckoning she stood in the hall where she raised a trembling hand to open the door. Outside it was dark and in the cold she shivered and a gust of wind forced her to adjust her step. Then head down she set off along the street, round the corner and up the hill. It was after nine so women and children were inside and any men out would likely be in the pub. To ease the discomfort she pressed her handbag to her tummy with both hands and concentrated on breathing slowly and deeply in an attempt to suppress a rising swell of panic. Behind her she heard the familiar metallic grinding and knew a bus was winding its slow way up the hill.   Of a sudden all became clear and she could see a new and more direct and infinitely simpler way to end her nightmare.   All she had to do was let the bus catch up then turn and walk in its path.   Her troubles would be over.

Slowing her pace she sidled towards the pavement's edge. Behind her she could tell by the increasing volume of the engine that the bus was in place and by now too close for the driver to brake in time to avoid her.   Turning she stopped and stood.   One step more and her heartache would be ended.   She closed her eyes, summoned her will but for no reason she could explain was unable to move from her spot.   The bus ground by while the suction of its passing made her stumble and almost lose her footing.   The moment passed and she checked up and down the hill.   No one was about so gathering herself together she set off again until breathless and panting she reached the top where she turned left into the tranquility of an avenue of tall Victorian houses.   At number sixty-four she unlatched the gate then shutting it behind her stepped carefully up the short path.   Then, taking a deep breath, she stood on the step and reaching up, raised the heavy metal knocker.

After what seemed an uncomfortably long time the door opened and the old man looked her up and down before smiling and clapping his hands.

"Why, my dear, good to see you.   You must be cold standing outside on a night like this.   Come in, come in."

She stood her ground.

"I'm so sorry Dr Patterson.   I know it's late and, in ordinary circumstances I would never dream of calling on you especially at this time but well I'm at my wit's end and I…"

Tears welled and she began fumbling in her bag.   The old man stepped outside, took her by the arm and led her inside, closing the door behind them.   Then he guided her down the hall, helped her out of her coat and hung it on a coat stand and led her into the living-room where he sat her on an armchair at one side of a roaring fire.

"Now you sit there and compose yourself while I get you a cup of tea – with a little drop of something in it that's guaranteed to help you see things in a different light.   Make yourself at home.

If you need the bathroom, it's the door ahead of you at the top of the stairs."

He was gone and she heard him bustling about in the kitchen. The fire was just too inviting so she tidied herself where she was, using her mirror and powder puff. She was just clasping her handbag shut when he returned bearing a tray which he held before her. She reached for the cup and saucer and placed it carefully on the small table at her side. The tray remained held before her and was pushed slightly more in her direction so taking the hint she took one of the biscuits and when it was still moved gently in her direction, removed the plate and set it down.

"If you don't mind, and indeed if you do, I'm having something a wee bit stronger."

He chuckled and turning nodded in the direction of his side of the fire where on a twin table of her own beside his armchair there rested a half empty glass and an almost full decanter. "I've never worn a nightcap but I've drunk a wardrobe full in my time and shared many a one with your dad as I recall."

With that he stepped back and headed for the kitchen.

Her father and Dr Patterson had been friends for as long as she could remember.   They had been at school together, attended the same university and then returned to follow their chosen professions in the city of their births.   She remembered her grandmother's pride in them both and how she loved to boast about her only son, Headmaster of the local Primary school and his best friend, the doctor.   Her mother and the doctor's wife had also become best friends and the couples had spent many happy hours in each other's company.   Now all were dead except for this kindly old man, the only one in the whole world she could turn to in her hour of need.

Her thoughts were interrupted by the doctor's return.

"Don't wait for me my dear.   Drink your tea or it'll be getting cold.   And eat a biscuit."   Approaching the fire he rubbed his hands together.

"That's doctors' orders."

Obediently she lifted saucer and cup and took a sip of the tea.   It was sweet and strangely bitter at the same time but she persevered and felt emboldened enough to reach for a biscuit –

digestives, one of her favourites.   With a grunt the doctor sank into his seat and reached for his glass which he raised and flourished in her direction.

"Cheers my dear. Now to what do I owe the honour of this visit?   Take your time and tell me what's troubling you?"

Finishing her biscuit and draining the remainder of her tea she settled the cup and saucer, took a deep breath and began.   To begin with she described her symptoms: the continued feelings of anxiety and panic; a growing inability to put up with almost any kind of noise; how she could no longer bear to listen to the radio or even read the paper; her dread of anyone coming to the house; not being able to put up with daylight and wanting always to have the curtains closed; her growing inability to encounter people; her wanting all the time to lie in bed; the truly awful sensations in her stomach; how she knew in her very being she could not face going to work; how she lacked the energy to cook for herself and anyway how her appetite had gone and most of the food she did make she could not eat and finally how desperately low and depressed she felt all the time and...   At this point she checked herself and was incapable of continuing. Some things were just too private to be aired in public; she was too ashamed to acknowledge her own awful weakness.

"And…"

Dr Patterson probed softly. Leaning forward he looked at her with such a penetrating gaze that she was forced to avert her eyes. He knew! Despite the insight and teetering on the very brink of confessing all she drew back and the moment passed. Dr Patterson looked away, leaned back, then stretched for the decanter and replenished his glass before raising it and taking a drink.

"My dear I'm going to pour you another cup of tea. This time I'll only put milk and sugar in it and I want you to eat another one of those biscuits. I won't be a minute." With an effort he raised himself from the chair. "When I return I want you to tell me what you think brought this on and remember," and he looked at her keenly, "I may be retired but I took the Hippocratic oath and as far as I am concerned, once a doctor – always a doctor. Nothing you say to me will ever go beyond these walls."

With that he left the room.

When he came back she told him about Peter, her marriage, his being called to the war and the telegram. Dr Patterson listened carefully to every word.

Then: " I remember when I was a much younger man practicing during the last war there were young soldiers I encountered who had been in the trenches and saw and perhaps did terrible things. Some of them were simply unable to cope. You know, my dear, the symptoms they described were not a million miles away from the ones you presented just now. Mm – now here's what we're going to do. You're not going back to work for at least a month. I'll contact Mr Jenkins Snr – we go back a long way - and he'll fix everything so you need have no worries on that score. I happen to know he has a grandson who is going to study accountancy and with the holidays coming up would love to help out since he will be taking over the business. So no problem there – look at it this way – you're doing them a favour.

"Now as for your good self; I'll have my successor prescribe a tonic to keep your strength up. Don't worry – you won't have to attend surgery or go to the chemist – I'll see to all that. My housekeeper will collect everything and she'll do your shopping

for you.   Let's see: Mona will call at your house every Monday

morning around eleven.   Give me your ration book and I'll see

she gets it.   Mona will buy your basics like milk and potatoes and

your meat ration.   I'll leave all that to her.   Don't you worry –

she's a good woman and knows what she's doing.   Mona is fit

and strong and she walks past your road each day on her way here.

She's the salt of the earth and I trust her completely so you have no

cause for concern.   Mona will see us both right.   Around twelve

when she's finished, Mona will drop the shopping bag at your back

door and knock, and you can pick it up at your leisure.   Mona will

tally the damages and leave it in a note with the shopping.   The

next Monday you can leave the monies in the shopping bag before

eleven and she'll pick it up on the way to the shops and Bob's your

uncle.   That way you don't have to worry about seeing anyone –

except me that is.   I'll drive down and check on your progress

every Friday at half past eleven.   Clear?"

She nodded.

"Good.   Now I want to show you something."

Dr. Patterson levered himself from his chair and placing both hands on his waist at the back pushed himself upright.

"That's better."

Tottering slightly he made it to the wall on his side of the fireplace where he pulled opened a tall cupboard door.   Inside was filled with bottles – dozens of bottles of whiskey.   His eyes twinkled.

"There you are; my secret hoard.   You know my dear; over all those years practicing in this city I must have done something right, something to deserve all this.   These are all from patients, my dear, grateful patients who insisted and who would simply not take no for an answer.   Your father used to help me drink it but now he's gone, God rest him, you my dear, you could give me a hand.   Believe you me; in the process you'd be doing us both a power of good.

"Now let's see – where did I put it?   Bear with me just a minute."

With that he wheeled and weaved across the room and she could hear him struggling up the stairs.   Minutes later he emerged carrying an old, battered brown briefcase. Placing one of the whiskey bottles inside he snapped shut the briefcase and bringing it over placed it on the floor beside her chair. Then he returned, shut the cupboard door, sat down and picked up his glass and draining its contents, smacked his lips.

"That's me for the night. Thank you for coming dear and for keeping me company. Now before I let you go there are just a few more things I want to say. To begin with I want you to do your very best to eat; even if its only bread and jam and I suggest you have porridge for breakfast. Potatoes are good; especially mashed with a bit of butter and milk or buttermilk. Oh and don't forget the salt!"

His eyes twinkled; he chuckled, and then continued.

"Now for the whiskey," and he nodded at the briefcase, "I want you to sip about a fifth of a glassful last thing at night. About that much," and with his thumb and forefinger Dr Patterson spaced out the amount.

"Have you ever tried whiskey before?"

She shook her head.

"Chances are you won't like it so add about the same amount of water and think of it as medicine. Trust me; it'll do you good. Now, my dear;" here he leaned forward in his chair and dropped his voice, "there's something else I want you to do for me. "I want you to gather together all the sharp knives in the house and wrap them in a towel and put them in that briefcase then set it outside your back door so Mona can pick it up on her way here on Monday morning. Agreed?"

Dr Patterson held her gaze, raised an eyebrow and inclined his head to one side.

She nodded.

After a pause where she felt sure he could hear the violent beating of her heart, he continued. His voice was gentle and even.

"Finally my dear, I want to reassure you. YOU WILL GET BETTER. Always remember that. It won't happen overnight, it won't be easy, you will have more bad days but I know how much courage it must have taken to walk up here and see me tonight and in the end it's that courage that will see you through. So there;

now let me get your coat.   My goodness just look at the time."

EIGHT

There is therefore virtually no feature of nineteenth or twentieth century fiction that is not anticipated by these early novelists. Irish writers made a lasting contribution to literature in English whereas in Ireland their cultural flexibility muted their effect. There the eloquence that really moved was being delivered by the revolutionary leaders of the United Irishmen. The organization had been inspired by the French revolution, with its conceptions of truth, equality and fraternity, and also by ideals embedded in the American War of Independence. A secret society led by Dublin Protestant Wolfe Tone, the United Irishmen was committed to severing any connection with England and uniting 'Protestant, Catholic and Dissenter' under the collective: 'Irishmen'. In the North, their armed rising of 1798 had the support of Presbyterians who, like the Catholics, were suffering discrimination under the Penal laws.

As ever their armed rising was extinguished with much bloodshed but the violence of the English response proved counterproductive and served to create martyrs which fueled the nationalist cause.   Historical irony on a grand scale occurred when the perceived insurrection by the United Irishmen prompted the imposition of direct rule from London that, in turn, led to the Act of Union of 1800.   In Ireland, fact was marginalizing fiction (however well intentioned) led by an Anglo-Irish Protestant intelligentsia.   Then fact and fiction were conflated when in 1881 the Dublin Protestant Robert Emmet led yet another disastrous rising against English rule in Ireland.   This time it was not the act of his rebellion, but rather the nature of his much quoted speech from the dock that had the lasting effect.   How could the Anglo-Irish writer of fiction compete with newspaper accounts of Emmet's words?   Although delivered in the nineteenth century, his speech distils the essential elements of a brand of Irish nationalism that had been fermenting in the eighteenth.

Let no man write my epitaph; for as no man who knows my motives dare now vindicate them, let not prejudice or ignorance asperse them.   Let them and me rest in obscurity and peace and my tomb remain uninscribed, and my memory in oblivion, until other times and other men can do justice to my character.   When my country

takes her place among the nations of the earth, then and not till

then, let my epitaph be written.

In a country where fact has often possessed the knack of

triumphing fiction this proved a particularly telling example that

had the effect of almost obliterating the Irish dimension from the

duality 'Anglo-Irish' in the province of writing.   From an Irish

cultural perspective these writers were seen more as belonging to

the English literary tradition.   A further irony surrounds the

contemporary recording of Emmet's valediction: were they the

actual words spoken or words written after the event?   No matter;

a cultural shift resulted and from this time forward Anglo-Irish

writers were compelled to confront more seriously the latter

portion of their cultural heritage.

Finally it has to be acknowledged that Dublin and the South

of the island have been the prime locations for the emergence of

the literary form that is the novel.   What about the North and why

was it so silent in terms of this cultural expression?

For a start, Dublin, rather than Belfast, was the island's artistic focus; in the eighteenth century Dublin was to Ireland as London was to England. In the North too, the Protestant work ethic prevailed, and this tended towards the promotion of a pragmatic outlook serving to marginalize the Arts as, at best frivolous, or worst, subversive: Science was a more valued form of human endeavour. There exists also in Protestantism an aspect associated with accepting one's lot; the moaning self tends to be suppressed, discontent is not revealed but all is internalized and tamped down inside, put up with and plaudits go to those who suffer in silence. By contrast the novel deals invariably with self-revelation, with confession; literature is about illuminating issues and not seeking to quench them. Then too, the six counties makes a very small space where the pressure of the watching countryside is intensified; a space where 'whatever you say, say nothing,' becomes a maxim to be heeded. Perhaps also the entitlement conferred by plantation bred parochialism tends to suppress the questioning process required for the production of great literature.

The northern Irish Protestant had no long term cultural heritage to mine and Protestant culture was not considered as artistically valuable.   Unionism tended to be more about practice than philosophy; ears tend to be shut to criticism; the mindset is set and the rationale becomes: 'Ours not to reason why...'   There may also have evolved a kind of self-fulfilling prophesy inherent in the appellation 'The honest Ulsterman'.   Writing Fiction as the title implies requires the ability to make things up: paradoxically novelists create a lie to arrive at their truth. It could be argued that plantation in a conquered land is to be involved in the creation of a lie and perhaps those eighteenth century Ulster Protestants clung too unquestioningly to the Anglo side of the channel: dependent acceptance does not provide fertile ground for artistic growth.   In their psyche novelists tend to be outsiders whose predisposition tends more towards disparagement than concurrence; they are crafts persons whose talents are more forged in perceptions of alienation rather than deference.   In short writing is to wrestle: not to submit.   Paradoxically their much vaunted 'No surrender' involved an all too eager surrender to the Anglo half of their duality and this in turn pushed them more towards the certainties of the sermon and away from the ambiguity of the novel. Their single minded focus perhaps outlawed the process of catechization required for fiction.

In short and nurtured in Religious practice, the significant quality and quantity of confession that is such an essential ingredient of the novel, came more naturally from the Catholic than the Protestant tradition.

CHAPTER SIX

Mercifully she encountered no one on her walk home. On the way she mulled over the visit. Dr Patterson was right – it had required great nerve (courage was too grand a motive for her) to go and see him in the first place. Then again he had always been such a good friend and since he had no children of his own had been especially kind to her and her brother. His wife – and then it clicked. Mona; Mona was a Catholic name and Dr Patterson's wife had been a Catholic. They had met at university and her father had been best man at the wedding. It had caused quite a commotion at the time; her grandmother had been particularly disapproving but even she came round due to her regard for 'the doctor' as she habitually called him. Was Mona a relative of the doctor's late wife? Anyway, what did it matter; she might never have to meet the woman. Then again surely she would have to thank her for services rendered. She would cross that bridge when she came to it. When she was fit and well enough.

It took nearly three months.

Twelve weeks when for the most part she lacked strength or will to even wash her hair; a nightmare time when sleep was her only respite and when the thought of hanging herself or hacking at her wrists or taking an overdose was constantly on her mind. That she resisted and managed to eat and drink enough to survive was down, in large part to Dr Patterson who was as good as his word and called each Friday, brought her another bottle of whiskey and gently propelled her towards recovery.   And then out of nowhere on one day she was able to pick up and read a little of an old copy of *People's Friend*; the next she switched on her radio and managed to begin tidying the kitchen while it droned away in the background and during this time the mice became butterflies again, the butterflies became moths that evolved into fruit flies until blissfully they too flitted.   Her appetite improved, she found strength to wash her bedclothes and wonder of wonders was able to carry them outside and hang them out to dry.   While it had never been her way to associate with her neighbours she felt no trembling at the thought someone on either side would appear and strike up a conversation.   She knew then she was on the road to recovery.

Well enough even one morning to approach the drawer in the kitchen table, open it and retrieve the telegram. With a quickening heartbeat she held it between thumb and forefinger of her right hand and steeled herself while she tapped it on the back of her right wrist; then impulsively she tore it open before over and over she read the printed words.

HE IS MARRIED TO ME AND HAS BEEN FOR NINE YEARS GET YOUR OWN MAN YOU BITCH

To begin with she was fearful that her awful illness would start up again and then when it did not something approaching calm and a kind of resolution took over. Never again would she allow herself to be dependent on any person but herself. For the telegram spoke the truth: of that she was certain. It explained why in all his talk he was so vague about the details of his own past; why he never wanted his photograph taken. That letter he was holding on their last night together had not been, as she had surmised, from the war office; it would have been from his wife, who somehow had found out about his double life. How could he – but he did. How could she – but she had. It was as simple as that. From this moment forward she would be strong and stop melting and being tearful when she saw children and parents together. That life was not for her; she would go back to work, attend church and fend for herself – by herself.

The week after, she resumed her old life.

She met Mona and thanked her for her invaluable support. The woman insisted she had done nothing out of the ordinary and they parted with the suggestion, on her part, that Mona must come and visit her sometime and have a meal. It was the very least she could do.

At work she was welcomed back without fuss, something else she believed was thanks to Dr Patterson. The old man himself refused to take any credit for his efforts and when she handed over his briefcase and he could tell by its weight there were full bottles inside he just looked at her, smiled a wry smile and shook his head.

"No need, no need," was all he said.

So her life returned to normal until the day when she returned from work to find a letter lying waiting for her on the mat inside the front door.   She recognized the handwriting immediately.   It was from her brother!   Short and to the point as always but that was his way.   The letter contained one significant piece of information: she had a nephew and his name was James.

James Carson.

THE NINETEENTH

CENTURY

ONE

Then we were all bustle in the house, which made me keep out of the way, for I walk slow and hate a bustle, but the house was all hurry-skurry, preparing for my new master-Sir Murtagh, I forgot to notice, had no childer, so the Rackrent estate went to his younger brother-a young dashing officer-who came amongst us before I knew for the life of me whereabouts I was, in a gig or some of them things, with another spark along with him, and led horses, and servants, and dogs, and scarce a place to put any Christian of them into; for my late lady had sent all the feather beds off before her, and blankets, and household linen, down to the very knife cloths, on the cars to Dublin, which were all her own, lawfully paid out of her own money-so the house was quite bare, and my young master, the moment ever he set foot in it out of his gig, thought all those things must come of themselves, I believe, for he never looked after anything at all, but harum-scarum called for everything as if we were conjurers, or he in a public house.

Almost a century before Mark Twain in *The Adventures of*

Huckleberry Finn (1884) heralded the breakaway of the American novel from the cultural imperialism of English Literature; the English spoken in Ireland had been presented in fiction by Maria Edgeworth (1768-1849) as illustrated by the passage quoted above. Her seminal work *Castle Rackrent* published in 1800 paved the way for writers as diverse as Sir Walter Scott, Thomas Hardy, Ivan Turgenev, and, as indicated, Mark Twain. Edgeworth's narrator is Thady Quirk a loyal, elderly Catholic Irish family servant who, in the brief quotation, is recounting preparations for the arrival of a new master at Castle Rackrent, after the sudden death of Sir Murtagh, the previous owner.

Unlike previous Anglo-Irish writers, Edgeworth elected not to deliver her text through the medium of Standard English prose and her employment of an original form of Irish dialogue contributed greatly towards the emancipation of the Irish novel from the confines of traditional English Literature, and inspired later writers from Ireland to produce independent voices. Another innovation was her appending dialogic footnotes and a Glossary to help explain her 'Irishisms'. These add another dimension, allowing the introduction of social and political comment and that irreverent humour so characteristic of Sterne in the previous century and Joyce in the next. So in reference to Thady's observation that:"…my Lady Rackrent was all kilt and smashed…", the author, adopting the guise of editor, appends the following explanation:

Kilt and smashed - Our author is not here guilty of an anticlimax - the mere English reader, from a similarity of sound between the words kilt and killed, might be induced to suppose that their meanings are similar, yet they are not by any means in Ireland synonymous terms. Thus you may hear a man exclaim -"I'm kilt and murdered!"- but he frequently means he has received a black eye, or a slight contusion - I'm kilt all over means that he is in a worse state than being simply kilt - thus I'm kilt with the cold is nothing to - I'm kilt all over with the rheumatism.

Maria Edgeworth's early years were spent in England where she was born in Black Bourton in Oxford shire. After the death of her mother, her father remarried when Maria was five and they moved to her father's estate, Edgeworthstown in County Longford, in the south of Ireland. There, Maria was home tutored by her father and studied subjects as diverse as Law, Economics, Politics, Science and Literature. She became her father's assistant in managing the estate where she observed and recorded details of everyday Irish life she would later employ in her novels.

Prolific in both adult and children's literature, her first novel *Castle Rackrent* was written and submitted for anonymous publication and became an instant success. The novel satirized Anglo-Irish landlords and within its pages she focused on the linguistic differences between Irish and English societies, while stressing the former as equal to the latter and thus challenging English stereotyping.

Another aspect of Edgeworth's originality is indicated by the novel's title giving prominence to a house, rather than as was previously the case: a person. After *Castle Rackrent*, the novel centering on The Big House in the country became a popular strain of Irish fiction being employed symbolically as a microcosm of the wider political situation. Edgeworth's novel is the chronicle of such a house through four generations of the Rackrent family, whose chief talent was in self-destruction. The sub-text can be interpreted as a gradual undermining of the old feudal ascendancy and its replacement by the self-made entrepreneur who has overcome the fore-lock touching deference exhibited by the novel's narrator, Thady Quirk. The 'new man' is Thady's son, Attorney Quirk who as an example of the newly arrived Catholic middle-class eventually assumes control of the Rackrent property in hard-headed business terms.

In *Castle Rackrent*, Maria Edgeworth presents to the English reader the customs and conventions of rural life in Ireland and in doing so demonstrates how artistic allegiance to national subject matter can enhance the wider cultural landscape. Her success proved inspirational for female writers; Jane Austen sent her a copy of *Emma* and praised Edgeworth's *Belinda* (1801) in *Northanger Abbey*.

While the Act of Union generated a shift in economic and political power from Dublin to London, *Castle Rackrent* stimulated interest in the ways of living of a nation little known to English readers. Place, death, the Big House, an outsider introduced to and then enmeshed within an unfamiliar landscape: all these became preoccupations of the novel from Ireland in the nineteenth century and all found expression in *Castle Rackrent*. Although published in 1800, the novel deals with an earlier period of Irish life. The title page announces the novel as *An Hibernian Tale taken from facts and the manners of the Irish Squires before the year 1782.* As a people undergoing invasion, land appropriation and exploitation, it has been remarked that the Irish have to keep remembering their history because the English keep forgetting it. Generally speaking, citizens of a colonized country continue centuries after the event to harbour feelings of resentment or gratitude arising from subjective perceptions regarding the treatment meted out to their ancestors during the initial invasion. All then becomes the stuff of oral account, of ballad and written record. Cultural claims become staked and positions with their attendant possessions are defended. Historical triumphs become the subject of ritual celebration, ensuring a divided past is kept alive in the present and for the future.   In such a society the artist

has little option but to respond.   From *Castle Rackrent* onwards, a

recurring theme in literature from Ireland would be how in that

land the past held in thrall, the present.

PART TWO

BOTH YOUR HOUSES

CHAPTER ONE

"Where," his mother would muse, "does the time go?"   Invariably she would answer her own question with: "There must be a great pile of it somewhere."   Then, "If only I could lay my hands on some of it - I'd make better use of it this time, that's for certain!"

The boy loved his mother; she was capable and strong and full of odd phrases and sayings that helped her and the whole family through the day.   When he concentrated really hard and thought back, his earliest memory was of a magical time when stumbling through a world of blinding white he came suddenly upon an icy, hard and scraping surface and then was falling before being gathered up in a sudden and warm embrace that soothed his hurt and made all well.   When he told his mother she was amazed he could remember something so far back.   He must have been just short of two and only learning to walk and it was a really cold January and he followed her everywhere even toddling through the snow to the clothes-line where he had come up against the sheets hanging frozen and had scraped his hands and was falling over when she caught him up and brought him inside.

Some years later his father whittled for him a pistol and he was John 'Kit' Carson, fur trapper, scout, hunter and Indian fighter, capable of gliding through the grass, reading signs no-one else could see, then diving, somersaulting before coming up pistol in hand and blazing away as yet another foe bit the dust.

Later still he swopped cowboy hero for true life outlaw. His target was Wilson's general store, small and cramped in the middle of a clump of shops on the edge of the estate.   The owner a large, balding man with spidery red veins mapping his cheeks knew his mother; she was a good payer and regular attender at the church where Wilson acted as warden.   The shopkeeper was always curious about their father, who never attended church.

"And how's the wee man today?"

"I'm alright, thanks Mr Wilson."

"Good and how's your mam?   Tell her I was asking after her; and what about your dad?   I don't see much of him these days."

Wilson was not the only adult who was curious about their father who kept himself to himself and whose religion and politics were not easy to place.   He liked to quote Groucho Marx who was, according to him, a better philosopher than Karl Marx: "I'd never join any group that would accept me as a member."

"He's fine thanks.   Here's the shopping list Mr Wilson."

Then when the shopkeeper turned away to find the items he snatched a bar of chocolate from the counter display, his hand flicking out and sliding back like a snake's tongue.

Once only he was caught in the act when on tip-toes, arm stretched out he had reached his prize, a coveted bar of fruit and nut chocolate and was drawing it back ever-so-carefully, held precariously between the tips of his fore and index fingers and just about to make transition to a firmer grip when the shop door was flung open and Wilson turned and there he was, caught with stolen goods in his possession and all because…   He spun round.   Two of his classmates stood inside the shop, staring at the drama played out before them.

"Heh, put that…what do you think you're up to?"

"You mean me Mr Wilson?"

"Of course I mean you!   Who do you think I mean?"

"I thought you meant them, barging into the shop like that."

"Not them - you, that's who I mean!   What are you doing with that bar of chocolate?   Wait till your mam hears about this!"

"Hears about what, Mr Wilson?"

"About," but his tone had changed; he was beginning to flounder.   "I mean that chocolate bar you have in your hand. You lifted it when my back was turned.   I've noticed stock has been missing here of late but you; you're the last person I'd ever have suspected.   Your mam…"

"It's for my mam; a present.   I saved up my pocket money and am ready to pay for it.   Here you are."   His heart had stopped beating fast and of a sudden he felt calm and in command of the situation.   Placing the bar on the counter he reached into his pocket.   Enough: he could gauge by the feel of the coins! Taking his time, making his triumph last he counted out the money.

The shopkeeper was all apologetic as he filled out the remains of the order and when his back was turned and in full view of his classmates he stole a packet of mints.   He waited outside the shop and shared the sweets with them on their way back to the estate.   They shared theirs.

There was a small gang of them from the estate: his younger brother Sam then two friends, Snap and Sean, and Teresa, Sean's twin sister.

THE RAID ON FERGUSON'S FARM

During school holidays they roamed freely combing the fields surrounding their council estate, their mams glad to see the backs of them.

That day they set out early assembling at the clump of trees in a hollow known locally as the fort.   A hike through the fields and they were huddled together beneath the high red brick wall surrounding the orchard and kitchen garden of Ferguson's farm. Ferguson: prominent land owner, chief cattle and sheep baron, another pillar of the church and he had heard his father comment, "Big in the Orange Order."

"You keep dick on top of the wall, Snap," he whispered. "If you see anything, whistle and we'll be out like snow off a ditch."   He liked to season his talk with some of his mother's sayings.   They passed unquestioned, even when he was not sure of their exact meaning.   "Right then, let's go.   Sam, you and Sean head for the apples, I'll get the pears; they're in the garden near the house."

As head of their small band he gave the orders and invariably claimed the most dangerous assignment for himself. That way he gained respect, appeased his inner competitive drive and (this was becoming increasingly more important) gained the admiration of Teresa.

"What about me?" she whispered urgently.

"You get the plums and goosegogs Teresa; they're next to the wall.   No need to worry – you'll be on the Pig's back." Whatever that meant; but it seemed appropriate and as always sailed by unchallenged.

"Right, you first Snap!"

His back to the wall he linked the fingers of both hands, then held them palms open between bent knees, providing a step for Snap to climb on his shoulders giving himself time to straighten before Snap sprang to hold the top of the wall with both hands, then pull himself up, toes scrabbling, to straddle the top.

"You're next Sam," and his brother went through the same manoeuver, albeit rather less deftly and requiring help from the wiry Snap who leaned down bracing himself with his legs tight against the wall on the orchard side and pulled Sam upwards.

"Right, Teresa."

With the girl on his shoulders he instinctively looked up and the weak morning sun shining through her dress was strong enough to reveal as if in some magic tent the thin legs parted above him, the white knickers loosely hugging her bottom, the scent, and the warmth before Snap reached down and she was up and up and away.   Sean was next and last, himself.   He retreated then ran at and up the wall to grasp Sam's pullover that Snap, held firmly by the twins, dangled down for him; then up over Snap's prone body, till he was there: on top.

They peered through plum tree branches weighted with fruit into the untidy, fruit laden orchard stretching before them to the neatly laid out kitchen garden with its rows of potatoes, lettuce, carrots and regimental canes supporting peas and beans.   Beyond all, the huge old farmhouse looked impressive and non-threatening in the dappled sunlight.   They reconnoitered anxiously; no signs of humans or dogs.

"Clean as a whistle," he whispered tersely, alert, in command.   "Let's go!"

Climbing down they were mindful not to attract attention by too much shaking of branches.   At ground level the orchard

was alarmingly silent.   Glancing up through the interlaced
canopy, he was overawed briefly by the religious hush of it all.
He glided forward, an Indian of the Wild West, surefooted, taking
care not to tread on any twig that might announce his presence to
the Whites in the settlement he approached.   There followed the
shivery sound of branches shaking accompanied by the thud –
thud, thud, thud, of apples falling.   Sam the clumsy eejit!
Ghosting onwards he reached the fringe of the trees where he
paused momentarily to scrutinize the house now looming grandly
only yards away.   Nothing at any of the windows, so crouching he
slid behind a row of peas taking care to stay in tight in case he
might be detected by anyone looking down from the top floor.
Then quick, pulling and snapping off the fat pods, cramming the
peas inside his shirt, their cool hardness causing him to gasp at first
touch, then snatching, snatching, exhilarated by the abundance,
until the terrifying sudden barking of a dog, followed immediately
by Snap's piercing whistle had him wheeling away, up and
dodging through the trees to the wall, leaping for a branch, hauling
himself up his heart thumping, reaching the top, turning round,
dangling down, his toes scraping the wall to check his descent,
hanging for a split second by his fingertips before letting go he
dropped, bending his knees when he thumped the ground, falling
sideways, then up and running, battling the slope of the meadow,
seeing ahead Sam struggling, then above him Sean and Teresa with
the unencumbered Snap in the lead and almost at the crest of the
hill.

"Come on!" he urged, catching up and then outpacing Sam
then up and over before fueled by exhilaration he propelled himself
recklessly down the other side, catching then speeding past the
twins, gaining on Snap then flung himself past him with a shout
and then when he was himself alone in front for all to see and only
then he slackened pace, eased to a halt, turned and looking back
and checking the stricken Sam had reached the top of the hill he

bent, placed his hands on his knees and brought his breathing under control.

Snap caught up first, then Sean and Teresa: all three red faced and breathing hard. Affording them no respite he turned away and walking casually to the hedge at the bottom of the field he squeezed through, and then strolled up the slope of the next field. At the half-way mark, he turned round, his heart beating uncomfortably fast. He scoured the meadow they had careered down; all was clear, no-one was following and not a dog in sight. Snap and the twins were approaching and below them Sam was squeezing awkwardly through the gap in the hedge.

"Come on Slow Coach!" he called and then when the other three caught up to him, "That was a close one. I only got away by the skin of me teeth!" By now Sam was within hearing range. "Did any of ye see the dog?" All shook their heads and looked at Snap.

"I don't know what you're all staring at me for? As soon as I heard the barkin' I whistled cos I didn't want to take any chances!"

"You did right, you didn't half. I saw it. Friggin' great black thing! It came round the corner of the house. Like a donkey it was and it ran straight for me, slobbering and roaring! Scared the living daylights out of me I can tell you, made me jump clean out of me skin! I didn't half take off! By the time I reached the wall it was snappin' at my heels so I had to turn round and boot it one! Did you not hear it yelp?

A bit of a risk here but the momentum of his fabrication propelled him onwards giving him the confidence to pause and look at each in turn until Snap, as he thought he would, caved in.

"I did, I heard the brute; you must have given him a right boot!"

"Actually, it was a left one."

Snap, Teresa and Sam all laughed; Sean remained stone-faced. Teresa looked sideways at her brother, then: "You know when we jumped down from the wall; I had a job keeping me knickers from falling down – with the weight of all the plums! I had to hold them up when we were running! Look!"

Unselfconsciously she pulled up her dress and displayed her knickers bulging ridiculously with fruit. Except for Sean, who if anything looked more set-faced than ever, they all laughed and hooted, then the wheezing Sam was overcome suddenly by a fit of choking coughing that was so intense it doubled him up and made him purple in the face. At this all, including Sean, set off jeering and guffawing and he slapped his brother's back as hard as he could and while, for now, harmony was restored, deep down he knew there was unfinished business between himself and Teresa's twin brother.

They set off on the trek back to their meeting place: the ancient Celtic fort, surrounded by a high ditch and a circle of trees. While it overlooked their estate, ensconced within its protection they remained hidden and sheltered. Here they sat and pooled their resources. First they attacked his peas, running their thumbs up the seams then parting the pods to reveal the full neatly packed contents they crunched, before flicking away the empty shells. Then the apples: crisp and juicy. Sam, ever the clown, gnawed three down to their cores without swallowing, then cheeks bulging began to chomp, juice dribbling down his chin and neck, eyes crossed hilariously before again being assaulted by a paroxysm of coughing causing him to blast out the whole mouthful and end up once again in a fit of wheezing, spluttering and gasping for air. They threw their cores at him, convulsed at his helplessness.

Lastly the plums, where sucking at the fruit he was overcome gradually by forbidden warmth. He became conscious he was staring at Teresa, and heart beating suddenly, he held her gaze, alive to the certainty that a vague conspiracy was growing between them. With her he was entering a new area of experience that was drawing him away from the boisterous posturing of Snap and Sam and as for Sean, why care about him?

TWO

In Ireland, as in England, the nineteenth century nurtured an increase in the number and significance of women writers. One such was Sydney Owenson (c.1778-1859), also known as the Lady Morgan she became through marriage to the surgeon and philosopher Sir Thomas Charles Morgan. The exact date of her birth is unknown as she was famously evasive regarding her exact age. The daughter of Robert Owenson an Irish Catholic and professional actor and Jane Hill, Protestant daughter of a trader from Shrewsbury, Owenson was educated by her mother and when the latter died when Owenson was approximately ten, was sent to private schools to complete her education. She subsequently became a governess, an avid reader, collector of folk tunes (to which she wrote lyrics) and following her father's example, an enthusiastic performer of songs and dances.

Through a prolific writing career and following the example of Maria Edgeworth, Owenson's achievement was to present Ireland to English readers, and she too set her fiction in the recent past. However, Owenson elected to write in a more romantic, sentimental fashion and achieved immense literary and personal fame with *The Wild Irish Girl* (1806).

Another memorable work is *The O'Briens and the O'Flahertys* (1827). The hero, a young patriot Murrough O'Brien, a volunteer and united Irishman, leaves Ireland after the armed rising of 1798 and after a series of exploits becomes a general in the French army. In a lively set piece relating a review of troops in Phoenix Park, Dublin, Lady Knocklofty and Lady Honoria have locked carriages and horns.

*'Do you call that love?   I call it calculation,' said Lady
Knocklofty significantly.*

*'Call it what you please,' said Lady Honoria, colouring slightly,
but 'tis good taste, pour le moins, and that is precisely what you
mere home-bred Irishwomen of fashion are perpetually sinning
against.'*

*'We home-bred Irishwomen!   And pray, what are you, my dear
pretty Honoria O'Callaghan, with all your country kindred...'*

*'Why my dear, to answer you...it is true, that as ill luck would
leave it, "I comed over to Ireland to be born," but I was never
dipped in the Shannon for all that; and thanks to my father, have
lived too much abroad, not to be fully aware of the absurdities of
my native home, since by divine indignation I have returned to it.'*

This constitutes a significantly different presentation of the
aristocracy of Ireland from that of Maria Edgeworth.   The male
Rackrents were to a man insular in outlook.   Sydney Owenson's
female characters (however risible) view attachment to fashionable
societies of England and France as a positive enhancement.
Incidentally, Owenson wrote a survey of French society and
politics titled ambitiously *France* (1817).   So successful was the
latter that it brought her a request to write *Italy* published (1821).

In their different ways, Maria Edgeworth and Sydney
Owenson sought to expose the shortcomings of the indigent
Protestant ascendancy.   The former revealed it collapsing in on
itself, then being revitalized by *nouveau riche* enterprise.   For
Owenson, deterioration could be averted by union with England
and openness to the wider civilization of Europe.   In a famous
letter to her brother written in 1834, Maria Edgeworth had opined:

It is impossible to draw Ireland as she is now in a book of fiction –
realities are too strong – party passions are too violent to bear to
see, or care to look at, their faces in the looking glass. The
people would only break the glass and curse the fool who held the
mirror up to nature...

Like Edgeworth, Sydney Owenson also became silenced by events in Ireland, with its agitation, led by the Catholic reformer Daniel O'Connell, for Catholic emancipation, ownership of the land by the people who worked it, and for Home rule. Emancipated though they were, for these female writers of the landlord ruling class, the realities evoked by O'Connell, proved too strong, too overpowering.

Charles Maturin (1782-1824) was born in Dublin and attended Trinity College. He became curate of St Peter's Church where he was celebrated for the power and persuasion of his sermons. So much so that in his obituary it was affirmed: "*...did he leave no other monument... these sermons alone would be sufficient*". Maturin endured much financial hardship and early literary failure till he turned his back on reality and produced instead the work that brought him fame: the Gothic novel, *Melmoth the Wanderer* (1820).

In return for a prolonged life, the eponymous hero, one of the most memorable outcasts of European literature, has sold his soul to the devil. Like Samuel Taylor Coleridge's Ancient Mariner (1798) Melmoth is compelled in his wanderings to pass on his burden of guilt and horror to another. In 1824 Maturin preached *Five Sermons on the Errors of the Roman Catholic Church* and his nervousness regarding the disposed Catholic majority and its struggle for equality surface in *Melmoth the Wanderer*. In fiction a turning away from holding 'the mirror up to nature' could provide ironic opportunity to do that very thing. How Swift haunts!

The Big House with its ruined isolation; the pathetic fallacy surrounding the storm; the turbulent emotions: a majority of the vital ingredients of Gothic fiction can be pin-pointed by the following passage from the beginning of Volume 1. Here the Melmoth referred to is not the hero, but a young student relative who has inherited the house in question.

Loud and sudden squalls of wind shook the house from time, and then as suddenly ceased. Towards night the storm came on in all its strength; Melmoth's bed was shaken so as to render it impossible to sleep... He rose and went to the kitchen, where he knew a fire was burning and there the terrified servants were all assembled... In a short time however, Melmoth perceived their minds were occupied with terrors besides those of the storm. The recent death of his uncle, and the supposed visit of that extraordinary being in whose existence they all firmly believed, were connected in their minds inseparably with the causes of this tempest, and they whispered their fearful suggestions to each other, till the sound reached Melmoth's ears... Terror is very fond of associations; we love to connect the agitations of the elements with the agitated life of man...

The passage above is presented by an omniscient narrator, but this is uncharacteristic of the novel as a whole, which is told through multiple viewpoints and a multiplicity of forms, including manuscripts, journals and letters. (Bram Stoker employed a similar technique in *Dracula* 1897)   All serve to promote the contention that the events, fantastic though they might be, are the stuff of real life.   Over twenty years later, Emily Bronte would display similar novelistic complexity in her *Wuthering Heights* (1847).   (Indeed, in their romantic isolation and blasphemous disregard for civilized codes of behaviour, parallels can be made between Bronte's hero Heathcliff and Melmoth).

Sheridan le Fanu (1814-1873) has been described as the leading ghost story writer of the nineteenth century.   Born in Dublin into a literary family (his grandmother Alicia Sheridan le Fanu and his great uncle Richard Brinsley Sheridan were playwrights) his father was a Church of Ireland clergyman and stern Protestant churchman.   Le Fanu studied law at Trinity College and was called to the bar in 1839 but never practiced, instead turning to journalism and subsequently he became the owner of several newspapers.   He campaigned against the British government's indifference to the sufferings endured in the Irish Famine where his support for the cause cost him nomination as Tory MP for County Carlow in 1852.   Characters in Le Fanu's fiction tend to be preoccupied with death's inevitable approach and this may well reflect reaction to the sensational reality of the Famine (1845-1851) which had reduced the population from 8 million to 6.6 million through disease, starvation and mass emigration to Britain and America.

In 1826 the family had moved to Abington in County Limerick where his father took up his second post as rector in Ireland.   During his upbringing there, Le Fanu would have been exposed to the violence and unrest in the countryside in the agrarian conflicts of the 1820's and 1830's where tithe payments levied by the established church on the largely catholic peasantry, were withheld.   As a consequence, the secure power and prestige Irish Protestants had enjoyed was threatened, and as the son of a

Church of Ireland clergyman, Le Fanu would have experienced in the family glebe house the vulnerability through isolation of the Big House in a hostile countryside.

Uncle Silas (1864) opens in such a Big House. It is winter and the conventional Gothic indicators are firmly in place. *"...great gusts were rattling at the windows, and wailing and thundering among our tall trees and ivied windows..."* The narrator is a young orphaned girl left in the charge of a sinister uncle. Alongside the Gothic trappings, Le Fanu grapples with a theme occurring throughout his fiction, and one very appropriate when referring to the condition of Ireland: the significant re-emergence of the past in the present. He touches also on the gradual disintegration of his own Anglo-Irish world.

Le Fanu's lesbian vampire novella *Carmilla* (1872) was a big influence on the most famous Gothic novel of the period.

How these papers have been placed in sequence will be made manifest in the reading of them. All needless matters have been eliminated, so that a history almost at variance with the possibilities of later-day belief may stand forth as simple fact. There is throughout no statement of past things wherein memory may err, for all the records chosen are exactly contemporary, given from the standpoints and within the range of knowledge of those who made them.

So declares the Preface of the novel introducing another celebrated outcast of nineteenth century Gothic: the eponymous *Dracula* (1897) by Bram Stoker (1847-1912). A sickly child, Stoker was born in Clontarf in the north of Dublin and raised as a Protestant member of the Church of Ireland. Often bed-ridden, his mother entertained him with stories and legends from Sligo, the area of her birth.   Educated privately and subsequently at Trinity College, Stoker became interested in theatre and became theatre critic for the *Dublin Evening Mail* where he became friends with the celebrated actor-manager Sir Henry Irving and then later business manager of Irving's Lyceum Theatre in London, a post he held for twenty-seven years.   At intervals during this time he spent several years researching European folklore and stories of vampires. *Dracula* is steeped in the folklore of Transylvania and was produced at a time when there was a revival of interest in the folklore of Ireland.   Thomas Crofton Croker collected oral legends for his incredibly popular *Fairy Legends and Traditions of the South of Ireland* (1825), while W. B. Yeats researched folklore for creative inspiration as did J. M. Synge and Lady Gregory.   To help create the illusion of eye-witness testimony, Stoker includes within the novel extracts, journals, diaries, a newspaper report, letters, a telegram and a transcript of a phonographic recording.

This trio of nineteenth century writers of Gothic fiction all grew up within the confines of the Irish Protestant professional class.   What prompted them to write this 'sensational' genre of fiction?

For a start there were, as is invariably the case, other literary models to provide possible sources of influence: Elizabethan drama and Mary Shelley's *Frankenstein* (1818); early English tales of terror (in particular Horace Walpole's *The Castle of Otranto* (1764) and in France the novels of the Marquis de Sade. The literary movement of Romanticism and the burgeoning of the Antiquarian movement played their part.   In this context Samuel Taylor Coleridge's *The Rime of the Ancient Mariner* (1798) was a significant text.

Castle Rackrent had introduced a theme in fiction from Ireland: that of the novel dealing with the Big House, isolated and storm ridden, the target of envy, gossip and sometimes hatred for the surrounding countryside.   *Melmoth the Wanderer, Uncle Silas* and *Dracula* all contain their Big House, each inhabited by a wealthy inmate who is somewhat of an outcast, misunderstood, feared and resented by the local populace.   The Gothic strain of fiction licensed this trio of writers from the Protestant elite to project fictionally what surely must have been the stuff of nightmare.   The threats were real enough with all around, agrarian agitation, violent murders, a growing nationalist consciousness fueled by inflamed rhetoric, everywhere envy insinuation and threat.   What if...   The Big House atop a hill imperiously commanding a panoramic view of the watching countryside could easily appear isolated and vulnerable when a siege mentality was induced.

There followed the whole business of inheritance.   How was the land to be divided?   What if there were no sons to pass on to?   What if no natural children to leave the property to?   What to do regarding fortune-seeking husbands for eligible daughters? The Big House was accompanied by a particular legacy of headache and heartache.   Questions related to the disposition of money and inheritance dominate Gothic fiction as do secret and unlawful pacts gradually coming to light and visiting retributive pay-back in the gloomy corridors, rooms and cellars of secluded properties.

Protestant Gothic in the nineteenth century can be read as a metaphor for the whole Anglo-Irish superstructure of an original felony leading to the unlawful acquisition of properties for privileged gentry.   Years pass, the transgression is resurrected and the tortuous process of retribution starts to unfold.   Within the covers of their fiction these Protestant writers of Gothic fiction could contemplate their history then present it in the form of cloaked confessions related to guilt surrounding their inheritance.

Then, as always, there was the matter of religion. Perhaps that should be a capital R – this is Ireland, after all. Charles Maturin, as we have seen had published a series of sermons attacking and criticizing Catholicism. It could be argued that residual insecurity regarding racial and religious identity propelled these Anglo-Irish Protestant writers to project latent prejudices against Catholics into their extravagant tales. Their fiction invariably included potent symbols of Catholicism.

The nineteenth century in Ireland was a time of religious enthusiasm for Catholics and Protestants. Secret societies on both sides like the Ribbonmen and the Orange Order ensured religious affiliation was difficult to resist. The Gothic novel plundered religious devotion and channeled it into a sensational form of fiction. Within its covers the cross was omnipotent; the reviving power of blood was featured; life after death and reincarnation occurred frequently while the main protagonist of the novels was often an outcast, reviled, spat upon, who possessed the often hypnotic power to recruit disciples who could be relied upon to spread his 'gospel'.

In the period, the interweaving of religion and politics led inexorably to violence. After a particularly violent passage in *Melmoth the Wanderer* the author appended the following footnote to demonstrate that such horrors are not confined to the enclosed world of fiction.

In the year 1803 when Emmet's insurrection broke out in Dublin – (the fact from which this account is drawn was related to me by an eye witness) – Lord Kilwarden, in passing through Thomas Street, was dragged from his carriage, and murdered in the most horrid manner. Pike after pike was thrust through his body, till at last he was nailed to a door, and called out to his murderers to 'put him out of his pain'.

Pre-Christian Ireland could also provide a source of influence for writers of Gothic fiction. From ancient times Ireland had a well-established oral tradition of storytelling. The ghost story has always been popular with performers as the voice can be employed to maximum effect to increase suspense and generate dramatic atmosphere. With its often gloomy and stormy weather, wild landscapes and isolated areas, Ireland displayed a fertile backdrop for the supernatural. Death was omniscient, accelerated frequently by wars and famine; the country was steeped in the cult of the wake. The location that produced the folklore surrounding the banshee could surely be relied upon to embrace the trappings of the Gothic.

These writers at this time, although protected from its ravages, would be aware of the horrors visited upon the population of Ireland by famine. The novelist William Carleton (1794-1869) is worth quoting in this context as he bears witness to events occurring in the epidemics of 1817 and 1822 before the Great Famine of 1845-1851.

To any person passing through the country such a combination of startling and awful appearances was presented as has probably never been witnessed since. Go where you might, every object reminded you of the fearful desolation that was progressing round you. The features of the people were gaunt, their eyes wild and hollow, and their gait feeble and tottering. Pass through the fields and you were met by little groups bearing home on their shoulders, and that with difficulty, a coffin or perhaps two of them. The roads were literally black with funerals; and as you passed along from parish to parish, the death-bells were pealing forth, in slow but dismal tones, the gloomy triumph which pestilence was achieving over the face of our devoted country – a country that each day filled with darker desolation and deeper mourning.

The sensibilities of writers of the period prevented them dealing directly with such terrors. The Gothic novel afforded the opportunity to locate dreadful happenings elsewhere and surround cruel circumstance, fearful suffering and injustice with the veil of the supernatural. The mirror, ironically ubiquitous in the literature of the Gothic was, in fact, not held as far from nature as one might suppose.

CHAPTER TWO

Reading became a passion; every comic he could beg, borrow, swap or steal and then the local library for all the boys' adventure stories he could find, then westerns, crime stories, Gothic and horror.   Primary school was about clocking in and clocking out and doing what you had to do in between but his natural aptitude for reading and writing and puzzle solving led inexorably to success in the 11+ examinations and promotion to the local grammar school.   There he learned to be ashamed of his council estate background, struggled for acceptance and countered by keeping his head down while inwardly he exiled himself from the whole system and its restrictive codes of behaviour.   Never part of the crowd, he found purpose in the role of spectator, standing on the sidelines, watching.

ME

Being alone

For me

Is playing

God.

I set myself

Apart:

Judge, jury,

Executioner

Alone

With my Sense

Of difference,

Indifferent,

Above, beside

Beyond

I confront

Myself

My impulse

To shock

Into awareness

Like a chalk

Scratching

On the blackboard of life.

One of his earliest adolescent outpourings written in the secret black notebook he had filched from Wilson's store. If the poem spoke to no-one else; it spoke to him.

In examinations he carried information printed carefully on neatly folded rectangles of paper he concealed in the pockets of his blazer. There he was: a candidate with a number on his desk, seated in the great hall, one among many sufferers, heart beating, waiting for the clock to reach the appointed time and for the solemnly intoned announcement: "Right, you may open your Question Papers and begin reading!"

A communal rustling as trembling fingers turned pages and eyes devoured the contents seeking re-assurance before alighting on possibility and then they were off. When the moment arrived and his heart beat increased he possessed from the beginning the facility to produce outward calm at times of inner turmoil. The stealthy hand glide to his pocket for the required note, a measured lifting of his head signaling pained concentration then the well-practiced draw as the invigilator stalked the serried rows of desks and was even now approaching himself. The increase in danger had the effect of producing a greater flow of calm and he looked the enemy straight in the eye, while maintaining his air of studied concentration but introducing a vacancy, a looking but apparently not seeing, while slyly his hand withdrew the note concealed between thumb and four cloaked fingers. The invigilator at his desk now, a tiny hint of a smile indicating just the proper degree of professional sympathy for this honest expression of mental ferment; then past, pacing with measured gait along the row. Danger averted, he scanned the crib's content then consigned it fluently to his lapel pocket.

Money his harassed mother left on the mantelpiece, he slipped in his pocket, knowing she was too overworked, too stressed coping with the four of them and a sometimes drunken, potentially violent husband to remember for certain whether she had placed it there or not. When the inevitable row flared he was briefly ashamed but sitting atop the stairs, hugging his knees, listening he became composed, serene almost, above and beyond home, school, the estate, everything and everybody.

"I never touched the money!" his father thundered.

"Well I'm sure I put it there, I…"

"You don't know whether you put it there or not!"

"I'm sure I must have…"

"Sure, you're sure about nothing!   You don't even know what day of the week it is!   You better not have lost it that's all I can say!   You'll get no more housekeeping from me!   You've had your lot!   I've more to do with my hard-earned money than waste them on a loony like you!"

"That's not fair, I…"

"Fair!   What do you mean fair!   You're lucky to get what you're given – especially since you can't manage it properly anyway!   Aw, stop whinging woman!   I've had enough!   I'm off out!   I can't stand any more of this!"

The house shook at the slamming of the door and he hugged his knees harder, spellbound by the drama he had provoked.

On Sundays, himself, his two brothers and sister were scrubbed, polished, dressed in their best and dispatched to Sunday school in their local Presbyterian church where later they would join their mother for the service.   The Sunday school congregated in the Church Hall: chairs set in circles, grouped according to age.   The wooden floor; the high ceiling; the tall rectangular windows and the uncanny absence of noise imposed by best Sunday clothing accompanied by dire warnings from parents related to certain retribution that would accompany any indiscretion.   This crowd at day school would enact Bedlam, but in this place and in this time religion waved the bigger stick.

A clap of hands and all was hushed. Reverend Brown made a few announcements: a meeting of the Boys' Brigade; a badminton match and, most exciting of all, details of the annual Sunday school excursion to the seaside. Then, after a nod in her direction a flourish of chords on the piano played by Mrs Brown, smiling and demure, introduced the hymn.

Jesus loves me

This I know

Cos the Bi-ble

Tells me so

Little ones to him belong

They are weak, but he is strong.

Yes Jesus loves me

Yes Jesus loves me

YES JESUS LOVES ME

THE BI-BLE TELLS ME SO!

They were divided into groups in the four corners of the hall, the chairs in a circle all facing the corners so the children had their backs to those in the other age groups. In his, the senior group led by John Armstrong, a gentle, kindly soul with ideas about becoming a minister in the church, they had bible readings followed by discussion.   It was more fun in the other groups, reading homiletic stories from religious magazines, having quizzes, or, in the youngest age group, colouring in religious pictures.   In all, prizes were awarded, and with his good memory and competitive instincts he had won his share for reciting verses of Scripture, learning the books of the Old and New Testaments and the one that assured a good turnout 'for regular attendance at Sunday School'.   Invariably prizes had been Bibles or Psalm books, but Reverend Brown, influenced perhaps by his schoolteacher wife, had introduced glossy backed editions of classics of English Literature: a kilted Rob Roy, claymore held high; Robin Hood in tights drawing his bow; Tarzan swinging through the forest; John Ridd wrestling Carver Doone: a glossy Black Beauty, mane streaming in the wind and strangely most memorable of all the pale, sad-faced Oliver Twist, standing, plate and spoon in hand.   He could summon at will the smooth touch of the dust jackets, the potent sniff of promise when he thumb-flicked the pages.

After Sunday school and a brief breath of air outside, their mam arrived, anxious and flustered and herded them into the musty church interior.   Their pew was half way down the centre aisle.   He in first, then Sam who contrived always to be beside him, their mother next placing herself in their centre, next Paul their youngest brother then last, Jane their eldest sister. Accompanying the congregations entry, Mrs Brown on the organ managed a tuneless dirge and when all were assembled her husband made his entrance, climbed the pulpit and all stood as the first hymn was announced.   One stood out in his mind, maybe not for the right reasons, but its lugubrious intonation brought the whole mirthless occasion flooding back.

On a hill far away

Stood an old rugged cross

Da, da, da, da, da, da, da, da, da,

And I'll cling to that old rugged cross

And wear it one day for a crown.

Not much there; despite all the attendance, only fragments of the content gained purchase.   Standing to sing, sitting to pray and listen to announcements and sermons.   He and Sam vied with each other to try and make the other laugh by pulling faces; mimicking the more outrageous singing styles and inserting irreverent words in hymns.   Their best effort and his own composition stuck in his mind.   He and his brother would belt it out straight-faced when accompanied by the congregation and Mrs Brown's flamboyant version of 'Eternal Father Strong to Save'.

It nearly broke her Mother's heart

When daughter Jane let off a fart

Its smell rose up around the pew

And the congregation all turned blue

As they held their breath and looked at Jane

Who'd smelled the church out once again!

Prayers, more hymns, announcements, sporadic coughing then the dreadful culmination: the sermon. Did anyone follow its mazy meanderings all the way through? Was not even the most fervent thinking of food or anything else but what the Reverend Brown standing above his congregation preached over their heads? With his aesthete's face, high forehead, cultured voice he would present his chosen biblical text then before all assembled, examine it, dissect it, place it in its historical context, introduce the most up-to-date biblical scholarship then link all in gentle, academic fashion to life lived today. For added colour he would include a fragment of personal reminiscence before completing the operation with a tentative reminder that they should all, himself included, try harder to lead fuller, less hypocritical Christian lives.

Reverend Brown: good cricketer, scholar, compassionate, sincere man. Genuinely apologetic regarding his vocation he was tentative in his expression of the message he was entrusted to deliver. His stage was the pulpit and from it he spoke in a still, small voice. What did his congregation make of him, this Anglo-Northern Irishman with his university education who was, in so many ways, divorced from them all? Yet there was, in his approach and example, some quality that gained grudging respect. *"There's no harm in him"*, was the phrase most often applied to Reverend Brown, and from these most reluctant praise-givers that was surely something. *"He means well,"* all concluded. Even his father who gave short shrift to any church visitor had time for Reverend Brown; and the latter liked him.

The service over, the minister passed first down the aisle then stationed himself outside the church door where he would shake hands and engage in brief, halting conversations.

"Good to see you Mrs Carson. Family all well I see. I take it that singularly clever young man is maintaining his good progress at school?"

The slight nod in his direction made him glow with pleasure but he kept his head down and turned away concealing his gratification.

"Good reports so far," their mam replied, while Sam, unnoticed, twirled his ears, stuck out his tongue and crossed his eyes.

"You have a lovely family, Mrs Carson and all with their special talents.   Send Mr Carson my regards!" he called as they turned away.

Clustered in front of the church were small groups of mothers and fathers with children lingering by their sides or risking chastisement for minor bouts of horseplay.   Lacking the support of her husband, their mam did not seem to fit in, so avoiding any standing to converse would doggedly march them all home.

After Sunday dinner, he and his brothers and sister were packed off to the Brethren service held in the Gospel Hall, a wooden structure with a tin roof on the edge of town.   Here their mam did not attend, and they were dispatched he felt, partly to clear the house and give her a well-earned rest, but also because their attendance made the family eligible for another excursion to the seaside.

Inside the sermon was delivered by Tom Crooks, the pink faced owner of a small hardware store.   He spoke without notes of any kind, summoning the words from within and displaying a power and passion at odds with his mild exterior.   Throughout, his sentiments were punctuated by fervent calls of *"Aye Brother"* which in this intense atmosphere, even the reckless Sam had the good sense not to mock.

"Are ye washed in the blood of the lamb?   Have ye taken the Lord Jesus Christ into yer life?   Are ye ready for the precious gift of everlasting life?"

Tom Crooks would jab his stubby finger at his congregation, thrust his head forward and confront them pugnaciously, eyes narrowed, gunning for weakness.

"Remember the words of the prodigal son when he left the family fold and lived the life of a sinner away from his father.   'I will arise and go to my father, and will say unto him Father I have sinned against Heaven and before thee and am no more worthy to be called thy son; make me as one of thy hired servants'.   That young man had strayed from the straight and narrow path that leads each and every one of us to salvation.   He knew it and it came to him in a rush how much he missed the love of his father. And what happened then, brethren?   The words of the Scriptures read (Tom Crooks could recite them from memory and he would hold aloft his Bible and wave it before them): '*But when he was yet a great way off, his father saw him and had compassion, and ran, and fell on his neck, and kissed him*'.   What love, what forgiveness!   And that love and forgiveness can be yours brothers and sisters.   What rejoicing and celebration in Heaven there would be if only one of YOU left off sinful doing and returned with humble and contrite heart into the arms of the Father who loves you!   Remember the greatest joy is for the sheep that was lost, and then found.   We are all the lost sheep of our Father in Heaven.   We are his prodigal children.   But we can all return to the fold, we can all experience his love and forgiveness."

Tom Crooks lifted his bible and held it before them.

"Remember how God sent His only son to die for our sins on the cross.   As the scripture tells us; '*He was wounded for our transgressions, he was bruised for our iniquities: the chastisement of our peace was upon him; and with his stripes we are healed*'. Healed and forgiven by the love of the Father, shown to us by the sacrifice of His Son who died to save our souls.   Who died so that we could be washed clean of sin and that we might have the precious gift of being born again."

Gently he replaced the bible, and then leaned forward, elbows and forearm on the lectern, his hands clasped, speaking slowly, beginning softly, then gradually raising his voice.

"Why not today, here and now in this gathering and before our assembled brethren, make witness and accept the forgiveness of the Father who despite all your sinful ways never, ever gave up on you, never, ever ceased to love you.   Rise up together and with full and contrite heart show you accept the risen Christ as your Saviour.   Come up Brethren!   Be saved!   Be saved!"

And row upon row the crowd succumbed, heeded the call, allowed themselves to be swept up by a communal surge that washed away their sinful past and buoyed them up with a renewed certainty of a better life to come.   Tom Crooks preached from no pulpit; he was before and among them, a man off and not above his flock, he could lift you up not just talk you down.   And one time, he did just that and succeeded in persuading him, prodigal lost sheep that he was to come in from the cold and surrender the arrogance, the superiority of the outsider.   For down deep he wished to be part of something positive, something that provided purpose and comfort to good men and women rather than clinging stubbornly to the outpost of cynicism.   Tom Crooks' message delivered with passion and directness spoke directly to him, he was called by a voice he felt compelled to hear.   *The lost sheep...the prodigal son…the sinner…our Father who art in Heaven…Jesus loves me…* Biblical phrases swirled in his head as he rose from his bench, dimly aware of Sam following and they joined the surge, accepted the pats on their backs, surrendered and allowed themselves to be saved.

The glow of their salvation lasted for about a week. Then they were back to their Godless selves.

THREE

Displacement was not a strategy employed by all writers in nineteenth century Ireland. The violence and anarchy of the period was faced up to in the fiction of writers from the Catholic middle class. Freed from restrictions imposed by the Penal Laws this new emerging force was now making inroads in the world of literature. Pioneers of this emergent Catholic intelligentsia were the Banim brothers: John (1798-1842) and Michael (1796-1874). Many of their works were published pseudonymously under the name 'The O'Hara Family'. John studied Drawing in Dublin then took up teaching in Kilkenny and subsequently moved to a career in journalism that took him to London. His brother Michael studied for the bar but could not practice as he had to take over their father's business. Later he served for many years as postmaster for Kilkenny. John was the more experienced writer (he became dubbed "the Scott of Ireland") while Michael provided invaluable background material based on his social observations in Ireland.

The Anglo-Irish of the Nineteenth Century (1828) is a noble attempt to bring to life a short period in Irish history for a predominantly English readership and simultaneously create a popular fiction: a challenging literary task. The setting is the close of the Napoleonic Wars and the prejudicial contempt of English and Irish Protestants for the Catholic Irish majority and the corresponding hatred for the oppressors are presented in unsentimental fashion. The novel spares neither side and perhaps this helps explain the Banims' desire for anonymity regarding authorship.

Frequently throughout *The Anglo-Irish of the Nineteenth Century* contentious issues are aired within conversations as in the following exchange that takes place over dinner.

"And when will they grow quiet, Sir?"

"When, indeed, General?"

"What with White-boys and Right-boys, United-men, Shanavests, Caravats, Threshers, Carders, and now, Rockites, I believe, all I have heard or read of them, since I left the country, shows that the old people of Ireland never can be peaceable as long as they remain what they are."

"Plainly shows it, Sir Robert."

"The mass of our half-countrymen are certainly difficult to govern," said the Minister, "I fear they may be said to give his Majesty's Councils as much continued' though petty trouble, as any people who are, or have been, our declared enemies"...

"It is however to be hoped," resumed the Minister, "that when the important measure of Union, as yet but nominally effected between the two countries, shall have fully come into operation, there will begin, in Ireland, a change of character, which must speedily repay us for the season of turmoil we now endure, and which will show itself as much the result of a well-squared dove-tailing with England, taking root during a necessary previous time, as the present sad state of things may be said to flow from a want of that close and kindly interweaving between the two people."

"If your Lordship means that Ireland will never be quiet, or prosperous, or worth living in, until English views, interests, industry – English character, in fact – take place of the views, interests, and indolence, instead of industry – which confer its present character – then I agree with your Lordship, said the General.

"In detail, Sir Robert, I mean that."

"In a word, until the great majority of the population cease to be merely Irish, and become, like the only portion of it who are now respectable, intelligent – ay, or civilized, - English-Irish," continued Sir Robert.

"Well, and my meaning allows for that construction too," assented the Minister. *"Yes; I like your word, Sir Robert; it defines almost to a point what I might admit to have been my own previous opinion; yes, my first cure for the evils of Ireland, certainly would be to make all her people English-Irish."*

Sir Robert's linguistic groping towards formulating an acceptable epithet for the Protestant plantation minority captures that group's own unease regarding their situation. The compound English-Irish illustrates the complexity inherent in colonization with the attendant split personality dichotomy of trouble associated with living in one country while accepting the sovereignty of another.

In the passage quoted above the view upheld is that Ireland should be defined by how it fails to measure up to 'proper' and therefore to 'superior' standards of English behaviour. This 'otherness' of Ireland, its categorization as irresponsibly wild and incapable of government could be traced back to administrators like Edmund Spencer in the sixteenth century who were sent to the country to report on the customs and conduct of the native population. The consensus was that they were just that: natives. This ethnocentric mind-set paved the way for legitimizing English policy towards its perceived unruly neighbour. Ireland could be classed with other 'savage' colonial areas and for its own good be subjugated towards civilization like any other outpost of Empire.

In *The Anglo-Irish of the Nineteenth Century* the Banims attempt to challenge this historical premise. When the novel commences, the hero Gerald Blount accepts the prejudicial view of Ireland and the Irish. Then when he is shipwrecked on its coast and encounters the country and its people at first hand, he undergoes a sea-change and settles down eventually, marries and stays, content to refute his status as an *absentee* landlord.

Another novelist from the Catholic middle-class was Gerald Griffin (1803-1840). Born in Limerick he was the twelfth of fifteen children in his family; his father was a farmer while his mother (a great influence) was well read and passionate about literature. When he was just seventeen his father, having failed in various business ventures, immigrated to America with his wife and several of the children leaving him in the care of an elder brother who was a physician in County Limerick. Griffin never saw his parents again. After failure as a playwright and while enduring much hardship, he turned to writing stories and his most significant work *The Collegians* was published when he was twenty-five in 1828.

The novel has a sensational story-line based on the actual murder of a young peasant girl, for which the son of a country gentleman and his servant were hanged in 1820. The novel introduces a wide cross-section of Irish country life, while the slightly pretentious prose and frequent allusions to an English readership indicate Griffin's desire to achieve respectability.

The English pastoral tradition is evoked in the description of the idyllic lifestyle of the Middleman Mr Daly, whose urbane, good-humoured gentility includes traditional benefits like a comfortable home, a magnificent view, an adoring family and a table groaning under the weight of food and drink. All is redolent of the opening chapters of Goldsmith's *The Vicar of Wakefield*.

In this way, behind the thrilling tale of violence and passion, Griffin takes pains to create a background of security and ease that is rather at odds with the social and political unrest of the times. The self-conscious prose style and apologetic, justifying intention are identifiable in the following passage from the end of Chapter 1V. The reader has just been assailed by successive chapters of blissful domesticity entitled respectively: 'How Mr Daly the Middleman Sat Down to Breakfast' and 'How Mr Daly the Middleman Rose Up From Breakfast'.

Such in happier days than ours, was the life of the Munster farmer. Indeed the word is ill adapted to convey to an English reader an idea of the class of persons whom it is intended to designate, for they were and are, in mind and education, far superior to the persons who occupy that rank in most other countries. Opprobrious as the term 'middleman' has been rendered in our time, it is certain that the original formation of the sept was both natural and beneficial. When the country was deserted by its gentry, a general promotion of one grade took place amongst those who remained at home. The farmers became gentlemen, and the labourers became farmers, the former assuming, together with the station and influence, the quick and honourable spirit, the love of pleasure, and the feudal authority which distinguished their aristocratic archetypes – while the humbler classes looked up to them for advice or assistance, with the same feeling of respect and of dependence which they had once entertained for the actual proprietors of the soil.

The Collegians is set in the 1770's and 1780's and in Griffin's presentation (that contravenes reality) the natural order in the Ireland of the times is well and truly in place. For the English reader, Mr Daly is the acceptable face of Maria Edgeworth's Jason Quirk. There is but a rose petal between the Munster Middleman and an idealized English Squire. The marriage at the novel's conclusion between Daly's son Kyrle and Ann Chute, daughter of a Protestant gentleman, could be read as symbolic optimism for reconciliation regarding Catholic and Ascendancy traditions. It reads as a literary rather than an artistic solution; like Mr Daly at breakfast, the marriage is more wishful presentation than realistic representation.

William Carleton (1794-1869), like Banim and Griffin, was a Catholic from the provinces; there the similarity ends. He was born in County Tyrone in the North of Ireland; his father a tenant farmer and his mother a noted singer. Carleton received a basic education in hedge schools (held outdoors to circumvent Penal laws forbidding education for Catholic children) then from a curate who taught a classical school in Munster. He studied for the priesthood but left after two years, then converted to Protestantism. He worked briefly as a bird stuffer (surely a detail worth including) in Dublin where he found lodging in a house that contained a circulating library and the landlady allowed him to read for up to 16 hours a day. To earn a living he began contributing to journals and in 1830 his publication *Trials and Stories of the Irish Peasantry* made him famous and from then on he wrote constantly. In his fiction he denounced bravely the excesses of both houses: the Protestant Orange Order and the Catholic Ribbonmen. With Swiftean forthrightness he concluded: *"I have never entertained any ill-feeling against the people on either side; it is their accursed systems which I detest."*

Carleton, like many self-taught persons was imbued with a pedantic desire to impress in his writings; he would even indulge in narrative suspension while he inserted his own opinion. A passage from his 1847 novel *The Black Prophet* illustrates the point.   After dealing, in fictional fashion, with the miseries of famine endured by the rural poverty stricken, the author can hold back no longer and appears in his story as follows.

The misery which prevailed, as it had more than one source, so had it more than one aspect.   There were, in the first place, studded over the country, a vast number of strong farmers, with bursting granaries and immense haggard who, without coming under the odious denomination of misers or mealmongers, are in the habit of keeping up their provisions in large quantities, because they can afford to do so, until after a scarcity arrives, when they draw upon their stock precisely when famine and prices are both at their highest.   In addition to these there was another still viler class; we mean the hard-hearted and well-known misers – men who at every time, and in every season, prey upon the distress and destitution of the poor, and who can never look upon a promising Spring or an abundant harvest without an inward sense of ingratitude against God for His goodness, or upon a season of drought, or a failing crop, unless with a thankful feeling of devotion for the approaching calamity.

There is much strong feeling here.   Not for Carleton the cool objectivity sought after by later practitioners of the novel; most notably James Joyce who opined: *"The artist, like the God of the creation, remains within or behind or beyond or above his handiwork, invisible, refined out of existence, indifferent, paring his fingernails."*

Carleton makes his presence palpable and allows subjectivity full rein.   So those he really objects to be a "viler class"; "hard-hearted and well-known *misers*" who *"prey upon the distress and destitution of the poor*" and demonstrate "ingratitude against God for His goodness".   This *j'accuse* style of writing is rarely lauded in the world of literature in English.   There, restraint and a detached ironic presentation are more celebrated, so that for example, Jane Austen will forever be esteemed above D. H. Lawrence.   Or Emily Bronte.   Carleton's reputation as a novelist has suffered as a result.

The Black Prophet despite its creator's meditations on the events is a gripping story dealing with hard times in the Ireland of its setting.   Within its pages Carleton includes the English he heard spoken in the countryside of his birth and sometimes snatches of the Gaelic.   All is illustrated by the following confrontation between the fiery heroine Sarah McGowan and her step mother.

"So," said the young woman, addressing her stepmother as she entered, "you're come back at last, an' a purty time you tuck to stay away!"

"Well," replied the other calmly, "I'm here now, at any rate; but I see you're in one of your tantrums, Sally, my lady. What's wrong, I say?"   In the meantime don't look as you'd ait us widout salt."

"An' a bitther morsel you'd be," replied the younger, with a flashing glance – "divil a more so.   Here am I, sittin' or runnin' out an' in these two hours, when I ought to be at the dance in Kilnahushogue, before I go to Barney Gormley's wake; for I promised to be at both.   Why didn't you come home in time?"

"Bekase, achora, it wasn't agreeable to me to do so. I'm beginning to get ould an' stiff, an' it's time for me to take care of myself."

"Stiffer may you be, then, soon, an' oulder may you never be, an' that's the best I wish you!"

"Aren't you afeard to talk to me that way?" said the elder of the two.

"No, not a bit. You won't flake me now as you used to do. I am able an' willin' to give blow for blow at last, thank goodness, an' will too, if you ever thry that thrick."

The old woman gazed at her angrily, and appeared for a moment to meditate an assault.

The passage above illustrates perfectly an enduring complication of literature arising when the world of the author is so different from the ambience of characters in the story. Stilted narration clashing with idiomatic dialogue is an inescapable function of the social divide agenda in literature wherever it appears. Indubitably the Irish peasant brogue, as it was rendered on the page, proved infinitely more foreign to an English readership than their indigenous working or rural class dialect could ever be. In William Carleton's fiction the Anglo-Irish writer's wrestling bout with his cultural promptings and the insistent voice of his neighbouring peasantry attains top billing. On the same page the reader witnesses a triumph for Irish experience then despair as English recital pins it down once again. In the end Carleton may be overcome through the intrusion of his own verbosity, but the spirit and verve he displays deserve applause. He makes a greater breach with the literature of England than any previous writer from Ireland and deserves therefore the accolade of Ireland's first national novelist and to be lauded as the father of modern Irish literature.

These three Catholic writers, Banim, Griffin and Carleton, elected to write about the recent past of Ireland, rather than the present they lived in. This may have been because, like Maria Edgeworth, they found the actuality of their time too unpalatably confusing to contemplate. Nevertheless they brought vision and vitality and contributed much towards the initiation of a new literature for the country of their birth. Unwittingly also they were enlisted as heralds propounding a new literary rarity: a Catholic literature for a Catholic land. Nationalist writing mines a slender literary vein so the idea was soon exhausted but did emerge briefly through the efforts of Canon Sheehan towards the end of the century. Sheenan (1852-1913), born on St Patrick's Day at Mallow in County Cork was a Catholic priest, author and political activist. His father owned a small business while the son entered the church and prepared for his priesthood at St Patrick's College, Maynooth in County Kildare before being ordained eventually in the Cathedral of St Mary and St Anne at Cork in 1875. There he wrote for journals, produced also a number of children's stories and poems but became best remembered as a novelist.

My New Curate (1899) is narrated by Father Dan, an elderly Catholic priest in a remote coastal region in Ireland, who has to cope with the arrival of a new and enthusiastic curate, Father Letheby. The novel does provide intriguing insight into the life of a rural priest, despite the fact that Father Dan is a somewhat over-sentimental narrator.

For what does modern literature deal with? Exactly those questions of philosophy, ethics, and morality which form the staple material of theological studies and discussion in our colleges and academies. Novels, poetry, essays, lectures, treatises on the natural sciences – all deal with the great central question of man's

being, his origin and his conduct. And surely it is folly to ignore
these discussions in the market place of the world, because they
are literature, and not couched in scholastic syllogisms? Dear
me! I am philosophizing – I, old Daddy Dan, with the children
plucking at my coat-tails and the brown snuff staining my waist-
coat, and, ah, yes! the place already marked in my little chapel,
where I shall sleep at last.

Other novels from the same vein were Gerald
O'Donovan's *Father Ralph* (1913) and *The Greatest of These*
(1943) by Francis MacManus. It has to be acknowledged
however that, while Catholic experience provided an envious
source of material, a Catholic literature for a Catholic nation was
an idea that never really found its time.

CHAPTER THREE

For their twice weekly attendance at Sunday school the family was
entitled to two outings each year. The best was the Presbyterian
excursion because this took them all the way to the sea-side.

Once aboard the coach their father would sit with Sam,
his favourite. Their mam would sit with the lively, non-stop
rabbiting - on Paul who maintained a whispered commentary on
gossip he had gleaned on others boarding the coach. He, as
reluctant sitting with Jane as she appeared to be with him, could
not help overhearing Paul and feeling all the while as jealous and
resentful of him as he was of Sam. It was the way it was and
there could be no changing it; all he could do was make the best of
his location on the periphery and be above and beyond it all.

"Look mam, there's the Smiths! Their eldest, Doreen –
you know Doreen, she works in Anderson's – she's going out with
Sam Black, you know Sam, he used to work for Davie Hamilton,

you know the milkman, helping him with his round.   Well, Mrs Smith thinks Sam's not good enough for **her** daughter so she put him, Mr Smith up to telling Sam not to come round to their house anymore.   There was a big row in the back avenue.   Sam and Billy Smith were shouting at each other and Mrs Smith – just wait till you hear this – came out and threw a bucket of water over him!"

"Who, Sam?" whispered their mam.

"Yes! Then Sam got real mad and Mrs Smith's dog, you know that wee, yappin' poodle was going past so he booted it and landed it over the hedge.   Mrs Smith flew at him and there was a right argy-bargy.   Somebody called the police and they took Sam away.

"Well I never," their mam would say, shaking her head.

Everyone liked Paul who with his ready wit and easy going disposition was popular with both boys and girls and who with no inclination to enter the secretive and lawless world of his brothers brought the shrouded world outside into their mam's kitchen.   When Paul came home from school, he told her all about his day and about all the news he had gathered from his classmates.   He talked to her and listened to her talk in a way not even their father or even Jane, were prepared to do.   Paul was even entrusted with the task of assisting with their mother's hair; putting it in rollers then combing it out and styling it to her satisfaction.   Natural competitor that he was, he hated losing to anyone, but in this area at least he realized early on, his brother had the beating of him.   So he backed off and left them to it.

On the journey they sang.   Inevitably:

She'll be coming round the mountain

When she comes

She'll be coming round the mountain

When she comes

She'll be coming round the mountain

Coming round the mountain

Coming round the mountain when she comes.

Just belting out the words, never paying any attention to the meaning, it was years before he twigged any sexual connotation.

She'll be wearing silk pajamas

When she comes.

For sure it must be a song about the joys of the female orgasm?   That would surely have put the wind up the Church and Gospel Hall organizing committees.   If they had known that is. The rowdy ones at the back of the coach where Sam and their father sat would turn up their volume on the chorus.

Singing I will if you will so will I

SO WILL I

Singing I will if you will so will I

SO WILL I

Singing I will if you will

I will if you will

I will if you will

I will if you will

SO WILL I.

Their father loved all this and would up the ante by urging Sam, who, where devilment was concerned needed little encouragement, to sing one of the silly, risqué songs their father had taught them when they were little.   Sam would have the coach in stitches with his rendering of:

Aunty Mary had a canary

Up the leg of her drawers

When she was sleeping

It was peeping

Up the leg of her drawers.

Their mam and Paul would look round, roll their eyes heavenwards, but to no avail, there was no stopping Sam now. Forever emboldened by any success he would round off with their father's best-loved:

Holy Moses I am dying

Just one word before I go

Set the pussy on the fireplace

And stick a poker up his

Hole-y Moses I am dying...

Hoots and whistles from the mob at the back, while their father cheered and clapped, their mother looked down, thumb and forefinger of her left hand pressed to her forehead while the silence at the front of the coach spoke volumes.

To Jane, Sam's buffoonery was meat and drink and she would laugh till, in her own words, she nearly wet herself. Paul shared his mother's disapproval while **he** could not bring himself to anything but tight-lipped, stone faced resignation. From birth it seemed to him their father had claimed Sam. The boy was his and that was that. Sam would be brought up in his image; he would spare the rod and spoil the child. Anyone else, as was the way with so many of their father's stances, could like it or lump it. He remembered the bitterness he felt at the closeness Sam and his father exhibited when they collaborated on various do-it yourself projects around the house. Sam had even been allowed to use their father's saw; a tool no-one else was allowed to touch.

A chorus of:

I see the sea

The sea sees me…

All heads turned, some on the isle's other side stood the better to gawk at the bluey-grey water flecked with white specks that initiated a general commotion as belongings were gathered in preparation for their exodus. Soon they were spilling out unto the promenade: the air, the cry of gulls, squeals of children, sand, ice-cream, sticky-splintering rock, the ever seductive whiffs of chips and vinegar. All this and the bright, warm sunshine that seemed always to cap their big day out.

Their father, as ever sticking to his guns, went off on his own. Never a mixer, he refused to make an appearance on the beach or in the amusement arcade with the rest of his family. He had his own day, perhaps in a pub somewhere for he would always stagger just a little when he returned, ever punctual, to the coach for the journey home. He would be dignified, over-controlled, but happy and in good humour, ready for nothing but fitful dozing in his claimed seat at the coach's rear.

His father: the man he feared more than anyone else. And admired, maybe even loved more than anyone else.

The man showed not the slightest modicum of interest in anything **he** ever did. All his life, in his father's presence a voice inside of himself was screaming NOTICE ME! ACKNOWLEDGE MY EXISTENCE! PRAISE MY TALENT! Yet always it was to no avail. His father withheld praise and yes, even criticism, in equal measure, perversely traipsing his own path, doing nothing like anyone else, yet winning respect and approval in a way **he** never could.

CHAPTER FOUR

The Twelfth: ostentatious celebration of the glorious day the Protestant William of Orange and his army battered the Catholic James the something and his, at the Battle of the Boyne. 1066 and 1690: two dates his fellow Protestants had emblazoned on their consciousness. The score: England nil - Ulster one.

"A crowd of bloody lunatics!" was their father's verdict who spent the day at home, alone.

That day! The ubiquitous red, white and blue proclaiming triumphal colorism over the opposition green, white and yellow all over-scored by the pounding tribalism of the lambeg drums. Crowds were lining both sides of the street and Union Jacks were flying from poles, and from upstairs windows, tiny flags waved by children and some mothers along the route and on cue, the sun shining. The mood was good humoured, relaxed with people smiling and small children ushered to the front to allow a better view. Then the bands: flutes, bagpipes, trumpets, accordions, huge belly-drums heard first in the distance, prompting a flutter of excitement then at first sightings, spontaneous applause, cheering as the first stirrings of a recognizable tune became distinguishable, then increasingly and overpoweringly the stamping authority of swaggering musicianship. The high tossed twirling tasseled stick caught then in a fluid continuation of the same movement birled round and round hand to hand back and front, then launched up and up…spinning…the swaying gold brocade banners proliferating with replicas of King Billy erect on the saddle of a white horse his sword pointing forward and upwards. All was uplifting, the music elevated while the pointed sword raised you skywards as did the swirling stick and the imperious Red Hand of Ulster; you were transported from the inevitable disappointments, concerns and sleights of everyday, to the lifting of all those loads on this day, when rich and poor, owner and owned, stood together and celebrated something greater, more instinctive, more emotional and powerful than the everyday could possibly afford.   The music captured and expressed it all; it was impossible to resist being swept up in the rhythmic surge of strutting release orchestrated with such dazzle and energy.

It is old but it is beau-ti-ful

Its colours th-ey are fine

It was worn in Derry Augh-r-im

Enniskillen and the Boyne.

M-y fath-er wore it in his youth

In the bygone day-s of yore

And on the twelfth

I love to wear

TH-E SASH MY FA-THER WORE!

Grim-faced Protestant men wearing dark suits, hard hats and white gloves, some displaying rows of medals won in wars with the British, and all with orange sashes draped over their shoulders, shuffled past, their arms swinging in time, the short steps maintaining solidarity while stopping just short of military parading.   The vast majority of fathers from the estate: all affirming a dignified solemnity with eyes to the front, only nodding occasionally to acknowledge a cry from the spectators. The Orangemen in their lodges all parading to the Field that belonged to Mr Ferguson, one of the huge sloping ones he owned, away from the main road into town.   He and Sam went there one gloriously hot summer's day.

Dotted all round families sat on the grass picnicking, children playing, fathers with shirt sleeves rolled, relaxed, indulgent, mothers harassed, disciplining while organizing food and drink.   The band members piled their instruments in set areas, and mingled with the crowds, the young men attracting the attentions of girls who snatched their hats, put them on their own heads and posed and giggled.   Cameras clicked, children tried unsuccessfully to breathe life into recumbent bagpipes, here and there a drum was bashed or a cymbal clashed.   Attracting most attention were the lads in kilts, nonchalantly fending off the bawdy innuendo of their mates while lapping up any flickers of attention from the girls.   Surrendering to the attractions of the occasion, people ate, drank and laughed and reminisced about previous Twelfths: how the sunshine made the day, the great turn-out, how you couldn't beat a good pipe band, the way you could walk behind it forever and not feel the slightest bit tired.

Over to the far end of the Field and down by the hedge, away from sight of the road a wooden platform had been erected and after midday chairs on it were filled with dignitaries like officials from the lodges, the local member of Parliament, prominent members of the town council and looking somewhat uncomfortable, the Reverend Brown.   Someone produced a loud hailer, and the crowd was assembled in front of the platform.   A familiar drumroll and all stood, throats were cleared, and crying babies were shushed.   The banshee wail of pipes stuttered then fired and the whole assembly rose to the occasion;

God save our gracious Queen

God save our gracious Queen

God Save the Queen

Da da da da

Send her vic-tor-i-ous

Hap-py and glor-i-ous

Long to-o re-ign ov-er us

G-OD SAVE THE QUEEN!

A brief silence, then a ripple of clapping accompanied by sporadic cheering, before silence was restored and the Reverend Brown led them to prayer. Then the speaker:

"Brethren, we live in dangerous times. We need to be as vigilant today as our forefathers were, for Ulster is under siege just as Londonderry was way back in 1690. I'll grant you it's of a different strain but it's a siege, make no mistake. Men, women and children stood firm then as we all need to make a stand together today. The enemy then was a Catholic army led by a Catholic leader, and on this day, the twelfth of July, we celebrate, as it is right and proper to do, their defeat and our famous victory." At this there was a volley of cheering and someone shouted, "Up King Billy!" The speaker raised a hand and order returned.

"The enemy then was a Catholic leader; the enemy today is also a Catholic leader. In the last century one of our brethren in the Orange Order wrote: *Popery is more than a religious system. It is a political system also: a religious-political system for the enslavement of the body and the soul of man.* Brethern, I tell you in all sincerity, the Pope in Rome is a threat to our way of life today!" Cheers and jeers from the crowd prefaced a defiant voice shouting, "No surrender!" Amid all the laughter and shushings the Reverend Brown looked pained and uncomfortable.

"Order, Brethren, Order!" A pause, then: "Rome never forgets and never forgives. Our wee six counties will never be forgotten and never forgiven for standing up against the might of the Catholic Roman Empire and crushing it at the Boyne on this day the glorious Twelfth of July!"

There was more cheering and whooping while someone somewhere banged a drum.

"Remember, the fight must go on! Today they seek to outnumber us by outbreeding us." Quiet reinstated now, the crowd were content to nod agreement. "And who supports their children? That's right! We do! It's the taxes we pay – yours and mine! Our welfare state! We support them! The British way! And never forget our forefathers were British! They planted themselves here and made this soil their own! They and we fought for Queen and Country and no power backed by Rome and Catholic Irish in America or anywhere else is going to wreck our union with the land of our ancestors! The Irish Free State is a foreign power whose very constitution threatens our position! They want to unite with us and claim us for Ireland but we are British, not Irish and must stand firm to remain so! We want no part of priest-ridden Catholic Ireland! We want our own way – the democratic British Protestant way! To protect it we will if called upon fight and we will be right, mark me Ulster will be right! God save the Queen, and for this time and for the future we pledge: NO SURRENDER!"

The Maguires were Catholic and attended a different church and school.

When they passed the chapel, Sean and Teresa would automatically make the sign of the cross. They attended chapel each Sunday but for them, instead of yet more attendance and house arrest, their afternoons were free. Sean would go for Gaelic football practice in a field somewhere behind the chapel.

In the lives they lived each day in the counsel estate these separate existences went unchallenged. They went with your birthright and were as natural an expression of selfhood as your boyhood or girlhood, conditions you received and over which you could exert no control. In **his** life and at that time what really mattered was how much nerve you possessed; how crazed a fighter you were; just how big your big brother was. The religion you were born into was way down the list.

The Catholicism he knew was gleaned from a host of dim sources that lighted on semi-distinct elements like; the Pope in Rome; Cardinals, Bishops, robes, ridiculous hats and palaces; Priests and Nuns; water in chalices changing into wine; biscuit into flesh; confession and absolution; three Hail Mary's, incense and the sign of the cross. Catholics seemed to belong to one unified tribe while his lot, the Protestants, was all divided and in separate castes like his, the Presbyterian, then Methodists, Church of Ireland, Plymouth Brethren; Jehovah Witnesses and maybe more he might not have heard about. Protestantism seemed generally to make less outward display with the buildings, the dress codes and the forms of worship all more muted. The common denominator, ah there was the rub, was faith. Faith was the nettle the signed up, on both sides, had to grasp; faith in a rise from death; faith that made you one of the chosen, to be yourself raised from death in an afterlife for all eternity in a blessed region above known as Heaven where you would be united with your Saviour, Christ. Faith too in the certainty that those who chose to ignore the message would be condemned to an eternity of everlasting pain and torture in a cursed region below known as Hell where they would be united with their chosen one - the Devil.

He could not, would not, commit or pay lip-service to any of it! Was it arrogance, intellectual separation, ego or sheer bloody-mindedness? When he thought it through it seemed to him there was a core message, a key to it all, that to be fair a few good men and women among the faithful did strive to live up to. *Do unto others as you would they should do unto you.* And: *love thy neighbour as thyself.* Christ, what simplicity, what wisdom! The problem was, the tablet proved nearly impossible to swallow. Digest it and the pomp and ceremony would surely have to collapse. You would give to gain and be ready always to turn the other cheek, humility would reign, you would love your brother and sister as yourself and everyone would be your brother and your sister. A sisterbrotherhood of all men and women – what revolutionary simplicity! Mind you, not everyone deserved to be embraced as your brother or sister and what then? Still true adherence to the faith should require that core tenant to be, at the very least, aspired towards, yet that was the truth church leaders and practitioners chose to brush aside. The authority of a faith should not require enhancing with ornate buildings, ceremony, vestments, ritual, icons, alters or even a pulpit. The most fitting church and form of worship would be a place where groups of men and women anywhere gathered together to reflect sincerely on their faith's contribution and response to issues of the day. For, he concluded, there would always be faiths. To him they appeared a response to some basic human need and people seemed relaxed about the attendant wealth and pomp and ceremony; were ready even to applaud and excuse the whole attendant paraphernalia.

Growing up in his time and place he could not help but wrestle with these issues.   That was the cross he had to bear. Sam, on the other hand, and everyone else he knew (apart maybe from Reverend Brown) seemed just to join in and get on with it. Ours not to reason why seemed the ruling attitude.   Religion and politics were not generally considered suitable topics for everyday discussion and were definitely not to be questioned.   They were there to be joined and subscribed to mindlessly; they were a tune you accompanied chorally with the same spirit and awareness you reached when you sang hymns in your church or stood and mouthed God Save our Gracious Queen.   Life was to be lived, opportunities were there to be grasped and the hand that fed you was not to be bitten.

At the heels of the hunt, he came to realize, ideology ruled you.   Grasp it and you could find yourself trapped in a dog-collar, a sash, or whatever.   To preserve his self he would stand alone.   A plague on all your houses!

THREE

Focusing on the rural areas of Ireland and introducing
melodramatic elements within the plot were significant features of
the novels of Emily Lawless (1845-1913).   Born in Ardclough,
Co Kildare and granddaughter of Valentine Lawless, a member of
the United Irishmen, her father Edward Lawless was third Baron
Cloncurry which conferred upon her the title of "The Honourable".
Lawless had a privileged existence on the family's large country
estate but all ended with her father's suicide (two of her sisters also
committed suicide).   Educated privately, she travelled widely in
Europe and a contemporary of Thomas Hardy, her fiction includes
the motif that fate or malevolent external circumstance can play a
hand in the destinies of her central characters.   Her most
celebrated novel *Hurrish* (1886) deals with the violent times of the
Land Wars (1879-91) and is a story of the Land Leaguers (Irish
farmers who resisted eviction and fought to control their own land)
and in general deals with the popular theme of Irish hostility to
English law.   Hurrish O'Brien, a hard working tenant farmer kills
a villainous landlord.   Later he goes to drink from a well.

*Hurrish hastily climbed the steps, and taking up a vessel, left
benevolently for the services of passers-by, drank long and
thirstily.   He was in the act, having done so, of putting the
drinking cup down again, when he suddenly perceived, with some
dismay that it was a skull; another and much older one, of which
this was evidently the successor, lay a little way off on the ledge,
half covered with green mold.   It was not exactly a pleasant
incident, especially to one whose morning's work had been what
Hurrish's had been!   It was a comfort to reflect there was nothing
actually unlucky about it.   On the contrary, skulls were formally
and in some places are still, considered absolutely indispensable to*

the proper efficaciousness of a holy well...Before the reader resolves to be utterly disgusted with this callousness, and to dismiss Hurrish O'Brien once and forever as a monster of brutality, he must first kindly consent to take the circumstances of his life a little into consideration. We are all children of our environment – the good no less than the bad, - products of that particular group of habits, customs, traditions, ways of looking at things, standards of right and wrong, which chance has presented to our still growing and expanding consciousness. Hurrish's history must so far have been imperfectibly told if it has not been realized that he was well disposed to use his strength for good rather than evil.

The quotation above displays many of the characteristics of nineteenth century fiction produced in Ireland. There is the sensational storyline and the concentration on a male protagonist. The author is typically intrusive and has no qualms about holding up the text to supply information regarding peculiarly Irish customs for the edification of readers across the channel. The phrase: *"...skulls were formerly, and in some places are still, considered absolutely indispensable to the proper efficaciousness of a holy well..."* illustrates the partiality for a suitably impressive prose style: the world of the character is definitely not that of the author. Then too the writer has her thumb firmly on the scales, weighing them firmly to favour her central character and leaving the reader in no doubt regarding where sympathies should lie. *"Before the reader resolves to be utterly disgusted with his callousness, and to dismiss Hurrish O'Brien once and forever as a monster of brutality, he must first kindly consent to take the circumstances of his life a little into consideration."* Nurture's influence over Nature was a nineteenth century preoccupation and Lawless is confident that the novel provides the proper forum for airing her views on the subject. *"We are all children of our environment – the good no less than the bad, - products of that particular group of habits, customs, traditions, ways of looking at things, standards of right and wrong, which chance has presented to our still growing and expanding consciousness."*

In all of the above there is omnipresent Dear Reader syndrome so beloved by writers of fiction in the nineteenth century. The novel was still relatively young and as yet in possession of youth's confidence; nervousness regarding the concealing of the writer's presence within the story would only arrive with age.

Heroes of eighteenth century fiction tended to inhabit the upper echelons of society, or if not, by the novel's close some benevolent twist would ensure that was their rightful inheritance. By contrast, Hurrish O'Brien is a poor tenant farmer and this signifies the more egalitarian concerns of the time. Whereas benevolence may have held sway in the eighteenth and early nineteenth century novel, by the middle of the century an increasingly malevolent fate (illustrated in the passage quoted by Hurrish drinking from the skull) became the more dominant controlling force.

Not all writers of the period sought to interpret rural Ireland in tragic terms. A comic approach was adopted by Charles Lever (1806-72) whose tendency was to represent the Irish peasant as a good-natured bumpkin taking a devil-may-care attitude towards poverty and suffering. Lever entertained his readers by playing light-hearted variations on what were considered to be acceptable aspects of Irish national character. The following passage from *Jack Hinton the Guardsman* (1842) serves to illustrate his very different approach. As part of a military exercise, a sham battle is being fought in Phoenix Park,

Dublin.   The bungling Irish approach to the scrap is light years away from the savage nature of the violence in the novels discussed previously.

The Louth fell back, and the yeomen came forward at a charge – Westropp standing high in his stirrups, and flourishing his sabre above his head.   It was just then that a heavy brigade of artillery, unconscious of the hot work going forward, was ordered to open their fire on the Louth militia.   One of the guns, by some accident, contained an undue proportion of wadding, and to this casual circumstance may, in a great degree, be attributed the happy issue of what threatened to be a serious disturbance, for, as Westropp advanced cheering and encouraging his men, he received this wadding slap in his face.   Down he tumbled at once, rolling over and over with the shock: while, believing he had got his death-wound, he bellowed out –

"O Blessed Virgin! There's threason in the camp! Hit in the face by a four pounder, by Jove.   Oh, duke darling! Oh, your grace! Oh, Holy Joseph, look at this!   Oh, bad luck to the arthillery for spoiling a fair fight.   Peter – this was the major of the regiment – Peter Darcy, gallop into town and lodge informations against the brigade of guns.   I'll be dead before you come back."

Lever's work was undoubtedly popular but his 'Oirish' approach did not meet with critical success and wounded by the criticism his subsequent fiction displayed greater sympathy with Irish national feeling.   Of a less sensitive nature in these matters was Samuel Lover (1797-1868) who unabashedly exploited

national stereotypes for the sake of comedy in, for example, his
Handy Andy (1842).

Lover was born into the Protestant middle-class in Dublin
and for a time worked in his father's stockbroking office.   More
interested in the Arts he left the office and family home aged
eighteen to try his hand at poetry, painting and playwriting; much
later with Charles Dickens he co-founded *Bentley's Miscellany*
where parts of *Handy Andy* appeared in serial form.   The novel
was written to amuse; within its pages Lover employs a direct,
almost colloquial narrative style that enables narration and
dialogue to merge quite naturally.

*Andy Rooney was a fellow who had the most singularly ingenious
knack of doing everything the wrong way; disappointment waited
on all affairs in which he bore a part, and destruction was at his
fingers' ends; so the nickname the neighbours stuck upon him was
Handy Andy, and the jeering jingle pleased them.*

*Andy's entrance to this world was quite in character
with his after achievements, for he was nearly the death of his
mother.   She survived, however, to have herself clawed almost to
death while her darling baby was in arms, for he would not take
his nourishment from the parent fount unless he had one of his
little red fists twisted into his mother's hair, which he dragged till
he made her roar; while he diverted the pain by scratching her till
the blood came, with the other.   Nevertheless she swore he was
"the loveliest and sweetest craythur the sun ever shined upon;"
and when he was able to run about and wield a little stick, and
smash everything breakable belonging to her, she only praised his
precocious powers, and used to ask, "Did ever anyone see a
darlin' of his age handle a stick so bowld as he did?"*

Like Charles Lever, Samuel Lover too, despite the harmless nature of his intentions, was castigated by home critics for subscribing to the cult of the stage Irishman, that unquenchable, pugnacious, daredevil, harum-scarum lovable rogue. For a conquered, colonized and planted people can prove sensitive when they find themselves the butt of humour; their skins are thin, their confidence fragile and their antennae ever primed to react to sleight.

A very different fictional world was portrayed in the collaborative novels of Edith Somerville (1858-1949) and Violet Martin (1862-1915). Cousins, passionately fond of horse-riding, the two embarked on a literary partnership which flourished throughout their lives and continued after Violet Martin died, Edith Somerville claimed, through spiritualist communications. They are best remembered for their Irish R. M. stories, in which the outsider Mr Yeates comes as a resident magistrate to the south west of Ireland and has to find his way in this horse-centered, eccentric and socially complex region.

The decline and fall of a 'Big House', that popular topic of Irish fiction crops up again and again in their work, while *The Real Charlotte* (1894) is their take on that popular fictional trope: the difficulty of divining purity of motive. On the surface, Charlotte appears well intentioned; underneath she is ruthless and vindictive in her desire to accumulate land and status and in this would not be out of place in Balzac's *Comedie Humaine*. The influence of Edith Somerville, who had studied art in London and Paris, can be felt in the following passage where the heroine Francie Lamber is struggling with her feelings for Gerald Hawkins, an insensitive soldier soon to leave Ireland.

At the back of the Rosemount kitchen- garden the ground rose steeply into a knoll of respectable height, where grew a tangle of lilac bushes, rhododendrons, seringas and yellow broom. A gravel path wound ingratiatingly up through these, in curves artfully devised by Mr Lamber to make the most of the extent and the least of the hill, and near the top a garden-seat was sunk in the bank, with laurels shutting it in on each side, and a laburnum 'showering golden tears' above it. Through the perfumed screen of the lilac bushes in front, unromantic glimpses of the roof of the house were obtainable – eyesores to Mr Lambert, who had concentrated all his energies on hiding everything nearer than the semi-circle of lake and distant mountain held in an opening cut through the rhododendrons at the corner of the little plateau on which the seat stood. Without the disturbance of middle distance the eye lay at ease on the far-off struggle of the Connemara mountains, and on a serene vista of Lough Moyle; a view that enticed forth, as to a playground, the widest and most foolish imaginations, and gave them elbow-room; a world so large and remote that it needed the sound of wheels on the road to recall the existence of the petty humanities of Lismoyle.

The passage quoted where the writer's eye is fixed serenely on the surroundings of a setting which are then sketched with care and artistry, is a rarity in fiction from Ireland where land, rather than landscape, is usually the focus. The land is inherited, then clung unto and fought over before once again becoming the provenance of wills and setting-off yet more disputes: it is the stuff of logistics rather than aesthetics, a place where artistic appreciation rarely gets a look-in. In fiction of the period, the land is for beasts rather than for beauty.

CHAPTER FIVE

Teresa was in their gang because she was Sean's sister and wherever her brother went she, his twin sister, would go also. More than that, she saw to it she would be accepted on merit so was as daring and resourceful as any in all their escapades. Without fumbling, Teresa could bounce three balls, one after another against a wall, catch each one and bounce and catch and bounce and catch for as long as she wished without pause or effort. He could not manage the same trick with two.

Where were Sean, Sam and Snap that day he and Teresa played cricket, just the two of them, her batting and him bowling furiously, underhand as they had agreed, unable no matter how hard he tried to hit the upended wooden box she guarded so expertly? He cheated, surreptitiously inching his pullover marker closer to shorten his bowling length, but to no avail. Teresa, chin jutting defiantly, defended brilliantly or the ball when it beat her bat would bounce a shaving wide. Now in a rage he sneaked his pullover even closer. His opponent retrieved the ball, turned and threw it back and he botched the catch vexed now with his-self, his foe, the game, the whole world. She ran back and took up her stance, patted the base of the old bat on the ground then looking up and at him leaned forward, alert and so looking the part while he stepped back, helpless doing his best to compose himself and quell the murder in his heart. Rocking back he set off and reaching his marker launched the ball at her wicket overhand. A throw! Teresa, the bitch, chin still jutting, not retreating one inch, swung her bat, middled the ball and propelled it soaring high and away, the meaty THWACK underlining the perfection of the stroke.

"You cheat, that wasn't fair!"

"A black moustache never was fair; it was only a joke!"

"No it was not!   You meant it!   You were mad 'cos you couldn't get me out!"

"I could've – if I'd wanted!"

"You couldn't, no you couldn't.   I saw you move your jumper!   Cheat!   Cheat!   Cheat!"

"Look, I was only messin'.   I never..."

"You weren't!   I know you weren't!   You meant it!   I know you meant it!   Boys hate to lose!   You're just like my brother!   You can't take it!   Cheat!   Cheat!"

Truth hurt he pushed her, while she, giving no ground drew back the bat to swing at him but he moved forward inside her arm-arc, positioned his thigh behind her legs and forced her back until she fell and he was on top, astride her, pinning her wrists to the ground while beneath him she writhed and bucked, writhed and bucked...

The gang constructed huts from branches.   They were secreted in a line of trees at the back of the estate and provided shelter, tribal security, a kind of back to the womb otherness but above all a place that, despite its shortcomings, they could call their own. Unlike family the hut group was a chosen one and provided a space where the rules were of their own choosing.   Inside, in summer, it was warm and from bright sunlight you saw little at first until gradually your eyes adjusted to the darkness.

They played at being Indians, stripped to their underpants, their faces streaked with coal dust, brandishing bows and arrows, wooden tomahawks, knives and lances, stalking each other through the trees.

That day they tracked Snap, a Blackfoot from a different tribe and kicking and struggling they wrestled him back to their camp where they tied him to a tree.

"What Blackfoot do here?"

"Why you come near our camp?"

"Where all your other warriors?"

"How is your belly off for spots?"

Whooping they war-danced round the Blackfoot, jabbing their lances at his chest before he, chief of the Crow nation, stopped, turned and held up his hand, commanding peace. Ceremoniously he planted his lance in the ground, withdrew his long wood knife from a string round his waist, held it aloft with both hands and approached the enemy, improvising as he went, playing to the crowd.

"Me Big Tool, son of Purple Nob and Swinging Diddies. You Little Prick of the smelly Blackfeet come to our land. You ask no permission, bring no gifts."

His warriors, sniggering, were crowding closer and he felt in top form, in control of his eloquence and the situation.

"You, we know are up to no good. You come to steal, take our horses, our women!" He looked solemnly at Teresa in her knickers and vest, held her gaze, excited by the power he felt over them all but inexplicably over her. Dropping his gaze he turned to Sam and Sean. "You Hairy Root and Crazy Chopper, hold his ankles, stop him kick! So Little Prick, you sent by your tribe to spy on our land. We make example of you. You come to take from us. We take from you!" Snap squirmed and yelled. "Little Prick become No Prick!"

Propelled now by the fearful logic of his improvisation he bent and yanked down Snap's underpants. Momentarily his warriors went silent then Sam saved the day by yelling and simultaneously slapping his mouth to produce his Indian call. To his relief the other two joined in. Snap started blubbing but within **him** the bully-beast was aroused and there was no stopping. Reaching out he pulled taut the pathetic penis.

"We teach you Blackfoot a lesson you never forget!"

He brought down the long knife and began to saw back and forth, back and forth...

They were collecting chestnuts: he, Sam, Sean, Teresa and Snap and he had on the gloves, black motor-cycling gauntlets their father had brought home one day and without explanation handed to him. "These are for you," he had said and that was that. It was enough and it was that gesture, the one and only time his father had singled him out and given him anything that made the gloves so prized. He wore them with pride, ritually pulling on tight each one, entwining the fingers of both hands before decisively smacking each balled fist unto his palms; aware he was on the cusp of ridicule, was asking for trouble, but then the gloves were his father's present.

The chestnut trees were in a small copse in a field not far from their estate. First they combed the ground, picking and bagging likely ones, then flinging a heavy stick into the spreading branches to dislodge even more. Then they would split the spiked mace-like yellow-green exterior to reveal the leather-shiny nut inside that squeaked with newness when rubbed between finger and thumb. They had nearly finished their harvest when the trouble came in the shape of four boys from the estate: enemies.

"Like the gloves, eh!"

The tallest, confident, with a strutting menace announcing out loud and no messing he meant business, while his mates looked uncertain, on the fringe of it waiting to see what stuff happened. He knew he could count on Sam, Sean and Snap but the problem was Teresa. Yes she could and would fight but that wasn't the point. Teresa was there and watching and that meant he handled this alone or died in the attempt.

"Think yer big, don't ya?"

They were face to face now, certainty was in the air and there was no backing down on either side. He stood, arms hanging loose at his side and shifted his weight forwards to the balls of his feet so when the expected ritual chest-prod came he was ready and up for it. Swinging up and over his right hand he open palm smacked his aggressor a slap on his left cheek so hard he felt the blow even inside the cushion of his glove. The boy staggered back, the side of his face suddenly red and tears, yes surely tears causing him to knuckle his eyes dry while **he** set himself, fists closed now, knees bent, left leg and left fist forward, looking the part: for Teresa.

Blinking, his foe rubbed his cheek and did his best to compose himself. He swept a look over Sean, Sam and Snap, then: "Got yer friends to back you this time," he whined face-savingly. "I'll get ye on yer own next time."

"You and what army?" he rejoined evenly, keeping it all simple, a triumph of studied underplaying, aware the spotlight was fixed firmly on him. All orchestrated to perfection and one of his finest moments. The enemy gone he pretended protest at his gang's praise and backslapping and smiled tolerantly at Sam's repeated enactment of the slap: his slap. Yet all temptation to join in and really enjoy his triumph he held in check in the consciousness that Teresa was present, confident now that she admired him, her hero.

He was dallying home from the library lost in one of his books when he rounded a corner, looked up from the page and in a flash his heart rate accelerated and he fumbled his books, only just managing to prevent them falling on the pavement. Before him stood an inconsequential acquaintance but accompanying him the feared, compact, muscular, bullet-headed figure of the boy's English relative, going home tomorrow after two weeks of terrorizing the locals. This boy was a street-wise, London tough who actively sought confrontation and fought with a bravery and brutality that had garnered fear and respect throughout the whole estate. Sam, not an exaggerator in these matters, had told him about the English, so privately he had determined avoidance was the best procedure and for nearly two weeks he had stayed out of the way and now at the very last minute…

"Wotcha, mate," or some such English-speak. The three were bunched together before the low wall of one of the small rectangular gardens that fronted each of a row of houses.

"Wot the feck 'ave we 'ere then?"

"Pardon, what did you say?"

"A smartarse: I've heard about you; think you're tough don't you? Well let me tell you, I've been looking for you. I'm here to teach you a lesson you won't forget."

Clearly there was no room for negotiation. Thinking fast he maneuvered himself to the outside of the pavement. The English was on the inside, setting himself, his back to the garden when he let go of his books and in the same movement darted forward and shoved - the low wall, as expected doing its trip-trick – propelled the English into a scraggy mess of dog-turds, assorted wrappings, razor blades, bottles and broken glass, car and motor-bike and bicycle parts, building rubble, barbed wire, empty tins, busted electric fires, wrecked radios, rusted roller skates: all the joys of an Irish country garden.   Eye-balling the hapless acquaintance he retrieved his books and fled the scene already composing the delivery of his triumph to the gang, but not first hand to Teresa.   No, let her find out from someone else.   With her, he sensed typical boys' swagger was not the way; for her he would create from within himself, another self.

Then, when things were going so well, it all went wrong, horribly wrong.

That day they were playing football in the estate's arena: grassy parkland ringed round by fenced off back gardens.   His team was playing Eamonn's, Sean's and Teresa's older brother. A year older than the twins meant he was the same age as himself but Eamonn was never a member of their or indeed any other gang, remaining annoyingly self-sufficient and a real loner who was popular without courting popularity.   Once in a while Eamonn would condescend to take part in their football brawl where he proved himself to be fearless, calm and a natural leader who made the absolute most of his team.

He hated him!

Especially he loathed and yes, envied, the way Eamonn had of running about at the rear of his troops so coolly and economically, reading and directing the play while he dashed about in front of his, ever in a frenzy, berating his teammates, cursing their ineptitude and growing madder and madder at his rival who appeared always in the right place at the wrong time, blocking the path, clearing his lines, controlling the game and winning it for his team.   Twice he had carried on ruthlessly through the tackle, barging into Eamonn but his opponent ignored his clumsy attempts at foul play and head high followed the ball, concentrating on strategy, more involved with team performance than personal vendetta.

Perhaps that was what annoyed him most: that Eamonn, this Gaelic football playing Catholic had more aptitude, more ability, at **his** game than **he** had.   For he knew Eamonn played Gaelic; had watched him practice that foreign run-a-pace, drop-the-ball, toe-tap- it- up- to- catch-sprint they did.   He had tried it himself and bloody difficult it was too; bloody stupid!   And here this taig, this Fenian bastard was poncing about, strolling round the park showing **him** how to play **his** game.   Just who did he think he was!

The ball appeared at his feet and he set off feinting past the full-back's lunging tackle.   He looked up, their goalie was off his line, chip him, no go round him so he pushed the ball forward, the goalie uncertain, now into the box, the goalie rushing out, he dummied left, foxed him, went right and there before an open goal! He drew back his foot to tap in, when sliding through from behind, a foot clean as a whistle stopped the ball, he stumbled and Eamonn slid past disentangling himself in the same fluid motion, rose and pumped the ball over the sidelines.   Too, too much!   Full of puff and huff he ran across and pushed Eammon in the back.

"Foul, that was a foul!"

"I went for the ball and I got it.   You know I never touched you."

"You did too.   I'd have scored if, if…"

"I took the ball."

"You never took the ball!   You couldn't have.   I was shielding it when you slid in and… Any road this is football – not fuckin' Gaelic!"

A circle had formed, he and Eammon were in the middle and as if outside of himself he could hear his voice and it was full of bluster and whine.   He felt also that sympathy had shied from him and transferred to his challenger so there was one and only one way out of this mess!   What was needed was the old might is right smack in the mouth that would show them and him who bossed this show so he did it and threw his punch only Eamonn's face had gone, his opponent had drawn back his head, making him miss and stumble, look a fool.   Right we'll see about this!   It was on now and it was all or it was nothing.   Setting himself he rushed forward swinging his fists before a clean blow to his nose stopped him mid stride, then another smack on his jaw and Eamonn wasn't there to be hit and his nose was bleeding and he was boiling mad now so he dashed forward again summoning himself to wrestle-boot-punch when he was assaulted with a flurry of blows: eye, chin, guts then crunch on the nose again.

It was over and he knew it.   He held up his hands, his foe held out his and he had to take it, had to shake it, attempt a smile and say nothing even though his pride bled and hurt so much more than his face.   Sam, Snap and Sean were there and that was bad enough but it was Teresa's presence that really crushed him.

A Reflection

Why not?   I mean who's to say when you sit at your desk and look down at the keys that you should do this or do that in this pattern or that pattern.   The only obligation you have is to go on going on but that comes from an inner prompt and not from any outer authority.   The writer is a dictator who dictates.   Form and tradition are there to be overturned so why not write an essay? Who is there to prevent me exercising the hard won right to freedom of speech and expression?   Not even you, Dear Reader, not even you.

THE TROUBLES

The root causes of the trouble and The Troubles in Ireland can be traced to sex and violence: too little of the former and too much of the latter.   Football can play a part in explaining the situation.

For a kick-off the pitch was too small for two teams to play without tripping over each other.   Then there were too many players in the opposition for them to be defeated outright so they always felt they were in with a chance.   In the South it was different: there the players on the opposite side were so few they hadn't the numbers to even raise a team.   Sides in the north, on the other hand had huge numbers to pick from, a deep vein of talent to be mined.

Things were relatively quiet when the Protestant side owned the pitch and the ball, laid down the rules, marked the sidelines and picked the players.   They could even, now and then, pick a few token Catholics.   The Troubles started when the Catholic side wanted their own pitch and ball, wanted their say in laying down the rules, marking the pitch and selecting players.   You could afford to be magnanimous when the few you picked did moderately well; it was a different story when the many resurrected their own team, changed the goalposts and the rules and started playing their own game with your ball on their own pitch and what was even more galling could also play your game on your pitch with your ball and your rules, as well and sometimes better than you did yourself!   That didn't half lead to some unfair tackles and when under pressure to some infamous own goals. That was when defenders and especially strikers on both sides came to the fore and exhorted their price.

When the game became too dirty and far too many fouls were being committed, English referees were brought over to restore order and establish control, but they were unable to comprehend the passions involved and soon were seen as biased and incompetent by both sides.   Powerless to call the tune the English referees lost it and started booking key players, giving them the red card, sending them off to the sin-bin, being subject to further abuse, starting to look as if it was a mistake to have come over in the first place and ever become involved in the game: the hate-riot game.

For in the end and for a while that's what it all came down to because hate you could count on; you could feel it, weigh it, measure it.   Hate had existed inside men and women from the beginning of time.   They could hate the cold so find clothes, shelter and fire; hate thirst and hunger so find food and water; hate loneliness so find a companion; hate vulnerability so find strength in numbers; hate indecision so elect a leader.   They would hate the animal or human that attacked them and tried to take what was theirs, so they would find a weapon and strike back.

Hate raised men and women from their knees and provided the spur for invention; hatred of injustice, oppression, inequality, slavery, poverty.   Jesus hated injustice.   Why else would he overthrow the tables in the temple? Why else make sermons about the difficulties of the rich ever entering the kingdom of Heaven? Jesus hated narrow, money-grabbing acquisitiveness – a message that has been played down by the rich and powerful who place the emphasis on the watery turn the other cheek; do good to them who hurt you: a carte blanche for the exploiter, the oppressor. Focused and maintained hatred can right wrongs; it is worth the effort of keeping it trim, in training. Enduring the status quo and making it to Heaven is all very well and good but what about stoking up the old hatred and making it on earth?

Racial hatred, religion hatred, nation hatred: these were the forces that ignited wars, but in the end it was hatred of the nation haters, the religion haters or the nation haters that stopped them. In the end what counts is whose side you are on in your hating. The world can be divided into those who have not and hate their condition and those who have and hate the thought of sharing what they have and the hatred is stronger amongst those who have. So they hold on more and more tightly and surround themselves with increasingly more sophisticated and powerful protection so that have-not hatred becomes powerless and sometimes finds outlet in sporadic eruptions of violence and crime. To a degree the haves can breathe more easily then and join in the ritual of condemnation and further marginalizing of the have-nots.

And love, what about love?

Lust, attachment, yes but love…was it just too abstract, too intangible? With hatred you dealt in certainties while with love you were mired in a tangle of questions? Did love provide the euphemistic expression of lust, a higher emotion concocted by men to confer respectability on their primitive compulsion? Was love a concept analogous to soul, spawned by men to persuade humankind it could aspire to a condition above the animal? Did love serve to persuade humans that monogamy was the ideal romantic union? Was love a man-made construct designed to subjugate women and imprison them within marital snares; to keep women at home while the male roamed free exploiting advantage under the guise of breadwinner? Did love persist to bolster capitalism by inculcating the premise that a guaranteed expression of its strength was the purchasing for the loved one of expensive goods? Was love promoted to keep in employment poets, playwrights, novelists, musicians, artists and religionists? Did the concept of love serve to persuade good men and women to fight and die for the cause of country? Was love a giant con, a sting perpetrated to entice humanity into the pursuit of a tantalizing ideal? Did love purge the minds and hearts of men and women and blinker their gaze to the inadequacy of present circumstance? Was love, like soul guilty of inducing confusion and making clear thinking impossible regarding the reality of the human condition? Did love coil humanity in transcendental tangles by exalting emotion and intuition and in the process denigrating reason and logic? Was it not the case that the power of the middle word in "I love you" could bring women and men to their knees? Did not love assist in adorning the idea of ownership?

In the name of love, Othello claimed he had killed Desdemona. All over the world, people are rejected, imprisoned, beaten, raped, killed; all in the name of love.

I feel better having got that off my breast. What about you, Dear Reader - for all I know, you feel worse. In that case I'm sorry you should be the one to suffer for my art for by right it should be the other way round. Enough! I hear your cry. Let's move on and turn the page together.

FOUR

The modern movement in literature from Ireland was initiated by two men towards the end of the nineteenth century.

George Moore (1852-1933) the eldest son of a nationalist Member of Parliament and trainer of racehorses was born at Moore Hall in County Mayo and thus experienced at first hand the decline and subsequent fall of an Irish Big House. While his early education was hampered by poor health, Moore nursed an ambition to become an artist with his own independent vision and voice and to this end he dedicated his life, leaving Ireland for Paris when he was twenty-one where he encountered new developments in painting, music and literature. His Parisian existence afforded accessibility to a succession of literary influences: Zola, Flaubert, and Turgenev, Tolstoy, the poet Mallarme and the essayist and critic Walter Pater. Moore became friendly with the painter Manet who sketched three portraits of him.

Setting aside any ambition he had to become a painter, Moore sailed for London in 1882 to write novels where he achieved uncharacteristic popular success with his *Esther Waters* in 1894. Previously he had employed a heroine as central character in his Dublin-centered novel *a Drama in Muslin* (1886) but *Esther Waters* was unique in restricting the point-of view to that of an illiterate servant girl, limited in perception and understanding; a technique later refined by, for example, James Joyce in the following century. Here is Esther, trembling at the prospect of employment as a kitchen-maid:

There would be a butler, a footman and a page; she would not mind the page – but a butler and a footman, what would they think? There would be an upper-housemaid, and perhaps a lady's maid, and maybe that these ladies had been abroad with the family, and would talk about France and Germany, about trains, hotels and travelling all night.   But she would not be able to join in: her silence would give them the tip; they would ask about what situations she had been in, and when they learned the truth she would leave disgraced.   But she hadn't sufficient money to pay for a ticket to London.   And what excuse could she give Lady Elwin, who had rescued her from Mrs Dunbar and got her the place of kitchen-maid at Woodview?   No, she couldn't go back.   Her father would curse her, and perhaps beat her mother and her too. Ah!   He would not dare to strike her again, and the girl's face flushed with shameful remembrance.   Her little brothers and sisters would cry if she came back.   They had little enough to eat as it was.   Of course she mustn't go back.   How silly of her to think of such a thing.

The carefully controlled empathy of this passage with its plain colloquial style echoes that employed by Gustave Flaubert in *A Simple Heart* (1875) another tale of a poor maidservant. Moore, as the passage above illustrates, utilizes an uncomplicated syntax allied to an interior monologue delivery with an accompanying repetition at key moments as in *"There would be..."* and the echoing crescendo of *"...she couldn't go back"* and *"...she mustn't go back"*.   James Joyce, himself musically adept, employed a similar technique in his tale of the servant Maria in *Clay (Dubliners)* 1914 and acknowledged the debt he owed to Moore when he rated *Esther Waters* as *"...the best novel of modern English life."*

In *Esther Waters* Moore, noted for the force of his personality and ostentatious display in social life, contrived to edit himself out of his work.   At a stroke he solved that recurrent problem of nineteenth century fiction: the gulf between the voice of sophisticated narration and lower class dialogue. For Moore's novel is presented in virtual first person and the single point-of-view is that of an illiterate servant girl; all the reader receives is filtered through the consciousness of this bewildered young woman. In this respect *Esther Waters* pre-empts key modern texts like Virginia Woolf's *Mrs Dalloway* or *What Maisie Knew* by Henry James. Moreover, Moore's is a brave novel, placing before Victorian readers at the centre, and not the periphery of the text, a *'fallen woman'* and one without redeeming beauty like Thomas Hardy's *Tess of the d'Urbervilles*.

In *Esther Waters* Moore tapped into the inspirational area of *'Ireland as Woman'*, for by relinquishing his male identity and adopting the voice of a woman, and significantly a sexually compromised woman from a lower class, (James Joyce achieved a similar metamorphosis with Molly Bloom), Moore paved the way a writer from Ireland could wrest independence from the artistic shackles of English literature. Freedom could be won through liberation of authorial utterance. If a sophisticated man could convince as an uncultured girl then, in fiction surely, anything was possible.

CHAPTER SIX

Snap's father was a Methodist minister; a man who believed in the essential goodness of young people. Freedom begat responsibility, he was fond of saying, tolerance triggered respect while kindness was repaid in kind. Besides, his son's friend was an upright young man from a good family, well-mannered and a model student. Two such deserved to be indulged; they were good for each other and set a standard to which other young people could aspire. The Reid's' family caravan at Portrush could do with an airing and the sea and sand and good clean air could only be of benefit to the boys who surely were old and responsible enough to be trusted on their own together. Mrs Reid, a gentle, sickly woman would nod nervous agreement at her husband's progressive views on the subject of child rearing. Whenever she could corner her only son she would draw him to her and hug and hug him, Paul had told their mother, and that Snap's mum had been told she was too frail to have children and his birth had nearly killed her and she called him her miracle boy.

Ruthlessly Snap exploited his parents' idealism and adoration. While outwardly appearing to permit their sermonizing and embracing, behind their backs this trusted and adored son blasphemed, gambled, drank alcohol, stole, fought and vaulted all over the rules, for his parents' faith and worship had bequeathed Snap a priceless commodity. What, through bravado, fear of failure and a constant, nagging prompting to impress, **he** achieved, Snap accomplished effortlessly from an unending supply of confidence. Any challenge was accepted because simply Snap was convinced he could do anything and anyway if failure proved a consequence, so what – you laughed, buried the memory, got over it and walked away.

With girls, Snap grinned and groped his way towards satisfaction; for him squeals and slaps were invitations, not deterrents and more often than not his audacity prevailed. Longing to fondle breasts and slide his hand up skirts with Snap's genial effrontery, **he** could be only uneasy and shrinking in the company of girls, unable ever to conquer an inherent reserve because, unlike Snap, he had no pool of confidence to draw from. On the few occasions he managed a sexual swoop the consequent alarm and inevitable rebuttal were enough to destroy the little confidence he had, so yet again his attempt would fail. Snap endured none such confusions and for this he envied him.

Later he would come to see their relationship as symbiotic; Snap stretched down a hand and raised him to heights of daring he would never have achieved alone, while his company conferred a veneer of respectability on their association. Further and of utmost importance, leadership struggles were never an issue; Snap's confidence required no such status symbol, his ego was secure and settled while for **him** command was vital. The title covered up the cowering creature he really was.

One Friday night Reverend Reid deposited them at the caravan leaving behind a cardboard box filled with groceries, the key and two ten pound notes.

"Are we the knees of bees?"

"Boyo are we a right pair of chancers?"

"Right bosun, empty the bilges, stow the gear while your captain peg-legs ashore for a barrel of rum that'll surely shiver yer timbers."

"Aye, aye, captain avast and aweigh and while ye be gone I'll polish me barnacles till they glow like doubloons."

"Then they'll light me way back.   But when I'm gone beware a blind man who can't see but can spot you a mile off."

Looking older than his sixteen years he had little problem procuring alcohol while the fresh faced Snap stood little chance.

Later, swigging down gulps of cider they prepared themselves for the night ahead.   Then with courage stoked they headed for the dance hall.   In the toilets they jostled as they splish-splashed the enamel while the room twirled and dipped and he found himself transported outside of himself, watching himself acting a part, even at times providing a running commentary.

"Steady there boyo, you'll be right as rain in a jiffy.   Why not give the hair a wee rake now?"

Drawing his comb, he set himself before the mirror, left arm loose, hand poised, right arm holding the comb extended and looped over his head.   The room tilted and he stepped back, frowned then resumed the position before drawing the comb through and patting smooth the result.   In command now, he willed himself back inside himself and with Snap in tow weaved his way to the dance floor.   Once inside the ballroom they split up while head spinning he sought his reflection in a floor to ceiling mirror.   He straightened his narrow tie; smoothed back his hair with the palms of his hands, then clasping his lapels between thumbs and fingers shrugged his shoulders more securely into the jacket's wide, padded frame.   Patting his pockets he found and withdrew his pack of Lucky Strike, shook the packet forward and swiftly back and for once it worked and a quarter inch of cigarette end protruded, just enough to take between his lips and winkle out the cigarette before replacing the packet and pocket tapping again he located and withdrew his book of matches. The cigarette tip was becoming moist so with the index fingers of his left hand he removed then stroked it, tapping both ends on his thumb nail before replacing it in between his lips then tearing off a match, sparking it then cupping his left hand, the matchbook snagged safely between his index fingers, with his right hand he raised the match and touched it to the cigarette, inhaling deeply, then letting the smoke escape evenly in equal measures from his nose and mouth. Man he felt good as he removed the cigarette, licked his lips and air-spitted free a fleck of tobacco while in the same breath blowing out the match before dropping it to the floor.

He was ready and the band was smouldering; all dressed in identical maroon blazers, narrow black ties, white shirts and black trousers, their slicked-back hair shining.

The trumpets wail as it wheeled away and soared free until it was chased then caught and scolded down by a chivvying sax until both were sent scattering by the drum's rip and the cymbal's clash. Then his favourite: the orchestral mayhem of the drum solo. It began slow, then wound up gradually beating faster and faster, louder the beatbeat bashbashcrashcrash smash of the whirring sticks making as only music could tiny hairs tingle at the back of his neck, the sustained maintained repetition exquisitely just bearable as the drummer worked his magic, transfixing everyone, holding centre-stage, holding all spellbound, holding, holding, holding, then timing the crescendo to perfection with a clashing cymbal's crash releasing and allowing the trumpets, piano and saxophones to effect release and restore normality.

He turned away, looked up and caught the eyes of a girl at the other side of the dance floor. She wore a dress with a tight bodice top low cut to reveal just the V at the crest of her breasts, then below a nipped-in waist that flared out over bunched petticoats.   Her hair was long and dark, her lips red while her eyes held his and drew him towards her.   Dodging between dancing couples he puffed at his cigarette before dropping the butt to the ground and stubbing it with his foot.   He looked up and into her eyes; they were brown and she held his gaze with no hint of embarrassment.

"May I have this dance please?" he managed and held his out his hand.

The girl took it and he led her to the dance floor, threading through the couples till he found their space.   There he drew her to him, his left hand firm in the small of her back, her hand resting on his shoulder, then he took her right hand and in the same movement slid forward his left leg, caught up with his right, shifted his weight and spun them both into the throng of dancers circling the floor, seeming to loom alarmingly towards collision, then at the last moment manoeuvring them towards safe passage with gliding ease fancy-stepping around and around, controlling their closeness through varying pressures of his left hand, commanding their direction with his left leg foot-push-turn and swivel-hip, while with his right hand he squeezed her fingers, gauging her reaction, sensing just the apt time to place that hand too on his shoulder, to enclose her in his arms, squeeze her nearer, press her cheek close to his and accompany the band's lead singer by crooning softly in her ear.

"Fancy a coke?"

"Yes.   Thanks."

He led the way to a table upstairs and bought and brought the drinks.

"Are you on your own?"

"No, my friend's dancing.   Look, there she is, down there!"

She leaned over the balcony, pointed and waved.

"I'm with a friend too. I can't see him but he's here somewhere."

Of a sudden all went black as his eyeballs were squeezed back into their sockets.   He stayed calm.

"Meet Dennis Reid - known to all and sundry as Snap. Watch those hands of his; they're always somewhere they shouldn't be."

He prised them from his face.

"I'm Paula and this is my friend Barbara."

Breathless and sweating slightly, a plump blond with freckled face slumped into a chair beside her friend.

"Give us a swig of that coke Paula.   Phew, it's hot in here."

"I'll get us one," Snap offered gallantly, then unseen by the girls he winked, formed a circle with thumb and index finger of his left hand while gently poking the index finger of his right in and out, in and out.   The girls told them they were waitresses in a local hotel where on top of their wages they received free board and lodgings.

"We're sailors on shore leave.   I'm Moby Dick."

"He's having a whale of a time.   I'm Captain Flint."

"Strike a light Captain!"

They nonsensed on, then Snap asked Barbara for a dance.

"He's a laugh, your friend."

Paula and he danced and he held her close, his cheek touching hers. He felt her breath on his face. Impulsively she clutched the hair at the back of his head and pulled looked him momentarily full in the eyes, and then brought her mouth to his, opening her lips, prodding her tongue between his teeth. At her touch his apartness deserted him and his desire was to cling solely to her.

Back at their table, Snap took over; they would all go back to the caravan for a drink, then they would see the girls back to the hotel. Outside he held Paula's hand, receptive to every tiny pressure of her fingers; she was special this slip of a girl and for the first time he felt truly protective towards another person. Snap, to give him his due, seemed to respond to his mood and wisely left off any add-libbing while back at the caravan he wasted no time overruling Barbara's giggling resistance and the two were soon kicking off shoes and snuggling under the covers of his bed. With Paula leading the way there was no option left but to do the same and when she unzipped her dress and shimmied it to the floor and stood briefly in her bra and panties before slipping under the covers he thought surely his heart would burst with a surfeit of love and desire. Shrugging free of his jacket he hooked his finger behind the knot of his tie jerking it away from his neck then tugged the loop over his head but it snagged under his nose so in his haste he prised and prised till the tie ripped and fell away. He struggled out of his shirt and vest, dropped his trousers and attempting to kick them free tripped and fell back on the bed where in the same motion he jack-knifed and wrenched free his shoes and socks, prised off his trousers, stood, lifted the covers and inserted himself under them and into his bed. Wasting no time, Paula ran her hand over his shoulder, down his side and was in the act of prising her fingers into his underpants when at her touch he spasmodically began to ejaculate.

On the way back to the hotel the girls whispered together and sniggered and at the dance the following evening Paula made it plain she was with Snap.   Heartbroken he did his best to pay some attention to Barbara but without any pleasure on his part: he considered her lumpish and course.   She danced with awkward enthusiasm so he spun her round and round the floor.   Afterwards in his bed under the covers he unclasped Barbara's bra, squeezed her breasts, even dared to touch her between her legs.   She slapped his hand but past feeling he was past caring.   Raising his head he could make out Snap's bed at the other end of the room, taking in the heaving covers and at the pillows a flaming red head bobbing up and down, up and down...

For him the rest of the holiday was a misery.   While he made it clear he did not wish to spend any time with Barbara, Snap made it equally apparent that Paula and he were inseparable.   Daytime he was left to walk the shoreline and fend for himself while nights he spent eating alone in a café and trudging round the town before returning to the caravan alone in time to creep to bed and do all he could to avoid contact with the ever together Snap and Paula.   A distance had set in between him and his former friend so he was glad when the holiday came to an end and the Reverend Reid came to drive them home.   As for Paula, she made clear her distaste for him which was fuelled further by his rejection of her friend.

The whole episode was a mess and he could not wait to be home and leave it all behind.

As he was diving into the back seat of Reverend Reid's car, Paula who had come to meet Snap's father and say her goodbyes, surreptitiously pressed a folded note into his hand. He allowed the car to drive some distance before he furtively opened the missive.

I HATE YOU.

BARBARA HATES YOU.

DENNIS HATES YOU.

ROT IN HELL JAMES CARSON.

Staring at the words he blinked several times and shook his head. He considered tearing the note into shreds then deciding against folded it carefully before secreting it in his pocket. He would dispose of it later.

FIVE

George Moore's work was always experimental and changeable and his traditional questioning of traditional forms and subject matter, allied to his imperviousness to adopting any moral stance, caused him to fall foul of establishment opinion.   Another such and a writer greatly influenced by Moore was Oscar Wilde (1854-1900).

Oscar Fingal O'Flahertie Wills, Wilde's parents were successful Anglo-Irish Dublin intellectuals.   His father was an acclaimed doctor, knighted for his work as medical advisor for the Irish census.   His mother was a poet who was closely associated with the Young Ireland Rebellion of 1848.   A bright and bookish child, Wilde attended Portora Royal School at Enniskillen in the north of Ireland where he fell in love with Greek and Roman studies and won a scholarship to attend Trinity College in Dublin. There he excelled academically, as he did later at Oxford.   At Oxford he became known for his involvement in the burgeoning philosophy of aestheticism, a theory of art and literature that emphasised the pursuit of beauty for its own sake, rather than to promote any political or social viewpoint.   Throughout his life he remained deeply committed to the principles of aestheticism.

Best remembered for the sparkling wit of his stage comedies, Wilde revealed a darker side in his novel *The Picture of Dorian Gray* (1891).   Inspired by an incident in his great uncle Charles Maturin's *Melmoth the Wanderer* (interestingly Wilde adopted the pseudonym Sebastian Melmoth in his last years in Paris after his release from prison where he had been convicted on a charge of sodomy), Wilde transforms the Gothic form into a detached dramatization of the triumph of art over experience. Like Melmoth, Dorian Gray barters his soul for eternal youth. The novel is a portrait of the artist as a young man; it deals with sensibilities and ideas rather than the sensation and incident that are the key features of the Gothic strain from which it emerged. In his famous Preface and in typically provocative aphoristic fashion Wilde presents some of his ideas on the art of novel writing.

To reveal art and to conceal the artist is art's aim.

There is no such thing as a moral or an immoral book.   Books are well written, or badly written, that is all.

No artist has ethical sympathies.   An ethical sympathy in an artist is an unpardonable mannerism of style.

All art is quite useless.

A central theme of *The Picture of Dorian Gray* is influence.   Here is Lord Henry Wotton revelling in his wit and sparkle as a conversationalist:

He felt that the eyes of Dorian Gray were fixed on him and the consciousness that amongst his audience there was one whose temperament he wished to fascinate, seemed to give his wit keenness, and to lend colour to his imagination.   He was brilliant, fantastic, irresponsible.   He charmed his listeners out of themselves, and they followed his pipe laughing.   Dorian Gray never took his gaze off him, but sat like one under a spell, smiles chasing each other over his lips, and wonder growing grave in his darkening eyes.

In the novel Dorian Gray is influenced also by the artist Sybil Vane and by an undisclosed book, while Gray in turn influences the artist Basil Hallwood.   With his constant preoccupation with the role of the artist in relation to his work, Wilde's novel could be seen as a harbinger for the whole modern movement in literature. Within its covers *The Picture of Dorian Gray* is permeated with epigrammatically rendered and sometimes contradictory opinions on the subject of art:

"Behind every exquisite thing that existed, there was something tragic."

"The true mystery of the world is the visible, not the invisible."

"Beauty is a form of Genius – is higher indeed than Genius, as it needs no explanation."

"An artist should create beautiful things, but should put nothing of his own life into them."

"Every portrait that is painted with feeling is a portrait of the artist, not of the sitter."

Much of this was influential on James Joyce, for example, who included his own theory of aesthetics in *A Portrait of the artist as a Young Man*.   Moore influenced Wilde, who influenced Joyce, who...   The significance here is that by the end of the nineteenth century, writers in Ireland (and elsewhere) were being influenced by writers **from** Ireland and not modelling their work solely on that created by literature from the English tradition.

The Picture of Dorian Gray was Wilde's longest prose narrative, and he experienced great difficulty with its composition. The difficulty was doubtless compounded by Wilde's inclusion in the novel of his own experience in relation to homosexuality; like his creator, Dorian Gray is open to the experience of love with both women and men.   In keeping with the times, Wilde's treatment of '*the love that dared not speak its name*' is suitably veiled, but still he dared to go where few had gone before.   It is worthy to note that, as suitable cases for treatment, Moore and Wilde should choose respectively an unmarried mother and a homosexual male; the outsider would figure as a character under fiction's scrutiny from this time onwards.   Ironically Catholic Ireland, where church censorship was a palpable threat, was spawning a fifth column of novelists who would contribute as much as anyone towards the dragging, albeit kicking and squealing, of that clergy-ridden nation into the modern world.

Labouring to find its own voice, the novel from Ireland written in English in the eighteenth century, aspired to imitate English speech rhythms and focus on English inspired subject matter.   By the beginning of the nineteenth century, the novel from Ireland was beginning to speak with its own voice and articulate its own experience.   By the end of the nineteenth century, writers in Ireland felt confident enough to embrace more experimental modes of expression.   The individual self was still a preoccupation, with the significant difference that the old judgmental concern regarding who was a good person was largely abandoned or became much more complicated.   George Moore and Oscar Wilde were foremost in introducing the concept that art rather than conduct was the novelist's primary concern and artistry was about the business of showing rather than telling: what was left out of a text became as important as what was put in. Previously the novel had tended to give characters a hard time and, through the creators' sign-posted morality, the reader an easy time; readers had been directed as to what to think and feel and with whom to extend sympathy. Within the pages of the book all was explicable. From Moore and Wilde onwards this certainty disappeared and the novel in English from Ireland was on its way towards Europe and the world beyond.

In their different ways writers from Ireland in the eighteenth and nineteenth centuries made a lasting contribution to the art form that is the novel. The language they wrote in was theirs and not theirs: like that ubiquitous hero of modern fiction their lot was to be born within their culture, yet remain alienated from it. This was a trope moulded further in their lives and writings by Irish writers like James Joyce and Samuel Beckett in the early twentieth century. For them too resistance to traditional literary forms became an essential feature of their artistic expression. With the magical realist Dean Swift at the helm and babbling interference from an undisciplined crew of Anglo-Irish innovators the craft of fiction was in good hands, freed to carry on regardful in the knowledge that conviction regarding destination was not of the essence, but rather significance resided in the jaunt itself.

Enough of scribblings from the past; it is time now to give undivided attention to mine in the present and remember we are fellow travellers in our time together you and I, Reader. One other thing before we set off once more: I promise no more interruptions.

You have my words on it.

CHAPTER SEVEN

Teresa and he drifted apart.   She enrolled in the young girls' tribe
of linked arms, nudges and cackles, an impenetrable society that
viewed the gang's activities with lofty scorn.   The gang broke up.
Their father bought a car and took the whole family on an outing to
visit his sister in Londonderry.   Somehow it was agreed that he
would take a bus and spend a month with her in the summer
holidays.   The idea did not appeal but his father ruled the roost so
what could he do?   He thought his aunt, mousey and old-
fashioned, loathed the smell of gas in her kitchen and hated the
way she hugged him, mussed his hair and made a fuss of him.
The only books on her shelves worth reading were a pair of Zane
Grey westerns but to be fair, seeing he liked to read she took him
to her local library and that way he could just about tolerate the
time spent and the boring trips across the border to the little seaside
town she seemed to take so much pleasure in.   The last day of
his stay she was putting some sandwiches in his suitcase when she
happened upon some trinkets he had found and there was a bit of a
fuss so that put paid to that.   He would not be going back.

He passed the eleven plus examination, gaining access to
the local grammar school and a new set of acquaintances living in
a world uniquely different from that of the estate.   Houses in leafy
avenues where a tranquil sense of order prevailed and plenty
abounded: plenty of space, of heat, of books, of food, of care and
support.   This was the world he felt comfortable in and knew
deep down he was entitled to inherit.   Beside it the company of
Sam and friends and acquaintances in the housing estate and the
members of his own family gradually lost their attraction.   More
than that he grew ashamed of his surroundings and associations
and wanted only to escape and leave all behind.

Study was the means, so he worked at his books with a competitive intensity that won him the respect and approval of his new acquaintances and their families.   Embracing the role of exemplar, the working class urchin who despite manifest disadvantages struggles to make good, he was welcomed everywhere as a corrective: if he could attain top marks then why not their sons with all their manifest superiority?   As for his own family, sensing he was breaking with the traditional mould, they left him to get on with it.   Except for Sam, who became perplexed and hurt, could not comprehend or accept remaining inside reading and making notes when fields and sun and later girls and pubs, beckoned so insistently.   Sam would not let go easily, cajoling, clowning and when that failed becoming noisy and abusive.   To no avail, and a distance grew between them that he stubbornly, single-mindedly did nothing to lessen.

Selfishly he slogged away and inevitably reward came. He gained the distinction of being the first in his family to escape, leaving their small country town for Belfast, the University, a student with a full grant and a room of his own.

Cards was the only game his family ever played together; except of course for Paul and their mother who were invariably to be found gossiping in the kitchen between bouts of making and drinking tea and assisting each other in kitchen-based activity.   In his father's hands the playing cards would come alive.   He would split the wrapping on a new pack, prise open the box and tip the contents into his hand, then pick out the Jokers before tearing them into pieces and flicking them on the open fire, on the pretext they were bringers of bad luck.   Then their father would tap the pack on the table, square them, split the pack in half, set the two halves side by side, then with his thumbs as he held them phutphutphut them together as one again and again before one-handed he would square the pack, cut and place it on the table before them. The ritual complete they were ready for the game.

To begin with they played partner Whist: himself and Jane against his da and Sam. Trumps were cut for; the cards were shuffled and dealt then picked up, fanned out, placed in suits and gauged before left of the dealer set down the first card and they were off. Invariably he set out a low card from a long suit in the hope his partner held the ace or, just as good had none and was able to play a trump card and win the hand. The Whist game over, Sam would be dispatched to the cupboard for the button-box, the contents spilled in the table's centre then picked one by one until each player had their stack for wagering during his favourite card game: Poker, or more specifically Five Card Stud. Of course you needed luck; the run of the cards but you could with skill, measured daring and bluff create your own luck and the more he played and the more buttons he won the more he realised he was good at this game.

He knew about cards.

The card school was held in a student's house behind the university. He found out about it from an acquaintance a year above him at school: Willy Hamilton, heir to a chain of furniture shops throughout the province, the moneyed son of a moneyed family. Willie could afford to lose and he did, persistently playing a Kamikaze game, taking risks with cavalier determination, making the most of student irresponsibility before his birth right claimed him. Flush with money from his recently cashed grant cheque **he** was in no mood for hazard so played the hands he was dealt with deliberation and as the night progressed won and won and won. At nearly two in the morning he was piling his winnings ready to stand, stretch, collect all and make his excuses when two blokes burst into the room. They had been to a party, were obviously tipsy, and the burlier of the two made a big thing of slapping backs and shaking hands, knew everybody, wanted to play and everybody agreed, why not, especially when he delved into his pocket, produced a wad of notes and slapped it down on the table.

It wasn't just the money; the man himself had a part to play. Unlike everyone else he didn't know him personally, had never been introduced, yet he had seen him around and he knew about him. The McCann's were wealthy: betting shops, a pub, a shoe shop, starting up in auctioneering. They owned no farmland like the Fergusons, but were into business in a big way and growing. McCann: rich Catholic with a private education, in his final year, studying Law, what else? McCann with his potato head, puffy eyes and big ears: he hated him as soon as he swivelled eyes on him so he'd stay, show him a thing or two, and teach him a lesson.

"I'm Kevin McCann, this here's Damian. What's the limit? I'll bet a fiver. Unseen." He wrestled out of his coat, dropped it on the floor behind and plopped into a chair scraping it forwards, before placing his elbows on the table and punching his right fist into his left palm.

"Come on!"

He dropped his head, considered his wad of notes, disengaged his left hand, peeled off the top one and spun it carelessly into the table's centre.

"Come on, it's only money! Who's with me?"

"I'm yer man McCann.   I'm Willy Hamilton and that shrewd boy there, that's James Carson; we're from the same neck of woods as you.   Ye seem to know everybody else."

"Aye I do that.   From the wee town are we and now up to the big city.   I know your family Willy – furniture isn't it?   What about you, what line of business are you Carsons into?

He ignored the probing.

"It's seven card stud, Jacks or better to open the betting. The limit was a pound but we can raise it if you like.   It's up to you."

"I'm easy."

"I'm out."

"Me too, I'm off to bed, big day tomorrow. See yourselves out lads."

They were left, just the four of them: McCann, his friend Damian, Willy and himself.

"Right, divvies up, I'll deal."

Clumsily McCann shuffled the cards and a few slid out face up on the table.   Not looking at what he was doing he scooped them up, smacked them in the pack wrong way up and shuffled.

"Shite I've boxed them!"

Taking his time he located the errant cards, turned them right way up, shuffled again, cut then dealt.   Then out of order, no respecter of etiquette, "Dealer can't go!   What about you Willy boy?"

"I can go!"

"Oooh bet you have a nice pair there Willy boy.   I like a nice pair.   What's yer bet?"

"I'll bet two quid," and Willie selected the notes and pushed them to the centre of the table.

"Oooh I like a man who puts his money where his mouth is.   Well Jamesy, you in?"

He hated talking card players and that Jamesy and all that ooohing…   He concentrated on the cards.   Two tens, so worth a go and he slid his money towards the middle.

"Damian?"

"I'm folding."

"So, tis up to me then!   Yer two and – ye see that five I threw in blind – well nothing ventured, nothing gained, I'll up ye five more.   Let's see what yer made off."

"Your five and I'll bump you five more!"

This was Willy's kind of game and his pair of tens seemed puny now.

"I'm out."

"A Loss of nerve eh Jamesy.   Well let's see now. Hmmm right, I'll go along.   How many cards Willy boy?"

"Three."

"Dealer takes three.   Well Willy, it's up to you."

Willy was smiling; he could be read like an open book. "I'll raise you five."

"Two pair eh Willy. Jacks and... Not good enough. Let's see: your five and five more." McCann rubbed his hands together, tossed the notes across, folded his arms and leaned forward with his elbows on the table.

This was getting out of hand. Willy fanned his cards, gazed at them, folded his hand and smiled. He was in his moment and enjoying it. Then true to form, "I'm with you: your five and five more."

McCann sat back in his chair, wiped his mouth with his hand, thought about it, then, "Too good for me Willy. Ye have the beatings of me. Look, King high. What did ye have? Show us your hand!"

One by one Willie placed his cards on the table.

"Jacks and threes; that's the best hand I've been dealt all night!"

Grinning and triumphant, Willy scooped the pot.

This McCann was a bluffer, a drunken loud bluffer who was there for the taking. He needed to be taught a lesson and **he** was the man to do it.

They played on until Willie had no more money left to lose. McCann lost too, **he** was up but the real winner was the silent, swarthy Damian, who played prudently, biding his time and seeming to have a sixth sense about when to stay out or when to make his bet.

"That's it," from Willy, "no more for me, I'm cleaned out! Jesus, look at the time, it's nearly four o'clock. It'll be light soon." He stood. "Are you coming James?"

"One more hand Jamesy boy, just one more for the road. There you go; I'll bet a tenner blind. Match that! What about you Damian, you in?"

"Naw, that's too rich for me. I'm quitting while I'm ahead."

That decided it: no card shark, just him and the gobshite.

"Your ten and," he smiled, "ten more."

Willy stopped, turned, crossed back to his chair and sat down. Damian who had been set back eyes closed, leaned forward with sudden interest.

"Sure ye know what yer getting into here Jamesy boy? Your ten and... Only pulling yer leg Jamesy. No need to get excited. Tell ye what, I'll go along. Let's deal three, and then we'll see how the land lies."

"It's alright with me."

McCann shuffled and then dealt. Outwardly he summoned calm but inside he felt a tremble as he reached for his cards, tapped them lightly on the table, raised them and fanned them open: a Queen, a ten, another Queen!

McCann picked up his cards.

"It's your call Jamesy boy."

He considered the stack before him and reckoned he had about a hundred and fifty pounds, nearly double what he'd brought.

"I'll go twenty more."

"Well, let me see: your twenty Jamesy and to make it interesting I'll raise you twenty more."

Bastard bluffer, lead him on.

"I'm in."

McCann dealt three more.   His heart beating fast now but surface smooth, he picked up the cards, tapped them lightly on the table, and then checked.   An ace, another Queen and he could hardly believe the evidence in plain sight before his very eyes – another ten!   Jesus, Mary and Joseph, a full house!   Easy now, stay calm and reel him in.   Eyes down, he reached for the note.

"I'll raise you twenty more."

McCann did not hesitate.

"Ok then: your twenty and twenty more."

"I'm in."

"Last card Jamesy."

With his by now familiar thumb and bent finger approach McCann emphatically prised away the last card, bending it with the force of his clumsiness in a way their father would have hated. Last card not needed so he reached for it unconcerned, then his heart beat accelerated once again.   A Queen!   Four Queens beat his previous best!   Steady now, don't scare him off whatever you do.

"I'll raise another twenty."

"Your twenty, Jamesy," and was it a new more focussed McCann (well he would be with the rising stakes) and was there a just perceptible exchange of glances with the ever impassive

Damian. He dismissed the thought, imagination surely. For once Willy was not animated, just absorbed in the drama and presenting a poker face he could do with wearing when he played the game.

"Your twenty Jamesy," McCann continued, "and let's see. Your twenty and fifty. Fifty smackers Jamesy, is what it will cost you, so how's about that then?"

McCann picked the money from his pile, slid it forwards into the pot, folded his arms, leaned back in his chair tipping its back legs off the floor and looked him full in the face.

He stared back, not really seeing. His thoughts were speeding, his heart beat increasing and he fought hard to erase any outward display. Fifty Quid! He made a quick calculation. There would be a hundred and seventy pounds in the pot. He could not afford to lose, it would ruin him. Willy could afford it. The Hamiltons had been business men for generations, money was their inherited right. The McCanns were in the business of making theirs. They fought harder, clung on tighter. Then again this, what was this all about? Was it a front? It had to be! He had to see him, was in too far to stop now. To raise the pot was not an option, he hadn't the money. Anyway if he had McCann would see it as an opportunity to raise the stakes even further; he was that thick-headed. Four Queens was enough surely. Unlocking his gaze at his rival he picked up the notes and placed them on top of the pile.

"I'll see you."

The smile gone now, McCann eased the front legs of his chair unto the floor. Picking up his cards he squared and then fanned them. "Mmm, let's see now." He selected a card and flicked it on the table, then another and another. "What about Kings and…"

The relief was overwhelming. He had to check himself from reaching out and turning over his own hand, showing this arrogant oaf what he was up against when McCann held up a finger as if to halt his progress.

"Three Kings and…" With surgical precision he selected a card and placed it face down on the table. Discarding the rest, McCann beat a drum roll on the table with his knuckles before, with a flourish, turning the card over.

"Three Kings and a fourth, what about that then, can you best that James?"

He was gutted. Of a sudden he was hot and sweating and thought he was going to be sick. McCann's voice, quiet and silky now had lost its country bluster.

"Lost your tongue, James? Come on let's see. Can't move, that's not a problem – Damian would you oblige, there's a good fellow. Aaah, Four Queens, well would you believe it? Queens and Kings: ever Ireland's trouble. Gather the spoils Damian, we'll be off now and remember any time you want a re-match, I'm your man."

It was that dramatic, life imitating art. His money was gone. There was no way he could return home, explain or beg for more. There was none to give. Anyhow he could only ever go back in some kind of triumph. Accounting for failure was not an option. To remain where he was, that was also not a possibility. The story would circulate. He would be seen as the loser, an instance of the country bumpkin blinded by the city's dazzle led helplessly along corruption's path; the innocent taught a harsh lesson. There would be sympathy and censure; he could stomach neither.

Penitent underdog was not a role for his repertoire. So, what to do? The only way was exile, a change of scenery where he could play a different performance before a new audience.

Willy would lend him money.

Next evening he was on board the overnight crossing and heading for London.

PART THREE

A NEW LOVE

CHAPTER ONE

At first her smoking cigarettes was a gesture, a signal that she was a changed person with a new outlook, then it developed into a habit, something she could look forward to that made her cups of tea taste better and without which her glass of whisky in the evening would be nowhere near as pleasurable.   At home after work she locked herself away and found a kind of peace in the gloomy interior where the loudest sound was the tlock-tlock of the grandfather clock in the front room.   She cooked, cleaned, tidied, talked to herself, sang sometimes, hummed, read the local paper, listened to the radio, flicked through *The People's Friend* and *The Radio Times* or lost herself in a library book.   Not a day passed when she did not think of him and their short time together.   In the beginning, outrage, anger, disbelief governed but imperceptibly as the days, weeks and months bled into years and as all hope of ever seeing him again receded, her frame of mind altered.

    The only person she had ever told the true story of his desertion and the shocking telegram had been Dr Patterson and the old man swore he would tell no-one else and moreover, he advised neither should she.   Better to say her husband was missing presumed dead; that little lie would be repaid by sympathy and would lay the matter to rest whereas the truth would only encourage gossip and feed fires of malice and bring out the worst in human nature.   As in all things she had listened to the good doctor's advice and in truth she never had to explain, as all those she knew assumed that was what had happened anyway.   So the secret remained hers and as the years passed in a strange way inside of herself, the lie evolved into a truth so real that sometimes, late at night when she had poured her drink larger than usual, in her mind's eye she would see his image, see him hopping on one foot as he had stubbed his toe and onetime she caught herself kissing the glass, pressing it to her thin bosom and rocking back and forth, keening her grief for love that was lost.

Then head down as usual, walking from the bus one evening, a glimmer of white on the pavement caught her attention. She stopped glanced around, no-one, and then bent to retrieve what she surmised was a postcard. The light was poor so she stepped under a lamp- post where she turned the card over and immediately her heart began to race. It couldn't be! The photograph was of a man from the waist up dressed in a soldier's uniform, wearing an officer's cap and then she realised it was not, could not possibly be, but the likeness… Footsteps were approaching behind her so she fumbled the photograph into her pocket and stumbled on her way. Once home she dropped her handbag, shed her coat, hung it up, retrieved the photograph and her handbag then raced for the kitchen, placed both on the table (the photograph face down), then dashed to her front room, the cupboard and the bottle of brandy she kept for emergencies then back to the kitchen, bottle on the table, glass from the cupboard, pour then flop in her chair and gradually deep breath, deep breath, slow her breathing and feel her heart-beat begin to dawdle and the room stop spinning. Raising the glass she swallowed a measure of the brandy and allowed the warmth to flow through her system, before reaching for the photograph and in measured fashion turning it over. It was not her husband, of that she was certain, but the likeness was unmistakable. In an instant she knew what she must do. Reaching for her handbag, she placed the photograph inside and snapped the clasp. Then, with a decisiveness she had not felt in years, she picked up her glass.

Next day during lunch-hour she took her time choosing a frame. The shop assistant proved kind and helped place the photograph between the glass and the backing and fix all firmly in place. All was wrapped carefully in folds of paper and presented to her in in a bag so alluring she decided there and then she would keep it forever.

At home she unwrapped all carefully, folded the paper neatly, placed it inside the shop's bag then took all upstairs to their bedroom and secreted it underneath her folded jumpers at the bottom of her chest of drawers.   Where to put the photograph? The kitchen was too commonplace and in their bedroom no-one else would ever see it.   The front room, on the mantle-piece was the place!   After all wasn't that the best room in the house, the one she kept clean and tidy, the one reserved for special guests. For, and at first the connection shocked and thrilled her, was not her husband *a special guest* and was he not **her** husband.   Dr Patterson had reminded her that when all was said and done they had been legally married, that was fact and you could not argue with that fact.   Your wedding ring, he had said, you should be wearing it, for in a fit of she knew not what, after the telegram she had torn it off and rushed upstairs and placed it in an envelope and tucked it away beneath her blouses in the top of her chest of drawers in their bedroom.   **Their** bedroom, for she had never stopped thinking of it in that way and never would, not till her dying day.   As in all he said, she had taken the doctor's advice and sped home, retrieved the ring, and had worn it openly from that day to this and would continue to do so for the rest of her life.

So the unknown soldier's photograph was placed reverently on the right-hand side of the mantelpiece where it would be seen as soon as she entered the room and where nestled in her favourite armchair, reading, sewing, knitting, crocheting or just day-dreaming she could look up and meet his eyes as she had done on those too, too few occasions in their short time together.   She took to deserting her kitchen after tea in the evenings.   Instead, when required she would light a fire after she came in from work or on week-day mornings so that gradually the room lost its damp, mouldy nature and became, over the years, her favourite place of retreat.

Visits from her brother were rare events, they exchanged Christmas and birthday cards and that was about that. They lived so far apart and he had his wife and family and his work kept him busy and he had never been one for holidays. Like herself, in that respect. They had not seen each other in years so it was a rare treat when she received a letter announcing he had recently bought a car and he, his wife and children were coming to visit not this Saturday but the next. They would be there around lunchtime and the news generated a flurry of preparation as she cleaned the house from bottom to top then back down again. She would cook his favourite ham, new potatoes and peas, a cake and iced buns had to be baked and she must not forget a new bottle of whisky. It was all go, go, and go.

The day they arrived was warm and sunny thank goodness so the children would be able to play out. With no experience of children and no resources to entertain them she was apprehensive but then again they would bring new life into the old house and, to be fair, it could certainly do with some. Her parents were dead now nearly thirty years and it had not received a lick of paint in all that time, nor had any of the furnishings altered. Except for the gas cooker, and that was about ten years old, all was as it had been when her grandparents were alive – but that was the way she liked it. The gloomy, smoke stained walls and ceilings, the dark wooden cupboards, cabinets, chests of drawers, tables and chairs, the sagging, lumpy beds and armchairs, the heavy fraying curtains, the few dull pastoral scenes enclosed in their dark frames, the old photographs of her parents and grandparents, the worn carpets and stained lino, and especially her beloved grandfather clock; she would not change any of it; not for all the tea in China!

The house spick-and span, ham in the oven, potatoes peeled and in their saucepan, peas shelled and in theirs, she stationed herself behind the threadbare lace curtains in the front room some half hour before the appointed time of their arrival. Now and then she would leave her post to wipe a speck of dust or adjust the angle of Peter's photograph on the mantle-piece. Her heart beat quickened when she heard the sound of a car. Concealed behind the curtains she could see it, shiny and black as it pulled up at the kerb-side outside her house. What would the neighbours think! Her palms felt moist so she wiped them down her front and then realised she was still wearing her apron so in a panic she pulled the wrong loop at the back and made a knot that somehow she managed to tighten and could not untangle and she was not going to greet her guests wearing her apron so all in a fluster she rushed to the kitchen and the drawer for her scissors. The door-bell rang! Where were the scissors? Scrabbling about inside she could find them no place so now in a frenzy she grabbed a knife, hacked her way through the tie, shed the apron, cast it in the sink and rushed to the door. On her way down the hall the door-bell rang for the second time. Opening the door she knew she would be at her worst, all flustered and red-faced but somehow in the hurly-burly of greetings, introductions, successive visits to the toilet, hanging of coats, delivery of gifts and eventual settling of everyone in the front room, attention was removed from her state of being and she found herself caught up in the animation of it all. This life and liveliness was completely alien to her yet to begin with she surrendered her will and let its ebb and flow buoy her and take her where it willed.

Her brother suggested a drink to celebrate their arrival. Obediently she stood and shaped an apology about being a poor hostess, not used to receiving guests.

"Don't worry, Mary and anyway," and her sister-in-law wagged a finger at her husband, "he's a right poor guest for suggesting it."

She was smiling and John, who was engaged in a mock wrestling match with his middle son Sam, pulled a funny face.

"I have lemonade for the children if they would like some."

A chorus of, "Yes please," confirmed she was on the right track here at least.

"I'll give you a hand," said her sister-in-law following her out of the room after she had disengaged from Paul and told him to remain with the rest of the family.

Grateful for the assistance she was apprehensive about being in the kitchen alone with Rachel. Her mother and grandmother had been disapproving over her brother's choice of bride, thinking his new wife, who came from what they considered a poor background was not good enough for their prized son and grandson and to be honest she had shared their opinion. John, as in everything had gone his own way and the divide between had widened. That was all history she reasoned, past troubles were past and she owed it to all concerned to make things right for the future. Then, with a start she remembered the apron in the sink – Rachel would think her a right hussy! Entering the kitchen she speeded up and at the sink she swung round placing her hands on its rim and using her arms to make her appearance as wide as possible to block her guest's view.

"What would you like to drink Rachel? The lemonade and glasses as you can see are set out already," and she nodded at the kitchen table.

"Don't you worry about me. I'll pour the lemonade and take it through and you see to that brother of yours. When I come back, I'll put the kettle on; I could just do with a nice cup of tea. I'll give you a hand with the food; it smells marvellous, roast ham, one of John's favourites – and mine."

As she chattered Rachel filled glasses with lemonade from the jug provided.

"I'll just take this tray up. It's very thoughtful of you. Our lot just love lemonade and they'll be thirsty after the journey. Don't worry, I'll see they don't spill any; you have to watch that Sam like a hawk or he'd be up to all sorts of devilment and sometimes," and she shook her head and rolled her eyes, "that brother of yours eggs him on; they're two peas from the same pod those two and that's a fact. Still, we all have our crosses to bear and when all's said and done I've made the rod for my own back."

She smiled, sped away with the tray, then stopped, turned again and set it down.

"Mary, we didn't want to say anything in front of the children, in case you got upset but, but we just want you to know, well time goes by and while we've been busy what with the children and everything we have been thinking of you; you've been in our thoughts and John, well he's not very good at speaking about his feelings but he's a great one for letting bygones be bygones and he was really upset when he heard about, about your husband and what happened and he would want you to know that, but somehow he could never bring himself to say so himself. Well you know what men are like. There's nowt so queer as folk, but men-folk; they're something else entirely."

Rachel shook her head.

She could feel the tears coming but mercifully her sister-in-law dodged any embarrassment by retrieving the tray and wheeling out of the room so she was able to salvage the apron, remove her glasses, bury her face in it and surrender to the sobs. Enough, now pull yourself together she instructed. Taking a deep breath she dried her eyes, put the apron in the washing basket, splashed water on her face, made for the bathroom and repaired as best she could the damage to her appearance. She was ready for the fray.

To her surprise and delight the lunch was a success though she had to admit that without the assistance of Rachel, her daughter Jane and astonishingly the boy, Paul, she would have struggled. Sam hung about his father begging for sips of his whisky. James, her eldest nephew kept at a distance appearing detached yet taking all in, saying little but comprehending all with an apparent perception she found disconcerting.

"Aunty Mary," why was Sam snorting with laughter when Paul addressed her as they were at tea and biscuits after the meal?

"Yes dear."

"That picture, the one on the mantelpiece, is that, is that, you know, is that of your husband, mam said was killed in the war when he was saving us from the, the Germans?"

The room went silent and all eyes dropped except for James who sat up looking at her even more intently. The bombshell had been dropped and now all she could do was pick up the pieces.

"That's right dear. If he was here now you would have called him Uncle Peter." Surprisingly words were coming easily and she found herself comfortable in the centre of attention. The children all had their stories or their parents had stories to tell about them or themselves and up to this moment with her life being so drab and lacking attraction she had felt at a disadvantage but now **she** had a story to tell; one she could warm to in the recounting.

"He was a lovely man, tall as your father and very kind and caring and brave. He, he would have loved you all because he was very fond of children, in fact we…"

Artfully she broke off at this point and reached for the handkerchief in her sleeve and though there were no tears brimming she removed her spectacles and dabbed at her eyes. She was aware you could have heard a fly land on the table. Replacing her spectacles she manufactured composure, inhaled deeply, then continued.

"We had a few, too few happy months together. Every day before he went to work he brought me up a cup of tea and when he came home in the evening he would help cook the meal and take a hand in the washing and clearing up."

Here she fought hard to suppress a glint of triumph when she caught Rachel giving a searching glance in her brother's direction. He, in response raised his eyebrows and held up his hands.

"You know, and this is the really special bit," she paused to allow all eyes to focus on her, "not a day went by that he did not write me a little note to say how much, how much…"

This was too much, a fiction too far and this time she felt real tears overflowing and had to fumble for her handkerchief and it took a real effort not to dash from the table and make for the sanctuary of her bathroom but then she would miss the sympathy and for once in her life she was revelling in being the centre of scrutiny – for that the red eyes and blotchy face were a price she was prepared to pay.

Rachel, with her shadow Paul in tow helped her clear up, wash the dishes and put all away.   The children, including the protesting Paul were then dispatched to the garden with strict instructions regarding good behaviour.   She was struck by how generally obedient and well behaved they were.   It could not have been easy for Rachel coping with such a brood but she had to admit her sister-in-law possessed the knack of making it all look easy and she and her brother appeared comfortable in each other's company.   It would not, she felt been her cup of tea to have such a large family, perhaps one, yes one child might have been…   In an instant she slammed the brakes on that train of speculation.

"Mary," the sound of her name jolted her back into the moment, "we were wondering, John and I," and here Rachel glanced at her husband, "if you would like James to come and stay with you during the summer holidays.   He passed the exam and will be going to the Grammar School; we thought it would be a bit of a treat for him."

"And for you too, Mary, you must get lonely sometimes being by yourself and what with, you know, well you know what I mean," her brother stumbled. "Anyway, if truth be told, it'll be one less mouth for us to feed and well two's company, a change is as good as a rest."   He looked across at her.   "Right that's that settled then, we'll put him on a bus and you can meet him at your end, Rachel will write and give you the details," and draining his glass, he held it out.   "I'll have one more for the road and then we'll be on our way."

The rest of the visit went well and all too soon it was time for farewells, piling into the car, her standing at the door waving and overplaying it all for the benefit of the neighbours. On the other side of the road a curtain twitched and for a split, silly, second, prompted no doubt by the whisky and a general feeling of lightness and ease, she envisaged making a curtsey then catching herself on, she slapped the back of her hand, turned and crossing her threshold, closed the door.

CHAPTER TWO

In August, as arranged the boy arrived on the bus and dutifully she was there to meet him at the station. As he stepped down among the other passengers, her driving impulse was to rush forward and hug him to her but she reined herself in and stepping forward attempted to take the small suitcase he was carrying. He pulled it away.

"How was the journey, James? You're a brave boy to come all this way on your own. Your mother said not to worry, that you would be all right but I have to admit I did suffer a few qualms, thinking about you all on your lonesome, all that way, by yourself, with no one..." Aware she was prattling she lost her thread, put off by the boy's blank stare and lack of response.

"Silly me, you must be tired and hungry I bet. It's not far and it's been such a lovely day here, all day."

For a split second she considered asking about the weather where he came from and about his brothers and sister, then thought better of it. No, she reasoned, this was probably the boy's first time away from home; he would be missing his family and friends and, she quailed at the thought, perhaps the whole venture was not to his liking. Perhaps he had had no say in the matter and his father had just railroaded the whole affair as, she knew was often his way. *One less mouth to feed*: it had been said as a joke but the sentiment had lodged in her memory and was now threatening to stain the whole event. For weeks, at any opportunity, she had boasted about his arrival and now here he was. She was more than the tragic, lonely widow her neighbours perceived her. Her new role had been bolstered when her brother and his family had come to visit in a car and now even more so for walking beside her, staying in her house for a whole two weeks, was her nephew, her boy. So who could blame her when she reached her street for deliberately slowing her pace and ever so gently hovering her hand above her nephew's shoulder, aware of the effect their little scene would be having on the whispering audience behind their lace curtains.

She spoiled him as much as he would allow. Before setting out to work she prepared sandwiches for his lunch, then made him a cooked breakfast. Just watching him eat his food brought her contentment and a surge of well-being. Ever watchful, he said little but that she put down to shyness and anyway, now she had someone to talk to, she was only too glad to chat away for both of them. So she inquired ritually if he had slept well, told him about her day at work, made as much as she could of any incident on her journey to and fro and talked at length of any item of interest from the local newspaper. When material was scarce she would re-visit her past and recreate memories of people and events linked to her brother, hoping he would remember and perhaps share them with his father.

At work she felt like a trapped schoolgirl impatient for the day to end. Her newly acquired impatience for home-time occasioned rare mistakes and those, as ever, were severely self-censored. At least now her errors could be employed as yet more matter to relay before the boy. The phrase *confession is good for the soul* came to mind and made her smile. It was.

Their evenings together were, for her, occasions of rare delight. Talking all the while, she would cook their meal while the boy laid the table and assisted with the washing and drying. On these occasions he was helpful and polite but self-absorbed, making no effort to initiate topics or elaborate conversation and replying only when asked a direct question. Apparently he spent the day when she was at work walking through the local park or going to the library, where, having learned of his love of reading, she arranged a ticket so that he could borrow books.

After the meal they would go for a walk and her joy was crowned if they chanced upon someone she knew so that she could introduce him and praise his cleverness, his good manners and quiet nature which was so unlike the majority of the young persons she knew or had heard tell of. Youngsters today were so ill-behaved; they had no respect for their elders. Mind you it was not always their fault. Look at the parents, they let them run riot and took no interest, and the schools, there was no real discipline she had heard, not like it was in her day. Invariably her acquaintance would nod agreement and offer up their own addition to the litany while the boy, head lowered, scuffed his toe in the ground.

On the way back she would make sure now they visited the corner shop where she allowed the boy to choose sweets. There again she would seek any opening to place him at the centre of admiring attention.

With him there her weekend could be looked forward to as an interlude filled with riches. On Saturday they took the bus across the border to the little seaside town where she loved to forage in bric-a-brac shops for the sentimental ornaments she placed all over the house. Together they walked along the beach and as it was sunny the boy was allowed to bathe providing he promised to stay close to the shore and never, ever get out of his depth. To her delight he appeared nervous and inept in the sea but appeared to take pleasure in the experience, now and then launching forwards and essaying a few frantic strokes before staggering upright gasping and spluttering, knuckling his eyes but with a wide grin on his face. Surprising herself she took off her shoes, discretely removed her stockings and paddled along the edge revelling in the sense of freedom and in the sensation of the water's cool lick.   She loved to fuss over the boy, over-riding his protestations as she dried his shoulders and back and ensured all the grains of sand were removed from his feet and between his toes.   Then they promenaded further, collecting shells, which she kept, as she kept everything, even old papers and magazines.

Later they lunched in a café where the boy's air of studied concentration on the bill of fare caused her heart to ache for love of him.   On the bus home, ignoring the stiffness of his posture she could not refrain from taking his hand and her happiness was complete when tired by the day's activity and the sea air, he fell asleep, and his head nestled against her shoulder.

On Sunday they attended church where glances and whispering explanations from acquaintances in neighbouring pews suffused her with new singularity and pride.   Outside she talked about the boy, his father and her brother to anyone who would listen, prolonging the conversations as long as she could to squeeze the last drop of sentiment bound up with this relationship that was becoming so precious to her.

Home from church, she cooked a traditional Sunday lunch of beef, potatoes, carrots, peas and gravy.   For pudding they had trifle, a treat she would not have contemplated making for herself alone.   The meal over and all washed up and put away and prompted by an idea that had struck her as they were eating, she proposed a walk.   They set off and up the hill.   The day was bright and sunny, her spirits high, so much so that in a moment she had grasped the boy's wrist and looped his arm through her elbow. On his part there was a just perceptible withdrawal then, as if he thought better of it, he remained attached.   Tenderness nearly overcame her and she had to blink hard to suppress the tears.   She had not been this happy in years.   Not since, not since…   They had reached the threshold of the avenue Dr Patterson had lived in and the thought of her old friend, long dead now, stemmed her emotion.

On up the hill she steered the way until they reached another avenue near the top that ran parallel to Dr Patterson's. For her this was a brave step, but the boy's presence gave her the courage she required. Two elderly maiden and distant relatives lived together in one of the tall Victorian houses in the middle of the avenue. She had not seen them for years and had lost touch but reasoned that the boy at her side provided the perfect opportunity to resume relations. Besides, now she had her own story to tell she required an audience, so taking a deep breath she unlatched the gate, steered them up the path and raised the door knocker.

CHAPTER THREE

The old ladies slightly more stooped and wrinkled than she remembered them, were surprised and intrigued and made it clear they were delighted to see them both.

"And isn't he the picture of his father at his age Agatha?"

"He is that Cassie, the living image."

And they were off reminiscing about her brother, a rascally favourite of theirs, and then of their youth and the changes they had lived through, of their relatives, and neighbours, the living and the dead until she despaired they would never ask.   Around four o'clock Cassie creaked upright.

"Right now, come on Agatha. We're off to brew a pot of tea and see to a wee something to eat.   It's no bother; we always have something around this time.   You stay there by the fire. We know what we're about and you know what they say, too many cooks spoil the broth."

"I'll just give the fire a poke and a shovelful of coal," replied Agatha who grunting with effort was as good as her word and together the two sisters padded out of the room.

As she expected the old aunts did them proud: there were sandwiches, fruit bread, cakes and shortbread all home baked and it was no hardship to heap praise on the produce and the providers. Offerings to help with the clearing up and washing dishes were rejected firmly.   No, no it was a pleasure to see them both and what was seeing to a few plates and stuff – they wouldn't hear tell of it.

"And what about yourself, Mary, we've not had sight or sound of you all these years.   We've often thought about you, haven't we, Cassie?"

"You're right there.   It was really thoughtful to come and visit and bring the boy, but what about yourself?   What have you been up to in all this long time?"

At last, now she had her chance.

"Well for a start time goes past so quickly and one day you're left saying where have all the years gone?   You never met your grandmother," she stalled, addressing her observation to the boy, "but she used to say there must be a big pile of them somewhere and if only she could find them… Now I know how she feels."

She paused, looked down then turned to the old women.

"I know it's been a long time, too long since I've called to see you but, well father died, then mother became ill and I was busy nursing her and what with work and one thing and another there just did not seem to be enough hours in the day.   Then mother died and well, for a time, I just didn't know where to put myself.   Then," she scrabbled around her cardigan pockets, then in her handbag where she retrieved her handkerchief, "well I met a man, a wonderful man…"

Alert now, both aunts leaned forward in their chairs, their heads raised.

"You, you met a man," Cassie managed; with she had to acknowledge inwardly, a degree of incredulity in her voice.

"What she means," and Agatha looked sternly at her sister, "is we never heard anything."

"Yes that's what I was going on to say," Cassie intervened, snatching the lifeline. "Mind you, that's not surprising, rattling around here in this old house, still, and not getting out anymore and never having visitors. Am I right, Agatha, or am I wrong?"

"You're right there Cassie," and Agatha smiled at her sister signalling equilibrium was restored. "You were saying, Mary?"

All the while she told her story of her meeting with James, their brief courtship, marriage, his summons to the battlefields and tragic death in action she was aware of the animated reactions on the faces of the old ladies who looked at her and each other with expressions that ranged through surprise, disbelief, sadness and concern. Causing greater discomfort was the, surely not, hostile gaze of the boy that never varied, nor wavered a fraction but seemed to bore into her consciousness with an intensity she found unsettling.

"You poor, poor thing," opined Agatha, "we had no idea, had we Cassie, no idea at all. You have certainly been through the mill, hasn't she Cassie?"

"She has that. I really don't know what to say. Sometimes I think we really don't know we're living, Agatha. I mean we complain nothing ever happens but it is surely better that way than having to put up with all the suffering that can and does happen to others like poor Mary here."

"Isn't it just," and Agatha shook her head sadly.

But was it, she reflected? She had lived the life of nothing ever happening, then a chance encounter had changed all that and brought with it sorrow and terrible loss but, and she was more convinced of it than ever, she would, given the chance go through the whole episode again and again.   Why - because it gave her a story to tell, one she knew she would go on telling for the rest of her days.   And there was more.   She still had not played her trump card.

"What makes it all even harder to bear," reaching down for her handbag, "is that there is no grave anywhere that I can visit. No opportunity to go and lay flowers and say a few words like I can do with mother and father."

Absolute silence in the room and all eyes fixed on her and the handbag on her knee.   "But at least I do have this. My husband had it taken specially to send over to me, in case, in case…"

She bowed her head, produced her handkerchief from her sleeve, removed her glasses and dabbed at her eyes, then a deep breath, glasses replaced but still holding the handkerchief she returned to her handbag, wrestled a bit then extracted her evidence. Reaching across, she presented it to Agatha.

The Friday night following, nervous and excited she waited with the boy at the coach station.   All was arranged, his and her suitcase was packed and they were on the brink of their adventure, together.   She had not been to the little seaside town since her honeymoon all those years ago, had never dreamed she could ever go there again but this boy at her side gave her strength. When the scheme first possessed her she had even considered booking rooms in **their** boarding house before conceding that would be too painful.   Besides, what were her savings for if not to spend on a little luxury now and then?   So she had found them adjoining rooms in a hotel and the prospect of being pampered and waited upon excited and intimidated her in equal measure.

Once aboard and their suitcases safely stored she gave up her favourite window seat to the boy and as she sat down beside him, retrieved his hand and looped his arm under hers.   As ever there was an initial rigidity but as the coach throbbed into life the arm became relaxed and he became absorbed in life passing through the glass while for her, as the coach wound forwards, her memory tracked backwards and she absorbed little of the passing landscape.

Peter and she had taken this same journey all those years ago and without doubt that was the happiest she had ever been in her whole life.   At times, thoughts of the terrible circumstances surrounding his leave-taking and that ghastly telegram would threaten to surface but she would push them down, hold them under with all her mental strength until eventually they lost strength and sank into the dark depths of her being.   Instead she allowed entry only to the good times and these she was determined to cherish and embellish.   Turning she gazed fondly at the back of the boy's head and had to check an impulse to reach over and stroke his hair, hug him to her, for he with his presence was bringing her such good times in the present.   Had things been different, and here again the bad had to be supressed; this polite, ever watchful boy would have been the son of her dreams.   If only, if only…   Absently she twisted her wedding ring before a thought made her start.   The boy was eleven!   Why not now?

Stealthily she disengaged the boy's hand.   He did not look round but remained concentrated on the world as it passed through the window of the coach.   Taking care not to disturb him she unclasped her handbag, reached in right down to the bottom and carefully extracted a tatty, cardboard diary her husband had started when he too was eleven.   That and his penknife, which she kept wrapped in tissue paper in the top drawer of her dressing table in her bedroom, were the only mementoes she had as keepsakes and she treasured them equally.   Of course there was the photograph, but that was special and in another category altogether! The penknife and the notebook she had found under the bed a few days after her husband had disappeared. He must have dropped them and well, in the state he was in...

It took time before she could find strength enough to handle the notebook, let alone open it and read the entries of the eleven year old who was to become her husband. She persevered and managed to make her way through innocuous entries dealing with money lost and found; bicycle rides; the hardships of an early paper round; football successes and failures and the highs and lows of brief spells tending chickens and rabbits. Then, and she knew she was being silly but simply could not stop herself from becoming upset and unable to continue, when her eye on the sloping handwriting had spotted trouble ahead and she was too much of a coward to go there, but now with the boy beside her all was changed. This was the moment to face the pages ahead.

Leaving her handbag on her lap she used it as a prop for the notebook, handling it carefully as ever, because despite her care, the years had taken their toll and leaves were beginning to disengage from the spine and a dark layer of cardboard backing had almost peeled away from the back cover. With the back of her left hand she stroked the frayed backing back into place, before employing just thumb and forefinger she began to ease the pages over, noting absently the black type indicating: Common Notes for Year 1909: Bank Holidays, 1909: Moon's Phases for 1909; Sun's Risings and Settings at London; Postal Information; British Weights and Measures; Foreign Timetable: British Moneys.

The diary could not be read until this solemn observance had been completed and when she thought about it her life, since her husband's disap... no death, death, her existence had become a series of performance rituals. So, in the morning she always prepared herself for the day ahead in the same fashion placing the left foot first into underwear, stockings and shoes, and then the left arm was always first into brassiere, slip, blouse and outdoor coat. Dirty dishes were always stacked meticulously on the left hand side of the draining board and after careful washing with a clockwise movement were just as scrupulously stacked on the right before filing in the allotted place. Each item recruited for setting at meal times was fetched and put down in a never changing left-to-right sequence; at all times curtains were opened and closed from left to right while before leaving the house she would complete a circuitous left-to right route from the kitchen to the top of the house following an obsessively pre-determined route that had to be re-started if she missed a step, as she checked gas taps, water taps, lights, windows and doors. She even hung out her washing with the smallest item on the left then working in ascending order to the largest on the right; they had to be collected in the same order and this proved problematical as she was compelled to stack them, smallest on top down to largest on the bottom. Time spent overcoming this obstacle was worth it to avoid the catastrophe she believed would surely ensue if she failed to complete her observance.

So with the diary; left to right softly through the opening pages of information, before pausing to read once again, as she always did, the enigmatic first entry she now knew off by heart:

January 1909

Thursday

Basil's birthday. Very frosty today. I put the wheel back on the cart. I hope that the results are in the Wizard tomorrow.

Who was Basil? There was a most unhelpful clue in the memo section at the foot of the page.

Basil is five feet seven and a half.

The Wizard she knew was a comic her brother used to read.

January 1909

Tuesday

Was nothing in the Wizard.   I only got 110, the reggubs!

Reggubs: where did that come from?   She smiled and then of a
sudden became conscious the boy was watching her, so engaging
his eyes she broadened her smile, but he started, turned away and
presented once more the back of his head.   The engine noise
changed and she realised the bus was slowing.   Looking ahead
she saw a small queue of vehicles and realised they had reached
the border with the South.   The part that pained her; she would
read it this instant!   Her practiced fingers speedily found the
place.

January 1913

Friday

*I met my dream girl for the first time today.   She is a brunette.
Basil was here and he got quite excited over her the swab!   We're
going to be rivals I can see!   Let the best chap win!*

Why did she find this precocious competiveness where girls were
concerned so disturbing?   Was it jealously and how could she be
moved so by events that had happened such a long time ago?
There was no sense to be made of it all, except that despite all that
had happened this was about the man she had loved, loved still and
would go on loving till her dying day.

A film of tears blurred her vision as she sifted on to the next entry.

Saturday

She came tonight!   Her name is Dora.   Got blue eyes.   By gosh she certainly is cheerful!   Absolutely hot stuff in fact!

Monday

It is now five o'clock and I have not seen Dora yet.   Gosh – don't you count the minutes when you are in love? – There – I've gone and admitted it now.

Fingers trembling she turned to the next entry.

Sunday

You're always in my arms –

But only in my dreams.   (More's the pity.)

More's the pity!   The bus juddered to a stop.   Unprepared her handbag and the diary slid from her knees so she bent forwards to retrieve all and in her haste struck her forehead on the metal surround of the seat in front   Despite all she saved the handbag and managed to stuff the notebook inside before sitting back in her seat, her heart beating fast.   Breathe deep, breathe slow she told herself feeling suddenly hot, dizzy and sick…

Voices in the distance, faint at first then coming closer, louder and at last more distinct.   Opening her eyes she saw faces above and around her and one in particular, moustachioed and reeking faintly of whisky, asking her over and over, "Are you alright dear?   Are you alright dear?"

Too abruptly she sat upright and vomited spontaneously over her best coat.

"Eew!" from the onlookers but she was conscious only of the boy turning away and the look on his face – that look!

After that it was all activity, and she acquiesced, feeling too weak to do anything as clothes were produced and the mess cleaned up as best it could.   She was able to communicate their destination, a wheelchair was procured, a taxi found, and eventually they arrived at their hotel where after a series of unbearable flurries she was escorted to her room and helped to undress by one of the maids.   A doctor was called; she was examined and given two pills she swallowed with a drink of water.

"You'll be right as rain after a good night's rest.   Just a little turn, that's all.   It's nothing to worry about."

Before she closed her eyes, powerless to do anything about it and too weak and exhausted to say anything she was only too aware of the boy on the fringe of it all.

He was taking all in with an unblinking stare.

CHAPTER FOUR

She wakened next morning with no more than a mild headache and a dry bad taste in her   mouth.   After the fiasco of the previous day her one desire was to put all behind her and repair relations with her nephew.   How she hated dramas and as she reeled back through her central role she shut her eyes and grimaced then shook her head with the result that the pain in her head increased.   A cup of tea, a couple of aspirins would relieve her tension and make all well.   She focussed on the room, concentrated on breathing deep and slow.   The cream and brown interior gradually worked its magic and her anxiety began to lessen.   Then in a vivid flashback she saw the boy's face and that look brought tears to her eyes.   What must he think?   Why had she made such a fool of herself – before him of all people?

Pulling back the heavy covers she slid her legs to the bed's edge, then pushed herself to a sitting position, stood cautiously and took a tentative step forward.   With an effort she stood waiting as the dizziness returned, her heart began thumping and she felt she might be sick.   Cautiously she stepped back and sat down on the bed and with eyes shut covered her face with her hands as coloured points of light flickered across the blackness before her heartbeat slowed and the sick feeling dispelled.   She was going to make it, she would be alright.

This time she stood warily then sidled carefully towards her suitcase on the rack by the door.   Opening it she located her dressing gown and was tying it together when a knock on her door made her start but she steadied herself and was reassured when she found it was the maid with, bless her, a pot of tea.   She asked about the boy; he was fine, had been up and about for about an hour so there was no need to worry.   She thanked the girl, asked her to put the tray on the bedside table and just in time remembered to ask about the aspirins.

The maid gone she splashed water on her face, brushed her teeth and applied her lipstick. By the time she had finished dressing, the girl had returned with the aspirins so she shook the tea-pot and poured herself a cup. It was now tepid and too strong but still, surprisingly refreshing. Then one at a time and experiencing her usual difficulty over tablets she managed to swallow the two pills, washing them down with another cup of the, by now, lukewarm liquid.

The boy must be frantic with worry. What would he feel like, abandoned in a strange place where he knew no-one? The whole idea was a selfish mistake; she had wanted to bury a ghost from the past, a past the boy had no part in. What could he possibly gain from being dragooned into accompanying an old maid in a scheme like this? And that frightful scene she had caused. At the very thought of it she grimaced and with both hands covered her face in shame.

On her route downstairs, she encountered the owner's wife who, in kindly fashion, asked after her health and informed her that the doctor would be calling round to see her after breakfast. The boy she was told was in the sitting- room and there she found him, lounged deep in an, arm-chair absorbed in an old Christmas annual. Cautiously she made her way across the room and coughed softly to announce her presence. He made no response so reaching forward she touched him lightly on the shoulder. Still no response; was it possible for anyone to be so engrossed in their own world?

"James," she ventured, "It's me, your aunt Mary."

A pause, a sigh and the book was lowered while with his thumbs, she noted, he still kept his place.   Then he turned and looked up at her, his face impossible to read.

"I'm, I'm so sorry about what happened yesterday.   I don't know what came over me.   I haven't had such a turn in years, not since, not since …"

Straightening himself the boy carefully turned over a corner of the page to mark his place and then standing carried the book across the room where he slotted it into its place in the bookcase in the corner.   He turned towards her.

"The maid said you were alright.   She said you would be down soon and then we could have breakfast."

As ever his eyes retained their unblinking focus.   Was it curiosity or a battle of wills?   Surely not she decided – it was just his way.   As her grand-mother used to say, it takes all sorts.

"You poor boy, you are right.   Here's me prattling on about myself and what does it matter anyway?   You and me – we're here to enjoy ourselves and you, you must be hungry. We'll have our breakfast together and then, well we'll see what the day has to bring."

Change the tone and be positive, introduce a note of lightness.   Of a sudden she was certain this was the way forward and the insight made her feel better.   Worse things happen at sea her grandmother would have said and as ever – she was right.

They went in for breakfast and as they entered the room she became aware of the small stir they caused as the waitress led them to a small, beautifully set window table.   For herself she chose poached eggs while the boy nodded assent when she suggested the full breakfast.   They ate in silence and during the course of the meal she felt her strength return. As for the boy, while he ate his eyes panned the room and she was content to watch him take in the grand and sometimes twinkling chandelier hanging from the ceiling's centre. His eyes followed the maid to the huge wooden dresser, noting her return bearing their tea and toast. He looked long at other guests and when he turned his head in an attempt to view a group behind she found the courage to inform him, smiling, that he should resist appearing so inquisitive. For a moment too long for comfort he held her gaze then lowering his eyes he reached forward and took up the heavy silver plated salt and pepper condiments and shook them as if testing their weight before setting them carefully back in their original positions.

During the meal she could not stop herself instructing him how to use his napkin and pointing out the presence of the correct knife for spreading butter and marmalade. Partly to puncture the silence and also because she felt it her duty as the adult to set a proper example, she found herself adopting an instructional role. She informed him about the value of please and thank you and how one should speak up slowly and clearly and never, ever while still with food in the mouth, and how elbows on the table were a sign of poor manners and how important it was not to hunch but to sit up straight in one's chair. He was assigned the responsibility of asking for another pot of tea please and when his clarity and politeness drew approving glances from an elderly couple at a nearby table, she positively glowed. During all he responded to her suggestions with an obedient mien despite persisting with his un-nerving habit of locking eyes for an uncomfortable few seconds too long.

Despite this she was happy, revelling in the companionship and so appreciative of the cutlery's weight, the shine on the sugar bowl, the texture and cleanliness of the table cloth.   The guests, some her age but the majority older were all her kind of people: she just knew.   Her poached eggs had been cooked to perfection; the toast, tea and marmalade were all lovely and she took rare pleasure in watching the boy eat and could tell he was enjoying every mouthful.   When he was finished she saw to it that he 'shipped his oars' properly, placed his napkin on his plate and before they left the table, tucked in his chair.   To her delight he seemed to have left off his habitual glare when instructed and this confirmed her intuition that she was doing the right thing. Fair enough, she was not a mother herself and that truth still hurt, but as the boy's aunt surely she still had a role to play; it was her duty and one she would not take lightly.

"And how are we this morning?"

The voice at first appeared far off, and then with a start of recognition she remembered what the owner's wife had said so was able to come to and compose herself before replying.   "I feel much better thank you and thank you also for your kindness.   I'm so sorry for giving you so much trouble."

"No trouble at all.   Glad to be of help and anyway, that's what I do."   They talked some more and she introduced the boy and explained their circumstances.   "You do seem to have recovered well.   Still," he looked around, "I do need to take your pulse.   We can sit at that table in the corner.   We'll be nice and private there.   Is there anywhere the boy…"

"I'll go and find my book!" and he was away before she even knew he was gone.   The doctor led the way.   He was kind and strong and she appreciated the masterful way he took charge of the situation.

"Mmm, still a bit racy. You still do need to take it easy."

"I'll be alright.   It's just a touch of angina.   I've coped with it for years."

"Still, you need to be careful.   Here."

He produced a prescription pad, found a pen and began to write.

"Take one of these twice a day.   I'll send the maid to the chemist's and remember, don't overdo things.   You need to take good care of yourself."

He looked her full in the face and smiled and she felt that familiar flush spreading up from her neck.

"I may call and check on you at a later stage; just to be on the safe side."

He raised himself awkwardly, his bulk catching the table and causing the ash tray to slide and rattle.

"Oops," he called, smiled again and then was gone.

CHAPTER FIVE

Immersed in her own thoughts she remained seated at the small table in the hotel's foyer.   Other guests crossed and re-crossed before her but while aware of their presence, she was oblivious in the face of their curious glances.   That brief encounter with the doctor had triggered a painful memory, one she had imprisoned deep in the dungeon of her consciousness and she was powerless and could only sit mesmerised as the recollection squeezed free and transfixed her where she sat.

Some three years after her husband's dis… death the boy's father had made one of his rare visits bringing with him a friend, a thickset man with powerful shoulders and a bold, outspoken manner her brother appeared to invite and encourage.   As often was the case there had been no warning of the visit but she had coped, as she had to, making sandwiches and opening a bottle of whisky.   Then late in the afternoon she had gone upstairs and was startled by the man's presence; he seemed to fill the whole width of the narrow hallway.   Without warning he had pulled her towards him and she remembered the whisky reek of him and shuddered.   She struggled but his strength was terrifying and he had backed her towards the bedroom, half carrying her in an embrace so tight it stopped her breathing.

She was thrown on the bed and he was on top of her fumbling with her clothing, making reassuring sounds and what with the heady effects of the whisky she had drunk, his bullish strength, her own physical weakness and yes, it had to be acknowledged all those years of emotion held back and frustrated desire she almost succumbed.   Somehow she hauled herself back, slapped him hard, made herself rigid beneath him and summoned her most chilling and commanding resources to browbeat him towards surrender.

"How dare you!" she had blazed. I shall call my brother! Leave me alone you brute! I'll scream! The neighbour next door will hear!" Then in a moment of inspired fiction: "He's a policeman! He'll hear me! I know he will!" The brute had halted and was listening. She pressed home her advantage. "He looks out for me - because I live alone. He hears everything. Once I tripped and fell over in this room and…" No more invention was required. Grunting he raised himself, prised himself backwards from the bed, stood, adjusted his clothing and left the room.

Eventually when she had gathered herself together and found the courage to go downstairs she found the man and her brother finishing the remains of the whisky; laughing and joking together as if nothing had occurred. While in part she was appalled, another self was persuading her that when all was said and done, the restoration of normality was what really mattered. Did her brother suspect anything? Had he, surely not, been a party to the whole episode? God forbid. The questions, her suspicions, the awfulness of it all were best banished, quashed down, hidden away never to see the light of day. She took herself off to the kitchen; they would need a meal to soak up the alcohol, something to sustain them on the road home.

Blinking she was back in the present and became conscious she was twisting her wedding ring. Her mind was made up. Never again would she allow another man into her life – not again, ever. She would be true to the memory of her dead husband, now and until the end of her time.

"Excuse me, ma'am." She turned. The maid had approached on her blind side. "I've brought your prescription. Dr Mulligan asked me to collect it for you."

Thanking her she took the small package and smiled.
Mulligan, she thought; well even if his intentions were honourable,
that put the cap on it.   He must be a Catholic and that would be
too much.   Her family and the neighbours, what would they
think?   They would not stand for it and neither could she.   She
stood, thanked the maid again for her kindness and set off in search
of the boy.

That day they went to the large outdoor swimming-pool
where for his sake she endured the shrieks, the splashing and the
hurly-burly.   He listened patiently when she instructed him to
remain only in the shallow end and never took her eyes off his thin
figure when eventually he jumped into the water.   He would
launch himself forward; essay a few frantic strokes before
disappearing briefly, making her heart pound, then emerging,
coughing and spluttering to repeat the same process.   Through it
all he appeared to be enjoying himself and once or twice she
caught him glancing in her direction seeking, she felt sure,
approval for his efforts.   At the thought, she glowed: from that
first evening when she saw him step from the bus she had been
drawn towards this withdrawn, watchful nephew of hers.   She
loved him as if he was her own child, would treat him as if he was
and would do anything within her power to make him happy for,
she knew now, if the boy was happy then she was happy too.

They ate lunch at a small café and in the afternoon she rested
in a deck chair while the boy occupied his time on the beach,
swooping in and out of the water at the sea's edge, licking ice-
cream from a cone and watching, apparently spellbound as a
religious sect imparted bible stories illustrated by small felt figures
that adhered to a cloth-backed frame.

When, as he had promised, Dr Mulligan came to see her she
was polite but distant.   When he smiled she did not respond and

she closed the consultation selecting her words slowly and precisely.

"Thank you doctor; I appreciate all you have done for me but I know I am going to be well now and what I need for the rest of our stay is a good rest." Here she paused. "And to be left alone; you understand don't you?"

She looked him in the eyes and did not surrender her gaze when he appeared flustered.

"Yes well I see, but if you do take any turn for the worse don't hesitate to, to get in touch. The maid can act as go-between."

He smiled but steeling herself and still holding his eyes she did not respond and in the moments before he stood and turned to leave, while her heart beat strongly, she felt suddenly empowered: she had stood her ground and won the day.

She was free.

The remainder of the week followed the pattern of their first day. The boy grew brown in the sun and each day she felt stronger. They went sight-seeing; she purchased souvenirs, gave the boy money, encouraged him to buy small presents for his parents, brothers and sister and took rare pleasure directing his choice of gifts. On their last day she had difficulty restraining tears when she was presented with a string of plastic beads which he must have selected because it matched the pink cardigan she wore so often. Putting them on, she assured him she would treasure them always and inwardly determined to keep her vow. She was so grateful that their holiday, despite its awful beginning, had been a success. In some way, with the boy at her side, she felt more at peace now with the memory of her dead husband. Facing the past, she realised had made the past easier to face and without a doubt the boy had been her saviour; without him none of it would have been possible.

The return home was uneventful and she basked in the normality of it all. As ever when she appeared in her avenue, she was conscious of the snooping eyes behind lace curtains but laden with suitcases, bags of shopping and accompanied by her nephew, she relished her part in the drama. Her house was as she left it and its familiarity brought her more comfort. They unpacked, made tea and she relaxed. The boy was going home the next day and to her surprise she did not feel sad at the thought. She needed time by herself to recover from all the excitement, to sort all out in her mind. The tlocking of the old clock was reassuring; the house was warm and friendly; content she slid towards slumber.

Next morning she left the boy at his breakfast while she went upstairs to conceal in his suitcase a present she had bought him. When he had presented her with the necklace it had touched her deeply; it was so thoughtful of him and the trouble he must have gone to matching it with her cardigan! She touched the beads lightly and smiled: he deserved something special in return. From her bedside cabinet she removed the carefully wrapped parcel containing her present: a gentleman's watch that had belonged to his grandfather with the strap altered so she was sure it would fit the boy's thin wrist. She had thought of presenting it to him before he left, to bask in the joy of his reaction, and then decided that would be selfish on her part.

Tip-toeing into his room she spotted on the bed his suitcase, all packed and ready as she had instructed. Taking care she clicked it open, cautiously pulled back some layers of clothing to ferret out a safe, secret nest for her gift.

At first she could simply not believe the evidence of her own eyes.

She had to touch it to be sure and then the full dread of realization made her heart race and no, not again surely she flushed dizzy and sick for there nestling in the boy's clothing lay one of her most prized possessions: her husband's penknife.

She would not faint, she would not be sick.   Dazed and somehow steadied by a growing suspicion, she searched mechanically through the suitcase – for what deep in her heart she knew she would find.   She was not disappointed: a pen, a cigarette case, and a few coins and surely not!   There at the bottom of the suitcase on their backs staring up at her were twin solid silver salt and pepper cellars.

The ingratitude, the thieving, the betrayal were all too much to bear; she felt soiled, spoiled.   This was all too, too much so dropping the suitcase lid she turned and sped from the room.   It was her duty to confront him and make him atone for the hurt he had visited upon her, the shame he had brought upon himself and his whole family.

Half way down the stairs she slowed – then stopped.   What good would a head on confrontation do?   It would serve only to break what was perhaps only her imagining of a bond between them.   Instinctively her arm rose and she touched the beads at her throat – surely not!   Perhaps they too were…   Immediately she arrested the thought and forced it down, down to the dark place where it could be interred with the others she could not allow setting free.   The relationship with this boy meant so much to her. If she confronted him now and won a victory, what then?   No amount of diplomacy could ever possibly heal his hurt.   They would become strangers from that time on and what kind of victory, if you could call it that, would that be since no true peace could ever be won, at any price?

On the brink she turned back and retreated slowly up the stairs.

All his spoils and her gift she placed as they had been in his suitcase, smoothed everything as it had been, placed the packet of sandwiches on top, then clicked all shut before leaving the room and closing the door behind her gently.   Then to the bathroom where she bathed her eyes, washed her face and applied powder and lipstick.   Apprising her appearance her eyes lowered to the pink necklace and of their own volition her hands were rising to remove it before she checked the impulse and looked at her reflection, into her eyes, searching, before with resolution renewed she turned from the mirror, walked into the landing and descended the stairs.

Hearing familiar sounds from the kitchen, she hesitated before the door, then breathing slowly; keeping all steady she pushed it open and entered the room.   The boy, at the sink with his usual absorption, was stacking his dishes.   She stepped forward.

"Never mind those, leave them, I'll do them later.   You get yourself ready.   If we're not careful we'll miss the bus.   It's getting late."   Obediently he stopped and turned to leave.   She could not resist: "I put some sandwiches in your case.   I thought you might be…"   Her voice tailed off as an awful truth drained her resolution.

He was looking at her and something in his eyes and in the tilt of his head gave him away.   She knew, he knew, she knew.   It was as simple as that.   She dropped her eyes, he left the room and mechanically she began to clear the table and wash and dry the dishes.   How she managed the walk to the bus station, the dreadful silence on the way, the perfunctory farewell and the long slow regretful tramp home was beyond her.   This time the silent audience of neighbours were of little significance and when she was inside, she closed the door and leaned against it to steady herself as the hallway slowly began to revolve, coloured lights pin-pricked and zig-zagged across her vision, her head thumped with soreness and she could not prevent herself slipping, surrendering.

PART FOUR

ACROSS THE WATER

CHAPTER ONE

London: sleeping rough, signing on, finding work on a building site, at last a room with an old gas cooker, a stained sink, wardrobe, single bed – his room.   Despite the squalor, it was a place of retreat where the real problem was that there he was forced to engage with his real self, the frightened, insecure him so far removed from the blustering bravado he played, had to play, to survive in the streets outside.   For that was the truth he had arrived at: it was possible to subsist if you were prepared to make all up as you went along.   At home he had fitted in by acting his part in the roles assigned to him; exile had forced upon him the realization that it was possible, necessary even, to choose his own parts.   If he could play convincingly the vagrant, the dole scrounger, the labourer, then what other characters might he essay? Time, he concluded would, as it was wont to, reveal all.   In the interim he would live in and for the moment and mark, mark and linger.

A born people watcher, the streets of London with their infinitely various clientele were ideal scope for honing a craft that required no expense to pursue and had the added asset of delaying self-confrontation in the confines of his room.   When the streets resources were bankrupt there was no better venue than a corner seat in a crowded pub.

"I would like a pint of lager please."

"Eh?"

"A pint of lager," but slower this time, enunciating deliberately but keeping his level low and even, or his harsh Ulster 'r' would mangle the word and he would be asked to repeat it again.

"I love your accent.   I hope you don't mind me asking but would you mind telling me – what month were you born in?"

A woman's voice behind him so obligingly he turned. Small and bulky and dressed entirely in black, a very short skirt, long straight black hair and a level fringe framing a chalk white face; she had long eyelashes and dark eyes.

"Pardon, what did you just say?"

"I know it sounds strange but go on tell me, what date were you born?"

He hesitated a moment: "All right then.   Twenty second of March…"

She shrieked and clapping her hands bounced up and down.

"I knew it, I knew it!   Aries, the fire sign!   I felt your aura," she confided, "Are you on your own?"   He nodded.   "You must come over and join us.   Here's your drink, I'll get it.   No, no I insist.   Barman, two large vodkas and tonic please.   Look, we're over there, see the girl with the long hair.   There's the money, he can keep the change.   You bring the drinks over; I'm off to the loo."

Peeved by the bossing he was never-the less intrigued, so deciding to play along he asked the barman for a tray and brought the drinks over, taking his time and summoning unconcern.   The blond girl's hair was bleached nearly white and she was thin with the same pale face and black eye make-up.

"Hi, I ran into your friend at the bar.   I've brought the drinks over."

Her face unreadable, the girl looked him up and down, then with the slender fingers of one hand picked up two empty glasses and held them up.

"Now, now Veronica hand me those, and the tray, I'll take them back."

Having appeared she was gone again leaving him with little option but the seat with its back to the bar affording him no view of the pub's comings and goings.   As for the girl she turned her head away as he sat determined to exude composure and resist any temptation to initiate conversation: two could play at this game.

"Right," from behind him, "introductions," and she flopped into place beside her friend and opposite himself.   "You've met Veronica, I'm Abigail and you're..."

"James."

"James, Jaime, the Supplanter."

"And that lovely Celtic lilt.   Are you Scottish?"

"I'm from Northern Ireland."

"You're Irish!"

She was right and freed from the manacles of home and country he determined to drop the nationalist qualification: he would be Irish and that would be that.

"A toast: to we three of the fire group, the Ram, the Lion, the Archer, quick to anger but just as ready to forgive; may our inner flames glow and may our radiations merge harmoniously.   Come on Veronica, raise your glass!   Let's drink a toast to us all!"

They clinked glasses and drank.   He looked at Veronica but she turned her head aside.   Apparently oblivious, Abigail pressed on.

"Your star sign James, you're an Aries; do you know about Astrology and just how important it is?"

He shook his head, convinced now more than ever that in this game silence was his strongest suit.

"Aries: strong personality, not easily discouraged by temporary setbacks.   You know what you want out of life and go after it with a passion.   To you, obstacles are temporary setbacks that exist to be overcome, there is always a way round, or over. You thrive on opposition, like to get things done and tend to become impatient when events or other people get in the way or refuse to move at the speed you wish.   You don't give up, you're resourceful and when setbacks occur you tend to bounce back. Am I right?"

He nodded.   Dammit, in many ways she *was* right.

"We're all planetary bodies, James, moving about apparently at random."   A couple at a table nearby were having an argument; ever nosey he strained to hear what it was about.   "We all emit radiations and our potential in the Zodiac is conditioned by date and time of birth and the other people constellations we connect with.   Do you know the time of your birth James?   James!"

"Eh, oh sorry…   You were saying?"

Anyone else would have taken offence at his loss of concentration but while Veronica sighed openly, Abigail showed no sign of irritation.   "I was asking did you know the time of your birth."

"Three thirty in the afternoon," he lied smoothly, "my mother thought it unusual, all the threes.   Three is a big number in our household.   My mother and father both come from a family of three; we live in the third largest county and would you believe, our house is number thirty-three."

Caught up in the improvisation he considered and then thought better about three little kittens.

"You could be our lucky star, James.   We need to look up an ephemeris for the year of your birth, and then proceed with a divination from that point.   We need to work out whether you are the Saint or the Sinner for your sign.   You have it in you to be callous and inconsiderate and too sharp tongued and impulsive. You could be too stubborn, unwilling to listen to reason, be nervous and irritable.   There is a possibility you could prove destructive."

Unruffled he met her gaze.

"What do you do?"   The question delivered in a slow drawl, came from Veronica.

"How do you mean?" he stalled.

"I mean," she paused to insert two slim cigarettes between her lips, light both, draw in smoke, then pass one to Abigail, "how do you earn a living?"

He thought fast.   Labouring on a building site had no clout; he felt compelled to impress.

"I'm a writer."   Where had that come from; why not, he'd told enough tales.   "Writers don't earn a living.   They starve in garrets."

Abigail clapped her hands.

"And despite the poverty and all the other problems you keep on persevering," and here she raised her glass and leaned forward towards him, "the true artist is faithful to his or her craft: adversity is part of the package and anyway is only a stepping stone towards greater things." She leaned back. "I think we're star-crossed we three. Veronica's painting, your writing, my fashion design: three creative forces from the fire group. Our paths were meant to cross. To us," and she swooped her glass, holding it suspended over the table's centre until first he, and then belatedly Veronica obliged and tapped her glass with theirs.

"What have you published?"

Another jab from Veronica but he had read it and was not to be floored.

"Nothing yet; young Irish writers have to try, then fail, then fail better before they ever get published. Samuel Beckett submitted *Murphy* over four hundred times."

He'd read that somewhere, not that he'd read *Murphy*, but sometimes little scraps of knowledge could make an impression.

"At present I'm working on a novel."

"What's it about?"

That shot from Veronica was too signposted; he'd seen it coming.

"I suppose like most young writers I have a compulsion to write my past out of my system. The hero's a young outsider who freewheels through life making it and himself up as he goes along. He's detached, distant, never laughs at what others find funny, is not sentimental about family or Christmas, loathes bunny rabbits, Val Doonican and Sooty, who would love for Tom to eat Jerry, one who…"

Abigail, acting the referee got in between them and stopped his flurry.   Damm, he was enjoying himself.

"Enough James, I can't wait to read it.   I'm sure daddy can help – he knows everybody, you'll have to meet him, I'm sure he'd like you.   Tell me, where do you live?"

"Well, at present I'm renting a room in…"

"A room, Veronica did you hear what he said?   A room, now look, I'm a Sagittarian, open, honest and plain-speaking, I don't deal in deceit, I put my trust in people I like and my impulse is to think the best of those I like."

"Careful, Abigail, don't go doing something you'll live to regret."

"Hush, Veronica, hush.   Being a Leo, Veronica likes to be the one in command and generally I'm happy to let her take the lead, only this time I know I'm right.   So James – you're living in a tiny room, right."

He nodded.

"Nothing to be ashamed about, but you have very little money.   Am I right again?   Come on, be honest with me."

He looked down.

"I can imagine.   Now listen and listen carefully."   She drained her glass.   Veronica twitched her head away and with a shrug, slumped in her chair.   "I've a house in Kensington that daddy leased for me.   Veronica has the top, she needs it for the light, for her painting; we've had it converted into a studio.   I'm on the ground floor." She leaned across; Veronica sighed and slumped more, "The middle's vacant, a friend," she paused and looked aside, "left recently. We're completely self- contained, have our own facilities: sleeping, washing, things like that – need to have, we're too independent to share. We would only get in each other's way. Look, collect your things and bring them over." She rummaged in her shoulder bag, found a pen and a small note book and began to print. "Here's the address," she rummaged again, "and a spare key."

"Abigail, be careful, you know nothing about…"

"Shush, Veronica, I know what I'm doing. That we three should cross paths was written in our stars, I'm convinced of it. I repeat: I know what I'm doing. We have to go." She stood; Veronica thought about it, and then rose brusquely and without saying goodbye made for the door. "You'll come."

He nodded assent.

"Good, that's settled then. Move in tomorrow. One of us should be there and if not, don't worry. You'll see us when you see us and don't mind Veronica, she's very protective of me; we're like sisters, only closer. She'll come round, she always does. Bye James, see you tomorrow," and she was gone.

He picked up the key and the slip of paper. A house in Kensington: not bad, not bad at all. And he was a writer – just like that! He'd have to buy a notebook and a typewriter. There was one he remembered, in a second hand shop he had even considered buying before. He had always scribbled: bits of poems, openings of novels, wise or witty sentences he chanced upon and he had mulled over trying his hand at his own work but the thought of being in his awful room alone was too much to bear. For as long as he could remember he had read and read; his mother used to joke he had been born reading. To write a book couldn't be that hard; all you needed was time and the proper facilities and Veronica's offer was too good to turn down. Write a book! Why not? *Catcher in the Rye, The Gingerbread Man, Borstal Boy*, something like that. After all, genius was ninety per cent perspiration and he had wasted enough of that breaking his back on a building site. He'd have to learn to type. The bloke in the shop would show him how it worked, so no problem there. He'd pack in the building site; it spoiled his image, say he had hurt his back and sign on. That Veronica was a strange one; he'd have to watch out for her. The only way would be to refuse to let anyone see what he was writing. Got it; he would say it was unlucky: bad star medicine!

CHAPTER TWO

Bit by bit he learned Abigail's story: the poor rich girl who paid in so many ways.   Time, effort and money were donated freely to buy the love she craved above everything.   In truth the money bit she didn't pay: daddy paid; thrice married daddy whose compulsive womanising drove his wives to desperation, or in the case of the first and Abigail's mother, to suicide.   Abagail was an only child.   In bits and pieces she told him her story.

She had met Veronica when they were both students at Art College.   From her mother, Abigail had picked up her interest in astrology and the occult and she had plotted Veronica's astrological horoscope and noted an uncanny resemblance in their birth dates and in the timing of their menstrual cycle.   The influence of the twelve houses of the Zodiac and the characteristics of the ten planets on the functions of the houses all indicated that she and Veronica had been moon pulled together and were destined to be life-long companions because their fates were intertwined.   Abigail's father found them a house and used his influence to find her work as an illustrator.   Veronica was the centre of Abagail's universe and she circulated around her pale companion, drawn to consult her at every turn.   Convinced their auras were compatible and that they supplemented each other's force fields, she contrived as often as possible to remain within radial proximity and if called away would telephone at regular intervals to maintain oral and aural contact.

He became the latest in a succession of star-chosen lovers. In a variety of ways the others had taken and left: Abagail gave and left no-one; she was the most promiscuous and the most faithful of lovers.   He was still a virgin when she came to his bed but she quelled all his anxiety by burrowing her way into his arms, then clutching, clasping, and crying towards orgasm.   On his part there appeared no requirement to please and no need for apprehension regarding performance.   His sole contribution was to be there.

Next day, Abigail insisted, should be theirs alone; after that the ritual of work could begin, but they had earned a day out in London together.   It was to be her treat.   On the Underground to Oxford Circus, Abagail snuggled up against him insisting on intertwining fingers, her head nestling on his shoulder and periodically tilting her chin to enable deep gazing into his eyes that invariably became the prelude to an embrace.   Deeply uncomfortable with this emotional display he offered no resistance, doing his ardent best to respond in kind and reasoning it was the price he had to pay.   He remembered reading *The Call Of the Wild* and the devotion of the dog (was it Buck) for his master.   What if he ordered Abigail to open the door of the speeding train and jump out – would she obey?

Abandoning the fantasy, he focussed on the carriage's interior and was instantly aware he was being watched.   An old woman opposite, dressed head to toe in black, was staring him full in the face.   He looked away, then looked back focussing on her but the expected unlocking on her part did not occur and the old woman continued to look fixedly at him, seeming to penetrate to the essential hollowness of his being, so to appease her he essayed a smile but there was no diminishing the shrewdness of her scrutiny and he was forced to look away while his heart pounded and anger began to swell.   To his relief the train crashed into their destination but he still felt the old crone's eyes fixed on him as they left the carriage and as they strolled past its window he peeked in and caught her still gawking with eyes that signalling blame, censure, accusation.   Shivering he inhaled sharply.

"What's wrong James?   Someone tread on your grave?"

"Eh!   What do you mean?"

"It's a saying – has to do with premonition.   At key moments in our lives we experience glimpses, insights, emotional contacts with our before and afterlives.   The insight makes us shiver or feel *I've been here before* or *I've met that person before.*"

"You mean déjà vu."

"That's right.   Split seconds like those give us an inclination of the complex web of past and future that determines our present.   Astrology can help unravel the mystery.

"Abigail, my love, you know what?"

"Yes, James."

"At times you talk like a textbook."

She frowned.

"But you're the prettiest textbook I know and I could listen to you all day."

Appeased, she beamed broadly."

Arm in arm they continued down Oxford Street and in the glare, the crowds, the bustle and the noise he was ambushed suddenly by nostalgia for his home town, for peace and quiet, clean air, familiar accent and some recognition.   He should write, let his mother at least know more than the "Don't worry, I'm all right" postcard he had dispatched about two months previously. Abagail was tugging his arm.

"We'll go into Carnaby Street, James.   Let me buy you some clothes."

Why not?   He was enjoying being a kept man and besides it didn't take a degree in Psychology to figure out that his provision of a suitable person for generosity was making a significant contribution to the continuing health of their relationship.   The morning sun brushed his shoulders and possessed suddenly by the anonymity afforded by the streets of London and by a crazy impulse that came from nowhere he drew Abigail closer, swung her to face him, clasping her hand in dance style then waltzed her around the pedestrians, crooning in her ear in carefree tenor:

"When Oirish eyes are smilin'

Shure it's like a morn in Spring.

With the lilt of Oirish laughter

You can hear the angels sing!"

Christ – where had that come from; there was no way he could carry-on like that back home.   As for Abigail, she seemed delighted with his performance, and when he was done she hugged him to her and when he looked down her eyes were shining and filled with devotion.   It was an appearance he was incapable of returning.   He returned the hug and looked away.

Abigail insisted on choosing for him a pair of black, patent leather boots, tight fitting black jeans, a thin, light, white polo neck and a shiny black leather jacket; all, she insisted had to be worn there and then.   He looked great.   She bought for herself a floppy wide-brimmed hat, and then they strolled into Piccadilly

Circus and perched in the sun on the steps under the statue of Eros and basked in watching and being watched.

"Do you drive, James?"

"Eh!"

"A car, can you drive a car?"

"Well no, I…"

"Not to worry. Neither can I, but I'm learning. Daddy enrolled me for lessons. I'll get him to do the same for you. No need to look like that, he loves doing things for me and always wants to know if there's anything he can do that would make me happy."

For just a moment she paused and appeared sad.

"Hungry, James?"

He nodded, so rising and brushing herself down, Abigail took his hand and guided their way to Shaftsbury Avenue, then into a side street and a small dimly lit Italian restaurant where after an excellent lunch and well into their second carafe of wine, she gave him space to complete some inconsequentiality, wiped her mouth with her napkin, placed it on her side plate, put her elbows on the table, reached forward, took his hands in hers and started: "You're an intelligent man, James, and by now you, well you could be forgiven for thinking we're playing our parts in that classic case history: excitement seeking rich girl wants to cause a stir by flirting with the attentions of a boy from the wrong side of the tracks but I, I want you to know, it isn't like that, not like that in any way."

She paused, and sensing high drama, he looked pointedly round the other diners and contemplated interrupting her outpouring before concluding it was wiser to stay hushed, so instead disengaging a hand he reached for the carafe and filled their glasses.

"James…" Christ she was crying, rivulets of tears leaking down her cheeks, streaking her face, causing her to look ridiculous. "I'm sorry, I'm being silly. It's just… Look, you order some more wine. I'll fix my face then…"

She was up and away and feeling he could get used to this life he signalled the waiter, outstared a couple at a nearby table, and then gave the order. While he hated the histrionics, he was beginning to comprehend they had to be endured as part of the deal.

"I'm sorry."

She was back, red-eyed and somewhat unsteady.

"I'm not going to cry any more. I promise."

Sitting heavily in her chair she reached for her wine glass, gulped some down, then speaking slowly continued:

"The point I was trying to make was, many women these days, intelligent women, often from privileged backgrounds, they, well, they seek out relationships with men outside their social group, often men from poorer, I mean financially poorer social backgrounds. It's in the, well in the air these days; the days of pleasing mothers and grandmothers are over."

She lowered her voice, raised her head and looked him in the eyes.

"I, it is important for me to let you know that it, it is not like that between me and you. Veronica," she lowered her eyes, "Veronica loves men and leaves them; her only lasting emotional relationship is with me. "You will have heard the background, how we met?"

He nodded.

"I knew one day I would meet a man who would mean as much to me as my star-sent sister, a man I would love and never leave. I," She drained her glass, set it down carefully and obligingly he re-filled it, in the process splashing wine on the tablecloth, "I cannot have children James, there were complications... So you, my star-sent lover, you are, are destined always to be, the centre of my universe."

Oh no, the tears were welling yet again. He picked up her wine glass and proffered it but with the back of her hand she brushed it aside causing more to splash over the rim and unto the tablecloth.

"You are the sun to my planet James and without your light, your warmth to bring colour to my life," her voice took on a tragic cadence, "without that. I would surely perish!"

Damn the woman, did she have to be so intense. Of a sudden he was angry and felt like reaching over and shaking her, giving her a good slap for making a spectacle of herself, of him, in this ridiculous fashion. Firmly he set down her wine glass.

"Abigail, pull yourself together, people are looking at us. We, why we've only just met, how can you..."

Under the impact of the transformation in Abagail's features, he lost his verbal path: gone was the anguish and now the emotion featured was approaching extreme dismay, almost dread and he realised in an instant how ill-judged his words were.

"How can you say we ONLY JUST MET when you, more than anyone should know that our meeting was never, could never be described as ONLY JUST!"   People at tables around were spellbound, the waiter was hovering but Abagail, totally regardless pressed on.   "I never thought you, of all people…"

He had let drop his guard he realised and knew in an instant that he had to change tact.

"Abagail, Abagail, no listen," he was insistent, allowing no interruption, "you don't understand, no listen, here take my handkerchief, and the wine, have some, go on, it'll do you a power of good, I promise."

He spoke soothingly, picking his way through the wreckage, stumbling but finding a path, a way back.

"You didn't let me finish.   I was going to say, now come on – don't start crying, listen to what I have to say.   Look at me."

He reached over and took her hand, bent his head low and holding her gaze engineered a tone of earnestness.

"I was going to say we'd only just met and how, how wonderful, how amazing it was that we, we experienced this instant rapport.   The 'only just met' was not as you interpreted it, it was well, it was my way of expressing wonderment, I was…" Nice one, he had made it, could see it in her eyes.   "I was attempting to express, groping towards saying how truly magical a moment for me our encounter truly has been."

Abagail's features were softening, the look of adoration he had found repellent began to glimmer, then intensified, and this time he endured and forced himself not to drop his eyes or turn away his head.   His was a lucky escape and a warning that in future he would be more tolerant and be careful to restrain any impulse to bite the hand.

"I'm sorry James. You have to forgive me. Sometimes I, I, well I know I become just too intense but you know it's because I care so much. I, I've behaved like this with Veronica too, so it's, I don't know why…"

"Look, now and then and often without meaning to, we can hurt people we love."

Risky that response but he need not have worried; she was back, singing to his tune.

"You are right. It's true – I hope I haven't hurt you; I certainly did not mean to."

"Well doubting my commitment was hurtful, I have to confess."

"I'm truly sorry."

She reached for his hand and he surrendered willingly.

The guilt transferred to her, they left the restaurant, blinking into the glare of Shaftesbury Avenue, then into Charing Cross Road and back to Oxford Street where they dulled the lunch's effects, window shopping all the way to Hyde Park. There they lay on the grass and fell asleep in the afternoon sun. Waking dry-mouthed they found a pub where he feigned tenderness, maintained eye contact and conveyed how much she meant to him and what great good fortune it was that their paths had crossed.

They took the Underground from Marble Arch and once on the train and in their seats, Abagail curled against him and was instantly asleep. His mind was too active for sleep. Being on the train had resurrected the memory of the old crone in black and the way she had kept on staring at him. A shiver ran through him and Abigail shifted then snuggled closer. The train juddered into Bond Street and an influx of arrivals jolted him back to the present. Struggling with a large suitcase, a dowdy, middle-aged woman stumbled down the corridor and fell into place opposite him, hefting the suitcase unto her lap. Two youths had been held up behind her and as they sauntered past, one tipped off the woman's hat. The doors of the carriage careered together and he sauntered on. Grunting and leaning sideways and down, the woman, her attempt impeded by the suitcase's bulk, attempted to pick up the hat but the youth behind kicked it forward and away towards the other who picked it up, held it out towards the woman, then snatched it away and skimmed it towards his mate.

"Cut it out ye wee skitters," the woman, by now well at the end of her tether, screeched. "Ye need a good skelpin' the pair of ye!"

A pause; the youths looked at each other, then, "Irish shithouse," the one with her hat responded evenly. He felt his face burn.

"Reckon there's a bomb in that suitcase, Towser?"

"A fecking Irish bog-trotter."

The woman put her hand to her mouth and helpless her eyes appealed to him. Why him? What about the others in the carriage who were studiously looking away or, in a few cases, also looking at him. Christ if he opened his mouth they would be unto him and what good would that do? The train began to slow. He glanced out the window: Oxford Circus!   They could leave here and wait for the next one and leave this sorry mess behind so he shook Abigail and dragged her towards the crowd by the doors, avoiding all eyes as they struggled through and unto the platform.

"I'm sorry, I felt sick, had to get some air," he lied and watched the train jerk into motion, flash past, turn its back on him and flee into the tunnel.

CHAPTER THREE

Nights he spent in Abigail's bed where she made passionate love
to him; by day *Gingersnap* was born and grew from childhood,
through boyhood towards the birth of young manhood.   The novel
was shaped by talk: Abigail would inquire what he had written, to
appease her he would make something up, make note of any of her
worthwhile suggestions, work on what he had the following
morning then two-finger-tap the result in the afternoon.

To begin with he had called it *The Higher the Climb*, but
Abigail had queried, suggesting his title was lacking in impact and
perhaps sounded a bit pretentious.   On impulse he had imprinted
his central character with red hair and she had approved of this
characteristic and suggested it should provide a fixed sign.   Why
not call the book *Ginger* – no too earthy, didn't have the right ring.
Snap – this time he objected; it was too close to home.
Gingersnap then, Abigail shrieked, bouncing up and down and
clapping her hands.

Gingersnap, born and raised the son of working-class parents
in rural Ireland, comes to England and there bobs and weaves his
way in the early sixties.   Without Abigail, his novel would not
have been written – or published.   She introduced him to her
father, convinced him of his talent and conveyed just how
impossible it was for a young Irish writer with no contacts to break
into the literary world in England.   Could Daddy not help?   She
would be ever so grateful and as ever her father did his best to
provide what his daughter requested and he could have done no
better than send round one time newspaper man and literary editor,
Sam McCready who took away the manuscript and returned two
days later.

"More literary borrowings here," he tapped the manuscript,
than from your local library."   A pause, then: "I liked the title but

after that," he scratched his head, "let's say there's a heck of a lot more work to be done to knock this lot into shape. The whole style needs tightening, for example your opening sentence."

McCready began reading in his broad Belfast accent, a look of pained exasperation on his face, running his fingers through his thick grey hair. As for himself, he had put a lot of time and thought into that sentence. *"Crabwise on a horizontal plane, the majority scuttle through the journey of life, but Gingersnap early on chose not to fraternise with his fellows, and instead determined to soar like a bird vertically, higher and higher until his pinnacle was breached."*

"What's all that detached authorial posturing got to do with anything? Tell the story man, tell the story. That *journey of life* and *soar like a bird*, it's criminal to signpost like that. Anyway that morality stuff is all just a pile of shite – why can't you let the poor bugger get away with it? You'd think you were wreaking some sort of literary retribution on the poor sod."

McCready paused and peered at him through narrowed eyes, then continued.

"Look, the novel by definition should be about the new. That old 'reap as ye sow" baloney is away with the fairies. Today there's room at the top for the Gingersnaps of this world." Again he scratched his head. "And there's no need for that sententious guff about the *pinnacle was breached.* No need for a limp cliché like that, no need at all: too much baloney. It needs tweaking."

McCready tweaked the opening sentence, then tweaked it some more until eventually it read: *On the pavements soft rain dwindled.*

For weeks after that McCready came to his flat, drank tea, smoked cigarettes and mussed with his hair until his 'baloney' and 'no need for' diminished as page by page *Gingersnap* was re-born and in the process transformed utterly.   His only break from the routine was the driving lessons that Abagail, true as ever to her word, had persuaded her father to countenance.

"You're good at this.   Why don't you write your own book?"

"No money in it.   Abagail' father looks after me and pays me well.   Tinkering with words, messing with somebody else's ideas, that's what I'm good at, what I like doing.   Anyway, I don't trust fiction, never read it unless I have to, like this. Journalism, current affairs, that's my interest and when I have time I read political biography.   Fiction deals in falsification."

"So does politics."

"True, but politics oozes from a world that is real and that's of greater significance than the stained reflection of reality the novelist presents.   Journalism or biography is the higher calling. There's no doubt that there you are often as not dealing with dishonesty, hypocrisy, corruption, but it's the crookedness and shadiness of the real world.   Journalists and biographers make an attempt to serve the truth, the novelist only serves lies."

Was this becoming personal, aimed at him?   There was no way he could afford to fall out with McCready, so he feigned interest.

"Novelists are egomaniacs who play God by bringing into being their own world.   Then they write their own bible to explain it.   They're all false prophets of the religion that is literature, and multitudinous are the converts to that holy writ."

McCready growled and gulped a swig from the hip flask he carried about with him at all times.

"The crowning glory of my religion," he raised the flask, "holy water.   Enough, now let's get back to work."

So with Admirable McCready at the helm and himself as cabin-boy the sinking ship that was *Gingersnap* was repaired and steered in the right direction.

Gingersnap climbed walls and trees, then scaled the educational and social ladders with friends and family left beneath gazing upwards, receding as he soared above, reaching university before being sent down having been discovered high on drugs then emigrating to England where a providential encounter in a pub led to work helping out in a touring circus till his fearlessness and talent for shinning up ropes was spotted and put to good use in the trapeze act and learning to walk the tightrope.   Then, before another fall he seduced, then married the owner's daughter and after inheriting the business he sold to a rival and bought his way into television, exchanging the world of the big top for that of the small box where he rose and rose, forsaking wife and children and springing off the backs of supporting players with their feet firmly grounded, till perched at the pinnacle of his climb contemplating the view from his apartment at the top of a towering skyscraper in New York as way down below dinky automobiles nudged and glowed, he swirled ice in his glass, raised it and sang the lyrics of a current and appropriate song from the charts.

"Would we not need permission to print those lyrics?"

"No need to worry.   Abigail's father takes care of things like that."

CHAPTER FOUR

And he did.   Not only that but when McCready was finally
satisfied, Abigail's father inveigled two leading publishers to
dinner and by the evening's end had them bidding against each
other for the rights to publish.   As Abagail forecast, his star was
in the ascendancy because the book, his book, was an almost
instant sensation.   Described as "a work that had found its time"
Gingersnap sold out in hardback, made two paperback re-printings
and the film rights were purchased.   It was noised abroad that
Albert Finney and Tom Courtney were vying for the leading role.

James Carson became a celebrity overnight.

Not only that, but he passed his driving test.

At Abigail's insistence, Veronica was commissioned to
design the cover for the paperback.   Purple- faced Gingersnap as
a boy resting on his hunkers and scattered all around the chewed
cores of apples.   He was choking with laughter while out of his
mouth spewed, not bits of fruit, but instead bubbles enclosing
binary opposed opposites: Protestant/Catholic; atheist/ believer;
individual/group; male/female/; saint/sinner; revenge/forgiveness
and love/ hate.   For himself alone she created and presented an
alternative version: same idea, only this time Gingersnap was
crouching with his back to the reader, looking over his shoulder,
his trousers round his ankles, presenting his bare bottom with the
binary opposites being shat from his arse.

Abigail was in raptures over his success.

"I told you.   We three focussed on a project are an unstoppable force.   Individually, our horizons would be narrowed
and our powers never tested to the limits of our abilities so that we

would in isolation from each other never achieve our true
potentials.   Together we can impose our wills.   You were right
about the number three, James.   The earth, air, fire and water
signs are each represented by a triangle.   Aries is the tip of the
fire sign and together we three make a powerful group, together we
form the three points of an arrow head that can be propelled to
heights none of us could ever achieve independently.   But," here
Abigail lowered her voice, "eventually the arrow must fall and
provided the three points remain intact it will fall naturally, its
shape intact.   Should we fragment," her voice took on an air of
tragic urgency and he had to suppress a compulsion to laugh aloud,
"then the lines of our force field would implode and the negative
aspects of our star signs would start to dominate and our arrow
would surely miss its mark."

They embraced.

Two nights later Abigail went to dinner with her father and the
new woman in his life who was to become her step-mother.   He
was pulling on his jacket about to go out he knew not where when
his door was flung open and Veronica, cigarette in hand and
looking dishevelled and appearing unsteady made her entrance.
Leaving the door open behind her she stood, legs apart, drew on
her cigarette and raising her head exhaled smoke into his room's
air.

"Thought it was about time we marked your ascendancy, oh
and mine too.   It's about time we two sides of the infernal triangle
came together.   After all, success breeds."

It struck him that if Abigail spoke like a textbook then
Veronica uttered dialogue like a character from a movie: a film
noir.   He could be Bogart to her Bacall.   A pity he did not smoke

now so that he could light one for her and him both like… no that was another pair, in another film altogether.   Oh yes, it was Bette Davis and…

Pulling her tight skinny rib top over her head Veronica uncovered her small white breasts and erect pink nipples.   She dropped the top on the floor, sidled towards him with arms raised and locking her hands behind his head drew his head towards her breasts and held it there rubbing herself against his face before pulling the back of his hair so fiercely he cried out in protest. Then leaning back she inserted bony fingers of each hand between the buttons of his shirt and with surprising strength ripped them apart, baring his chest.   Stepping away she snaked her hips free from her jeans peeling down her panties with the same movement, revealing incongruous against her pale skin a dark triangle of pubic hair.   He wrestled free from his clothes, she pushed him back unto the bed and was upon him, roughly tugging his penis, guiding him inside her, leaning back, bringing his hands to her breasts when over her shoulder a figure materialized in the doorway and he knew without having to register consciously who stood there. Reading his face Veronica extricated herself, stood and turned to face her friend, while he could only raise himself and draw his knees together in an ineffectual attempt to conceal his nakedness.

Her hand to her mouth, Abigail took in the situation then her face contorted she beat her sides with her fists closed and screamed and screamed before turning and swaying aside.   They heard her along the corridor and beginning to descend the stairs.   Without turning his way, Veronica began to pick up and climb into her clothes and he felt he had no option but to follow.   She was slipping out the door and he was pulling on his trousers when he heard the screech of brakes.   Frantically, not bothering with socks or tying laces he thrust his feet into his shoes and slide stepped out of the room, along the corridor, down the stairs and through the open front door.

Beneath him on the road were curved black tyres marks; a car was stopped at an angle and behind it was laid a mangled prone body. In the distance he could just discern the faint sound of a siren and wondered how it could be arriving so fast, then reasoned this was London where siren noises were as common as sheep's bleating from where he came. Most likely it was not connected to this particular tragedy and so it proved. Veronica was engaging with a man in a business suit who was leaning against the bonnet of the car kneading the back of his head with his hand while along the road, doors were opening and people were making their way towards the scene. He bent and began to tie his shoelaces feeling already detached, apart from it all. Anyway what could he, or anyone else do except leave it to those who were experts in dealing with the situation. Should he call an ambulance? Most likely someone would have already done so – the houses in this area all had phones but he had to do something. For a moment, standing on the doorstep watching events unfold he deliberated, then his decision reached he turned and entered the house.

CHAPTER FIVE

Sales of *Gingersnap* continued to climb and the press speculation regarding his relationship with Abigail and her tragic demise served only to add polish to his celebrity sheen.   He affected dark glasses and cloaked himself in an aura of dignified grieving when he escorted the even paler and thinner Veronica on a circuit of literary events where they looked good and made an intriguing couple.   In reality they had virtually nothing to say to each other and back in the house there was no more lovemaking; they kept to their separate rooms and neither made any attempt to talk about Abagail or the fateful accident.

At the funeral they had met Abigail's father, a small, bald, slightly overweight man wearing large rimmed, black framed spectacles.   His manner was quick and decisive and despite his short stature he exuded command.

"I know how you feel, you two.   You'll be blaming yourselves, arguing over and over about what each of you could have done differently to prevent what happened on that awful day, that terrible accident.   You need to remind yourselves that that is what it was: an accident, pure and simple.   There is no point in attaching any blame to you or on your part seeking in any way to feel responsible for what happened.   Believe me, I know.   We cannot and should not blame ourselves for the actions of others outside our control."

He looked around and moved closer placing a hand on each of their shoulders, as if drawing them both into his inner circle.

"No one knew Abigail better than I.   It was written in the stars that one day her emotional nature would lead to calamity.   I always had an intuition something like this would happen.   So remember," he looked up and at them both, "it was mischance, misfortune, call it what you will, but no-one, including that poor driver, was to blame so there is no call for any feelings of guilt."

He paused, gripped their shoulders tighter then dropped his arms and stepped back. "Stay in the house as long as you like." His voice had become suddenly business-like. "I bought it for Abagail and I am sure that is what she would have wished. I'll send a van round to pick up her things before I make any decision about her room. What are you working on now?"

The question was directed at him and its abruptness un-nerved him. Before he could summon any resources Abigail's father cut in decisively:

"An acquaintance of mine has this idea for a brief critical work on the novel written in English from Ireland; from its earliest beginnings in the eighteenth century to the end of the nineteenth, from say Dean Swift up to Oscar Wilde. Ireland and England are still making waves. There's a market for the kind of work we have in mind, I'm sure there is. The research is already done: background history, potted biographies of the main protagonists, a list of the works to be considered, even key quotations copied out. I put a team on it and they know what they're about. All I need is for someone to collate the work and put his name to it. My colleague is too busy to do the job himself. For my money it should be right up your street what with your background and to speak frankly, your present celebrity status could do no harm to sales. The project could keep you busy during this time of grief. I can arrange for all the material to be boxed up and sent round in the next few days. What do you say?"

What could he say?

"That's settled then. By the way Veronica, I was talking to an acquaintance the other day. He's looking for an illustrator for a series of gardening books.   Lucrative field," he smiled, "I mentioned your name so when you feel up to it, give me a ring and we can sort things out.   Remember both of you: life must go on."

Veronica moved smoothly from his arm to that of Abigail's father.   A week later she moved out of the house, leaving him the briefest of notes.

No offence James.   A girl has to live.   I know you'll understand.

He understood.

CHAPTER SIX

It took him nearly a year: a year of rising each morning at six and then with a devotion that was akin to the religious, absorbing himself in study.   Initially it was all reading and making notes, then when he had enough material he began the writing process. Thereafter it was writing in the daytime and reading in the evening. The research was meticulous, all arranged in chronological order in a stack of black hard backed files while two tea chests contained the novels.   The delivery men also arrived bearing tools and two long wooden planks they constructed into shelving.   Abigail's father thought of everything.

Purposeless reading had been his enduring passion and he had a talent for fast scanning and retaining information for a short period.   He found also that he possessed a knack for summary and penetrating to the core of an argument, so while it was hard demanding work the immersion and fidelity to a strict regimen provided purpose and a daily sense of achievement.   With the inspiration provided, all he had to come up with was the perspiration and when initial concerns about his suitability for the task were resolved in the doing, the days, weeks and months passed till the inevitable transpired and he was done and once again Sam McCready was in residence.   Never one to be complimentary, at least this time the process went both swifter and more smoothly and with a great deal less head scratching and muttering and in this way *Dean Swift to Oscar Wilde.   From Ireland: the Novel Written in English* by J Carson went to press.

What to do now?   Financially he had no worries: the *Gingersnap* advance and the ready income from royalties took care of that. He lived frugally; breakfasting on cereal and toast; a self-constructed sandwich of cheese, tomato and mustard for lunch;

while his evening meal varied between pie and chips and fish and chips. Who could ask for anything more? Residents came and went in the apartments above and below his and beyond the occasional greeting he took pains to avoid further contact. London, he was beginning to discover, was a great place for those who did not mind, not minding other people's business.

He found it all unsettling and an insight arrived and would not go away: he was at heart a settler. Acting as bit player in the London literary scene was not for him. He longed for quiet, a place away from all the noise and surface glamour, somewhere he could concentrate and be concentrated upon, because for sure someone with his achievements did not deserve all this anonymity. He needed peace and quiet - and recognition. Home was peace. Home was quiet. At home he would be recognised. The idea began to nag. He would be returning in triumph, a celebrity and surely all the world loves one of those and he could gloss over his past, polish the narrative of his university debacle and portray the menial labouring in England as staging points in his grand design; all undertaken for the sake of the novel he had been planning to write. Back home he could sculpt his image and build on the myth he had fabricated already for the English media. That losing card game could yet prove to be the best thing that ever happened to him.

There was but one way to find out.

CHAPTER SEVEN

STATEMENTS

FRONTISPIECE

O for a Pound

Of Ezra

To give my words

More weight.

VOW

I will weed out the pride in opinion

That so often comes with age

And fend off the claim to experience

That snuffs out youth's artless rage.

STATEMENT

The poems beneath are ponds.

Look into them

Swill your head around

And seek out any glints of thought

That lie there lurking to confound.

THE MUSE HELPS THOSE

Faced by a blank sheet I panic

And thoughts zigzag around my brain.

Scene from my window:

A sprawling unfinished house,

   No insight there

So I lift my eyes

To fix un-seeing on sky

Clear, albeit smudged smokily

By a factory's finger.

A boot scrape unhinges my gaze

And I begin the aimless doodling

Of patterns I'm compelled to complete.

Neat curves and eyes, always eyes.

This way madness lies.

A VAIN ATTEMPT

Do I view you typewriter

As some kind of status symbol

To be placed centrally

A beacon for my ego's eye?

For since that monetary commitment

I have sidestepped closer contact

Bypassed your cryptic stare

And embraced lesser woes.

Typing this is my vain attempt

To stem your staring discontent.

CONFESSION

I long to experience myself in print

To spawn a stir through the written word

To be interviewed by Him and Her

Then smash the illusion, reveal it's absurd.

Van Gogh's an exception that proves the rule

The garret is warmed with ambition's flame

It's all a scam, you can take my tip

The quest for Art's just an ego trip.

COMMENT

They lived their lives

Delaying;

Ignored they were

Decaying.

MANEFESTO

We're not of the right

Nor the left

Or the centre

We're neither for the workers

Nor the men in charge

And we might trade unions

For manage meant.

We're not of the bar

Or the lounge,

Neither bitter

Nor mild.

We're neither hawk

Nor dove

We're bees

Who have stung our sting.

We'll tolerate almost anything.

Really we don't give a damn

But we do care.

MEDITATION

In every situation

There is an area beyond fact

That should be allowed for.

Fact is a cage

Potential trills the true essence.

TO SHE OF THE SPECIES

Beware

For once you could stop

And look outwards and upwards

But now you've clocked on

And heads must look down

In the market machine.

TO THE YOUNG HE OF THE SPECIES

Take care

You whose binds are

The local pubs

The local lads

The local girls.

At your age

You should be on your bike

Boldly seeking out

Newer and greater limitations.

TO THE PARENTS OF THE SPECIES

Adhere to practicalities

And decline judge mentalities.

TO GRANDPARENTS OF THE SPECIES

It's hard but right to accept

That the teacher

Can be the taught.

TO THE GOD OF THE SPECIES

If you're there

Then you're to blame.

If you're not

It's not your fault.

You cannot be there

And not be blamed

And if you're not

The fault is ours.

TO A MONARCH FOR THE SPECIES

In the Golden Age yet to come

The Prince married a black Catholic man

And his father, the King declared

"One day he'll be your Queen!"

TO THE INDIVIDUAL OF THE SPECIES

Down deep we know

The world is split

Into two powerful forces

With the first

Much more powerful

Than the next:

These are

ME

And the rest is you.

Each certainty

Wraps round a seed that destroys.

Every group you join

Slivers another slice

From the purity of the self

You donate to the cause.

A SHORT

Neat

Heady dram

A poem is.

Language distilled

Word

By

Word

To crystallise meaning.

FLEETING PUB THOUGHT

Better

Anthropologist

Than

Drinking

Tribesman.

Why should I sacrifice

My liver

For my living?

PRETENTIOUS, EPIGRAMMATIC, SOCIO-POLITICAL POEM

Ism

Equals

Schism.

A CERTAINTY

The real truth

Is what we know to be true

But don't ever like to hear.

A KIND OF LOVING

Where one force prides itself

On just how much torture

It can inflict

On another abject

That prides itself

On how much torture

It can endure.

THE MIND'S NOT...

Once swishing up wetted coal dust

A polished nugget plopped down an unbarred grating.

Stooping and scoop-diggering confident fingers

I prised out, pale, dwarfed pig-like, a drowned mouse,

Rubbery hairless with china-fine curled feet.

The electric shock of it jolting my elbow

Propelled it free and I shuddered away.

On the edge of my brain an analogy teeters

But for some days now has refused to spill.

The mind's not an unbarred grating

To be entered with self-assured skill.

A KIND OF REALITY

In formaldehyde in jars the snakes coiled staringly.

As first formers we played a simple chicken game

Slithering the heavy jars to the edge of the stone sill,

Leaving them precariously teetering while sir droned on.

The world of the jungle was in the classroom

Without the sweat, the tangled growth, mosquito bites.

Vicarious experience became an opiate, later induced

By TV dosage in our sitting-rooms.

Until one day a jar powdered splashingly

And oiled snake elasticated across the room's floor.

What riot terror then!   I remember screaming.

Life made more real.   Not living dreaming.

MOMENT RECOLLECTED

On the steps of the Tate gallery

My vision was blurred

Then flicked to consciousness by a drama in progress.

Pushing ridiculous furniture in a battered pram

Her Munch face splintered with tears,

A woman trailed past three descending children.

A grey wind made nonsense of her thin dress

And I followed, voyeurism battling concern

While oncoming tourists stared then passed.

An older, over- coated man caught up

And recrimination began, the big-eyed children

Completed composition and added poignancy to the frame.

Then furious progress, gesticulation and gasping tears.

I'll give her my jacket!   A plague on objective viewing,

This time I'll step inside the frame.

The row becalmed, she raised a shawl.

Had Art contrived to fool us all?

DO IT YOURSELF

You never let me saw

I only held the wood.

Despite the murderous thoughts

I helped you all I could.

"A chip of the old block,"

Family and friends would say.

The chip I shouldered grew

And would not fall away.

I felt myself excluded

Used only to impress

Always kept outside you

A type of formal dress.

At least that's how I saw it

So one day resentment's elf

Prompted me to cut you with

The barbed, "Do it yourself!"

BROTHERLY LOVE

That day I grudge-tugged Sam and Paul to the Pictures

Their four and five an elder brother's heartache.

Firm father-like I spent the conciliatory thruppence

On penny gob-stoppers, a sure half-film suck.

Once inside the velvety Aladdin's cave

I basked in the benevolence of Sultan- ship

And forgave their tell-tale pact against me

Assuaged by the eminence of my role.

Then Paul (it would be him) cough-shot his sweet

And it stickily rolled, shattering content.

Bugger responsibility!   It trapped you every time.

I punched him hard; then swiftly gave him mine.

THE RAIDS

We did the ecumenical thing

When we robbed the priest's orchard one night

Led over the walls and through the gates

By Catholic friends, so to keep the thing right

Next time we brought them to our Minister's place,

A silly mistake that sprouted ill-feeling,

For the lack of fruit proved a total disgrace

So we never again mixed religion with stealing.

WHY

Is it just arrogance?

This gritty resistance,

This refusal to be scrubbed

Into unified opinion.

Hearing the everyday replies

On, prices, politics, my God,

I laugh (inside my head),

Yet I am their culture drunk.

I too was reared to stay

On my own side of the fence.

Why then am I not brethren bound

A man who struts his common ground?

GETTING BY

We merge our self into opinion

To avoid bites from argument's teeth

Change colour or creed on the outside

Try to stay what we are underneath.

INSIGHT

Weed is a linguistic

Category

That should not be binding

On you or me.

MORE ENCOUNTERS

Yo big man

Just a minute of your time

The street hawker rapped.

I shook my head

And walked on by

But that *big man*

Buoyed me up that whole day.

Good morning

I risked cheerily

To the black postman.

Ya boss

He replied.   He really did.

I sauntered on

A party to

The mystery of it all.

MORE UTOPIAS

Since to my cost, unarguably I am

That singular, monstrous creature, man,

One free to choose, as far as freedom goes,

The highway of thorns or the path of rose,

The former is the route I spend my time

Avoiding when I can, since I wish mine

To be the scented lane, the road to bliss

The petalled causeway to my happiness.

So why is it when I could spend my time

In hunting pleasure rather than this rhyme

I find myself trapped in the track of thorn

Rueing my fate, the day that I was born

To be the one pursuing with regret

The chimera of a rhyming couplet

And if that was not enough to frame her

In squared iambic pentameter?

The reason's plain, I say it without shame:

Like many more than me, I seek acclaim.

To publish and be dammed is my desire.

For that I'll take life's pain and risk hell's fire.

And Fame is not alone what I pursue;

She has a sister, Truth, I seek her too.

These rarely stray into the scented way

Rather the place of thorns is where they stay.

Pain's pleasure then, the paradox is clear

When Fame's the game and Truth is just as dear.

What need for fame, why not seek truth alone

The single quest is just, and on one's own

Could be pursued with honour and with pride?

Acclaim is for this world; we cannot hide

We live in it; it prompts our every thought,

Our only hope is change, to bring to nought

Competitive desire, the sad old game

To have what others have, to make a name

To be remembered by.   To change all this

We need a new world and the old dismissed.

The nation-state, it could provide, while we

Pursue our individuality.

A charitable sign is what we seek

Donated by the strong to aid the weak.

Food, shelter, warmth all we require to live

Together, should be ours so we can give

Thought and attention to the way we are,

Look to our inner selves, ignore the far.

Our daily wants provided, proffered free

By that machine-slave, our technology.

The humdrum gone, our shoulders off the wheel

We then could sing and play and think and feel.

Instead of competition there would be

Time to create, and then to be the me

I am, to seek the way I wish to go

To find the truth, ignore acclaim and so

Increase our opportunity so we

Can reap the benefit and see

The paths clear to our valued happiness

With Truth not Fame the aim of our success.

No need for charity because the State

Supplies the basic needs.   No longer Fate

Determines whether we succeed or not;

Allows a few to bloom; the rest to rot.

All come inside and none are turned away

We work from choice, fulfilment is our pay.

In a brave new world freed from Envy's sting

Each accent would be music that we sing.

No single sound rhymes better than the rest.

All prize their own voice; surely that is best.

The song I sing looks forward to a time

When all pursue their individual rhyme

Satisfied that the thoughts they speak or write

Will be respected and there is no fight

To be accepted, be one of the crowd.

Denying freedom should not be allowed.

We'll sing for joy; Truth the aim of the game,

No need for Envy or the quest for Fame.

IN THE WINGS: TREMBLING

I wait to make my entrance

As here I stay standing

Waiting to compose myself

And then I can appear

And be

The Me

The one

 I'm in this place

And meant to be.

CONCLUSION

My thought is a northern flinty kind

Where reason thrives and soft words die,

It finds no peace in peaty sentiment,

No resting place in a past's sad sigh.

CHAPTER EIGHT

Then there was one that came from nowhere; a kind of automatic transcript he penned one night when, notebook at the ready and senses alert waiting to be inspired he found his self, composing:

The singers of songs

Are as various as shells

Yet all share one common spring

That is sourced from the parents

Whose love or neglect

Paves the way for their creative fling.

Such a one was Andros

Whose resentment was born

Of parents who never stayed still

Instead toiled all the time

And slaved for their son

Till they made themselves feeble and ill.

The parent needs die

For the son to be freed

This Andros knew to be right

So ever the coward

He avoided a scene

And slunk off like a thief in the night.

Andros: where did that come from?

There it stopped and try as he did he could make no more of
it so he called it *The Singer of Songs,* folded it carefully twice and
inserted it into the old worn leather notebook he had discovered in
his aunt's house all those years ago.   It had turned out to be
someone's diary but the contents did not interest him.   It was the
feel of it, its soft texture and sense of musty age that transformed it
into a kind of talisman.   It brought him luck, he was convinced of
it.   He was not religious but retained traces of superstition – one
and the same thing when you thought about it.   An argument
could be made that religion was but the literary intellectualization
of superstition: he should write a poem about it.

He had needed to keep his hand in so that and the idea of
cashing in on his bit of fame had prompted the flurry of poems.
Many he had written already (he had always been a closet
scribbler) and as an afterthought and because he could not bear the
thought of destroying them he had stuffed the tatty exercise book
in his bag that night he left Ireland.   They appeared in a slender
volume he entitled *Statements.*   In what he considered a clever
ruse to fend off possible criticism he penned a poem as a
frontispiece.

REACTION to a REVIEW

The pejorative *...clutching his slim volume...*nettled me

Weighing as I am, my vulnerable collection.

That word 'slim' prompted the pain.

Yield is important, supply needs be maintained.

While already I can sense resources being drained.

His publisher decided to print his poetry along with the work of
another two emerging writers in a slim volume entitled *TRIO*.   In
the event it made about as much stir as did a spoon in a mug of tea.

Then again Hollywood was reported to be taking an interest in
Gingersnap and stars like Dustin Hoffman and Al Pacino were
reported to be vying for the central role; it was rumoured he would
be invited to work on the screenplay.   The literary history was
moderately well received and all things considered a barrowful of
luck had helped propel him to heights he had never dreamed of
reaching but his fortune could run out.   He was aware and
frightened of that possibility.   What he needed was quiet, a place
away from all the noise and the surface everything, the temptation.

Home was quiet.

He would be returning in triumph, a celebrity.

Abagail's father agreed saying he would have his personal assistant handle the arrangements.   There was a mass of left un-saids suspended between them that he sensed neither would ever make the effort to remove; simultaneously it bound them together and kept them apart.

They shook hands and the die was cast.

By the end of that week, the papers had their story.   James P Carson sated by the excess of London society was proposing a return to the rural innocence of the country of his birth, turning his back on false hype and insincerity, seeking instead emotional stability and creative regeneration among his own people.

What a load of baloney!

Nevertheless, home he went, to be greeted at the airport by a straggle of gawping onlookers, flashing cameras and a request for an interview with Ulster television.   Why not, any publicity… The questions were posed by a humourless, focussed presenter, affecting black-rimmed spectacles and adopting that Anglo-Ulsterese of what passed for the intelligentsia of the region.   Not long out of university, destined no doubt for a career in English television and nobody's fool, she succeeded in making him feel wary.   A kind of veiled hostility was in the air that propelled him towards formality and a careful, stilted delivery he was aware could come across as unnatural.

So what?

He was the writer and why should not a writer discourse like a book? Be aloof, superior, intelligent he told himself. He'd done his preparation and repeated mental rehearsals of interviews, knowing people would be suspicious, antagonistic because of his success. He knew because that was exactly how he would respond to anyone else in his position. Umpteen encounters had honed his interview technique; he was ready, primed and in good shape and took care to spurn any hospitality alcohol, electing instead to sip from a glass of water.

Let verbals commence!

Q. *Gingersnap* has been described as a refreshing breeze blown through the Irish literary landscape. What is your reaction to that comment?

A. Interesting image. My initial intention was to create a Bildungsroman. (*Sure there was nothing like a portmanteau word to set the tumbrils rolling. The best joke he saw in a Queen's University Rag magazine was a drawing of a man-hole with underneath the single word caption: HERMAPHRODITE.*) Joyce's *Portrait of an Artist* was my literary model, but this time focussing on a Protestant upbringing, an area of the literary landscape, to borrow your phrase, that is relatively unvisited. Joyce, as I am sure you are aware, ended the novel with his central character exiting his native land to seek his fortune in the world outside. I thought it would be interesting to follow a vaguely similar path with Gingersnap and see how he fared. I suppose you could say if I blew any, it was a kind of Irish/Anglo breeze. How refreshing is for others and not myself to say.

Q.   I notice you place "Irish" first in your category.   The English press describe you as an Irish novelist.   How would you describe your literary identity?

(Tread carefully here.   The old nationality minefield and this was Ulster television where viewers (if any) would have their ears and eyes more tuned in to this response than any of the remainder his literary blathering.)

A.   Well, as to that, my background is Ulster Protestant and I harbour no sense of shame as a result.   Rather, I am proud to acknowledge it.   *(That should keep them happy).*   In artistic terms I view myself as a colonizer of the English literary landscape, treading in the footsteps of worthier trailblazers like Swift, Sheridan, Yeats, Wilde, Shaw, Beckett and the like.

Q.   A way to classify those writers you describe would be to call them Protestant Anglo-Irish from the south of the country.   How would you react to George Russell's observation and I quote: "Unionism in Ireland has produced no literature."   *(Jesus! Ulster TV's no pushover.   Still he'd taken the shilling.   Thank God for that research material.)*

A.   I'm aware of Russell's comment.   I can think of a number of reasons why Protestant culture in the north of Ireland might not appear as alluring as that of the Catholic tradition in the south. To begin with there's the identity issue you referred to previously.

Historically nationalism, despite the suffering and death in its wake, has always been viewed as a viable ideology. The union with England scenario appears to be condoning the colonization process that has become vilified in so many places all over the world. Protestant culture in Ireland is not seen as having artistic merit. Unionism is more about practice than ideology. (*He was beginning to struggle*). Its narrative appears duller, less dramatic and has failed to produce as many colourful martyrs to the cause.

Q. What is your opinion of the Unionist cause?

A. (*What had he let himself in for?*) I have to declare I'm even less qualified as a political commentator than as a literary critic. (*A dab of humility should do the trick*). However you did ask me the question, and I did agree to appear on your programme. Let me put it this way. Art of any kind is about establishing some kind of order on the randomness surrounding us all. The artist in me strives to reconcile polarity; to attempt to create a degree of harmony where discord prevails, so in purely artistic terms cohesion appears the more desirable solution. (*Was that woolly enough?*) Then again I'm an Ulsterman fettered with pragmatism and a cultural tradition and folklore I cannot circumvent.

Q. You're saying that any commitment you would make to a united Ireland would be confined to artistic grounds?

A. That's about it, yes.

Q. Unionism: a practice lacking a recognisably respectable literary body of work. You said there were other reasons for the apparent lack of productivity in literature.

A. Well, perhaps the Protestant work ethic has something to do with it. Maybe writing is not perceived as proper work. Generally speaking the Arts in Ulster are viewed as either frivolous or subversive. The practical Protestant mind-set tends to value Science above Art. Also, in large part, there's the fact that the Protestant outlook is to do with accepting one's lot and that's not such a bad lot in this part of the world. The tendency of literature is to question. Then there's the tradition of Confession on the Catholic side.

Q. What do you mean?

A. (*What did he mean? He was beginning to enjoy himself. Tread carefully!*) Well the novel, in large part, is a kind of extended confession. Ulster Protestant tradition tends to value suppression of the self, inner thoughts and emotions tend to be concealed rather than revealed. Button up, whatever you say, say nothing, keep all inside. There is surely an inhibition related to artistic expression lurking within the Ulster protestant psyche. The inhibition is increased by the small, closed nature of the community that prevails in the wee six counties; the feeling of critical pressure from a watching countryside. Allied to this are feelings of security, belonging, dependence, gratitude created through attachment to the protecting Big Brother, England. All this is not good for the artist who needs to feel an outsider, away, above and beyond it all. The true artist harbours feelings of oppression and exclusion.   Perhaps that's why women have enjoyed such success as novelists.

Q.   Interesting point.

A.   Then (well into his stride now) there's the self-fulfilling prophesy factor in the stereotyping 'Honest Ulsterman'.   To be a writer, to tell stories requires an act of make believe, or to tell the truth, of lying.   Our Ulsterman is too open a book, too easily read, too forthright when he declares, "Ulster will fight and Ulster will be right". The true artist is spawned from doubt rather than certainty.   The other side of the coin, the paradox inherent in the character of the Ulster Protestant, is that despite his core conviction, he is too self-effacing.   Of course the extremists, on both sides, can make a lot of noise, but generally speaking the Protestant mentality goes hand-in-hand with private judgement; any grandiose posturing, an essential requirement for creative practice, is thus supressed.   As I have already pointed out, the Ulster Protestant prefers to keep himself within himself, be civil and accommodate himself to adverse circumstance.   As a case in point consider their reaction to the *ne temere* decree.   (*Detecting her startled look he smiled innocently. Would any of the Protestant viewers know what the hell he was talking about or how many Catholics?   A little research could go a long way.*)

Q.   Perhaps, for the benefit of our viewers, you could elaborate on that point.

A. (*Hand to hand it to her: that was an astute move. As his mum would say, this one was no goat's toe.*) As, I am sure you are aware, I refer to the Catholic church's insistence that children of so called 'mixed marriages' be brought up in the Catholic faith. That edict has been received with the self-effacing politeness I have been talking about. Enduring self-effacement and politeness, those denominators of a basically staunch Christian people, are not I am afraid, qualities linked to sustained achievement in the Arts. (*Phew!*)

Q. To turn to your own work. I am aware you will have been asked this on more than one occasion but your reply would still be of interest: to what extent are the characters of Gingersnap and the milieu surrounding him, based on your own life experience?

A. Gingersnap is of my imagination and that imagination has been fashioned by my life experience just as the imaginative world of any author has been formed by their particular life experience. Inevitably there is a connection between the lived and the imaginative world of all writers. In that sense, Gingersnap and his world are as much and as little to me as are, say, Lemuel Gulliver's were to Jonathon Swift.

Q. Back to your world then James Carson. Much has been made of your return here from across the water; indeed in some quarters it has been hailed as an attempt at a sort of sea-change. What is your version of the event?

A. Well, to begin with I'd be loath to describe my homecoming as any kind of 'event'. (*That little sally should keep the viewers happy and joy of joys surely he detected a slight wincing round the mouth of his interrogator.*) I'm an Ulsterman. This is where I spent my formative years. London has its attractions; perhaps too many attractions. Things occurred there I need to put into perspective and to do that I need to distance myself from them. I've returned, and I hope it doesn't sound too pretentious, for a spell of reflection, to re-acquaint myself with the slower pace of life here where people are not as isolated from each other or as obsessively absorbed in the pursuit of their own ends. There's talk about *Gingersnap* being made into a film and there's the possibility that I may be invited to work on the screenplay. Bearing all that in mind I believe I'll find more peace and quiet back home here than I would back in London.

Q. Won't you find us too dull, too insular?

A. Dull never, insular maybe, but insularity is not an ignoble condition. The world, I am afraid, has much, much worse to offer.

Q. I'm afraid our time is up. Thank you James Carson, we wish you success with your screenplay and welcome back.

CHAPTER NINE

Driving home, the car (waiting for him at the airport curtesy of Abagail's father and his machinations) loaded with presents for the family, he assessed his performance.   Gradually, during the course of the interview hostility had lessened and by its ending he had sensed he was in with a chance with her if he made the right moves.   Truth to admit he was tempted but he allowed discretion to rule, feeling any relationship would be too high profile.

The literature of his native land had been a mainly closed book to him when he had left for England: he had read *Borstal Boy* and that was about the depth of it.   Then when *Gingersnap* was published and became a sensation he was labelled an Irish writer and at parties and interviews was expected to account for his place in the tradition.   He thanked his lucky stars the parties came first for early on he latched onto the silence that un-nerved, projecting thought while saying nought.   There was, he discovered always someone who could be relied upon to fill a sound vacuum, argue your corner for you and create a defence against the verbal assaults and taunts success invites when alcohol prompts.   Almost totally ignorant of his cultural heritage it made sense to allow others to assemble it for him, shuffle the pack of Irish writers, arrange them in suits and produce them with triumph.   In the London literary circuit he had found many equipped to play that game.   He watched and learned, took mental notes, sometimes after a really memorable retort would later even make a written note, and in that way built up his confidence until he could begin to engage in the diversion himself.   Then the literary research landed in his lap and he had a font of authority to draw from.   He had seen that *Unionism in Ireland has produced no literature* stab coming from a mile off; had encountered and countered it on numerous occasions.

It was, he reflected odd that *Gingersnap*, written when he had no awareness of the contribution of others had sold so well while his book of verse and his literary work were not nearly as successful. Was a little knowledge proving a dangerous thing? Mind you, if it hadn't been for Sam McCready...

To be fair he had made an attempt to have McCready's contribution acknowledged on the title page, but Abigail's father had dissuaded him; it would not look good, Sam had offended important people in the past so it would naturally make the novel more difficult to publish. Besides those with insider knowledge might spread rumours that the man's contribution was greater than it really was. Better to keep it under wraps. McCready had done what he'd been asked to do and been well paid for his services. Forget him.

The car handled well and having learned to drive embroiled in the swells and eddies of London traffic this was plain sailing. Fields, houses and trees he passed by un-heeding; he knew where he was going and was in no particular rush to complete his journey. His thoughts turned to speculation regarding the welcome he would receive. When he'd left Belfast he had composed a brief letter explaining he had decided to put off going to university to make an attempt at experiencing life in the real world outside; he was going to England to find work and no-one need worry about him as he had plenty of offers of places to stay. Then swirled round by the turbulence of London life he had stopped writing. Abigail had wanted to meet his family but he blocked that in the certainty that her gushing ardour and astrological leanings would be granted short shrift with the practical, no-nonsense folk of his community. When *Gingersnap* came out he sent everyone in the family a signed copy with a personally tailored message inside.

Sam McCready was wrong when he castigated novels for being lies: novels were truths disguised as lies. Familiarity formed the material of production, the life lived was the mine the writer dug, sifted, cleaned despoiled, then manufactured to be sold on the open market. So he had quarried the proggings, the skirmishes, the game-playing, Sunday school, church, the excursions, the Twelfth, the week-end in Portrush, the card game…the visit to his aunt. Novelists not only used, they also abused. What Sam had made of it, Teresa, Snap…? Of course he had changed names, deliberately kept places ambiguous but there was no concealing the reality beneath the artefart. Surely too, the connection between Snap and Ginger, *Gingersnap,* was too obvious. It had bothered him at the time but, he recalled, he had wanted to please Abigail who had come up with the title.

So what? Novelistic licence bestowed permission. In the end weren't we all potential material for each other's stories? As a writer you used what you found and made of it what you wished. The novel had always been a criminal form, autobiography disguised as fiction; it was all about pretending and persuading, and surely he had a right to pretend and persuade as much as anyone else.

It was dark when he drove into the housing estate and pulled to a halt outside the house. His hands were tight on the steering wheel so taking a deep breath he flexed his shoulders and did his best to instil calm before switching off the engine. Across the street he spied a curtain flutter, then another. Affecting a smile he climbed from the car, stretched, clunked shut the door, and then began to stroll towards the front gate when the front door opened and light spilled across the path.

"James," and his mother approached her arms outstretched. They were not a hugging family and he was for a moment uncertain how to respond but he rallied and reaching out clasped her hands in his.

"Come on in, you'll be foundered out here. I'm sure you're starved. I've made sandwiches."

"Thank you. I've got some presents in the car. I'll get them, bring them in."

"I'll give you a hand. Good to see you."

It was Paul and his easy-going friendly manner quelled any awkwardness on his part. They shook hands and then Paul and he carried the parcels into the house. Inside a coal fire was stacked and burning brightly, making the room cosy and warm. His father's chair was empty: no Sam. Jane came towards him her arms reaching out like their mother's had then, reading his face volunteered, "They're out. You know what those two are like, gone to the pub. It's past closing time, so they'll be here any time now. They clasped hands.

"You're looking well. You'll take tea. I'll bring the sandwiches in. If you're not hungry, don't worry. Nothing goes to waste in this house."

"I'll give you a hand."

Jane and his mother were gone and he was left standing with Paul who was the first to speak.

"Have a seat and sit down as they say in this part of the world, or if they don't who cares, I'll say it anyway."

Paul had grown taller than he remembered him and his easy-going friendly manner was infectious. He sat down opposite him inwardly admiring his neatly pressed jeans and tight fitting short sleeved open necked, checked shirt. Sacrosanct, their father's empty arm-chair made its presence felt: it wasn't fair, they should have been here to meet him, and instead they were at the pub! Together!

"I'm in Belfast now, sharing a flat with a friend. I've come home for the weekend. I'm working in a salon, training to be a hairdresser. I want to open my own place, perhaps bring a bit of glamour to the old town."

Paul prattled on but he could not fully engage; his mind was on the pub with his father and Sam. Dimly he became aware of a change of tone so he summoned attention.

"You won't have heard James but our aunt Mary died. Apparently she'd not been well for years and our dad, well you know what he's like, had not been in touch with her. He had phoned her one night about a year ago but said she was drunk and out of her head. Kept blethering on about some notebook and a penknife but he couldn't make head or tail of it and slammed the phone down on her. We did go to the funeral though and our dad kicked up a big scene when he found out she had left her money and the house to some Catholic woman who had been doing bits and pieces for her when she had been bed-ridden. So what do you think of that then?"

"Things happen."

He remembered the old fuddy-duddy and how he thought she'd kick up a fuss about the artefarts he'd purloined. That stupid old notebook: he'd only pocketed it because he liked the feel of it. *REGGUBB*: what was that all about? It was funny how the daft word had stuck. It was some kind of silly diary and he only kept it for good luck.

"Tell us about London, James."

"Like here with knobs on," he managed hoping the wisecrack would suffice. He was too upset to speak at length and besides the topic was too big and surely worthy of a larger audience.

"Right you two, get stuck in. You know our mum, she hasn't changed. Still measures how much people like her by the amount of her food they eat, so no picking."

Jane to the rescue, handing out plates, proffering sandwiches, pouring tea and blethering on about leaving enough room for the cake baked especially for the occasion. His mother appeared and immediately Paul's focus shifted to her, praising her efforts with the spread then igniting the fire of local gossip that so warmed them both while Jane hovered ensuring everyone ate and drank their fill. They were the family these three and in a moment of insight he realised that was the way it had always been. They were the hub, the heart of it all, whereas he, Sam and their father... Suddenly he felt an impetus to shrug off all the introspection and join in, become a player and warm his self in their family glow.

"These sandwiches are just what the doctor ordered," he ventured, "you should open a café mum, we'd all be rich." She looked pleased. "Look, I've brought you all presents, let me hand them out now, we can all..." His resources left him. They were shaking their heads, looking at each other. Then, as one, they were staring at him.

"You know we couldn't James, we couldn't start without your father, whatever would he think?" His mother tut-tutted disapprovingly. She was right of course, but still his resentment flamed: his father and Sam were jealous and had taken themselves to the pub to spoil his entrance.

"Try to understand, James. Don't be angry. You know…"

"Yes I know; I know what's what."

From outside the sound of voices then the front door opening, followed by feet clomping in the hall. Paul looked at him and he found he was rising from his chair, standing awkwardly feeling nervous and apprehensive. His father came first through the door. Then in ludicrously exaggerated fashion, he stood to attention, clicked his heels together, discharged a silly flourish of a salute and ignoring **him** addressed their mother.

"Apologies captain, the first mate here," swivelling his head and staring pointedly at the figure in the hallway behind, "and I would have been back and aboard ship by eight bells, but we were press-ganged by low company landlubbers and beggin' yer pardon captain, the lower the company, the more the first mate loves being press-ganged."

Christ, the boring old 'shiver me timbers' routine, how often had they heard that one down through the years. And now Sam was being dragooned into the act, probably being made to feel a right…

At this Sam stuck out his tongue, crossed his eyes, slowly and rigidly rotated his head, then inched his face forwards till his nose was almost touching his father's cheek. A moment's silence, their father's mouth began to twitch, then he lost it and crumpled forwards snorting with laughter till he was assaulted by a coughing fit, and hawked and spluttered while Sam thumped him between the shoulder blades and their mam ran to the kitchen, returning with a glass of water, while Jane plumped the cushions in their father's chair by the fire and Sam and Paul helped guide him towards it.

Hapless, he might as well not have been there for all the attention he commanded.

"He'll be the death of me that one. So the prodigal has returned. Greet your long lost brother, Sam. Doubtless the fatted calf has been slaughtered. I could do with my portion of it at this minute."

Compliantly his mam and Jane made for the kitchen, while Sam stepped over and proffered his hand. Then silence until Paul released them: "James has brought us all presents. We're dying to see what we've got but he wouldn't let us see them till you two were back." Paul avoided eye contact and silence reigned: dammed if he was going to bring it to a halt.

"Come on everyone. Mum'll be in in a minute with a fresh pot of tea. Polish off that lot and mind there's more where they came from. All you need to do is give us a shout."

Gradually Jane bossed the mood towards domesticity, but on his part he found it difficult to conceal his hurt. No warmth from his father, and Sam was behaving like they were strangers. What had he done to deserve this treatment? Become successful, that's what; they were jealous, it was as simple as that.

"Good to see you've not returned after all this time of hardly ever hearing from you, with both arms the same length."

Feted by his womenfolk, attended to by two of his sons, in his chair by the fire, in his house their father assumed command. He was to be the focal point and all would proceed under his direction. The emotional temperature was to be controlled by him. Resistance would only invite rows and distress and from past experience all present knew the rule: appeasement was the cup that sobered. This time, on this special occasion, HIS homecoming, he would cow- tow, but after this no more.

"Let distribution commence," and his father smirked, rubbed his hands together and sat upright in his chair affecting excessive anticipation.

Seething, his thunder robbed, he did as directed. Many times over he had rehearsed this scene in his head: himself the star attraction, one by one doling out the gifts, the sole recipient of gratitude, oohs and aahs, embraces and backslapping; instead a general hotchpotch, everyone tearing off wrapping paper, showing each other, exchanging knowing looks, making a mockery of his event.

"That coat's real leather," then in spite of himself, or perhaps through spite, "cost a bomb."

His mother raised an eyebrow, all eyes fixed on him, accusing him. Blaming him for what? For generosity! What was wrong with this family? Anywhere else the exile returned would be made to feel welcome, be shown you were glad they had returned, while here... Other fathers were happy when their sons made good, while his... Umbrage swelled suddenly towards anger, his heart began to thump, suddenly he was past biting his tongue, ready instead to turn on the ungrateful host of them, tell them a thing or thirty, when Jane sidled over and hugged him, shook him.

"James, the coat is lovely, James! The presents are all lovely, but you shouldn't have spent so much money!"

"Jane's right. Don't be in a strunt James. With me it's all about, 'You'll never see what I'll give you', but even as a boy you always brought home great presents. Remember the time you stayed at your aunt's and bought us that lovely heavy salt and pepper set: we still have them. I'll be a real swank wearing these earrings and this necklace. I think I'll give them an airing at church on Sunday and really give them something to talk about."

"They'll call you a right hussy! Mrs Smith will swallow her false teeth for sure. Mind you, I'm one to talk, wait till they see me in my new Carnaby Street jacket..." and Paul was off and away, making things right. Sam looked contented, absorbed in assembling his new fishing rod. His father's chair was vacant. As always he had been the difficult one – what to buy for the man it seemed impossible for him to please, the man he had wished to please more than anyone else? In the end he had settled for Harrod's and a ridiculously priced bottle of whisky.

"Whisky without an 'e', the English brew. I thought I'd share my good fortune. I've put white lemonade in the ladies, and in Paul's. Sam and I'll have ours straight, we like our drink undiluted." The bottle on the tray his father carried was half empty. "What about yourself, a drop of water, white lemonade? How does the London gentleman take his drink?"

In that instant he gained insight into the twinned nature of love and hate, understood they were spawned from the same cell. Holding the tray his father stood before him, smiling. Beyond rage lies a doldrums region, empty and chill. From there he summoned, "From a glass, from a glass, we London gentlemen take our drink from a glass."

At the first opportunity he made his excuses and left. He was renting a bungalow on the edge of town and in a simmering rage he drove there, regretting already his decision to return.

The bungalow stood on Stanley Ferguson's land and originally it had been built for the eldest son. He had been killed when a tractor overturned on him, and his widow had returned to her people. It stood on a hill, isolated and well back from the main road: an ideal location that should afford him the peace and quiet he craved. Surely here, if anywhere he could focus his attention and commit to the profession that had chosen him.

This time words did not tumble. Without desperation or competition to goad him, his inherent lazy, hedonistic nature could not be submerged. By any measure he was now a success: his money invested secured an adequate income, by nature he was not a spendthrift and that losing card game had cured any propensity for gambling. Besides, here there was little in the way of temptation on which to fritter money away. Added to this he was finding that with a resourceful agent (and Abagail's father had secured him that) the literary world could be cajoled to look after its own. There were offers to review books and he was still copy for press interviews, radio and possibly even television appearance. He could occupy himself also working on his version of the screenplay for the projected film version of *Gingersnap* so he could coast along evenly taking up the odd proposition here and there. His own man: not bad for a twenty-four year old. Not bad at all.

His landlord was the old man, Stanley Ferguson. Semi-retired now, he was still a commanding figure in the area. A bullish womaniser, he was reputed to have spilled his seed where and when by taking full advantage of the inherent deference granted to land-owning position in this otherwise prudish, church attending community. Till now his only contact with the old man had been seeing him from a distance on that platform on the field on the Twelfth.   Now he was to meet him face to face.   It had been arranged that on the first day of each month, he would pay his rent.

Cash only, Ferguson would have no truck with cheques.

CHAPTER TEN

That first occasion he set out around ten thirty in the morning. Deciding to walk, he chose a meandering route, strolling through narrow lanes with a switch in his hand, flicking at tall grass in hedgerows, halting now and then to outstare a placid, dead-eyed, chewing cow in an adjacent field.   There was contentment: you stayed put, accepted your lot, and existed in a state of unruffled indifference.   Let anyone stare, like them think what they liked, just turn away, maybe shake your head and go about your business. There was an irritating triumph attached to this supreme indifference: he was impressed.

Approaching the solid white farmhouse, he reeled back to the walled orchard at the back and the day he, Sam, Sean, Snap... Snap!   Had he read the novel?   How would he react to the blatant parallels?   He'd have to look him up and gauge his reaction.   Then there was Teresa: Teresa on his shoulders, her legs parted above him.   The image excited: he needed a woman. Teresa?   This mad impulse to return; had it subconsciously been prompted by her, a call to which he was responding?   Perhaps it was so.   He must try to find out.   Look up Sean, that was it, and then through him find out if he could get to her.   Working out the logistics had carried him to Stanley Ferguson's front door where he beat out a rat-a-tat on the huge knocker, eliciting immediately a deep ringing barking from inside that set off a progression of yelping round the back of the house.

The door was opened by a tall, handsome woman.   Her eyes were dark brown and they addressed him calmly and evenly. Her hair, flecked with grey, was coiled in intricate fashion that in her case did not decree severity.   Over her clothes she wore a black and white dotted smock, yet her carriage and everything about her made the household garment an irrelevancy.   The woman stood her ground, the faintest hint of a smile about her mouth.   He felt the impulse to explain himself.

"Hello, ah, sorry to disturb you, my name's Carson, James Carson.   I'm renting the bungalow at Green Lane, and as agreed, I've called to pay the rent."

"Ah yes do come in Mr Carson."   She spoke firmly in clear, cultured fashion: no ordinary domestic, this.   "I assumed you must be Mr Carson.   We have been expecting you.   Stanley said you would be along some time this morning.   I'm Sarah Patterson."

Graceful, decisive she extended her hand, making the point that they met as equals; she was nobody's menial.   He took her hand, impressed by the agreeably firm grip, meeting her eyes and smiling.   You did not, he decided, mess with Sarah Patterson. She was a real force and she somehow made him feel it was significant to be accepted by her.   Being approved of by this woman was he felt, a type of yardstick by which humankind, especially the male of the species, could be measured.

"This way, follow me Mr Carson."

"No please, call me James."

She smiled and from handsome melted to beautiful.   Christ, bet she looked lovely with that hair down.   You could see what the old man sees in her.   Wonder if…   He followed her into a wide, wooden floored hallway, past rooms to the left and right, then down some steps into a long, low-ceilinged, stone-tiled room at the back of the house.   Warm and cosy, the room's central feature was a solid plain wooden table with chairs tucked in all round.   At the back was a monumental farmhouse range, the source of the heat, and at the side, on a large ancient leather settee: the old man.

A picture of Churchill came to mind, sitting and leaning forward on an armchair, legs planted apart, between them a walking stick kept perpendicular by his hands folded on top. Male bulk squatting solidly, past his best now but the bulk conveyed power and the physical presence still intimidated.   They made a remarkable couple, he and Sarah and dream material for a novelist.   Who knows, maybe…?

"Mr Carson.   Ye'll be here to pay the rent.   Trust you find the accommodation to your liking.   Ye'll know who I am.   Sarah ye've met.   Give us the money then; sit yourself down and we'll have a while of your crack.   Ye'll have a cup o' tea."

Commandingly the old man held out a large gnarled hand; for the money, not the shaking.   From his inside pocket he withdrew the envelope containing the cash and handed it over. Then obligingly he pulled out one of the chairs from the table and sat.

"A famous name, Carson, in these parts: yer not a member of the lodge?"

The directness was disconcerting.   Beneath white tufted eyebrows the astonishingly clear and keen blue eyes pierced through him.

"No, ah, I'm not."   On the brink of bluster he snipped the sentence short, aware that Sarah, pouring tea, was also observing him.   "I'm not a joiner."   Making amends for his false start he continued, "I make a point of never joining any group that would accept…"

"And yer da," the rudeness of the interruption was shattering, but impervious to social nicety the old man just bullied on, "I don't know him.   He's not a member either."

Sarah brought the tea, handing each a large china cup and saucer, offering milk and sugar, providing time for him to summon resources to create some form of resistance. Her duties complete she took her seat at the other end of the settee. Jesus, what a pair! Sipping his tea, he felt trapped, then angry, then suddenly belligerent. Just who did this old codger think he was talking to? Another sip, then, "My father's his own man Mr Ferguson. He brought us up to think for ourselves."

A pause: Ferguson managed not only the talk, but also the quiet. The old man narrowed his eyes then, to his relief, laughed.

"Aye, thinking for yerself. Not much of that, in these parts, and a good thing too. Yer work, being a writer that helps; yer expected to think for yerself, allowed to," another pause, "up to a point." Then abruptly, "Do ye go to church?"

Jesus, what next? *What colour's yer underwear? Are ye wearing any?* To hell with it: he'd had enough.

"Used to: I'm a lapsed Presbyterian, a perfectly noble calling."

Sarah, he noticed, smiled but the flippancy had no discernible effect on the old man.

"Yer da doesn't go either, I'm told. Seems to me," another pause, "seems to me, yer less yer own man than ye let on, Mr Carson."

"Would you like more tea James?"

The timing was perfect and the soft utterance of his Christian name quelled his mounting anger. Sarah rose, Ferguson looked up, something passed between them and the old man smiled. What a woman, wherever did he find her, where did she hail from;

too good for the old bastard who doesn't deserve her? What to reply? Leave it out: when in doubt say nowt.

"Can I get you another?"

"Yes please. I'm sorry I was elsewhere. I'll have another cup, thank you."

"I hear ye went to University, and then left before even starting the course. What did ye set out to study?"

He heard a lot.

"My intention was to follow a course in literature."

"We've had university men in our family: law, medicine mostly. Our lot have little time for the Arts. Reading for the sake of reading can't help you farm land, hold it, can't keep you well. The world's the way it is because of doers, people who join in and get stuck in. Readers," a pause and those alarming blue eyes held his, "and writers are well and good as long as they don't try to be too clever and ridicule the rest of us. The Lodge, the church, there's worse places, much worse. Manys the good man's been a member of one or the other."

He paused again and again those eyes bored into his. The mouth was firm, inviting challenge. Best leave it: there was no chance of victory on this ground. Silence, then unexpectedly, "My son, Kenneth asked me to give you this."

From his side pocket the old man produced a white card, then grunting with effort and levering himself with the aid of the walking stick, stood up.

"Here ye are." He held out the card. "I'm off out to take a turn round the yard. Sarah'll see ye out." He turned and shambled away, opened the back door and was gone.

"Phew, not many like him that's different.   There's Ulster will be right, if ever there was."

She laughed.   "There's principle there too, James."

"Is that what you…?"

He stopped suddenly conscious he was going too far, too soon.

"See in him.   More, much more, more than you, or anyone else for that matter could ever know."

Genuine feeling was conveyed through the soft voice and clear delivery.   She had the old man's way of looking directly at you.   He dropped his eyes and focussed on the printed card:

Mr Kenneth Ferguson and family

Request the pleasure of your company

At a small gathering in their home

On Tuesday May 24th between 7.30 and 8pm.

"Will you go?"

"Yes, why not and what about you, will you be there?"

"No, I'll be here.   We don't go out much.   I'll let Kenneth know you're coming."

"Right, well then I'll be on my way.   Pleased to meet you, Sarah, perhaps…"

"Yes we'll see each other again but not, I don't think, before next month, when you come again to pay the rent."

She accompanied him to the door, and then as he stepped out, "By the way, for the most part, I enjoyed your book."

Formulating a response he turned round but the door was closed on any possible retort.

Strolling back he homed in on the new twist.   Kenneth, Stanley's surviving son, the first born, went to University in Belfast, then lived briefly in England shortly before his brother Harold died in a tragic accident.   Land, wealth and privilege did not secure protection from pain and suffering, he reflected.   What had Kenneth studied; Law probably.   The Fergusons were more than farmers, much more: they owned a cattle mart, an estate agency, a funeral business, were big in auctioneering.   A lawyer in the family would be a real asset, holding together and expanding an operation like theirs.   Harold, the dead son, had been brought up to inherit the farm.   He remembered him from school, a huge, ruddy-faced genial lad, often teased due to his slow wits, but not beyond a certain point, due to his fierce temper and great strength. It must have been a big blow when the accident happened: a tractor he was driving had turned over and pinned him underneath. Kenneth would have come home to help run the enterprise after his brother's death.   The mother had died soon after and it would have been some time after that Sarah Patterson arrived on the scene.   Had she been employed to help run the house?   Had Stanley known her before?   Had they been...?   No matter. There had been a lot of talk at the time and now he wished he had paid more attention.   Not to worry: Paul would know.

"A small gathering": he was intrigued.   Somewhere he had heard Kenneth's wife was Swedish.   They had met when she was attending finishing school in London. Wonder what old man Ferguson made of her?

The times they were a-changing.

A crack-crunch underfoot and he disengaged his shoe from a snail's wreckage.

CHAPTER ELEVEN

Kenneth Ferguson's place rose from a five-acre plot at an edge of his father's farmland; the edge nearest town. Land rose then fell away from the dwelling, providing the effect of it floating like a becalmed ship on an ever high tide. The association was compounded by porthole shaped windows and turret-like structures protruding from a long, low hull-like base. Lit up at night the sea and ship connection was unmistakable. The locals shook their heads and muttered about 'Ferguson's Folly' but would have undergone keel-hauling to have been invited inside. The land surrounding the house had been machine gauged and planted up with wave upon wave of trees and bushes: altogether, a landscaped seascape.

Kenneth was back; a son announcing to the locality he was his own man, with a Swedish designer wife whose father, rumour broadcast, had been a sea captain. Having met old man Ferguson, all became understandable. To emerge from behind his presence and make yourself noticed you had to do something radical and to give him his due, the old man would have proved big enough to understand. He would not have given ground easily and perhaps Sarah Patterson (who better) might have had to intervene to calm the waters, but in the end the danger of losing two sons would have been averted. Then again the old man would have gleaned a perverse pleasure from the disapproval of the clacking countryside.

Anyway when all was said and spun, Kenneth did not extend his rebellion to any of the truly significant areas. From Paul he had learned that Kenneth and his wife attended church regularly; he was President of the local Round Table society, high in the ranks of the Orange Order and most likely master of the Freemason's secret handclasp. So, in that sense, despite the ostentatious display of ownmanship, Kenneth Ferguson was still his da's man because that was the way it was in this corner of the world where the fathers forged the sons.

Not always the case.

In an effort to find out about Kenneth Ferguson he had invited Paul for a drink. They convened in McCann's bar in the centre of town and it was there that his brother, after filling in the background to the Ferguson situation and in the process knocking back several gin and tonics, dropped his bombshell.

True, he had always known Paul was an exception to the rule that fathers cloned the son. Paul broke into and was embraced by his mother's world. His friends were his mother, his sister, their friends and the women of the estate who loved him and accepted him in their world of tea, gossip, laughter and tears. Sam, Sam was a man's man, Paul a woman's man, no a woman's woman-man who could be trusted embraced, confided in and accepted. He was a brave original who'd learned to sew, knit and cook at home with his mother and sister. When he completed his apprenticeship, Paul too intended to return home and charm the bank manager so that he could rent and equip a place he had his eye on. His plan was to convert it into a unisex hairdressing salon; it was to be called *Ginger's* and inside, all round the walls, blown up photographs of Ginger Rogers would lend glitter and romance. He intended to cap it all by playing taped soundtracks of music and dialogue from his favourite scenes of her films with Fred Astaire. He'd met a young builder who was as excited about the project as he was and they would work together on the venture. That way he would save a lot of money.

"It's my round, I'll get us another. I've something I want to discuss with you; I have to tell someone and you're the only one I trust. I'll tell you all when I get back."

As Paul weaved his way to the bar he sat back in his chair and blinked rapidly several times.   Matching Paul's gins with whisky was beginning to take its toll so that for an instant the room began to revolve and he began slapping his cheeks with the fingers of both hands.   In a corner of the bar diagonally opposite a small group were setting up equipment.   A young girl sporting large black horn-rimmed spectacles stepped forward with a microphone in her hand and a fiddler began playing a plaintive melody.   Head down she listened, and then softly and with increasing volume and authority commenced to insinuate her voice into the music.   The ballad was new to him while the performance was mesmerising: never one for paying attention to lyrics there was something about this singer and this song that made this moment special.

As he joined in applauding the girl and the fiddler he was overwhelmed suddenly by a clarifying insight.   Drinks in hands, Paul was making his way towards their table. And at the sight he was stirred by a surge of affection for this brave brother of his.   It was no little thing also that he was the one chosen to be the confidant, for Paul would not have broached the subject to anyone else, of that he felt certain.   The next hour or so would be diverting, on that he could count.   Things could change on the island of Ireland.

Well, at least some things could.

CHAPTER TWELVE

Ingrid was petite, blond and spoke with a quaint veneer of foreignness. A perfect hostess she flirted exactly the acceptable amount with everyone, then to counteract the wrong signals being received she would disengage and home in on her husband. She would hold his hand, clutch his arm, whisper in his ear and make it clear to all that he alone was the man of her choice.

Kenneth was bulk smooth, a quiet and careful speaker with a firm handshake and eyes of a blue piercing quality similar to his father. Beneath the sleek exterior was the hard muscle of the one-time rugby player tipped for international selection until injury precipitated his retirement from the game. He projected his father's self-belief, his intelligence and undeviating purpose; so what was this beast of a man doing, cooped up in this rural backwater circumscribed by the palpable net the past cast over all? Comfort, luxury, the easy life would surely not be sufficient; there would have to be challenge, risk, hazard and where to find that here?

"I saw that piece you did for Ulster TV when they interviewed you at the airport. Impressive (*pause*) performance. Saw it yesterday."

"You – how, it must have been over a month ago?"

"Oh, if you have the means you can always find a way. It's remarkable what technology can do these days. It helps also that I have a friend in the world of surveillance. He owns his own company and it's amazing what he can get his hands on. I like to know what's going on." Another pause then: "I thought you coped well with that question on divided loyalties."

Here we go again: another room, another grilling.

"To be fair I had seen that one coming. In Ireland it pays to be mindful when treading that particular minefield."

"Ireland. Not often in this part of the world, called that by one of our persuasion. The exception of course is when we play Wales, Scotland, France, or the old enemy." Then smoothly and with no discernible gear change: "What ball do you kick with James?

"The round one, I kick the round one."

Kenneth laughed, then, "Real balls are oval shaped; surely everyone knows that." In an instant he was business like and signalling formalities had ceased. "Come with me, there's someone I think you'd be interested to meet."

At once he was conscious of other guests in groups standing, drinking, and chattering. The room was spacious with a low ceiling and painted entirely in white but with long blue curtains framing a huge rectangular window and paintings on the walls predominately coloured in blue. The guests were all out of hearing. Kenneth had obviously stage-managed their conversation to talk to him un-disturbed. Why? The man was purpose personified and had no need for any petty diversion a writer could possibly provide. There had to be something else. What? So what? For a writer they were all excellent material: the father and the son. From his point of view they were wasted on life.

Kenneth led the way and he followed to another room across the hall where the only light flowed from a large half-wall from behind which multi-coloured tropical fish were darting and gliding. A female figure, her back towards them stood watching the fish, her main feature a mass of copper reddish hair.

"I'll leave you two to catch up on old times. We dine at eight thirty."

Another staged collision. Old times, surely not…The figure turned and the merest pulse of the gawky girl pulsed.

"Teresa. Well I never…"

"Never what James; are you surprised to see me?"

God she was beautiful. The lie spilled easily

"No. I had a premonition we would meet. What about Sean?"

She ignored his question while again a vision of the skinny kid standing on his shoulders blipped across his consciousness.

"What are you smiling at?"

"I was thinking of the day we played cricket. You were batting and no matter how hard I tried I couldn't bowl you out. Remember?

"I remember you cheated and…"

"And the plums, I remember where you stashed them that time we progged Ferguson's orchard."

"That's not fair, James."

A black moustache never was fair."

Together they laughed, and then both turned at the sound of footsteps.

"There you are – Kenneth said I'd find you here. Mind you I should have known. She likes to feel sorry for the poor creatures," nodding towards the fish, "to-ing and fro-ing for our pleasure, constantly under surveillance."   He paused and extended his hand.   "How do ye do, James Carson?   Remember me? Kevin McCann – Teresa's husband."

PART FIVE

RELEASE

CHAPTER ONE

"I'm Barney, Barney McCann, Kevin's father. You're James Carson the writer fellow. Understand you and Teresa used to play together when you were little. Am I right or am I right?"

The encounter with Teresa and the jolt of McCann's appearance had left him bereft, so after managing very few platitudes he had set off in search of a drink. Grabbing a whisky from the tray of a passing waiter he was turning away when he was accosted by this small man, his thinning hair slicked back, with crow's feet wrinkles round the eyes, a mixture of the sly and the pugnacious crowned locally (the ever reliable Paul had once informed him) as that 'cute wee hoor'.

"*Gingersnap,* eh a good read that one. Kevin gave me a copy. I keep it in the toilet. You never know when it might come in handy."

What could he say or do? He smiled and mercifully a gong sounded announcing the drift towards supper so he disengaged and joined the flow where he accepted his plate, piled it with food, grabbed a drink and set off for a corner near a shelf where he could place his glass, fork his food and observe. The buffet and wine were excellent and attentive waiters and waitresses ensured all were well served. He began to relax. Returning home had its compensations; he'd done the right thing. Being a writer guaranteed access; there was no side to it, Kenneth Ferguson wanted him here because of who he had become, not because of who he was. After all, in a tiny rural community a writer coming back from London was somebody surely? He scanned the room and locked focus on a dark-haired, shapely waitress bending to retrieve fragments of glass after her tray had been knocked aside. There was something about her he recognised and he was about to move forward and offer assistance when: that face: great domed bald head, glinting steel rimmed spectacles, huge, stooping, shambling figure, coming towards him, hand offered. Another smaller and younger man followed behind.

"Hello, remember me? You were in the shop just a couple of days ago."

Accepting the large fleshy hand it came to him.

"Yes, the unfamiliar surroundings threw me; I didn't recognise you without your white coat. How are things?"

Ivan Campbell, chemist, and in this part of the world valued not only for his human treatments, but also for the medications he provided for sick animals: another inheritor of a family business.

"Things are good thank you. I'm afraid I have to confess I have not got round to reading your book, far too busy for cultural pursuits. Trevor has."

No more introductions. Just Trevor: medium height and compact build.

"I loved it." He was soft spoken with shiny grey eyes that held his, unblinking. "Very true to life, I thought. I loved the early scenes like the stealing sweets from the shop and the progging of the orchard."

Kenneth Ferguson had overheard their conversation and he lurched forward, "Criminality. We know all about that here. What say you Ivan the terrible?"

The chemist looked distinctly uncomfortable. Ferguson laughed.

"Observe the blushes. What dark secrets do you think this man is hiding?"

Others were turning in their direction; Trevor, he noted, was sidling off, while Ferguson appeared goaded on by his victim's agitation.

"I know; it's in the shop, all those potions to be mixed together secretly, then…"

"Kenneth, the feelms are ready.   You must say the guests to come."

Ingrid knew her man: the scene was dissolved.

"Right, come on, come with me James, I'm sure you'll find this stimulating, even if it's not to everyone's taste."

Here he glared pointedly at the hapless Ivan.   For his part he smiled at the chemist, shrugged his shoulders and then followed across the room and out the door and into a corridor and up an open staircase into a darkened room, a sort of mini-theatre with tiered seating.   On impulse he claimed the first seat at the end of the right-hand row.   For a brief second Ferguson halted, then shaking his head jounced his way down to the front row where he seated himself heavily.   The audience was entirely male.

The first film: a young woman checks into a hotel, takes the key and goes to her room, undresses and lies naked on a huge double bed.   One by one three men enter.   They undress; climb unto the bed and man-handle the woman towards its centre where they feel her all over her body, then take turns mounting her, the soundtrack a cacophony of sigh, moans and gurgles until satiated the men rise, pull on their clothes, toss bundles of notes on the bed and make their exit.   Ecstatic the woman throws the money in the air, rolls in it and it sticks to her body.   The scene fades.

A perfect amorality tale: he was aroused.

Another film and yet more naked couplings but after the initial excitement he felt a gradual boredom and an overwhelming sadness. He knew suddenly he had to escape, so carefully he stood and eased his way through the door, closing it gently behind him.

He had no difficulty tracking down a stiff drink but had no luck seeking out Ivan Thornton or his friend Trevor. The few men and the women were in tight groups laughing and talking so he knocked back his whisky and procured another. What to do? A sliding glass door leading to a balcony outside was ajar and beckoning. Why not? Glass in hand he strolled through and there in a far corner looking out into the darkness, Teresa stood alone smoking a cigarette.

"Like one?"

"No thanks."

"Enjoy the feelms?"

He was thankful for the dark as he sensed his discomfort might be apparent.

"Not really. What's going on Teresa?"

"Oh, I don't know. I suppose even here the Sixties swing. Men will be men. I suppose it's still about power corrupting the way it always has; that sort of thing."

"Kenneth's wife – what does she make of it all."

"This is the wee six counties, James as you well know. Here, wives don't have much of a say. As I well know. Any road, don't let Ingrid fool you. She probably introduced him to the stuff in the first place. She's what they call a liberated woman: a rare breed in this part of the world."

"And you, if you don't mind me asking, what about you, where do you fit in?"

"Fit in?"

"That was clumsy, I'm sorry. You know what I mean."

She hesitated, took a deep last drag of her cigarette and flicked the butt into the darkness, then: "Kevin...wanted me. I was flattered. He was so assured, so different from any of the hapless young men I was acquainted with. At the time it seemed a good thing that I would not have to think for myself, to worry about the future. Kevin would smooth the way, do all that for me. He was big, strong and successful and I was to be his partner. He was so certain he made me feel certain. There was no need for courtship. We met and we married. I fit in...because he wanted me to fit in. Now he goes his way, does what he wants to do while I...I fit in."

She looked at him, her face serene, her brown-green eyes teaming with expression he dared not read.

"Do you love him?" The wrong card; he knew it and immediately regretted its slippage. It was too late now. "I'm sorry, I..."

"No need. It's a perfectly natural question. I love him for his weakness. How about that? And what about you, James, is there someone special you can tell me about?"

"No."

"Is there not someone you love James?"

What could he say, so he stayed silent, impassive, his eyes fixed on hers.   She broke the spell.

"We live in a house up the road.   Newly built too, but not as futuristic as this one.   Kevin and Kenneth were at university together, in the same year, that's where they met."   She stalled, then: "Kevin told me about the card game.   He's not mentioned it?"

"No, neither have I.   Not likely to.   What's past is past."

"If only that were true: in this part of the world what's past is rarely, if ever, past.   You lost and left."

"Yes.   Best thing ever happened to me."

"Had you stayed we might have met before now James."

"You were at the university?"

"Yes, studying literature.   I wanted to be a journalist, a TV personality, maybe an actress then in that first year I met Kevin. He changed my life too."

"You won and left."

"Winning, losing: two sides of the same coin."

"Like comedy and tragedy."

"Like orange and green."

She laughed and he laughed and then before he could choke on them the words spilled.

"Teresa, could we meet, I mean, get together and talk over old times."

"A dangerous game that. This is not London, James. In these parts we have a watching, gossiping countryside to contend with."

"I know. I've lived here, remember, only sometimes risks are worth taking."

"It's not boys' games we're talking about here, is it? You know the old tit-for-tat stuff: he took from me, now I take from him."

"That's not got anything to do with it, Teresa! The thought never even entered my head!"

She looked at him for a time, then: "I believe you." She thought for a moment. "Kevin and his father have just started promoting boxing matches. There's some new young fighter they're involved with. I hate it, all those people baying for blood. Kevin knows I can't stand it and give him his due, he understands. Next week they're in London for some tournament. Tuesday night, after dark, around eight o'clock, you could call round. We're further up the road, on the right, the only one so you can't miss it. They'll be out soon; I'm off to freshen up."

She was gone. He stood gazing out into the darkness before a shiver made him aware of a chill in the air and he turned and strolled inside.

The men were descending the stairs to a general buzz as all began gathering their belongings in preparation for leaving. Teresa meandered across the room, stood behind him and started whispering.

"That one's a judge, over there a Member of Parliament. The big man there talking to Kenneth, he's high up in the police. They're all here, the cream of Northern Irish society; Church unrepresented – as far as I know.

"What am I doing here Teresa?"

"I don't know, although I imagine Kenneth and Kevin have plans for you. They know what they're doing. Whatever you do, don't underestimate them."

An impulse made him turn and look behind. Kevin, his face frowning, was staring in their direction. He smiled: no response.

Kenneth saw him out.

"I'll call on you sometime next week. I've a proposition for you."

Now was the time to say no, he knew, but to do so would be impolite, an offence against the laws of hospitality. Invited to a stranger's house, wined dined and entertained meant you owed and so any reasonable proposition you would have to consider. Kenneth would know all this and was taking advantage of the situation. Of course, that was the way with the Fergusons of this world: and the McCann's. What did their union bring to each party? It was easy to work out from the McCann perspective. Through Ferguson they gained access to the world of the judiciary and a Protestant ascendancy that had the power to confer privilege and even immunity. Unfair enough, but what did the McCanns bring to the table; more of an embarrassment, surely.

Be careful, Teresa had counselled and he intended to heed the warning.

He rented a television set.   On the night it had been installed he lounged half asleep watching the news.   A march, some housing protest, talk, then police charging before laying into the demonstrators.   One in particular – a policeman in uniform beating and beating, his hat falling off in his frenzy, revealing silvery white hair, then fumbling, replacing his cap, before looking about furtively then rushing forwards, baton raised.

The Troubles had started.

CHAPTER TWO

"Am considering embarking upon one of my infrequent excursions outside the perimeter of the ancestral demesne and wondered if you would accompany me in a fraternal libation.   The venue I suggest is that of the unworthy McCann in Main Street.   I propose we convene in the lounge bar at two thirty, by which time I should have terminated my transactions and would appreciate a soothing cup of usquebaugh made assuredly more agreeable by the presence of your civil self."

All delivered in a drawling, perfectly enunciated fashion in an accent that surpassed affectation to verge on the ridiculous. No one else, surely, would possess the gall to speak so slowly, so mellifluously and in such a self-indulgently convoluted manner. No one that is, but Cuthbert Adair, past president of the Debating Society at Trinity College, Dublin, and present master and sole heir of what Paul had described as "the crumbling ruin" that was Adair Hall.   Like that on the telephone and arguably even grander in person, well over six feet tall, he propelled his angular frame with a calculated slow motion grace.   Aged around fifty, impeccably presented in a heavy three piece tweed suit, he wore highly polished brown leather boots and a wide brimmed tweed hat. From the top pocket of his suit sprouted a multi-coloured handkerchief.   Half an hour late, he crossed the room unflustered and unapologetic.

"MacGillycuddy Reeks," he announced, extending a large, soft hand, "as do I.   The cattle mart is not conducive to the maintenance of odoriferous sanctity.   Now sir, as Hamlet ought to have said and never, ever in soliloquy, "What will it be?"

It was all empty verbiage, but entertaining so he allowed it to roll over him; in truth any diversion was welcome when the alternative was a date with his typewriter.

"I'll have a bottle of Guinness and a whisky please."

"Sapiently selected sir, I approve. Despite your brief residence in the land of Angles you have chosen to maintain your Irish quaffing mannerisms. Beer, unaccompanied and in pint proportions is a certain indicator of inherent gastronomic deficiency, typical of a nation whose experience of the staff of life does not embrace either the Soda, the Wheaten or the crusty Pan. Landlord, your presence is requested."

Adair babbled musically while the dark wood and subdued lighting oozed tranquillity. He sipped his Guinness, savoured its smooth bitterness, licked the foam from his upper lip and summoned attention.

"The bubble that is reputation advertised your presence while modesty propels me to observe I may remain an enigma to such as yourself. Cuthbert Adair, sir, solitary progeny of deceased and much regretted progenitors; last in a protracted succession and predisposed, I confess, to so remaining. My house and I have covenanted to waste and wither as one body. Life's but a walking shadow and this poor player has determined his line will strut and fret no more. I remain jubilant to enmesh in affiliation with you, James Carson."

He raised his glass.

"As I am with you. Your name, by the way is not unknown to me and I have often heard your family spoken of, and with affection, in the area."

Cordiality established, glasses were clinked and he settled back, at ease. Adair, he sensed was a social being, who despite his affiliation for solitude, craved a discriminating audience and that was a part he was content to play: all he had to do was act like he was listening while here and there making approving comment.

So, as long as he found Adair entertaining it was a small price to pay. Was there a price to pay? Probably; wasn't there always?

"That infamous Reek of MacGillycuddy I alluded to in my salutation seems to be spreading. It indicates there exists something rotten in the state. I am intrigued by your reaction to the situation."

He started: a question and one that was not rhetorical. This was not the script he had expected. He would need his wits about him after all.

"You mean the news, last night."

"You have tuned in, sir, to my wavelength."

Another interrogation: in this wee neck of the woods there was no need for a secret police; the citizens did the job. What team would Adair play for – the Liberal Ascendants? To hell with it!

"The status quo, to my way of thinking, is coming under scrutiny. Up till now the privileged belonging class pocketed their perks quietly, accepting them as their right. Times are changing and youth in particular is not up for quiescence and in television they have a new, and very powerful ally; one arguably more potent than the old ways with the bullet and the bomb. Christ knows what might transpire if you had television *and* the bullet and the bomb."

"Therein, dear boy resides the rub: these civil rights marches, honourably undertaken and provoked regrettably by sterling grievance can be viewed by our brethren of a less flexible morality as a crime against the established order. Perceived provocation invites righteous indignation that can ennoble harsh response and what will poor Robin do then, poor thing?"

"What indeed and what about Cuthbert Adair, what will he do?"

The big man lifted the glass of Guinness, drained half, then set down the glass and flicking the handkerchief from his breast pocket, wiped his mouth before prodding it back in place. He reached for his glass of whisky.

"Cuthbert Adair will do will do what his Plantation forefathers have done since the dawn of the seventeenth century." He rotated the glass and the liquid swirled. "Planted in this fertile soil then we dug in, germinated and propagated and withstood the famine and seasonal insurrection to which this island is heir. We were not extirpated then; if anything we dug down deeper." In one smooth quaff he swallowed his drink. "I am the last withered tendril and to my last fibre I will resist uprooting. Here I was born," he smiled, "and here I intend to die." The emphasis completed he hoisted his empty glass. "It is now your turn to procure access to inebriation dear boy."

CHAPTER THREE

"Be a camera; better still be four cameras all rolling simultaneously."

That had been the advice Sam McCready had proffered about writing a screenplay so he took to walking round the estate, eying up Wilson's shop, his old schools, the Church and Gospel hall, the orchard, the Twelfth field, Portrush, Londonderry and the area his aunt had lived in, Belfast and the University.   He tramped round all the major locations, taking photographs and making notes. Such research, he convinced himself was vital to the project, besides it was fun, it helped pass the time, and best of all stalled the process of writing: the part he dreaded.

Still it had to be done and he was at his desk trying to concentrate and block out Teresa's image flickering through: standing, back towards him in the half light, her hair glowing, then turning and the ghost of the child guttering through; sitting and the smooth rasp as she crossed her legs...   Tyres swished, followed by the muffled thwunk of a car's door shutting, then the crunch of footsteps and the bell ringing.   Kenneth Ferguson was not in the business of wasting time.   He let him in and offered drinks.

"I'll have a whisky, Scotch if you have it.   I find the Irish a bit rough."

"And it appears to me to be getting rougher by the look of things."

"Our R U C can be relied upon to police the situation."

"The situation and how would you describe that, then?"

A pause and when he punctured it, Kenneth's voice had a trace of impatience denoting anger suppressed.

"Don't let the veneer of urbanity fool you James. Back to the wall I'm my father's son – as you are yours."

Where had he heard that one before? The eyes, the thrust of the jaw signalled the conversation was closed. Kenneth settled himself in his chair and sipped his drink.

"Writers: to do the job properly they need to research?"

Off balance he stumbled.

"Well yes. As a matter of fact…"

"Good you need to constantly be in search of new material."

Where was this going?

"To my way of thinking, travel is the best bet. A new book might benefit from more exotic locations, places like Paris, Amsterdam, Berlin or New York… You should go; you know you should and stay in the best hotels, walk around and soak in the atmosphere. It could be arranged; in fact I could arrange it, all expenses paid."

What was going on here? Ferguson was serious; the proposition was so preposterous it had to be genuine.

"I don't know what to say, I'm… Why ever would you?"

"Never mind the why. That is not your concern. Look at it this way. You could write a sequel, take your Gingersnap on a journey to places new and far away, write what he finds there, how he reacts and the scrapes he gets himself into."

There was no doubt there was merit in the concept. Already his mind was racing.

"What would I have to do? Here, let me top up your drink."

Kenneth placed the palm of his hand over the top of his glass and shook his head.

"A few simple instructions, but you would be required to follow them, as they say, to the letter.   Your flight, to wherever, there and back will be booked on dates previously agreed.   Your hotel will be arranged, spending money taken care of and you will, provided you agree, be given a suitcase.   In it you would pack clothing and toiletries.   When you arrive at your hotel unpack everything then go about your business sight-seeing, gathering material, whatever.   On the morning of your departure, before breakfast, prepare yourself for return home, pack the suitcase, lock it and leave it on top of the bed.   What could be easier?"

"You will arrange for it to be switched?"

"Maybe, maybe not: don't you see, that's the beauty of the whole thing.   You're completely innocent, you don't know anything.   All you have to do is collect what you believe to be yours and return home with it.   One of our people might retrieve it from you on your return or they might not."

"What would I be carrying?"

"Invariably you will have nothing.   Sometimes…"

With his forefinger he touched the side of his nose.

"What if I'm caught?"

"Not much chance of that, who would suspect you?   Anyway, if you were all you would have to do would be to deny everything.   Just say the suitcase was not yours; perhaps it had been switched somewhere, which remember, it well might have been."

He must have looked hesitant, for Ferguson leaned forward in his chair, his voice urgent.

"Look, you're a celebrity, an artist. No one would ever suspect you. Anyway you know nothing about the wider picture. All you have to do is pretend; pretend to be a tourist, a novelist researching his next book. You can pretend innocence because well, frankly, you are innocent."

Kenneth rose to his feet and extended his glass.

"What do you know about any crime – if crime there is?" For a moment he left the question be. "I have to go."

"Why are you approaching me?"

"You, because you're perfect for the role: you're single, you have no ties and as a writer you have the ideal cover. Look at it this way. Writers are used to pretending, to being armchair people not having to cope with real life, real excitement or real danger. It goes with the territory; living life on the side-lines, never getting the knees dirty. This gives you a chance to play a part. Take my word for it; for you it's a win-win situation."

"In my experience there is no such thing: there's always a price to pay. As a matter of interest, how much would those spends to which you referred amount to?"

As if making up his mind, Kenneth stood still for a moment then abruptly sat down. "You would receive four thousand pounds before you set off. On the successful completion of your trip you would receive another four thousand. Enough stake money there to fund any gambling urge – should you so wish."

"I don't play anymore."

"What a pity. I and a select few convene for a game once a month.   The venue is either my place or at Kevin Mc Cann's.   I believe you and Kevin have met before?"

He allowed the bait to slip past.

"I would need time to get my passport sorted.   When would the first trip be and what would be the destination?"

"Late next month and to Barcelona, so you would have plenty of time.   No need to worry about Spanish currency or travellers' cheques.   We'll take care of all that."

"Who are these we you refer to?"

Ferguson ignored the prompt.

"You'll go?"

Why not play along and see how the cards fell?   He nodded.

"That's settled then.   Right, this time I've got to go. Thanks for the drink.   Oh, and we'll be having another little get together soon, you are not on the guest list this time but I alert you because one of your family is"

"One of…"

"You'll find out; in due course all will be revealed.   I'll let myself out."

One of the family: what did that mean!   Evidently Ferguson loved flirting with intrigue; probably a power thing, an obsession with control.   What would he be carrying: money, drugs…   Was McCann involved?   What was it Teresa had said?   Something about Kenneth and Kevin having plans for him.   Ferguson obviously knew about the poker game.   What was going on here? Not to worry!   Eight thousand pounds: should he have asked for more, raised the stakes?   Barcelona, the best hotel – he could certainly do with a holiday, and what scope for experience; a novelist's dream!   It was time to cease probing into the gift horse's mouth.   Trust in luck; for he was lucky.   Even when he lost, like in the Poker game or with losing Abagail, in the end he came up trumps.

Ole!

CHAPTER FOUR

On a chill, wet evening he set out for Teresa's. No car: empty parked vehicles stirred speculation in this snooping community, and the only taxi driver wasn't nicknamed Nosey for nothing, so shank's mare it had to be. Turning up his coat collar, he stuffed balled hands deep down in his overcoat pockets and bending forwards from the waist drove his shoulders against the slanting rain. His father's generation would be sensible in a brimmed hat while in London, rain and umbrellas went hand in glove. Not here: in this code bound region umbrellas were for women, while the ubiquitous flat cap signalled farmer or lower class or, as in England: aristocrat. Cuthbert Adair cocked his snook at all the stereotypes. Had he ever received an invitation to a Ferguson hooley? Probably not; there was yet another divide there: long standing landowners and the nouveau riche tended to lead separate lives.

Trudging forwards he shook his head and wiped his face with his hands; water leaked under the collar of his shirt and he shivered. He looked up and the lit monstrosity that was Ferguson's home loomed out from the driving rain. The narrow lane had no footpath and he picked his steps cautiously, listening to water gurgle in the adjacent ditch. Suddenly headlights blinded him as a vehicle charged towards him from a bend in the road forcing him to jump clear and drenching him with a heavy skim of spray. Cursing, he stumbled on holding his sodden coat and trousers away from his legs, till through narrowed eyes he gleaned dimly splintered lights and the blurred shape of a building on his left. It must be the house, but he had barely touched the gate when a heart-stopping barking made him jump back cursing, fit to burst.

"Down, Paisley down, be quiet! Stay! Stay!"

He recognised the voice.   The door opened and light flowed, washing the path.

"Come in James.   You must be soaking.   Don't mind Paisley, his bark's worse than his bite."

"I surely hope so.   Who would call a dog Paisley?"

"Kevin's idea; he loves saying he's buying Paisley a new collar or he's having Paisley castrated – that sort of thing."

"That kind of humour could be dangerous."

"Only the best kind is James, surely you know that."

"That is fair comment: a good speak as they say."

"Kevin never cares who he offends and maybe that's why he gets away with what he does.   You're wet through; I could hear the rain outside.   How did you…"

"I decided to walk; singing in the rain is one of my favourite pastimes.   Mind you, I wouldn't have been so wet if I didn't have to take evasive action when someone attempted to run me over on that bend below the house."

Instantly the mood was transformed and Teresa was alert, tense and anxious.

"What colour was the car!   Did you see who was driving?"

He shook his head.   "I didn't see anything, it was all so sudden.   It was over in a split second; the car was gone before I had my wits about me."

Teresa seemed lost in thought, then, "It's really dark down there, especially in this weather.   I've been at Kevin to speak to the council about a lamp-post but he doesn't seem bothered and anyway, you know what councils are like. Give me your coat. The bathroom's at the top of the stairs; you can dry your hair. I'll fix us a drink."

The stairs and landing were thickly carpeted; not for this couple the ubiquitous lino favoured by his parents' generation. The wallpaper looked and felt of good quality and the whole was warm and cosy owing to strategically placed central heating radiators; none of that biting cold outside the radius of the fires in sitting rooms he remembered so well. On the wall above the bathroom door an image of Christ glowed. The house signalled conventional Catholic respectability with no desire to declare itself through any outward show.

Towelling himself he reflected on Teresa's reaction to his encounter with the car. Was she frightened that some neighbour had recognised him? Surely there was little chance of that in the dark and the rain. Still, he felt uneasy. What was he doing here? Combing his hair he stopped and stroking his chin took stock of his reflection in the mirror. He needed to be careful; there was no city anonymity afforded in these parts. What if McCann found out he had visited his home without his knowledge? Gripping the sides of the sink he bowed his shoulders till his forehead touched the cool of the mirror's glass.

He would have his drink, make his excuses and leave as soon as politeness allowed. That decided, he gave his hair a last comb and with some toilet tissue wiped the smear his forehead had caused from the mirror's surface. A final check of his appearance, a straightening of his tie, a shrug of his shoulders and he was ready.

CHAPTER FIVE

The whiskey was just what the doctor ordered.

"I put Paisley in the kitchen.   You mustn't mind him – he's only a pup."

"So's his namesake.   Wait till he grows up."

"I suppose you're sorry you came back, the way things have turned out.   Did you catch the news tonight?"   He shook his head.   "I'd hate to be living in Belfast.   Houses and cars burning, stone throwing, there's been gunfire.   British troops are being sent over to protect the Catholics in the Falls Road.   You should have stayed in England."

"Then I wouldn't have run into you again, wouldn't be sitting here with you."   He watched for her reaction: nothing. What the hell!   McCann was away and when the rat's away… "I feel happier at this moment than I've felt in a long, long time. Any sacrifice, if sacrifice there be, is worth it for that."   Then some playful impulse he could not control prompted: "Why don't we run away together Teresa, why for once not give into impulse and do something meaningful together, you and me."

"That's the whisky talking, James.   Have another."

"Thanks.   You're right I suppose; reason should prevail. Still, if you'd said yes, I'd have gone."

"Would you?"   She paused and looked away, then her voice trembling slightly: "There's a hotel in Newcastle, the Slieve Donard.   I'm going there next weekend, Friday to Sunday. I've been before.   There's a forest park you can get lost in and the beach is magnificent.   There are times Kevin likes me to get away.   Like when he's holding some men only do here.   I don't know what they get up to and I don't want to know.   You could come down.   We could walk, talk, and be together there.   That's about as impulsive as I can be – as I've ever been."

"You amaze me Teresa, I didn't expect…"

"You didn't expect me to make the first move."

"I'm sorry; I didn't mean to sound…   I'll be there on Friday."

"Be there by seven in the evening.   We'll meet in the bar and we can take it from there.   Register in a single room and use a different name.   Kevin has friends everywhere and if he ever found out…"

She stood and he set down his empty glass, rose and stepped towards her.   Teresa turned away.   I'll see you on Friday, James. You'd better leave now."

Hiking home he reflected on the accelerated pace of his life. Two improbable proposals within the one week!   He'd sort out his passport, and search out bus connections to Newcastle – safer than by car.   The way things were heading you didn't want to drive into the wrong area.

CHAPTER SIX

Wailing, the wind rattled the window panes and a splattering of rain pelted the glass.   Away from the shoreline, high waves rolled and smashed while white smears of foam glimmered and faded. Inside the room's womb he was warm and thrilled by the helter-skelter craziness of the whole venture.

McCann's wife: did that confer a frisson, make Teresa more alluring?   No, he knew now he had always loved Teresa, knew too that she knew it.   They were meant for each other; fate had sundered them then, as was its way, nudged them together again. Sure it was high risk but, for both of them, the prize was worth the playing.

He had checked in as John Cooper and while showering and dressing he mentally composed his autobiography. He was a writer, travelling and researching a book on… fishing, that was it, arguably the world's most popular leisure pursuit. He had travelled to this area to check out ports along the coastline: Kilkeel, Ardglass, Portaferry, and Bangor, then up to Larne, Cushendall, Ballycastle, Portrush and Portstewart. Knowing little about fishing himself he was approaching the subject from the point of view of… fishing families who for generations had made a living from the sea. When you tell a lie tell a whopper, was his motto and this one he felt confident he could spin out for as long as he needed.

Around seven he bounced down the stairs to the bar. The hotel was a tasteful balance of Victorian restraint and modern lighting. Muted colours, splendid high ceilings and glittering chandeliers; all made their contribution to enhance the mood of peaceful, hospitable efficiency. The barman was one of those who had seen it all before; the way he called a customer sir did not denote deference but served only to put them in their place. When he caught his attention he felt singularly honoured, was grateful to be served and concerned whether his, "Keep the change," was sufficient recompense.

Turning round he paused, sipping his fizzing drink, and surveyed the room. There in the corner, a table where he could sit and enjoy an uninterrupted view of any proceedings. Taking his time he sauntered across doing his best to exude confidence and self-sufficiency, and then seated, surveyed the clientele.

They were mainly men in suits in groups, chatting and taking no special interest in him, just the odd casual glance except... standing alone at the bar, small, dark, compact, vaguely familiar, where had he seen that face? The man looked his way, then hurriedly swept up a cigarette pack and lighter, before whirling away and scurrying from the room, leaving his glass unemptied. He flicked back through memory: England, no, had to be here, school, could be, University... Teresa made her entrance and all heads turned as she stood, looked about her, saw him and walked across and he stood, all thought annihilated by the force of her presence. She held out her hand, "John Cooper, as I live and breathe, well fancy meeting you here."

"I caught a glimpse of the name on the hotel register, thought it might be you. I read somewhere that people using false names invariably select one with an echo of their own."

He must remember that. Her hair pinned up threw into relief the long lines of her neck and the fine curves of her cheekbones. "What will you have to drink?" Teresa leaned forward, took up his glass and sipped.

"Mm, gin and tonic, I'll have one of those and tell them to send over the menu. I'm starving."

True to her word she cleared her plates, now and then accompanying a pleasing mouthful with a just audible moan of pleasure. Her passion for the food was entrancing and for the first time in his life he experienced the sensation of privilege conferred by the presence of another. Somewhere he had read a line about how much better it was to love than to be loved. Until this moment he had failed to comprehend how that could possibly be. He thought of Abagail and knew it to be true. In his whole life he had never been happier than at this time in the company of this woman who for all he knew was so absorbed in the act of eating that she was not granting him as much as a thought.

"You enjoyed the meal Teresa."

"Yes, I love eating out. It never happened when we were children and Kevin... Would you like a cigarette?"

"You forget that I don't smoke, but if I did I think I would give them up at this very moment, to fix this meal with you in my memory for all time."

"You surprise me James."

Teresa opened her pack, took out a cigarette, held it in position between her lips, and with the other hand flicked flame to her lighter. She inhaled deeply, and then settled back in her chair her right arm under her breasts, her bunched fist providing a resting place for her left elbow. The cigarette nestled between the forefingers of her left hand and for the first time he noticed – no wedding ring.

"I never took you for such a romantic."

"There's a first time for everything. Teresa, you and Kevin..."

"Careful, be careful." A waiter was approaching. "We'll have coffee and brandy. Can you serve it in the lounge please?"

They made for the lounge and settled on a corner table; the only other customers a group of middle aged men, some sort of sales conference, he guessed. Teresa lit another cigarette as the waiter busied himself with the order. Be patient he counselled himself, stay quiet and let her do the talking. Then countering his

resolution he was propelled towards a sudden query.
"What about Sean; how's he diddling?"

"I don't see much, if anything, of Sean these days.   Sean is Sean, his own man.   He never liked Kevin, or Barney, never came to the wedding.   Family – you know how it is."

He nodded.

Teresa took up her glass, gave the brandy a spin, then in one movement tilted her head back and drained the contents.   Setting it down, she reached for her cigarette packet.

"I know I smoke too much; you did well not to develop the habit."

"I tried for a time, and then gave up when I left for London. To be honest, at the start of my time there I simply never had the money.   It's only recently I've come into funds, but I figure it would be folly to start now."

"You were asking about Kevin and me."

"I'm sorry, I didn't mean to …"

Shut up, let her talk he instructed himself.

"I have much to be thankful for: a lovely home, money, freedom within reason to go as I please and yet…"   She sipped her coffee.   "Kevin's only reading is a balance sheet or one of his, one of his magazines.   He would never dream of going to the theatre and the only films he ever watches – well you know."

"Would you like another brandy?"   Teresa shook her head. "What about another coffee?"

"I've had enough for tonight. I think I've drunk myself sober. I did enjoy that meal. I felt that for a short time the cage door opened, I spread my wings and flew free."

"You could still soar away from it all Teresa. I mean people do it all the time don't they, leave mistakes behind, carve out new lives. Have you ever considered divorce, for example?"

A step too far and he knew it, but he was genuinely interested in her reaction.

Teresa shook her head.

"Not in this part of the world and certainly not for those born into my persuasion. The Church would never condone it. Apart from that, the back-biting and malice it would instigate would be a setback for Kevin's business interests. And besides, he would never grant me a divorce. Here, and we're not unique in that regard I'm sure, public face is everything. The veneer of respectability has to presented and maintained. Anyway, as I've said, Kevin would never agree. I've come to believe he never had a high expectation regarding marriage. It had to be done to confer respectability but once accomplished the one chosen would become his possession for life. Already I, I know too much and he knows a wife cannot testify against her husband. My fate is that of my mother-in-law, except that unlike her I'm not prepared to stay at home, eat for comfort and play the role of martyr in isolation. I've advanced the cause that far at least."

"And where do I fit in, in the grand scheme of things?"

Teresa opened her handbag, gathered up her lighter and cigarette pack and popped them inside. She snapped the clasp shut.

"To begin with, like many I suppose, I was intrigued by your reputation, your having written a book, your being a celebrity. That night we met at Kenneth's party I'd had too much to drink; you must have thought I was a right hussy asking you back to the house like that."

"Not at all, I thought…"

"Then, when you came and told me about the car in the lane, I lost my nerve, and then because I felt guilty, false pretences and all that, I invited you here." Unclasping her handbag she reached inside and began scrabbling around its interior. "My tissues, I could have sworn that…" In his trouser pocket he located his handkerchief and handed it to her. "Thank you." She dabbed her eyes. "I'm a mess, half the time I don't know what day of the week it is and while we're on the subject, it's so embarrassing, there's something else I have to confess." She lowered her voice. "I'm, I'm on my period.   I never thought about dates or anything. I'm sorry; I so wanted us to be together, really together, but now…"

Tenderness, an emotion so far alien to him, welled.

"Never mind, I understand.   Hopefully we'll have many more times together when we, we…   What I mean is, let's enjoy this weekend as friends getting to know each other again after being a long time parted."

For he knew, was more certain of than anything, that being in this woman's company was reward enough.

CHAPTER SEVEN

His agent phoned; the Students' Literary Society at Queen's University would be prepared to engage him to give a talk. A good idea: increasingly youth was the age to be. The student campus was a place of ferment in America and France so accept, but be contentious, have a bash at the establishment, let them see what side you are on. Lack of respect for the system went a long way to explain *Gingersnap's* appeal so why should not his creator come across in the same way and (this last swung the argument) it could give sales a boost.

Why not? He was bored with the screenplay and could do with a bit of a diversion. His agent had sent some material, so he employed himself preparing *Confession*. Bizarrely he had this title from the outset and his head was buzzing with ideas which he had found was invariably the way when he possessed only a vague idea about what he was talking about. That was not really a handicap he mused when you were opining about the Arts: with the Crafts it was a different story. He resurrected his barely concealed loathing of the entitled, University educated chatterers at literary soirees in London.

There beat a heart of darkness in University departments of Literature. From their every pore there seeped the whiff of long dead Athens. Rather than facing the canon, chair-bound professor generals, men forever looking backwards, polishing and displaying medals won in their past; their rallying cry, *Allusion not Illusion*, held up their arms and surrendered. Why forever exhume, dust off, then pick over the dry bones of Homer, Aeschylus, Sophocles, Euripides, Aristophanes, Menander? What did they know of writing who only writing knew? Why the Saint Jane Austen mentality and the canonization for High Church in English Literature of the American Henry James? Why was the Irishman Jonathon Swift not acknowledged more widely as the true founding father of the novel written in English?   Has not English Literature to much Pride and too much Prejudice? Queen's University; Queen's English: there was an Irish literary highway to march up and down.   Why didn't the Professor Generals get off their arses and pave the way along that turning? That way you could circumvent the English Canon, establish and fortify positions of your own and light fires in the bellies of your own troops.   Buzzing, he thought he would pen a poem that would make some sense of it all: maybe not a good idea, but was there not a place in literature for dogged pursuit along a false trail? Why not have his poem printed and distribute copies at his lecture; it could do no harm surely?

HI PRIEST

His alter-ego

First habit by now

Signifies devotional geniality

While incense of humour

  Sweetens the air:

Yet beneath all simmers

The zealot's potential

To overthrow the tables

And censure.

Congregations everywhere

Consume his holy writ

And it becomes

Their stuff of life.

The craftily wrapped homily

Solicits harmonious concord

Austenian solicitude

Through wit and word.

Multitudinous are the converts

To this secular religion

This aunty establishment

School of fart.

The hall on the day was packed and he was initially un-nerved by its mahogany sumptuousness and by the portraits of grim-faced and gowned academics lining the walls. Earlier the Dean of the English Faculty had disconcerted him by the apparent warmth of his welcome. Momentarily he was disarmed and made to feel an apostate in the face of such civility. He was relieved therefore when from the podium gloves were touched and hostilities resumed. The Dean's introduction was an exemplar of crafty shaftmanship.

"Were, ahem, literary accolades to be conferred primarily through the mechanics of the marketplace, then our invited speaker this evening," turning, looking at him and commanding the moment, "would surely be held in the highest esteem. For, ladies and gentlemen, James Carson has probably hawked more copies of his slender text than the grand total of all published work presented by myself and," pause, "by all my fellow academics present on this occasion. It is difficult to stand one's ground in the path of such a wave of popularity and to contend as I did in my review that the *Gingersnap* I prefer is the one I take up with relish and then dunk in my tea in this establishment's English Common Room." The laughter, he noted was patchy and was followed by one loud and theatrical groan that triggered a greater volume of hilarity.

"Personal preference aside, James Carson is welcome here this evening. He was, as some of you will be aware, admitted as a student to our university, but holds the spurious distinction of taking his leave before attending even a single lecture – unlike some here present who make a doomed attempt to stay," removing his glasses and tapping his upper lip with the stem, "without attending a single lecture."

Cheers and clapping. The ould git knew how to play to the gallery.

When his turn came he was nervous, but had a sense he was more in step with the student audience than his elderly opponent could ever be.

"The professor's penchant for gingersnaps has been well documented. Personally, I find them rather sweet, while dunking in tea is a ritual surely imported from that neighbouring island of which the professor is a native."

The ensuing laughter helped settle his nerves.

"Out of curiosity I tried the English way but found that gingersnap not only too sweet, but soggy too – like too much of the literary diet – the English literary diet – your body of students are undoubtedly force-fed in this institution. Small wonder that the roughage in my *Gingersnap* should stick in his craw." Laughter, sporadic applause and some stamping of feet: the students were on his wavelength and he would push any buttons it took to keep them there. Members of the Faculty, he noted smiling and applauding: the English way.

A bout of brain wrestling gave him what he considered a more appropriate title: *The Irish/Anglo Crew of the Good Ship Hibernia.* Basically his lecture was a potted version of his previous work on the subject and he had a field day dropping names like William Chaigneau, Thomas Amory, Charles Johnstone, Frances Sheridan, Henry Brooke, Thomas Leland from the eighteenth century and Maria Edgeworth, Sydney Owenson, Charles Maturin, Sheridan Le Fanu, William Carleton, John and Michael Banim, Gerald Griffin, Emily Lawless, Charles Lever, Samuel Lover, Edith Somerville and George Moore from the nineteenth. He made much of his admiration for Jonathon Swift and pointed out how the ship was in good hands with the likes of James Joyce, Samuel Beckett and Myles na gg GCopaleen.

"Fair play," he concluded, "that *Queen's English* should be celebrated in *Queen's University* in the North but there was and remains an Irish contribution to be acknowledged and studied also and this, I fear may not be accorded its true value within this institution. I rest my case."

Great was the applause, some even standing and inviting others to do the same. Standing his ground he revelled in the moment before holding aloft his hands and restoring sound to a buzz.

"I have written a short poem that crystallises some of my thoughts on this evening's lecture. You are welcome to pick up a free copy on your way out. Thank you for being such a warm and attentive audience."

A hand on his shoulder and he was aware suddenly of the Professor beside him at the podium."

"Ladies and gentlemen, before you exit and go your various ways I think this an appropriate moment to apprise you of a little secret."

Silence restored all eyes on him now and the hand still resting on his shoulder, he lowered his voice.

"For some time now we have been engaged in talks with the powers that be and I believe I can safely say that a new Faculty attached to the English Department, but devoted solely to Irish Studies, is in the pipeline. Who knows, perhaps our invited speaker this evening will be invited to make a contribution. Thank you for your attendance. Good night and safe home."

In the Students' Union Bar later he was confronted by a tall, rangy raw-boned young man and a small, solid mini-skirted young woman with long straight brown hair.

"Michael and I are on the committee of The People's Democracy Party."

Her manner signalled no-nonsense directness, like the country people he had known who would spit on the palm of a hand, and then vigorously rub both together before setting to. Her accent was an unapologetic version of the one he had done his damnest to lose. The young man was equally forthright.

"We're after equal rights for men and women: one person, one vote; fair electoral boundaries; houses on need; jobs on merit; free speech and repeal of the Special Powers Act." As he spoke the young woman looked up at him unblinking, her flat American Indian features impassive.

She drew deeply on a cigarette, then: "We're planning a march, setting off in a couple of weeks, New Year's Day, from the City Hall at nine in the morning. Our aim is to walk to Derry city. We believe strongly that direct action is the best and only way to maintain the momentum of the Civil Rights movement. Would you agree?"

Wow! Stanley Ferguson, that's who she reminded him of, she exuded the same challenging directness. He became aware of a gradual fall in the hubbub around them and had a sudden insight he was being manoeuvred into a corner. Time for a spot of boxing clever and at that moment he recalled his agent's advice: youth is where the times are, think circulation, be a guru, a potential pavement-sitter and street-clasher. He could play that part. All he had to do was a bit of summoning the lines and improvisation. He could manage that.

"You're right.   Look at what's happening in Paris and in Alabama.   You need to be out there, on the streets and be seen to be out there.   You young people," he was aware now of the room's virtual silence, of students crowding closer; it was not only these two he was addressing, "you probably don't realise it but let me tell you your fight here is making its contribution to a, a bigger battle that has the potential for igniting other struggles in, in places all over the world.   Your generation has the potential to challenge and who knows, even change the status quo.   In so many ways the older generation have had their day and we can see the mess they have made in it.   It's your turn now and…"

"And we intend to take our turn."

The startling forthrightness of her interruption un-nerved him: this sixties St Joan would go far and in this time and in this place there would be no end of volunteers ready to light a fire under her stake at crucifixion hour.   It was left to the young man to pour oil.

"We're in a rush, another meeting.   As for the march: Paisley and Major Bunting will be against and we're not sure whether we can rely on the police for protection.   We thought when we reached the Maghera area you might join us for part of the road and give everyone a boost before we head for the Glenshane Pass."

"You're on," he heard himself agree and ever the leading man, centre-staged himself by extending his hand.   They shook, a camera flashed, the clamour rose gradually in volume and the young man turned away.

His companion was already gone.

"Not two to forget in a hurry," he addressed a couple nearby, "especially the female of the species. Who were they?"

"That was Michael Farrell," the man said, "and the female as you called her – that was Bernadette Devlin."

CHAPTER EIGHT

Abagail's father's connections were still burrowing away to his advantage. The text of his address was circulated widely and was generally received positively, particularly in America, where bizarrely he received invitations to speak on the University campus circuit. He was tagged as 'An Angry Young Novelist' and once again publicity's hot air swept him up and beyond his station. The Northern Irish Press focussed attention on the political rather than the literary: *The Irish News* – PROMINENT WRITER PLEDGES SUPPORT FOR PEOPLE'S DEMOCRACY MARCH; *The Belfast Telegraph* – MISGUIDED ALLIANCE. Beneath each headline the same picture of himself and Michael Farrell, smiling and shaking hands.

He was in a deep sleep when the telephone rang. The bedside clock glowed 12.20. Alert at once he swivelled from his bed and padded swiftly to the telephone in his study where he groped for the receiver and pressed it to his ear while money was being processed at the other end. A call box, then his sister's voice: "James, sorry for calling so late but this is an emergency. It's our dad. He's in the hospital. Can you come? It's not so good."

"What's wrong Jane?"

"It'd take too long over the phone and anyway I haven't enough change." Her voice was tearful. "I'll tell you all when you get here. We're all here. Mum went in the ambulance. Be here as soon as you can." The phone went dead. Unbidden, the line "In the midst of life…" flared in his head. He did what he could to expunge the last bit but with little success.

Struggling into his clothes he ran outside and unlocking the door threw himself into his car. He drove fast, hedges skimming past on the narrow road. Then out of a corner and about to accelerate on a straight stretch, he could barely discern something like a red light moving horizontally back and forth. Easing down his speed he made out figures on the road, five men, no mistake, their faces covered with woollen balaclavas, all dressed in paramilitary clothing. They stood in line across the road their arms folded across their chests, except for the one in the middle who swung the lantern. In silhouette, in the car's headlights the group's menace was palpable and his heart throbbed in his chest as he slowed obediently to a halt, switched off the engine and breathing deeply, wound down his side mirror.

The man with the lantern set it down deliberately and set off slowly towards the car, his heavy boots crunching impressively on the gravelly tarmac.

"Show us your documents!"

"I'm sorry, I rushed out, there's an emergency, and I've left my licence…"

"Get out of the car."

Trembling he did as he was told.

"Put your hands above your head." The man searched him, patting him down and running his hands along his sides and down his trouser legs.

"Give us your name!"

"Carson, James Carson." In his fearful state he responded automatically before cold realization spread. In this part of the world, names could be dangerous give-a-ways.

"Carson, well now what is the purpose of your journey?"

The clipped military style sounded ludicrous delivered in broad Ulster-speak; not a discrepancy he was on the brink of disclosing.

"I'm on my way to the hospital.   My father's been taken ill. I think it's serious."

"This is what's serious, Carson.   You watch yer step. Watch WHERE YE STEP!   Ye get my meaning."

"Well, yes, I…"

"Think about it.   Ye have been warned, so take heed. Now you can get on yer way."

The man jerked his head, indicating he should get back in his car and trembling with fear he did so and started the engine.   The men in front stood impassive, arms still folded, their menace blatant.

In the hospital corridor he heard the ringing click-clack of high-heel shoes and round a corner Jane appeared, running.

"Saw your car from upstairs.   Let's go outside for a minute."

"This is all down to you.   If only you hadn't come back, then none of this would have happened!"

Sam, his face flushed and his fists balled at his sides was striding towards them.

"Take it outside Sam. This is a hospital. People are ill. This is no place for fighting and arguing."

Between them Jane stood her ground. Her words worked and Sam strode ahead down the corridor and they followed after. Inside his head was buzzing. The hooded man's *Watch yer step* and Sam's *all your doing*: what was going on? Surely not...

Outside Sam swung him round, his face pressed so close he could smell the whisky on his breath.

"We were coming back from the pub, out for a drink together, doing no harm to man nor beast when five men jumped us. Two of them held me while the other three beat the living daylights out of our dad." Stiff armed Sam pushed him back. "He was knocked to the ground and they booted him and booted him! Ye've no idea, ye..." Sam's shoulders shook and he covered his face with his hands. "When they finished and our dad was lying there on the ground one of the ones holding me said that was only a taster. There'd be more if big brother didn't get the message. He said the only march he wanted to see you on was on the Twelfth of July. It's your entire fault! All you're interested in is getting your face in the paper!" Sam was so incensed he slobbered and spittle spilled. Jane scrabbled in her pocket and handed him a handkerchief.

As for himself his worst fears were being confirmed. What could he do? What could he say? He had to say something.

"Who were they Sam? Did you see their faces?"

"Did I see their faces? For your information they were wearing balaclavas." The anger was still in his voice but Sam seemed at least more in control. "Did I see their faces? And what difference would that make? Ye don't understand. Ye've been away; ye don't know what it's like here now. You write about us but you don't really KNOW us. All you know is books and sticking your nose in where it's none of your business. It's all a game to you. You, you stand on the side-lines and watch, and then you turn away and leave while us, we…" Having lost his way Sam bent his arms, balled his hands and shook with frustration. "I'm off to see what's what with our dad. Just remember what I said. You go on that march and it will be the last walking you do for a very long time."

Turning away Sam sloped off. Jane came closer.

"He's in a bad way. It must have been terrible for him watching our dad take that battering. They have always been so close. He means what he says."

"I don't doubt it. What do you think?"

"Me, I don't think – I KNOW that Bernadette Devlin's a dangerous hussy. If I was you I'd stay well clear of anything she was connected with."

"How can you say that? You don't even know her."

"You're right there, but I know people who do know her, and they're not the sort to tell lies. That Michael Farrell, he's cut from the same cloth."

"*Not the sort to tell lies; I know people who know people, cut from the same cloth.* What sort of way is that to talk?"

"Look, you've a way with words James, but you can't read the signs. Sam's right and you need to make your peace with him. You know how much our mam hates to see us fighting between ourselves. This is a time we should all be sticking together."

She was right and her words hit home.

"How is she?"

"She's taken it bad."   Jane's eyes filled with tears and she reached into her pockets.   "Damm, I forgot me…"

"Here take this."   He handed her his handkerchief.

"Our dad's not good."   She pressed the handkerchief to her eyes, then: "We're not even allowed in to see him yet.   He's unconscious, in a coma."

When his father finally and thankfully regained consciousness Jane phoned and informed he wished to see him alone.

In his heart's heart he knew for certain he loved this man who lay tubed and drip-fed, his face pale, lost in the whiteness of the pillow only crying out, the black bruising round the nose and mouth.   He went on his knees beside the bed.

God make him better please.   Forgive me I'll do anything. Only grant this one wish.   Make him better please.

Religion, he reflected: the last refuge and first port in the greatest storm.   Like crossing your fingers; touching wood; saluting a single magpie you dared not leave it out – just in case.

Reaching out he covered his father's hand with his and squeezed gently, then blinked tears when his fingers were pressed in return.   The swollen lips were moving and he raised himself, bending across, the breathy words causing his cheek to tingle.

"…need to stand your ground."

"Don't talk dad, the doctors…"

"Listen. Listen to me. Don't give in. You be on that march. Don't let them hoors win. You hear me. You promise."

"Easy now, easy, don't be…"

The grip on his hand tightened. His father's voice was an un-natural rasp and blood began to leak from stitches round the pounded mouth. He raised his head and was staring at him wild eyed. Unbidden a sliver of thought entered his head: *what in England is histrionics, here is history.*

"Hear me now and promise! Promise me! You will be on that march! Promise me!"

The eyes burned.

What could he do?

"I promise."

CHAPTER NINE

From the seclusion and comfort of his armchair he sipped whisky and watched TV coverage of the People's Democracy March: an historic event modelled on the march led by Martin Luther King between Selma and Montgomery in 1965.

Through the screen he was witness to the Loyalist jeering as the march set out; the confrontation with Major Bunting and his supporters outside Antrim; the forced detours at Randalstown and Maghera.   Wincing he viewed the onslaught with stones and bottles on the Derry – Clundy road and literally cried out against the beatings with crowbars, chair legs and lead piping at Burntollet Bridge.   Incensed at police inaction, he was stirred to further outcry at the sufferings of the marchers still left when in Derry they were showered with stones, sticks and petrol bombs.

Scraps of quotations floated through his consciousness: *I am not Prince Hamlet nor was meant to be...; I have something to expiate.   A pettiness...:   The best lack all conviction, while the worst are filled with passionate intensity.*   His literary retreat did little to quell his sense of shame.   He should have been there, could have been in that leading group; **should** have been in that leading group.   Yet deep down in that rarely accessed subconscious region where a man can be honest with the only person in the whole world he can be truly honest with, he knew. He knew he had no intention of ever taking part and in all likelihood Bernadette Devlin who was nobody's fool had seen through him from their first meeting.

Later that evening his relative calm was interrupted by the rare sound of his doorbell.   Fearful of prying journalists and their potentially embarrassing questions he had taken his phone off the hook.   Who could it be?   In an instant he had a premonition and his dread was confirmed at the sight of his sister on the doorstep, her eyes dry now but red from crying and that look: that look on her face.

"Our dad died about an hour ago.   We thought he might pull through but it was not to be.   I tried to get you on the phone but it was engaged.   Then I thought the walk would do me good so I came to tell you in person."

Her voice was hoarse, devoid of feeling, almost matter of fact.   He could feel the effort she was making to conquer emotion, to overcome it and focus on her new role as family decision maker. There was so much he wanted to talk about.   To ask had their father been aware of the details of the march and in particular had he known about his non participation.   Then again, say nothing seemed the best approach.

"Come in Jane," he managed, "let me get you a drink.   You look as if you could do with one.   I mean, given the circumstances, I mean…" he faltered.

"No I have to be getting on.   There are things to do and I know our mum will need seeing to.   As you can imagine she's in a right state."

He could imagine.

"One thing more before I go.   There's no use trying to talk him out of it.   We've all tried.   Sam has applied to join the B Specials.   He's been accepted."

At the funeral he felt awkward, marginalised, relegated to the side-lines as he watched and waited while the rest of the family coped as a unit.   Paul had left Belfast, moved back to his old room in the family home and was in the process of renting and converting a premise for a hairdressing salon. A great comfort to their mother, he was at the centre of everything radiating warmth and good will. With Paul constantly at her side it made it impossible for him to talk to their mother on his own and as the days went by he gradually lost the compulsion to make it happen. The single contribution he had to fight hard to make was to pay for the funeral expenses.

On the day, during the funeral procession he shouldered his corner of the coffin and tried his hardest to confer significance on the occasion and wrestled to subdue any sense of self-esteem attached to his role in the proceedings. The cortege made its slow way to the cemetery and they edged in round the graveside with the men in heavy overcoats, their heads bowed as the Reverend Brown intoned his piece. Jane, sole female present, stood between himself and Sam, linking their arms, compelling them to be together, to be family. Their mother had been too upset to attend and since Jane was of the opposite persuasion, Paul had volunteered to remain with their mother at home. Unable to focus on what Reverend Brown was saying, he looked around at the faces of the mourners and recognised none. To him his father's life had been a closed book, just as his had been to the old man. His father had left home in the morning, done his day's work and returned in the evening. No one questioned him and he gave nothing away.

Sam would know.

The coffin was lowered, earth scattered and the ritual hand-shaking commenced. A cold wind swept through the headstones and he shivered, and disengaging his arm from Jane's pulled up the collar of his coat.

"Sorry for your trouble," was the best the succession of men in their heavy coats could offer yet their mumbled understatement struck a genuine note while the press of their hard hands afforded a relieving sense of fellowship that was soon dismantled by a stocky, little white-headed man who shook his hand squinted up at him and then opined, "If ye become half the man, yer dad was, then ye'll do." Growls of assent expelled him once again to the margins.

Back at the house he and Sam made their peace.

"What I said at the hospital; I was upset, not in my right mind. Our Jane said I should apologise. So there," and Sam reached out his hand. They shook.

"I understand Sam, you and our dad were always close."

"Aye we were that. Ye did right not to go on that march. The family has to come first."

"You're right," then meaningfully, "it's what our dad would have wanted." Mercifully in the pause following there was no comeback. Not from Sam or from their mother standing within earshot. The risk had been worth the taking. In for a penny... "Sam those men who, you know on that night you..."

"Forget it, it's best not to think about them, or that night. What's past's past."

"Fair enough, but what about the police. Did you..."

"Huh, the police - you can forget about them, they don't want to know. I'm telling ye, for your own good and everyone else's just leave well enough alone."

They fell silent. An image of the young Sam, eyes crossed and cheeks bulging with stolen fruit pinged across his consciousness. Then they had been inseparable, while now there was a divide between them that he was finding impossible to bridge.

"Jane said you're joining the Special Constabulary."

"Special Constabulary shows how in touch you are with…"

"Sorry, I forgot the…"

"They're called the B Specials."

"Alright, would you like to say why you're joining?"

"Ye get a licence to kill," Sam grinned and for an instant the mad boy was revived.

"I'm only coddin."

PART SIX

RESBITE

CHAPTER ONE

The gatehouse was in ruins and the driveway was over-run with weeds and pitted with potholes. On the roof of the big house, tiles were missing and the guttering sprouted green shoots. On the ground floor, some of the windows were boarded up. He remembered his mother referring to Adair House as *that right paracus* and *a real poultice.* As for Cuthbert, she had opined that someone needed *to give that man a good clout.*

Of late Adair had certainly become an irritation, but to give him his due, the big man was big enough to realise the fact. Hence the invitation: more than likely. The problem was Adair had a problem and no matter how entertaining a drunk's act might be on first viewing, after a while it lost its spark and dwindled down to lesser variations of the same. Besides the role of audience member was not one he was equipped to play for any lengthy run. Never mind, the invitation was welcome and he was curious to discover how this other half lived, so here he was at eight o'clock precisely, a bottle of whisky tucked underneath his arm and his mind instructed to be pleasant, enjoy the experience and rein in exasperation. Sure Adair meant well, so live and let live. There lay the problem as Adair failed abjectly to fulfil his side of the bargain. In his befuddled world, normal time scales were an irrelevancy and he had taken to phoning at outrageous times like two, and once four in the morning. In times like these his meandering locutions had the effect of maddening rather than amusing.

One time, in a blind fury he had slammed the phone down only to have to answer it again, feign penance and endure yet more of the manufactured eloquence while in his head, rage pounded and his one fixation became how to sever the babble at the line's end. Last time the violation of his privacy, the severance of his sleep, the repetitive vapidity of the monologue had so enraged that he heard the adult, intelligent and reasonably civilized man who was himself screaming down the mouthpiece WILL YOU JUST SHUT THE FUCK UP before crashing down the receiver, then lying back, heart racing, racked with guilt yet this one time so demented that he knew with certainty that if the phone rang once more, he had it in him to top his last verbal assault with one so devastating that any rapprochement would be an impossibility. Fortunately the phone had stayed silent and anyway, to give him due credit, Adair possessed an astonishing capacity for either forgiveness or forgetting and the afternoon following had phoned again, making no reference to the previous evening and invited him to dinner. Perhaps he had been so out of his head, the altercation had simply not registered but who cared: better they tear up the scene, forget all about it and start afresh.

So here he was.

Overhead, crows or rooks cawed and flapped despondently, circling tree nests at the rear of the house. The crumbling ruin, these winged harbingers, the less than splendid isolation, what a setting. Melmoth, Uncle Silas, or Count Dracula: none would have been out of place at Adair Hall.

He tugged the bell.

They ate in a spacious, draughty dining room with a log fire doing little better than partially removing the chill from the air that exuded a dank, musty quality. Paper was peeling from the walls and the hanging portraits were faded and cracked. On creaking, rickety chairs they perched at opposite ends of a large and ornate table, stained and scratched from years of abuse with the upholstery on the chairs frayed and torn.

"Alas the dumbest of dumb waiters has not graced these proceedings for many a year so I am forced to fend for ourselves."

And fend Cuthbert did: busying himself presenting and carving a roast of lamb and passing round potatoes and peas. A generous host, he plied his guest with food and wine, drinking copious amounts himself, while eating little. The observation served up a conversational opportunity.

"I can't help noticing that while the fare you have taken so much trouble over and brought to such a, a high standard (he could detect a stumbling effort at Cuthbert's circumlocution in his delivery) is not being, being, appreciated fully by your good self." From his host a blank stare. "I mean you are not, not eating much of your own excellent dinner."

"Ah, a perspicacious pronouncement dear boy: the pleasures of the flesh and their myriad attractions interest me no longer. Liquid is my element sir, the way of the half measure is not mine so that always my cup overfloweth. In the full flourish of manhood I have determined to commence my descent and quaff my portion." He poured more wine and held up the bottle. "Not, I regret to disclose a remnant of our cellar that I do not regret to say, I caroused away some years ago. A man should at all times misspend his inheritance, how say you dear boy?"

Enough of meandering, pandering: he needed to assert himself and bring some clarity to the table.

"Cuthbert, why do you drink so much?"

"To expiate residual guilt from my forefathers," Adair pronounced solemnly. "I'm that Protestant with a horse. I'm the direct descendent of progenitors who invaded, appropriated the best land, planted ourselves and ours and left the rightful owners the remnants.   Then I claimed you as my people before proclaiming you nasty, brutish and low, silencing your native tongue and force feeding you our alien parlance."

Was he being serious?

"None of it was mine."

"Ah yes I forgot you too are a descendant of a seedling planted and not of indigenous Celtic extraction.   Still, not being the beneficiary of the Big House, you are a more acceptable variation of the species and it has to be acknowledged, the peculiarity of your condition, as you have discovered, confers the power to open doors."

"And what condition is that?"

"You are an Artist, dear boy, a state of being to which I, after my fashion, aspire."

"You write, paint, you compose?"

"I consider myself guilty on all counts.   The art form I allude to however, while it embraces all afore mentioned is of a higher calling.   My lifetime virtuosity is no other than myself and the perfection of the art of dissolution, of genteel disintegration."

He could contain himself no longer.

"That's a load of pretentious…"

"Bullshit is the expletive you shilly-shally before dear boy."

"I'm sorry Cuthbert and while I'm about it, I'm also sorry for my outburst on the phone.   You see…"

Cuthbert waved his hand.

"Apology not required, totally redundant.   Sometimes," he
paused, "I am prone to a spate of becoming forlorn, of feeling my
predicament more acutely.   When the black dog is upon me it
comes in the clichéd wee small hours and when the last bottle has
been drained.   Human contact can help take my mind off my
predicament.   You, dear boy," he cleared his throat, "have
become the port I turn to when the storm becomes too fierce too
resist.   My inheritance has become the albatross round my neck.
You see any envy you may excite due to your aggregate of fame
and fortune can never measure up to the resentment directed
towards such as myself.   The spirit of Captain Boycott still rides
this land."

"Is that why you drink?"

"I drink because alcohol," he stretched forward and filled
their glasses, "provides the illusion of indulgence.   The spoiled
child can pretend he is still spoiled and only.   Seeking inebriation
I continue to be irresponsible, unchecked, mollycoddled, spoon-
fed.   An elimination of reality can be achieved and the outcast can
achieve some consolation.   At the end of it all I've little left but
my character and that, dear boy, I bequeath to your fiction."

"What can I say but thank you?"   He raised his glass.   "I
may take you up on that.   One day."

After that dinner he took to avoiding Cuthbert Adair and ensuring
the man took the hint.   He had lost patience with the flamboyant
oratory; the staginess of the performance, the neediness.   Having
plumbed his shallows he reckoned the demands on his own time

were too onerous.   He had work to do and places to go and worthier people to see.

CHAPTER TWO

The star attraction at Ferguson's next gathering was not his self, for as Kenneth had forewarned him he was not invited. He would hear about it from the member of his family who was. Jane told him, so he went for a haircut.

Paul had converted his dream and made it real by charming the bank manager, then renting a small property and with the assistance of his builder friend Trevor, transforming it into what was in all likelihood, the North of Ireland's first Unisex hairdressing salon. He had christened it *Gingers* and inside and all-round the walls, blown up photographs of Ginger Rogers lent glitter and romance that was enhanced by taped soundtracks of music and dialogue from her films with Fred Astaire. After a slow start the concept had taken off and recently Paul had acquired adjacent premises, knocked through with the help of his friend (*Trevor*: it rang a bell and he racked his brain) an adjoining wall and extended. Paul was a new man: a beacon announcing things could change in these parts.

So *Gingersnap* had been followed by *Gingers*.

The coincidence was exploited ludicrously by an American academic who produced a literary paper on the association. His premise: *Gingersnap* was a rites of passage novel dealing with initiations into the world of adulthood while for primitive tribes, hairdressing also functioned as a symbolic rites of passage induction ceremony. Thus James and Paul Carson were enacting artistic rites of passage, by severing connections from umbilical types of dependency. Together they were seeking and formulating new identities, freeing themselves from the restrictive confines of family and society. **Ginger** noted the academic was derived from zingiberaceous plants of the genus Zingiber and was cultivated for its spicy underground stem. Paul and he had lain dormant in the womb of the family and society until their inner resources of creativity had caused them to uproot and present their spicy offerings for appreciation. The choice of *Ginger* in both titles of their *texts* (for was not everything a text) was but a Freudian signifier of the academic's contention.

Yer bum!

Inside the salon was pure Hollywood kitsch; artificiality elevated to an art form. The dominant colour was white, dazzling from walls, floor and ceiling. In one corner a raised dais with a white piano displaying gleaming black and white keys with a shiny black top hat and cane placed artistically on the piano top. He was halfway in before he realised the perspective was all achieved through paint: no dais, no piano, no top hat and cane but all pretence, a design on plaster. From the ceiling there hung a huge pearl drop chandelier. The overall impression, in what was in reality a small space, was of a sumptuous film set with the full length photos of Ginger Rogers in frozen dancing pose supporting the illusion. In front of black framed mirrors the chairs were white and clients sat, their upper halves draped in black capes as two young men in flouncy white shirts and tight black trousers and shoes tended their hair. At his entrance one detached himself.

"James, well this is an honour. You should have made an appointment. Now let me see, I have to finish a perm so I can be with you in about twenty minutes. You'll have a coffee? Daniel!"

Paul snapped his fingers, and then sallied round the shop, stopping at various points to check his assistants' work, teasing his customers' hair: a man in his element. Sitting, sipping his coffee he browsed through one of the magazines, all old copies of *Film News* and flicked through static images of Victor Mature, Alan

Ladd, Montgomery Clift, John Wayne, Rita Hayworth, Elizabeth Taylor, Joan Crawford, Bette Davis, Hedi Lamarr, Joan Fontaine...

Inside the cinema was musty, dark and exotic and pregnant with promise. That jaunty, raucous cockerel announcing Pathe News with its flashy black/white photography and racy commentary before a lion's snarl or rippling muscled man crashing a great gong heralded the main feature: saturnine Robert Taylor lance at the ready drumming along the lists as Ivanhoe: teeth bared Burt Lancaster swinging acrobatically as The Crimson Pirate; sneering Basil Rathbone forced on his back foot by the athletic swash and buckle of Errol Flynn's Robin Hood; James Stewart's slow burn from drawling pleasantry to vicious anger; John Wayne framed in a doorway back turned before that swaggering walk away; Van Johnson bursting into the saloon swinging a pickaxe handle enabling Alan Ladd's Shane to bone-crunch his way through the baddies; James Cagney's machine-gun delivery; George Raft's rasping deadliness and best of all Humphrey Bogart smiling through his teeth wisecracking Elijah Cooke Jr. towards impotent rage...

"Sorry about the wait. Come on, follow me, I'll deal with you now."

Paul led the way and following in his wake he reflected how his brother's choice of cinematic fare had always been uniquely different. Not male macho content for him but against the grain as always he was more at home with the romantic melodramas of stars like Bette Davis and Joan Crawford. Paul had never left the cinema riding a horse, shooting guns or mimicking sword fights. After Fred Astaire, his favourite male lead had been Paul Heinreid and he recalled how on one memorable occasion he bemused the family by parading round the house repeating endlessly with different emphasis but in the same awed tone: "Why ask for the moon when we can have the stars?"

Why indeed?

Paul sat him down, flapped one of the black capes, then draped it round his torso, tucked it in securely around the neck, then combed his hair.

"How would you like it?"

"I'd like a curly perm please; I'm seeking a new image, one I can be comfortable with."   He smiled, admiring his reflection in the mirror and taking in his brother's frown of concentration as he focussed on the job in hand.   "I don't know, round about the same but tidied up.   You know."

Paul began clipping.

"I love your décor.   I'm sure I've seen a clip somewhere of Fred and Ginger dancing on that dais round that piano.   It had me fooled for a moment.   I thought it was for real."

"Like the chandelier?"

"You mean that's…"

"Cardboard and tinsel; that's what I love about Hollywood – you really can fool all of the people all of the time.   It's too real for Sam, he can't bear to come in here; somehow the overall effect is all too much for him."

"And our father, how did he react?"

"I never asked him."

"I hear you were at Kenneth Ferguson's latest soiree." He checked in the mirror: no reaction. "I've been at one of his. Did you see the peep-show? I'm sure we'll all have to fork out in the end. There's always a price to pay"

Was he going too far? Watching Paul's face, he noted the shadow of discomfort and was time-travelled back to their childhood and occasions when he and Sam had taunted their younger and so very different brother.

He felt guilty.

"This is not the place James. Look when I'm finished I'm due a break. I have rooms above the shop. Why not come up and we can talk. I think we need to talk, you and I."

Paul was right so he nodded agreement. Sam and he needed to talk but somehow he knew they never would. Like his father and he had needed to talk and never had.

Job done and payment refused he followed Paul to the back of the salon and through a door on the right hand wall then up a narrow flight of stairs to a door at the top that Paul opened, leaned in and switched on a light then stood back and bowing with a theatrical flourish, bid him enter.

"Wow!"

The floor was snuggled with deep pile blue carpet while the walls appeared to be hung with what appeared to be floor to ceiling light blue curtains. Strolling across the room to the hearth Paul clicked a switch at the side that lit up an artificial log fire that cast its glow on a red leather settee and matching armchairs. Then he sauntered to the wall, drew back the curtains to expose a view of skyscraper buildings at night time like you would see in…

"New York, it's a mural, all pretence, but heaps better than looking out at our main street. From here I can be in Broadway, Times Square, wherever. I can put on my film music and I'm there, not here, there."

"Why don't you go?"

"Go where?"

"Well America, New York, Hollywood, any of those places you only ever dream about."

"I suppose because deep down I know the dream will always be better than any reality could ever be. I've always been a great one for pretending. That way I've found you really can make the world a better place than it appears to be in real life."

"Without a shadow of a doubt Paul you are the bravest man I know."

"Braver even than John Wayne," he laughed. "Would you like a mug of tea or would you prefer something stronger?"

"Tea would be fine; it's a tad too early for the hard stuff."

He followed Paul into the kitchen where everything was white, including the taps and kettle. Paul filled the kettle, wiped it with a dishcloth and switched it on. Humming, he opened a cupboard and extracted a white teapot and matching white cups and saucers. The kettle boiled, he poured hot water into the teapot, sluiced it around, and then poured the water into the sink. From another cupboard he fetched a white tea caddy, measured out two heaped teaspoons into the pot then switched the kettle on again to re-boil the water. He poured the boiling water into the teapot, stirred the mixture with the spoon, replaced the lid then ran the spoon under the tap, dried it, replaced it in the drawer, then wiped the worktop with a teacloth he found hanging in the cupboard beneath the sink.

"Do you take milk?"

"Just a drop thanks."

Paul occupied himself with the same deft efficiency he had displayed with his scissors in the salon.

"Who designed this place?   Who built it?"

"You like what we've done?"

"I think it's just fabulous."   He could tell his brother was pleased.   "It's so original, so…"

"Outrageous is perhaps the word you are searching for."

"Well, certainly not what you'd expect to see in this part of the world, but then there's always been too much simplistic assumption regarding what people presume to see here.   At the moment I suppose the outside world imagines we exist in a state of permanent siege with all the images of damage related to bullets and bombs and burning buildings, cars and buses."

"I hate all that."

"Don't we all, or at least the vast majority of us.   Seriously though, with your flair and skill you could go anywhere and be successful.   Have you never thought of leaving?"

"So many questions; let's take this lot through to the other room.   We can be more comfortable there."   With the teapot and his cup and saucer in hand Paul led the way then placed both carefully on a low marble table. "You give the tea a twirl and pour and I'll fetch some shortbread." Obviously enjoying acting as host he spared no detail, even down to the black napkins he placed on their side-plates.

"Let's see now. First question the design: that was my own. I chose the colour schemes, the material, everything. The builder you have met already."

"Have I now?" His mind raced. "No, you have me beaten."

"At Kenneth Ferguson's house, think."

He trawled through his memory of the evening.

"No, you must be mistaken; I don't remember being introduced to any builder."

"Trevor," a faint stirring, "Ivan Thornton's friend; you remember." He did: the softly spoken young man with the intense gaze. "Trevor and I are friends. He's very talented, was wasted working for someone else. I persuaded him to go out on his own. We went to the bank manager together. Now he has his own van, is his own man and doing very well. He did the alterations to the salon and the flat: plumbing, plastering, tiling, electrical wiring, the lot. If you ever need a job doing, Trevor's your man."

"I'll bear it in mind."

"There was another question."

"Apologies for the inquisition; since I've been back, people have been quizzing me constantly, so I'm using you to get my own back."

"I don't mind. I remember now, you asked me why didn't I move away? I've thought about that often. Would you like another cup?" He shook his head and Paul poured himself more tea, added milk and then: "The emigration thing I mean, there's two directions you can take. There's the external route you take by plane or ship, then there's the one I chose. From a very early age I emigrated **internally**. I took off into a world I discovered inside myself and in that sense I emigrated a long time before you did James."

"Of your own bat or were you pushed?"

"A bit of both; Sam and you could be pretty cruel, as could our father. My place of refuge was the kitchen. That was the place where I felt most at home, where I felt safe and happy."

"I'm sorry for the part I played in any of that Paul." Saying it he realised he was saying sorry too often recently. In some film he recalled John Wayne saying that apologising was a sign of weakness. He had better watch out.

"You said our father…"

"He had little time for me and the feeling was mutual." Paul's forthrightness was impressive. "Sam was his man – you must have known that." He nodded. "He had even less time for me than he had for you. We shared an equal amount of lack of respect for each other. I told him once I'd take a knife to him if he came home drunk just one more time and shouted at our mother. That happened not long after you left and I think he knew I meant it too. Your macho world at least has one thing right. Violence and threats of violence mean you do at the very least, get listened to."

"Why do you say **my** macho world?"

"It's more yours than mine."

"Fair enough; so our dad and you…"

"We never got on and I know it's a hard thing to say but I don't miss him now he's gone.   Our mam told me how he treated her.   She could talk to me, tell me things, she needed me.   That was another reason I decided to stay put.   Someone needed to be there to protect her."

Was there a whiff of accusation in his brother's last remark? Fleetingly he contemplated a defence, then just as swiftly decided against.   In truth, in many ways his brother was correct.   He remembered the rows, recalled his part in one and felt a surge of shame.   Best to let sleeping dogs lie and switch the subject.

"Families: they're all the same and always different.   The Fergusons for example, they're a rare breed.   Our Jane said you were at Kenneth's the other evening.   How did that come about?"

"You mean, how come a humble hairdresser manages to wangle an invitation to such a society event?"

"Aw come on now, you know I didn't mean…"

"I know you didn't; I was only pulling your leg.   In part it's down to Trevor.   He's doing some work for Kenneth's wife, Ingrid.   He got the job after she came to see his work on the salon.   We got to talking, then she came to have her hair done and hence the invitation.   She wanted me to see her house and really enjoyed showing us around.   Ingrid likes our company and we like hers: that's all there is to it.   Kenneth wasn't there; he was away on business somewhere so…"

For the splitting of a second there was an eerie silence, a sensation vacuum, then a singular increase of expectation that was

confirmed by a thunderous explosion that blasted shards of glass
and debris through the room and he caught the horror on Paul's
face as the ceiling showered on them and he jack-knifed forward
covering his head with his arms and the floor trembled then
sundered and he was falling past his stomach till he crash-landed
and all around him ceiling smashed and powdered and he screamed
"Paul!" but heard only a hoarse whisper and he spluttered and
retched till a deafening crash close by made him cower in terror
and he cried out and felt a wave of unconsciousness swell and he
knew he must not succumb that reason would save the day so
began reciting his tables: one ones is one two twos is four three
threes is nine four fours is sixteen… above he could hear
scrabbling and the faint sounds of voices then a siren blaring
louder and louder… start again one ones is one two twos is four
three threes is nine four fours is sixteen five fives is twenty five six
sixes is thirty six seven sevens is forty nine eight eights is sixty
four nine nines… start again… the scrabbling was closer now he
could hear voices

"Here help me lift this!   Give us a hand here, easy, steady
now, and steady!   Heave!   Heave!"

There was a sudden whoosh of air and he began to choke
and splutter.

"There's someone here!   Help me, help!   Take it easy.
This one could be alive!"

CHAPTER THREE

In literature it would have been considered too pat: Paul goes out after coming out.   Or there would have been barbed accusations related to killing off the token gay.   Life took no heed of criticism of its coincidences; instead it continued blithely serving them up.

He had not gone through any protracted grieving process related to his father's death; to do so would have involved some dwelling on his own feelings of guilt in the whole sorry episode so he had simply repressed the memory and expelled it from consciousness: obliterating his own shoddy compliance meant he had to eradicate all.   With his youngest brother it was different and paradoxically with no reason to blame himself this time that was exactly what he found himself doing.   Had he not gone there in the first place would Paul still be alive?   Was there not something he could have done when the explosion occurred? That look of horror on his brother's face haunted him.

In hospital he learned the IRA had accepted responsibility. The bomb had been meant to target the local police station but it had gone off prematurely, killing two volunteers in the blast. From now on a police and army checkpoint was to be set up at the north end of the town.   It was no consolation when the IRA released a statement saying they deeply regretted the civilian casualty; miraculously everyone on the ground floor in the salon had survived death or serious injury.

In the aftermath, caught up in the wake of personal involvement his political balance tilted.   Now, as far as he was concerned, a campaign for civil rights pursued through democratic channels was being hijacked by a plague of ruthless murderers who affected military status and sought to justify murderous atrocity by calling themselves Freedom Fighters.   Yes the Catholic grievances were justified and yes the authorities had reacted in shameful fashion, but surely nothing served to justify carnage of this type and of this scale. Acts like this would not, could not be forgotten or forgiven, so the whole cycle of retribution would once again stir into motion. Even the title of the tragedy conferred a degree of normality: not The Terrors, The Outrages, The Horrors but the understated, the low key – The Troubles.

Sorry for your troubles Ulster.

Greyer than he remembered and stooping slightly the Reverend Brown visited him in hospital, said a prayer by his bedside and spoke earnestly about how he could understand how he might be feeling but how important it was to keep sacred a tiny corner in his heart where forgiveness and compassion could be nurtured. In the end we were all God's creatures, there was a grand scheme so we should not dwell overmuch on one particular instance, not a sparrow fell but He knew and cared, vengeance is mine saith the Lord so we should never entertain the notion of taking the law into our own hands.

Not that he ever would. While in his mind he could conjure avenger retribution it was not and never would be a reality. While not a pacifist, the path of violence with gun in hand was not his way. As for the Reverend Brown he allowed the piety to wash over him and let the man do his job, let him Rev on.

"I know how you must feel. I'm sorry for your trouble in these troubled times. We reach for the same platitudes in times like this and while I know about the power of words I am aware that they can seem so inadequate in situations like this."

Reverend Brown stopped, sighed then leaned closer.

"We have an unfortunate history in common you and me. My father lost his life in the First World War and I had a brother who was killed fighting in the Second. I come from a military family and to some extent I suppose I'm their black sheep. My mother wanted me to be an army chaplain but I could not take on any role that would lend credibility to the ways of violence. Deep down I have always been a conscientious objector and I feel that calling so strongly that, and I don't mean to sound arrogant, that if called upon I would have been prepared to give my life to uphold that principle."

He believed him and could not help but feel a renewed sense of respect for this sincere man of the cloth. The blue eyes held his and he steeled himself for the religious assault he could sense was imminent.

"Your father was a strong man, a man of principle. Unfortunately I never got to know him as well as I would have liked, but I respected him and I sensed the feeling was reciprocated. Not many in this community stand their ground; there's always pressure to subscribe to this or that group."

The Reverend Brown continued to look him full in the face.

"Your brother Paul was another man of principle. He too, in his own way, was his own man and I respected that in him too. Enough said." He slid further forward in his chair and his voice had a whiff of urgency. "At any time men like your father and your brother would be a loss to a community, but at this time…" The inference was allowed to speak for itself: we know what we know was the message. "What your family and what this whole community needs now is another man of principle, someone who could be relied upon to fill the shoes of your father and brother." A pause then, "I hear your brother Sam has joined the B Specials."

"So I hear but what has that…"

"Come the Day of Judgement we will all have to present our own account," the Reverend Brown offered enigmatically and then from nowhere dropped his bombshell. "A pity, and of course I understand you must have had compelling reasons, but a pity never-the less, you were unable to participate in that People's Democracy march. Through, of course no fault of your own, you disappointed a significant number of good people who were looking to you to give them inspiration, leadership even.

What could he say? His visitor stood.

"Have a think about what I said. You know, Paul went to church every Sunday with his mother. Not many men the age he was are to be seen in the congregation now. I'll miss him; the whole congregation will miss him. The surgeon says you'll be out soon and should, as your mother would say, be as right as rain. I don't need to point out that it would mean a great deal to her if you could, at least some of the time, stand in for Paul and share with her, in the worship at our church. I know it's a bit forward of me to but I'm thinking of her and at this time she needs all the support she can get."

"I'll do my best Father," he lied then reddening, appalled at his mis-representation, "I'm sorry Reverend; just don't know what I was thinking about."

"No offence taken; don't worry about it," Reverend Brown smiled, "my son."

Jane came to visit. Their mam was in a bad way and not fit to leave the house. She would see him when he came home from hospital: an encounter he was not looking forward to but there it was. His sister, bless her, had brought him a notebook and pencil he had requested and he was working on a poem after she had gone when he became aware of a bit of a commotion at the far end of the ward. The shock of hair was unmistakeable and he braced himself.　Snap, older and a little heavier was bouncing towards him, then he noticed the carrier bag and heard the bottles chink and was relieved to be in the vicinity of one to whom offence could be given, yet none taken.

"Snap," he folded the notebook over the pencil, placed it on the table beside him, raised himself in the bed and held out his hand, "I was on the verge of seeking you out when the tidal wave struck.　For a time I thought I'd been Long John Silvered and me timbers had been shivered."

Sam's freckled face was a mixture of perplexity and annoyance, and the realization that in his nervousness he had conjured the wrong tone left him floundering.

"I'm sorry, it's, it's the after effects of the drugs they pump me full of; for the pain you know; half the time even I don't understand what I'm prattling on about.　It's good to see you, and good of you to come."

To his consternation Snap had not accepted his outstretched hand and his failure to respond in kind was proving unnerving. The void had to be filled.

"Take a seat.　A couple of days ago I had a visit from one of your dad's vocation, same cloth but a different cut.　The Reverend Brown, you know…"　Mid delivery he called a halt; there was no way talk on his part would smooth this situation, something was seriously wrong.　Let Snap deal with the silence; for once he had fallen out with the sound of his own voice.

"In case you get the wrong idea the contents of the carrier bag have nothing to do with you.　They're just some messages I picked up.　We live here now just down the road from the hospital."

We: for a fleeting moment he considered making inquiries then ruled out the option.   Given Snap's bristling demeanour he had a feeling he was about to be told.

"Paula and me, in case you're interested, and knowing you I'm sure you are.   You remember Paula."

"I'm not sure I…" then a vivid flashback: Portrush, the dance at the Arcadia, his failure back at the caravan, that note she had foisted on him.   Then unbidden, an image of Snap, a little boy tied to a tree, naked and vulnerable while for his part, he…

His former friend was holding himself in check, speaking evenly and selecting his words carefully.   His speech had a rehearsed quality: the bed was in a corner at the bottom of the ward and Snap's back was a shield against prying eyes and thankfully he was speaking quietly.

"I read your pack of lies and saw you being interviewed on television."

Snap paused to give him a chance, but he had made up his mind to endure all as a monologue. He sensed the situation was combustible and a carelessly dropped word from him could set the whole alight.   He heard the clatter of dishes: down at the bottom of the ward a tea-trolley was being stacked so surely an end was in sight.

"You have no need to worry – I'm not going to make a scene.   What would be the point?   You don't attack a man in a hospital bed, at least I don't.   I waited till I heard you had recovered, heard they're letting you out soon so thought it was about time I came and had my say.   We both know that not in a month of Sundays would you have ever come to see me."

The tea-trolley stalled and rattled and Snap's voice raised a fraction.

"I'm no expert on literature and I'm sure all writers borrow bits from their own experience, but surely it's not right to steal someone else's life and, and stuff it into a fiction to make money and gain fame." Red blotches were spreading on Snap's face as his anger swelled. "People here aren't fools and they know how you robbed bits of my life to, to spread your lies. And there were bits and you know what they are, that it was just not right, not fair, for you to, to put in your trash. You know what I mean."

He knew.

"You're a pretender Carson: your book is a pack of lies and your life's a lie. Your brother Paul was an honest man and now he's dead; you're a liar and who's to know but you may go on from strength to strength."

The tea trolley was upon them. With a swift turn of his head, Snap acknowledged its presence and made a quick assessment before raising his voice and thereby ensuring all heads were turned in their direction.

"You remember this. This is a law abiding community. Stealing and lying are not tolerated in this part of the world. For that kind of behaviour there has to be a price to pay, a price to pay. You mark what I said!"

With that, Snap spun away and looking neither right nor left, made his way down the ward and to his relief, no stopping, turning round and firing another dramatic round before he made his exit. The trouble was now he was left centre stage with an audience spellbound and anticipating his response. Stage struck dumb he had no lines to deliver. Then mercifully, a cue: "Milk, no sugar Mr Carson."

CHAPTER FOUR

STILL LIFE

When the bomb thundered in our town

People were locked in mid stride

Flecks of debris spiralled high

And somewhere a baby cried.

Then like a snapshot granted life

There was movement and purpose once more,

People strode on their way while a curious few

Rushed to gawk at the town's new sore.

That and:

A THIN SUB-CONSCIOUS LAYER

The saddening news keep seeping in

And now it's grieving time once more.

Names sign if Protestant or Catholic dead

While all condemn the tolling score.

It's not fellow-feeling shared by all

That stops prejudice from tribe-ling out

But only a thin sub-conscious layer

Fragile, wind-blown and subject to doubt.

These two were his only artistic response in his spell in hospital. A premonition came that he had drained dry the well of his creativity and any road he felt the rhyming mode had ploughed its furrow. The way ahead was too narrow and winding, too problem-strewn to be corralled within its boundaries.

Yet not all was lost.

From strength to strength Snap had forecast and so it proved. A letter from his agent in London informed him that *Gingersnap* was being reprinted and copies were selling fast. There was a new surge of interest generated by the publicity surrounding the deaths of his father and brother and the circumstances of his own miraculous escape.

There's a price to pay. That theatrical caution bubbled up and swamped him in anxiety. He felt deeply the Ulster reticence related to dirty linen and its public cleansing. He felt now he was wrong to rely so openly on Snap and his lived story in his fiction. He should have left out the childhood humiliation and their time in the caravan but, at the time, he saw them as scenes that just seemed too good for life, that were made for his story, and when all was said and done, it was he and not Snap who was the true creative source behind the novel. So what? Snap didn't and couldn't write it. He, on the other hand, could and did and anyway, it was part and parcel of the writer's trade to borrow or steal from wherever he can. The lives of other folks were not resources you had to pay to mine. They were there for the taking and any enterprising entrepreneur was free to make of them what he wished. There was no price to pay, so there was nothing to be worried about. Snap was over-reacting: he had always been a tad delusional, so let him stew in the juice of his own making. He had more important things on his mind.

Where was Teresa? He had been in hospital for nearly a month and not a word from her? That could be explained he supposed: in this community married women did not visit menfolk outside their own family circle. How to explain then the lack of any visit from his mother and when he attempted to find out from Jane or even in desperation from Sam, their evasive mumblings did nothing to reassure him. Something was seriously wrong.

His agent's letter and a few relevant clippings were contained within a large envelope and the final curiosity he left till last: a tiny black, rectangular envelope with on the outside in white calligrapher's pen and in ornate spidery style, his name. Inside there was no letter, just a small carefully cut item from what he surmised was *The Times*.

On Saturday May 27

We announce the marriage of publisher Leonard Bloomfield

To artist and illustrator Veronica Lane.

The ceremony will take place at 11.30 in The Registry Office

Kensington High Street and later at Claridges Hotel.

He folded the card, tore it in small pieces and in the toilet cast them into the bowl where, when he flushed, he watched them swirl round and round before they sank.

Jane brought him clothes and accompanied him on the taxi journey home from the hospital. Outside, photographers jostled, there was a television crew and microphones were stretched towards him.

"What do you think of the men who were transporting the bomb? Can you ever forgive them for their part in the tragedy? What are your views on the IRA targeting town centres? Do you think the security forces should be given special powers to intern known suspects? What are your plans for the future?"

To all but the last he stayed mute, looked serious and affected stoic resignation.

"I'm going home to rest; perhaps I might take a holiday. That's all I have to say."

They were in the taxi and away.

"If that's fame," Jane opined, "then I, for one, could do without it."

"It's the price you pay," he countered automatically and then shivered at the personal import of his words. He seemed to be encountering that sentiment often recently: too often for his liking.

"Are you feeling cold?"

"No, just someone was walking over my grave." He shivered again. "That's all."

For the remainder of the journey they remained silent, aware of the interest taken in their every word by Nosey Parker in the front, driving.   They reached his bungalow, Nosey was paid and sped off and Jane took the initiative.

"You alright to drive – as far as our house I mean."

"I'm sure that would be in order."

"Let's go inside first.   I'll make us a cup of tea.   I've brought some milk and biscuits.   Then we can get it over."

The "get it over" sounded ominous.

Inside the bungalow smelled musty and Jane bustled about opening windows while he checked the fridge and poured soured milk down the sink and bagged up a few rotting vegetables and bacon and eggs before placing them in the bin outside.   His legs were stiff and there was a pain in his right thigh but thankfully there was no permanent damage and no need for crutches.   He had been advised to walk, short distances at first then increasing gradually but leaving off when he felt tired or there was any trace of discomfort.   A walking stick was suggested and the Thespian aspect appealed so he had requested that Jane bring him one of their fathers' sticks, who had never used them but they were a legacy from *his* father, kept for sentimental reasons in a stand in the hall.   Jane had brought him a shiny, knobbly blackthorn, not the prop he desired; that was a smooth silver-topped job so he was impatient to be in his mother's house to affect a swap.

When they had settled down with their steaming mugs of tea, Jane typically wasted no time.

"I'm afraid neither of us is in our mother's good books."

"What have I done," he blurted selfishly," before creating he hoped a better impression with, "more to the point what could you possibly…"

"I'm going to have a baby, James," and then to his complete bafflement his tough sister, the one he, all of them leaned on, crumbled right there and then and wailed and shook, leaving him helpless and not knowing which way to turn.

"I'm going to have a baby!   Our mother, you know what she's like; things like this bring out the worst of her country ways. All she could say were things like *bad scrant to ye* and *ye're neither use nor ornament.*   She says I've brought shame on the family and wants nothing more to do with me or as she puts it *I'm nought but a wee skitter* and she gives *neither hilt nor hare* what becomes of me because I'm no kin of hers.   She's practically thrown me out already and I've nowhere to go.   Sam won't speak to me, he doesn't want to hear anything I have to say, I've no one to turn to, I'm…"

"Steady on Jane.   Here…"   He groped for a handkerchief, had none, "Wait, I'll get you a hanky."

He stood too abruptly and a searing pain shot up his leg causing a yelp of pain he did his best to stifle.   Jane's pain was the one to concentrate on and fleetingly he marvelled at and was pricked with pride at his new found solicitousness.   Perhaps suffering really did have redemptive side effects.   In a drawer in the bedroom he found a handkerchief.

"Here you are, wipe your face with this.   Don't worry yourself about being thrown out or any of that nonsense.   If the worst comes to the worst there's always a spare room here," he heard himself say.   "Never mind, it's unlikely ever to happen. The whole thing will blow over in the end like these things do.

Look at it this way: you're affording me the opportunity to play big brother in a positive way and remember a trouble shared..."

"Don't you want to know who the father is?"

"You know him already."

"Do I?" He was intrigued. "Someone I know." He played the game and did his best. "No you have me beat. I give up."

"Eamonn Maguire."

"You mean Teresa's... Sean's brother?"

"That's the one."

He remembered the football match, Eamonn's self-possession and poise and his humiliation and the fair tackle and the brawl.

"But how did you..."

"We met about a year ago at a dance in the Town Hall. I'd never known Eamonn, had not run into him before. He was away from home. He had won a scholarship and went to a boarding school in Londonderry. When he finished, he took a year off before going to university, to do charity work in Africa. He was back home when we met and now he's home permanently waiting to go to college to become a teacher. We're really struggling to make ends meet. I've got a job as a receptionist but the money's not up to much and..."

"Are you, does he..."

"Want to make an honest woman of me, you mean. Yes, our plan is to get married."

"Then what's the problem? Eamonn will get a grant surely. You won't be rich, you might have to…" Jane folded her arms, leaned back in her chair and stared him in the face. "What's wrong? What have I said?"

"James, listen to me! It's not the way it was anymore when we were children playing together. We're grown up now and that seems to be the part you've missed out on in the different world you've lived in from the rest of us."

"You mean…"

"I mean I'm Protestant and Eamonn is a Catholic and whether we like it or not that's what we are and there is nothing we can do about it and in this part of the world where people will put up with a lot, the one thing they will not put up with is marriage between the likes of us. If Eamonn was Protestant our mother would be busying about helping with wedding preparations, but he's not so I'm a wee hoor and she's at her wit's end."

"What about the Maguires? Has Eamonn told them?"

"He has. They're for us getting married, but it would have to be in a Catholic Church, not here but in a different parish. There are papers to sign and I must promise our child will be brought up as a Catholic, go to Chapel and attend a Catholic school."

"What's your feeling about that?"

"I love Eamonn, James. I want to be married to him. He loves me and we want to be together. Our mother… well you'll see. If we can work it out we'll go to England. Our plan is to go there in any case but Eamonn would rather we go with his parents' blessing. He doesn't just want us to run away together. As for me I just don't care anymore. I just want out. You don't have any idea what it's really like.   Maybe someday we'll come back, but now there's too much hatred here; it's no place to bring up a child.   All we want is to be married, have a family, be together and be left alone to live our lives but you can't do that here given our, our circumstances.   People won't let you.   They won't leave you in peace."

No, he thought, some would rather leave you in pieces. Jane was right.   She was right also about his living in a different world from the rest of the family.   So little of all this had impinged on his experience.   It was true that in abstract terms he was aware of divided loyalties in the North of Ireland, but they had never really impacted upon him personally except...   He summoned up the football match where rage had booted his macho red blur into retaliation against Eamonn.   Perhaps beneath the surface of all on this island there smouldered a sectarian fire waiting for circumstance to set it alight.   Who knows?   But that was a rare, an extreme case.   Surely, in the main, reason and compassion ruled and the Grammar school, library, University, those venues were places of retreat away from the drums' banging where you could aspire to become part of a cultural clan and in the long run accoutrements like the sash and hard hat clashed too ridiculously with the cap and gown – even if you never got to wear the cap or the gown.   Then there was the study: he had chosen to keep his head down, burrowing in his books and had as a consequence neither the time nor the inclination to be pied-pipered behind King Billy and his pointed sword.   The exams passed, he had been allowed entry to a new social spin that whirled him away from received mores and brought into question and even ridicule, the ways of his fellows.   Then again he was not and never could be a team player: he had instead been born to play for himself.

All for one and one for one: that was more his motto.

Later he drove Jane to their mother's where he was more than taken aback by the change in her appearance. In just a short time his mother had become old: her eyes were watery, her shoulders slumped, her back was rounded and she was painfully thin. Gone was any of the softness he remembered in her face: her cheeks were sunken and in her expression there was no welcome but instead a pinched malevolence focussed, he sensed, most acutely in his direction. His attempt to embrace her was rejected and she jabbed him back and on the doorstep started up screaming at him and attacking him physically, beating at his chest with the sides of her fists. The neighbours would be having a field day so he bundled her inside, into the living room and let her screech her piece.

"Why did you have to come back? Why couldn't you stay away and leave us alone? We didn't want you – or your presents! When you weren't here we all got along just fine – even that wee tramp was no bother then, whilst me and Paul, me and Paul…" Her hands clenched into fists and she wrapped her arms around herself and wept. Acting on instinct he moved towards her but she backed away, released her arms and then raised them palms extended like, the thought flashed across his mind, some threatened female in a silent film. "Stay away – stay away from me – I don't want you around me anymore – I couldn't care less if I never see you again – you've always seen yourself as a cut above the rest of us. If you hadn't come home your father would still be here and if you hadn't called on Paul… You never attend your church and, and your book is a pack of filth and lies! You're no son of mine! Get out of my house, get out, GET OUT!" Spittle was running down her chin. "Out I said and take that one with you! Your father must be turning in his grave while Paul, Paul…" She placed her palms on her ears and screamed and screamed.　He thought of Edward Munch, turned on his heel and made for the door.　Jane ran after him.

"James, don't…"

"Do you think she's trying to tell me something?　Look, either I slap her face to try and bring her to her senses or I remove myself from the scene.　You hear the screaming's stopped.　You stay.　Better ring for the doctor and have her checked out. Remember if you need a place to stay and any help, papers to sign or anything, I'll do it for you with the greatest of pleasure.　From what I've seen and heard, you're better off out of all this."

Outside a small cluster of neighbours clustered and he scanned their faces looking for Mrs O'Neill who had lived with her family next door for years, been a good neighbour and especially close to their mother.

"Where's Mrs O'Neill?"

There was a hush.

"She left last week; went to another estate."

"A Taig one," another added defiantly.

So that was where things were headed: separate schools, separate churches and now separate streets: the Shankill and The Falls in the countryside.　The women were scrutinising him closely, ferreting for any nuance in his response.

"My mother's ill, probably suffering from a delayed reaction to what happened with our father and Paul.　Jane and I think she may be suffering a breakdown so I'm off to…"

His words were extinguished by the muffled phut-phut then deafening machine-grind of a helicopter overhead.　Grateful for the clatter he made his escape and climbed into his vehicle. Damn, the walking stick: in all the commotion he'd forgotten to pick it up. He sat in the car and drummed his fingers on the steering wheel, then his mind made up he struggled out of the vehicle, marched through the group of women and up to the house. "Shit! Shit! Shit!" He had pulled the door shut. Mercifully the helicopter's clamour allowed him to purge his passion in private. He rang the bell till eventually the door was opened.

"James, something told me you'd come back. She's calmed down, still shaking but quiet at least. I've phoned for the doctor and he should be here any minute. That's probably him now."

He checked any mention of the walking-stick and allowed Jane's definition of the situation to stand.

The doctor, a small corpulent man with red veins sketched across his cheeks and the sides of his nose, was crisp and business-like in his approach. His layman's prognosis proved accurate.

"Your mother is going through a nervous breakdown. I've seen quite a lot of it recently." Taking off his glasses he held them up to the light then began polishing them with his handkerchief. "It's the Troubles, and Mrs Carson has suffered more than most: losing a husband and then a son, too much for normal times but now... I've given her a sedative." He checked his glasses against the light. "I'm going to prescribe Valium. You will need to ensure she takes only the recommended dosage and keep the tablets in a secure place out of reach of the patient. In a month or so she should be on the mend and then we can think about gradually decreasing the prescription." Putting on his glasses he went to the table, took out a pen and small paper and began writing. Then when he had finished: "Who do I give this to?"

They looked at each other before Jane, as he knew she would, relented.

"Give it here.   I'll see to it."

The doctor gone, she looked at him and sighed.

"As our mother would say, you never know what's round the next corner.   And as she has often pointed out, this certainly puts the cat among the pigeons.   I'll do what I can and stay as long as I can.   This delays things for a bit but maybe that's a good thing. Perhaps we could do with a breathing space but in the long run Eamonn and I will still be getting married and we're still heading for England."

"I understand, and remember any help you need, I'm there for you.   I'd better go.   No need to see me out."

He went into the living room where his mother was sitting in their father's chair.   She was breathing more easily now, but the look she aimed told him all he needed to know.   He turned away.

"I'll trust you to say my goodbyes," was his parting shot to Jane.

In the hall he slotted the blackthorn into the stand and extracted the silver topped cane.   He ran his fingers down the satin smooth surface, considered, and then immediately expunged the notion of a Chaplin twirl: the hallway was too cramped. Stepping outside he pulled shut the door, then hammed it slowly down the path: a walking wounded suffering with dignity, projecting a brave front to milk the pitying glances and sad head shakings of his audience of neighbours.

CHAPTER FIVE

After Bloody Sunday, the news spiralled downwards till it became increasingly and more bloodily depressing. You had he knew a duty to keep self-informed and he did his best to resist adding to the spread of a 'let them get on with it' mentality, but it was proving difficult to resist. This insignificant little corner of the world was being transformed into a violent cul-de-sac where the word 'atrocity' was becoming commonplace. "What a bloody awful country", Reginal Maudling was supposed to have said and there were times he was forced to agree.

Home from his mother's, he slumped in front of the TV to be ambushed by flickering images from yet another abomination: the Abercorn restaurant in Belfast city centre, crowded with afternoon innocents had been torn apart by a bombing. No warning, two dead, four had lost both legs. He rose and switched off the set, then crossed to the window and looked out across the fields. *"No worst, there is none. Pitched past pitch of grief."* More words: yet words were all you had. Did having literary reference points at hand aid access to a higher, purer form of feeling? He doubted it.

The journalist's cliché "escalation of the violence" floated through his thought flow and then lodged and became jammed. Escalate where, how – what could be worse than carefree, ordinary folks going about their harmless activity to suddenly out of nowhere be maimed and killed? One sunny second people were nodding, laughing and chatting, the next they were ripped to shards in the terrible pursuit of the heads, legs and arms race.

"Paul, Jesus, Paul!" Wordless, impotent, he wept for his brother and for the whole awful, bloody mess.

The following evening Jane called, accompanied by Eamonn: tall, curly headed wearing little round spectacles.

"Sean sends his regards."

The voice was gentle and the handshake firm. He remembered the last time they had shaken hands, and felt his cheeks burn.

"Jane tells me you know about us and are willing to help. I appreciate that."

Like the boy, the man controlled the situation, but this time he did not mind: this match was Jane's.

Eamonn's house was in a terraced row at the edge of town. They went in the dark with Eamonn driving his father's old van and Jane and he squeezed beside him in the front. On arrival they were led up the path, round the side of the building, then straight through into the back kitchen: no front of house welcoming. The mother and father were polite but ill at ease, doing what they could to make the best of a situation that was not to their liking. He shook hands, considered an ice-breaker remark and then cancelled the impulse. When in Rome…

He took tea, accepted a sandwich and a slice of cake and played his part in the small talk. Eamonn appeared relaxed and unaffected by the general air of embarrassment. Then a tiny vignette spoke volumes: Eamonn winked at Jane and the old woman clocked the wink and Jane's smiling response. He watched her face: eyes narrowed, nose pinched and mouth set hard in a look of distilled hate focussed on his sister. All reeled him back to his mother and the distaste she directed towards himself. Aw God bless them – the mothers of Erin. He rested his eyes on Eamonn's mother and let her know he knew.

There was a knock on the back door.

"That'll be him now," Eamonn's father declared and the mother stood in response, scraping back her chair on the tiled floor.   Taking his time, Eamonn strolled across and opened the door.

"Come in Father."

The priest was small, stocky and grey haired with a leathery lived-in face: like a boxer with a dog-collar.   His eyes were dark, small, set back and they darted about with a fierce alertness.

"Shure would ye take a gander at the Lurgan spades on the lot of ye."

The voice was as lively as the eyes, a stage southern Irish brogue projecting shure Jaysus it's all a level playing field and I'm no different from the rest of yis.

"Ye'd think by yer fizzogs this was about a funeral and not a wedding."   He rubbed his hands together.   "Woman o' the house, I'll take a sup o' that tay an' a slice o' yon cake.   Father Phelan O'Rourke: God bless all in this cosy wee kitchen."

Father O'Rourke shook hands, ate drank and won over all assembled with an intrusive jocularity the devil himself would have found hard to resist.   A man like this was wasted in the church: put him in politics and he would sooth your troubles, Ireland.   Then again that might be stretching things just a wee bit too far.

"They say never recommend that an Irishman go to war – or to marry.   He's too hot tempered for both."

The priest swigged the drains from his cup, placed it back on the saucer and handed it back to his hostess who having hovered all the while in attendance by his side was there at hand to receive it.

"Well Eamonn, despite that excellent advice yur determined to claim Jane here as yur lawfully married wife."

"Yes Father, I am."

"And as for you Jane I can tell from the smile on yur face that you're a consenting party.   Aaah to be shure you young ones; what's to be done wit ye?   The best advice I can give both of yis and indeed all present is never, never rub yer eye - except with yer elbow."

Even he found himself laughing.   So far Father O'Rourke had played a blinder but he sensed the preliminaries were coming to an end and events were about to kick off in earnest.   Eamonn was watching him and he sensed he too was bracing himself for a different assault.   With his elbows Father O'Rourke levered himself upright in his kitchen chair, brought his hands together and interlocked them, making a steeple with his index fingers.

"When you got down to it, the bedrock of any stable community comes from marriage and family.   There' any amount of bad news about in these troubled times so all the more need for the good news of the gospel to be proclaimed to all without exception who are called to the holy union that is marriage.   Sure wasn't the family attached to the wellbeing of the whole of society like the shepherd was to the fold and didn't God's plan for marriage and the family touch all men and all women in the fullness of their daily existence."   The brogue had softened, the vocabulary cleansed and there was no doubting the seriousness of the delivery.   "Many and various are the threats to the sacred nature of the family structure: notions concerning the freedom of spouses to act independent of each other; changing ideas regarding the nature of authority between parents and children; then God help us the proliferation of divorce, the evils of abortion and the whole cancerous growth of the contraceptive mentality."

The priest was pulling no punches and here was he a grown man allowing himself and his sister to be pummelled without summoning any degree of resistance. What would his father… He looked down, avoiding Jane's eyes and let the words wash over him. They were only words.

"…Couples like you two entering what is termed a mixed marriage have special responsibilities." He looked up. Father O'Rourke had a smile on his face but his voice had a slightly sharper edge. He saw Eamonn cover Jane's hand with his own. "It is incumbent on the non-Catholic partner in such a union to recognise that there are certain obligations that require to be fulfilled if the marriage is to receive our church's blessing."

Father O'Rourke paused and in the silence ensuing, he was conscious, for the first time, of the kitchen clock's loud ticking.

"There is for example an obligation to ensure that the baptism, schooling and upbringing of any children are nurtured within the boundaries of the Catholic faith."

That was it: his cue.

"We have no problem with anything you have said, Father. Jane and I have discussed the situation and I've spoken with Eamonn. I'm sure if our father could have been here, he would have said the same. Any papers there are to sign, I'll do so gladly. All I want," keep it simple, "is what I'm sure Mr and Mrs McGuire want too," and he nodded in their direction, "is for my sister and the man she has chosen as her life partner to be happy together."

What a performance: there should be applause, a standing ovation, and shouts of "Bravo! Bravo."

Outside in the dark Jane embraced him. "You were great, James."

Eamonn took his hand.

"I appreciate what you have done. It meant a great deal to me; to us both. I won't forget."

He attended the wedding: no Sam and no Sean. Teresa sat in the chapel but there was no sign of Kevin. During the proceedings he looked across and tried to engage with her but she was impervious, remaining fixed ahead and she failed to turn up at the meal afterwards. Sam, siding with his mother, had refused to take any part in the event and in a way both Jane and he were glad of his absence. They both considered him too much of loose cannon. Sean was another matter entirely. Where was the man? Most likely he and Eamonn had had a bust-up; it was the only feasible explanation. It would not be because of the wedding, of that he was certain. Sean would not be like that. So what then? If Teresa was not incommunicado he could have found out from her and he did not possess the gall to raise the issue with Eamonn and certainly not with either of the parents. Would Jane know what was going on? The problem was that in all the hustle and bustle of the service and its aftermath it proved impossible to make an opportunity to talk to her on her own.

He had agreed to drive Eamonn and Jane to the docks in Belfast so that they could catch the overnight crossing for Liverpool. He recalled the time of his own flight from the city and in a trice Jane the rock and centre of their family was more fragile and vulnerable than he could ever have imagined her. He hugged her close and pressed an envelope with money into her hand.

"Take it, you'll need it.   Let me know when you're settled." He disengaged, turned aside and looked Eamonn in the eye. "Look after her, she's…" then he was flummoxed and had the breath knocked out of him when his brother-in-law stepped up, threw his arms round him, hugged him close then slapped his shoulders.   Then he wheeled away, took his sister's hand and they were on their way up the gangplank and onto the boat.

The wind on his face was making his eyes water, so he wiped them dry before turning inland.

CHAPTER SIX

Interrupting his dream, a distant ringing sound that became increasingly persistent then insistent till it belled through that someone was outside ringing his bell, so he jarred awake and snatched the bedside clock and glared in disbelief: four twenty in the morning!

Who in hell's name at this God forsaken hour?

Wrestling with his dressing-gown he lurched out of the room and down the hallway, feeling for the light-switch and half closing his eyes against the glare. The ringing ceased.

"Who's there?"

These were changed times: you didn't leave doors unlocked or throw them open with the old abandon.

"It's me Sam; for Christ's sake switch off that light!"

Instantly he obeyed, and then opened the door where stood his brother in full uniform, even carrying his rifle and with a green duffle bag slung over his shoulder. Without protest he let him in, closed the door then followed him into the living-room. What else could he do?

"Can I get you anything: a mug of tea, whisky or..."

"I've no time for any o' that. You sit yerself down and take heed o' what I have to say."

While **he** had shaved off the rougher edges of his accent, Sam had the swaggering assurance to sport his with pride. His bulk seemed increased by the uniform. Recently he had put on a deal of weight and most of it had settled on his stomach. Grunting he heaved himself free of the duffle-bag and dropped it on the floor, then creaked down onto the settee, holding the rifle like a spear with its butt to the rug at his feet.

"Ye see me here tonight and God willing I'll be here again tomorrow night, though as far as you are concerned, neither time have I been here at all if ye see what I mean."

He saw and his pulse began to race. Sam was trying to involve him in some shady dealing and he knew he must do his best to resist. His mind flitted back to when they were boys and he had led Sam into many a scrape and now his brother was leading him into God knows what. He had to fight back but how to in pyjamas and bare feet against that bulk, those boots and that gun. He would have helped Paul in any way he could, he helped Jane, he was the older brother and now Sam needed a hand. What could he do?

"Look Sam I'm..." What: a respectable un-married man; a person of some standing in the community.

"I've no time for flannel!" True to type Sam adhered to the rhinoceros school of diplomacy.

"I'm, I'm trying to get my bearings here. Look it's four thirty in the morning and you burst in here wearing uniform, carrying a rifle, speaking in riddles and you expect me to react as if the whole shebang is the normal run of things. Well I'm sorry but..."

"Keep yer hat on. Now here's the way it is. There's a change of clothing in that duffle-bag. I want ye to take it and put it somewhere safe and then give it back to me when ye see me next, which if all goes to plan should be tomorrow night. It's as easy as that – so what do ye have to say?"

What could he say? Trapped by circumstance, the force of his brother's personality and by his own inability to stand his ground or even to protest he could only comply.

"If it makes you happy I'll do what you say," then he considered giving it one last try. "Do you mind telling me what I'm letting myself in for? Surely I've a right to know."

"Ye have, I'll grant ye that, only this is not the time." Sam heaved himself to his feet. "It's time I was on my way. Don't worry yerself about any of this; I've got everything in hand. Just remember to hide the duffle-bag and I'll see you tomorrow night. We'll get drunk together and I'll have a while o' yer crack. Put it there."

They shook hands.

"How are you getting home?"

"I'm just off patrol. My pals are waiting in the jeep – that's why I can't stay. Now mind, tomorrow night or just maybe in the wee small hours. I'll let myself out and you close the door behind me – no need to slam it and no need for a light: I can find my way. Just remember, you haven't seen me tonight and you won't see me tomorrow night, if ye see what I mean."

At the open door he stood and watched his brother stride across the garden then over the fence before disappearing as he headed for the road below. He waited, and then moments later caught the muffled cough of an engine and remained till it faded away into the distance. Outside it was still dark. Over the fields a dog barked setting off another. He shivered, wrapped his dressing gown tighter and then turned inside closing the door quietly.

Those men, and they would be men in the jeep, must be involved in whatever Sam was contemplating.   He recalled the night he had gone to visit his father in hospital and those men on the road.   These were dangerous times and he was allowing himself to be yanked up some blind alleyway.

Up a blind alley and wearing a blindfold: not a good situation to be embroiled in especially when led by his mad dog of a brother.   He needed a drink.

CHAPTER SEVEN

The next morning he tidied the house and then set off for a walk across the fields. His legs were strengthening and he needed the exercise. Anyhow writing, even reading was impossible as Sam's visit had blown his concentration. Regretting returning the blackthorn he fashioned himself a stick from an ash plant in the lane; his cane was too dainty for tramping in the countryside. The air was crisp and frosty, the sky a pale blue while the sun afforded light but little in the way of warmth. Fields and hedgerows were…fields and hedgerows. He had an instinctive contempt for notions of the countryside as pastoral landscape: as far as he was concerned it was a working environment. He breathed deeply and with his stick swiped at the heads of a clump of daffodils smiling at him from the hedgerow. In this corner of the universe land was for profiting from, owning and holding onto, passing on and inheriting; the emphasis was on scrape and not scape.

Back home he pottered about, did some tidying, cleaned the windows and made himself a sandwich for lunch. Then suddenly the Sam situation came to him in a rush. What had he let himself in for? How could he have been such a fool to agree to implicate himself in whatever his brother was up to? Suppose it was something illegal, then he could be convicted as an accessory and then he might even end up in prison. His reputation could be destroyed. What a fool he had been! He paced about, his thoughts speeding, circling, whirling faster and faster around any action Sam might take. This not knowing, this being helpless, this waiting was no role for him. Of a sudden he remembered what Sam said when he told him he was joining the B Specials: he would have a licence to kill.

Without warning his breathing became restricted, he felt his chest tighten and was fighting to force air into his lungs or he knew he would suffocate. The only way was to take short shallow breaths. Easy now, control, control, you can fight this. His forehead felt hot and he thought he was going to be sick but gradually he imposed his will and the symptoms began to subside, his breathing became easier and the pain spreading in his chest began to lessen. His shirt was sticky with sweat, so he removed it, washed and phoned for a taxi.

Ivan Thornton's bald head gleamed under the artificial light in the shop. He explained what had transpired and added to the drama by saying it had happened a few times since the explosion and Paul's death. The big man nodded sympathetically.

"Don't worry: you did the right thing to come to see me. What you describe is symptomatic of what we call a panic attack. Since the Troubles there's been a significant increase. Normally a doctor would prescribe Valium, soon half the town will be on the stuff." Where had he heard that before? "The drug companies are making a fortune out of this part of the world. It's an ill wind... For starters I think you need something stronger. Just hold on a sec."

Thornton disappeared into the back of the shop, while he continued concentrating on breathing slowly and evenly. He became aware of the curious glances of other customers, could feel his anxiety level increase and began to feel more agitated, felt hemmed in and started to sweat and tremble.

"Here we are. You're not driving." He shook his head. "Better still; we can fix you up straight away. Take these two tablets, mind you're shaking so watch you don't drop them. Here's a drop of water to wash them down with.   You'll be as right as rain in no time."

The man was as good as his word.   Gradually things became removed and he was at a distance, detached, viewing the world and the other customers with an amused tolerance.   The trembling receded and his worry regarding Sam faded then stalled someplace too far away to pose any threat.

"Take this pill-box."   The voice was ever so slightly disconnected as was the ting of the shop's cash register as an assistant served someone else.   "There are ten tablets inside. Take two any time you find an attack coming on.   They'll make you feel drowsy and if you can, give in to them and sleep.   It's still the best healer.   This instance may just be a one-off so it might not happen again.   Can you think of any particular trigger that might have set you off?

He shook his head.

"How much do I owe you?"

"Don't worry; they're on the house.   Paul was a lovely man, he was someone very special, I miss him," was there a catch in his voice as he looked away, stayed silent for a moment, then, "the town misses him.   He will not be forgotten."

"What can I say?"   His own voice sounded external to himself but he felt in control, with time to choose the content precisely.   "My brother was unique in life, at home and in his work.   Like you, all in the family miss him deeply.   Your kind words and deed will not be forgotten."

Extending his arm he shook hands with Ivan Thornton, then glided from the shop and slid into the taxi, where on the journey back Nosey Parker cost him not a single thought.   On arrival he paid, eased inside, lay on the bed and slipped into sleep.

CHAPTER EIGHT

The room was dark when he drifted towards awareness and lay back allowing the silence to settle around him, buoy him, in a sea of serenity.   Dreamily he peered at the bedside clock and worked out he had been asleep for almost nine hours.   No headache but a touch dry-mouthed, so he slipped from the bed and coasted into the kitchen where he ran the tap, then drained a glass of water.   It was nearing midnight so his brother could be here at any minute but he accepted the premise neutrally with no tinge of personal involvement.   He washed, changed clothes, made and laid out sandwiches, plates and glasses, a bottle of whisky and cans of beer; doing all in a placid sense of otherness.   The duffle-bag: he fetched it from a wardrobe and placed it at the ready.

The door belled.

It was Sam, clad in black overalls, clutching what looked like a black woolly hat wrapped round some heavy object.   He blundered past into the living room, trailing behind the reek of male sweat.

"Aaah good man!" and carefully he placed the cap and contents on the floor, then grabbed and snapped open the bottle of whisky before pouring himself a generous measure he downed in one go.   Wiping his mouth with the back of his hand he retrieved his bundle, unzipped his duffle-bag and placed it inside, then took all up and left the room closing the door behind him.

For himself all was still mercifully at a distance but to be sure he retrieved the pill-box from his pocket, undid the top and placed two more on the tip of his tongue then swilled them down with a shot of whisky before sitting head back and eyes closed in his armchair.   What will be will be he intoned and in a jiffy he was snapped awake as his brother bustled into the room, washed and wearing casual clothes, the duffle bag over his shoulder.

"Ye got a spade?"

"Well yes, in the shed round the back.   I can get it for you. Just let me get my torch."

"No you stay here.   Where's the torch?   Is the shed locked?"

"It's not locked.   There's nothing valuable, only a few tools inside.   The spade is just behind the door.   The torch is on the worktop on the kitchen.   You can go out the back door from the kitchen.   Be careful of the step, it can be…"

His brother was gone so he left him to it, sipped his whisky and composed himself so that when Sam returned he sailed through the waters of host playing and mentally prepared himself for the squall he knew was about to break.   He did not have long to wait.

"We found out who planned the bomb attack; the one you got injured in and our Paul, our Paul… well you know."

"How did you…"

"The Brits: we share intelligence with them.   We've got a man who tells us things but we couldn't make an arrest, no proof, nothing that would stand up in a court of law.   So the murderer would have been laughing, walking away scot-free, except me and my pals had other ideas.   Yer own brother and what harm had Paul ever done to anyone; there wasn't an ounce of harm in him. Ye see, often we know who the bastards are but the law, the law that should see justice done, stops them from being punished.   It drives me crazy just to think about it and when it's yer own brother…"

He closed his eyes and stopped himself from concentrating on each individual word; the general drift was all he could bear.

Sam and his accomplices weren't prepared to lie down and let the murderer go unpunished. Scum like that deserved no mercy so they watched him and watched him and plotted his movements. They found out he would be going to the big Gaelic match across the border and knew he would be coming home late. They also had the number of the car and knew the road he would be taking home. So they set up a road block and stopped the car. At this point Sam reached for the whisky bottle and filled his glass to the brim, slopping some of the liquid onto the table-top. He slurped from the tumbler then placed it down carefully.

"There were four of them in the car." Sam had his full attention now. "The one we were after was in the back. We ordered them all out, looked at their papers and searched them, then ordered the other three to get back in the vehicle and drive off. We said we were taking their companion in for questioning. They knew, he knew what was going on, but there was nothing they could do."

Sam picked up his glass, raised it to his mouth, then reconsidered and held it in his lap.

"We watched them drive off and waved the waiting cars through. Our man said nothing, just kept looking at me, looking and looking." He stared down into his glass. "We packed up the road block and drove to a place, a quarry and…" Draining the glass he held it out for re-filling. His hand was shaking. "Ye have to understand. This is a war, but even in a war there are rules and scum like that one, they think they can break the rules, kill innocent people and get away with it.   They have to be taught there's a price to pay."

He took back the glass and cradled it once more in his lap.

"He was in the back seat between me and another fellow.   I swear I could hear his heart pounding.   When we arrived we dragged him out of the car and threw him on the ground.   He rolled over then tried to run on hands and feet up the side of the quarry but he kept sliding back on the loose stones.   It was kind of funny in a mad sort of way so we let him scrabble on for a spell then, well then we shot the murdering bastard, executed him for the crime of murder of an innocent victim who happened to be our brother.   Then we wrapped the body in a tarpaulin and drove back and dumped the bundle on the roadside in a place where he'd be found so he can act as a warning to the rest of them.   To let them know we know who they are and that some of us at least are not prepared to stand back and let them bomb and maim and kill us all."

The whisky was having its effect; Sam's face was flushed and his speech was becoming slurred.

"This wasn't only about Paul though God knows, that's reason enough.   Scum like that murdering bastard claim they are freedom fighters, soldiers fighting for a united Ireland.   But we're British and we have to stand up for our right to remain so.   If they take the law into their own hands then it's only right that we, we take the law into ours to, to defend the Union we hold dear.   So Ulster will fight and Ulster will be…"

Shite, he irreverenced mentally and sipped his whisky as his brother gulped his, becoming more and more zealous in his efforts to dig himself behind a cause that might provide a ditch against the enormity of his crime.   Eventually Sam ceased his babble, slurped his whisky, and then staggered to the bathroom where he heard him retching then throwing up. He wrestled him into bed, cleaned up as best as he could, knocked back a couple more pills, then sought his bed and access to oblivion.

The following afternoon, Sam appeared, shivering and with a blinding headache. He found him aspirins, Sam showered and later they drank strong tea and watched his account verified on the evening news: a dead body had been found riddled with multiple bullet wounds. The victim's identity was not being released until relatives had been informed.

When it was dark, Sam set off across the fields. As far as the world was concerned he had been in bed all day recovering from a bout of flu, too ill to answer the door. The ammunition they had used was not official issue so there was no way it could be traced. He was in the clear.

As for himself, now he realised surely an accessory to a murder, he remained at home blocking out reality with doses of the blessed Ivan Thornton pills. On TV some days later he watched a news item: a line of men wearing balaclavas and military style jackets, pants and boots in a graveyard standing to attention around a coffin. The camera picked out the neatly folded tricolour then panned back as the men raised hand-guns.

He winced at the crackle of bullets.

Somehow before Sam told him he'd known who it was. Sometimes in life you are prompted towards an intuition of the ending before its enormity is revealed. Sometimes life manufactures ironic coincidence that would not be deemed feasible in the realms of fiction.

Mad, sad and dangerous to know. Mentally he conjured up the boy sitting cross-legged, cross-eyed, his cheeks bulging with stolen fruit. Sam was born to be mad – the sad part came with age. He thought back to their day at the field that Twelfth of July: who would have imagined his brother would ever subscribe to that kind of rhetoric and that one day he would recite it as justification for the murder of his childhood friend?

They were careering towards him down a hill: Sam, Sean and Teresa. That it should come to this: indirectly her brother had contributed to the death of his brother and his brother had participated in the death of her brother. The tangled web of it all clogged his consciousness to the exclusion of all else. What could he do? He knew he should go to the authorities but knew also it would kill their mother. Then what about Jane and Eamonn? An image of Sean guttered to life, crab-like, scrabbling up a quarry-side, slithering down then frenzying up, down, up till the bullets cracked, thudded and tore and he rolled over dead.

Paul was dead and his father, dead. And now his one-time friend Sean was dead too.

He should never have returned home.

Unbidden an image of that old crone on the London underground came to him and he shivered. Then he thought of Abagail and her obsession with star signs. Was he star crossed, star bossed – star bollocks! All he had learned: you can be in the right place at the right time or alternatively the wrong place at the wrong time. Life was a four letter word: stuff happened.

The telephone rang.   He did not recognise the voice on the line.

"What size shoes do you take?"

"Nine," he replied automatically, "but..."

Click.

The phone went dead.

CHAPTER NINE

He had heard no car so was shaken when his doorbell rang. Ten-thirty so it would be dark outside. Switching on the light above the outside door he considered calling 'Who's there' then ruled out the thought. To be restored, normality had to be maintained, so he cracked the door open and vaguely recognised the compact, neatly suited figure standing in the porch, a rectangular box tucked under his right arm. Then it hit home: Newcastle, in the hotel with Teresa, the man in the restaurant, the one he thought he had met before.

"Can I come in?"

He considered.

"We've met before. I caught a glimpse of you in the Slieve Donard Hotel in Newcastle. You were at the bar and you left suddenly leaving, if I remember correctly, your drink untouched."

"And what about that night outside the McCann homestead?"

"Outside... It was dark. You, you tried to run me over."

"No, no if I'd wanted to do that you wouldn't be here now. No, that was just to give you a bit of a warning. You and Teresa needed to be put on your guard."

"What do you mean me and Teresa? Just who do you think you are coming round here and...?"

"Look, can I come in or not? It's cold out here and rest assured I mean you no harm."

He thought it over.

"Come on in then.   I suppose I should offer you a drink. What would you like?"

"A glass of water would do fine."

"You don't drink?"

"Alcohol, no, nor smoke and don't go to church either."

"You're an unusual man for these parts."   He gestured where his visitor should sit then sidled into the kitchen and ran a glass of water.   "Here you are," and he lowered himself into the armchair opposite.   "There's somewhere else I've seen you but I can't quite…"

"That's understandable, it was very late at night or to be more accurate very early the next morning and you had more important things to focus your attention on and I, well I was only a bit player."

Still puzzled he stared at him: *a bit player.*   Then in a flash it came to him.

"You're Kevin McCann's friend…"

"Damien, so now you know.   Try the shoes on and see if they fit."

"Look I'm a writer: digging up unusual plots is part of my stock in trade, but this…"

"Try the shoes and I'll drink the water."

He thought about it for a moment before deciding to comply. Why not?   Damien had placed the shoe-box on the floor between them so grunting he stretched down, retrieved it and placed it on his knees.   Opening it he saw a pair of shiny new black shoes and instinctively he raised the box and sniffed the leathery aroma: surely something primitive there.   Self-consciously he removed his slippers, pulled the shoes on, stood up then padded around carefully, the shoe soles feeling slippery on the rug.

"They fit perfectly.   Now perhaps you can tell me just what the hell is going on?"

"Give me the right shoe."

Who did this Damien think he was?   He thought about standing his ground or at least formulating some corrective related to the importance of the word 'please', but something in the dark eyes, in the tilt of the chin, held him back.   So once again he did what he was told.

Damian placed the shoe on the floor between them and hunkered down before him.

"Now watch carefully."

Reaching inside he pulled back the insole.

"The trick is to take it just to here.   Do it carefully and evenly and you'll know just when to stop – it becomes difficult to pull back any further."

"Look, just what…"

"Never mind the questions; all will be revealed in due course.   Just take the shoe and do what I told you."

"Were you in the armed forces?"

No reaction so he reached inside the shoe and performed the task.

"Good, now give the shoe back to me and again watch carefully."

Deftly Damian inserted poised thumb and forefinger in the newly exposed space beneath the insole then daintily prised away a tiny, clear, flimsy rectangle of plastic.

"Know what this is?"

"Yes, for your edification, I think I do."

"Go on then."

"Well since it's a certainty no one in their right mind would go to all this trouble to hide just a bit of plastic it's my bet there's some kind of information on it.   If memory serves I think it must be what is called a microfiche or a microfilm, one of those two."

"How would you know that?"

"Through watching all the wrong films – I suppose that's how."

"You put it back."   Damien handed him the shoe and microfilm.

Obediently he took the flimsy plastic, settled it carefully in place, sealed it carefully with the insole and then placed the shoe neatly beside its partner on the floor.   He sat back in his chair.

"So, come on what's this all about?"

True to form, Damian ignored his direction and started up his own path.

"Kenneth Ferguson approached you.   He wants you to take a trip, all expenses paid.   Some place abroad, a port.   You're to travel using his luggage.   Am I right?"

"Yes, what you say is true."

Denial would be pointless. Damian was too well informed. Anyway he was intrigued about where all this was heading.

"First off there's two things you have to understand. To begin with you have to know that behind Kevin Ferguson, there's Kevin McCann. The whole operation is at his instigation – he set it up. Kenneth is only a sleeping partner and that's the way he wants it to stay. This secrecy thing is at his instigation. The business with the shoe is Kenneth's idea; some friend he knows took care of the detail. He never wants it made public that he is in any way in partnership with Kevin McCann. Those two go back years, to their time together at university. Kevin was making contacts even then. That's always been his way, inveigling himself into people's lives, letting on he's only out for a good time. You saw it at the card game."

He remembered. Damian shifted forward in his chair.

"Kevin seems to have some hold over Kenneth Ferguson. I met them both when I was at Queen's. I needed money and Kevin needed someone to drive him around, to stay awake at card games, to stay sober. I fitted the bill and gradually over time I've become more and more involved and more and more indispensable."

Reaching down, Damian retrieved his glass, drained it and then placed it back on the floor beside his chair.

"That's why they trust me with little tasks like this. What I'm about to tell you, keep to yourself – believe me when I say you would be risking life and limb if you ever spoke to anyone else about what I'm about to say. Now before I go any further is that understood?"

He was in too far to back out now. Besides, he was
intrigued and felt compelled to find out more.

"I understand. What you have to tell me will not go beyond
these four walls. Your secrets, as they say, are safe with me."

As he spoke, surrendering to superstitious illogicality and
taking care to conceal his betrayal from Damian, he crossed his
fingers.

"Right then, that's agreed. I'll tell you all you need to
know." A pause, then: "Kevin and Kenneth, and it has to be kept
secret, are going into business together. They are in the process
of setting up a road haulage company. They intend not to limit
themselves to this part of the world but to operate abroad, in
Europe. Kevin has made contacts. They will be exporting beef
mainly but there are plans for other types of product to be
transported. That's all you need to know and trust me when I say,
the less you know the better. The microfilm contains details of
the truckers' destinations: dates, times loads, that kind of thing. It
is all information that is of interest to the big players in the
operation and stuff they wish to be kept secret from official
scrutiny if you get my meaning."

He nodded. What else could he do? Deep down he knew
that in this case, the less he knew as Damian had pointed out, the
better for himself.

"Go on this trip; you're too far in to back out now anyway.
Wear the shoes. On the first night of your arrival leave them
outside your hotel room as if you want them to be cleaned.
That's all you have to do. They will be collected and replaced
and you have no need to worry because there is no way any of this
can ever be traced back to you. The information on the microfilm
will end up in safe hands.

"You said there were two things."

"Well remembered and from your point of view this second is the most important."

"Well?"

Damian slid forward to the edge of his couch and his voice became more urgent.

"McCann hates you. You need to know that since the night of Kenneth Ferguson's party he's assigned me to watch Teresa."

In an instant he was consumed with dread.

"You mean he knows about Newcastle, the hotel, I saw you there so he will think, think…"

"Calm down, I didn't tell him, not about that or about the night you visited his house. If he found out you would be in big, big trouble. You have to understand, McCann is possessed by jealousy. You may not know it but he already hated you because you knew Teresa before he did."

"But that was when we were only children."

"For him that makes no difference. When he's drunk he rants and raves about how he saw something between you two at Kenneth's party and he's convinced it's connected to when you knew each other in the past. Then there's the card game."

"But I lost."

"Not in his eyes."

"Eh! How does he work that one out?"

"Look at it from his perspective. Because you lost at the card game you left Ireland and went into exile. There, you won fame and fortune and returned triumphant. McCann hates that and above all hates that he was the instigator of the whole caboodle. For him the worst thing his enemy (and believe me when I say that's how he sees you), the worst thing his enemy can do is to prosper and let me tell you, McCann is not the sort to lie down under a perceived injustice. He's out to get you and he will."

"So what do I do?"

"From where I sit it's as clear as day; you play along, do as you're told and then you disappear from the scene. I happen to know this first trip is a dummy run. You go but you don't come back. That way you remain in the clear. Out of sight and you're out of mind. That's the way it works with McCann. Believe me – no one knows how he ticks better than I do."

"Why are you telling me all this; why let me in on all their inner secrets?"

"Let's just say I've had enough of McCann and particularly that bastard of a father of his, that Piggy. I'm getting out, going to America: I have family and friends there. I've had enough of the McCanns and this whole country. I want to make a clean break from it all."

Fair enough he thought. Damian and he were singing from the same hymn sheet. He had a thought.

"What about the money?"

"Up to you, but if you want my advice, I'd leave it alone. That way you wipe the slate. Take it and you only give McCann reason for getting back at you."

It made sense

"There's just one thing more."   Damian reached forward, picked up the shoes, stood up then bending forward looked him full in the face, narrowed his eyes and his voice was suddenly urgent and filled with menace.   "McCann must never find out about any of this.   If ever you…"

"No need for threats.   You can rest assured that this stays between us.   No one else will ever know."

He meant what he said.

CHAPTER TEN

"He seems to have some hold over Kenneth Ferguson."
Damian's observation nagged him.   What was the connection?
Paul would have known.   Curiosity willed this cat.   Where could
he find out?

The rent was due again. So a dander over to old man
Ferguson's was in order.   Having recovered from the effects of
the explosion, the cane was un-necessary but he determined to
affect it anyway: attendant sympathy might make any probing
more tolerable.   The last time he had called the only response to
his knocking had been the barking of dogs so he had posted the
rent through the letter-box.   This time surely she would be there
and he might just be able to manoeuvre some time with her alone.
Sarah Patterson would be the one to turn to.

The early morning sun was beginning to glow.   In the
fields, cows and sheep grazed, ambled lazily or lay down exuding
an impressive lack of aspiration.   Sod off human they projected:
we care not about you, your father or your brother.   One from the
field stared at him with the detachment he felt only contempt could
have bred.   One day human, one day we'll see what we'll see.
Instinctively he raised his cane, marched forward aggressively and
whacked the beast full on the snout, causing it to shake its head,
turn and pad disdainfully away.

He felt good.

Sarah Patterson answered the door and he followed her into
the back kitchen.   She appeared pre-occupied, not as friendly and
open as when they had first met, and he was soon privy to the
reason why.   Old man Ferguson looked now the eighty-plus he
must have attained.   His shirt collar was too large, his whole

frame appeared shrunken and the hand he extended for the money trembled.

"Sit yerself down."

The voice was as potent and commanding as ever, and beneath the tufted eyebrows his eyes had lost none of their blaze.

"Ye'll take tea."

He acquiesced and Sarah obliged.   The cup and saucer rattled alarmingly when the old man accepted them, but he took his time, drank deeply, and then quietened all in his lap.

Time steals.

"So," the blue eyes probed, "Ye've lost yer father and a brother."   A pause, then, "True grief will be yours if ye ever lose a child."   Another pause to allow the effrontery to fester before: "I take it yer still not converted to the benefits of joining.   Ye'd find comfort in the Church – or the Orange Lodge."

"Some might.   Many I suppose do, but not me.   I prefer to serve my suffering time in solitude."

He was determined not to huff.

"And yer sister marrying a Catholic; does that cause you to suffer – in solitude?"   Sarah looked cross and the old man smiled. "No need for you to ruffle yer feathers," he said softly, "let's see how he stands on his own two feet."

He was conscious this was another of those significant moments when invariably he could be counted upon not being among the counted.   This time it was different: he was leaving and you could push a man, even this one, too far.

"I do no suffering for my sister and Eamonn Maguire.
Those two love each other in a true and brave fashion that points
the way forward and shows that tribal allegiance can be conquered
and bigotry defeated."

His voice was shaking but he forged ahead, sustained by an
emotional uplift he had never experienced nor ever dreamed he
could achieve.

"What makes me suffer is the hatred, the prejudice, the
shooting, bombing and the needless death.   When I see love in
life, then I rejoice."

A silence ensued and then a still small voice.

"What do ye think of that, Sarah?"

"You know what I think."

"Aye, I do that lass; I do that."

Their eye contact excluded him and the whole world.   Then
grunting with effort the old man launched himself from his chair
and stood tottering slightly, arms extended, both hands clasping his
prop, his walking stick.   Sarah too had stood up and was hovering
close.

"Don't fuss woman, I can manage.   I'm off out round the
yard.   That was a fine speech.   At least some of your opinions do
ye credit."

He shuffled away then stopped and turned.

"That other brother of yours; I hear he's made of the right
stuff."

Christ, just what did that mean?   In an instant he was on the defensive.   For weeks now Sam and what he had done had ground round and round in his head, till eventually the groove had worn smooth and purchase almost ceased.   Now this from Stanley Ferguson flushed all back.   What did he know?   What if he knew…?

"I'm sorry I…"

"I mean he joined – the UDR.   Yer brother's prepared to make a stand, to do something, to do what's right.   What about you, eh?   Yer an able man when it comes to words," he raised the walking stick and shook it in his direction," but what kind of a man are ye when it comes to deeds?"

Not waiting for a reply, Stanley turned his back and scuffled off.   Just as well for he had nothing to respond.   He had no deeds and he had neither the energy nor the inclination to explain that his only response would be to try his best to forget.   Not forgive, that he would not, could not ever do.   No more than he could stop himself thinking murderous thoughts and entertaining fantasy, violent revenge, but to translate this into deeds – never.   It was not in his nature and never could be.

"He's dying, James."

"A dying breed," was the response he regretted the moment the impulse spilled.

Sarah, her hands covering her face was convulsed with grief. He stepped forward compelled to wrap her in his arms, then halted.

"I'm so sorry, I didn't mean to sound callous.   Forgive me."

From her smock pocket she delved for a handkerchief and pressed it to her eyes.

"I understand," she sniffed then continued. "You, everybody, you only see his worst side – the side he chooses to present. It's all pretence – he's really not like that, not like that at all." She blew her nose, then: "He enjoys provoking people, everybody, and he's at it all the time, all the time, prod, prod, and prod again. It's his way of annoying anyone and everyone, to invite retaliation so he can provoke them even more. He just loves to make people angry and he's been like that for as long as I've known him. And he doesn't pick and choose; he's that way with everybody."

Sarah smiled fondly.

"It's his way of, of testing people's mettle, seeing what they're really made of I suppose. The trouble is," she stared at the handkerchief, folded it and then tucked it away, "the pretence has taken him over, become a way of life, one he could no longer shed even if he wanted to. And the certainty is only an act. When you really know him as I do, then you find he is as full of doubt as anyone; he just doesn't think it's manly to let it show. All that stuff about joining is only a load of huff and puff. At the end of it all he's as full of contradiction as the rest of us."

She smiled again.

"From his earliest years he screamed at the world, *Stanley will fight and Stanley will be right.* And no-one ever took him on and they certainly won't now, now that he's in his final thrashings." Her voice broke. "Now he's getting weak and frail they think he deserves sympathy and he hates that. He's impossible."

"And you love him."

She nodded.

"Sarah, before I go there's something… Perhaps you can help."

"Try me."

"What hold does Kevin McCann have over Kenneth Ferguson?"

"She hesitated, then, "Can I trust you to keep a secret?"

"Trust me, you can."

"It's really very simple. They're brothers – twin brothers."

PART SEVEN

RESOLUTION

CHAPTER ONE

Sarah told the tale concisely and without embellishment. As a young man, Stanley Ferguson had made pregnant the twins' mother – a Catholic girl and a servant on the farm. When the pregnancy became evident a farm-hand, Barney McCann was persuaded to marry her and as a sweetener the young couple were given free accommodation above a cobbler's premises the Ferguson's owned in town. McCann proved to have a shrewd business head and he made the most of the opportunity and soon opened a shoe shop and was on his way. Stanley was already married but his wife was sickly and they had no child, so when the boys were born it was decided the Fergusons would keep one and the McCann's would have the other.

"Who decided?"

"Stanley's father, that's who, the man was a complete tyrant. He ruled the farm with a rod of iron and woe betide anyone who stood in his way. The stubborn, contrary Stanley you see today came into being as a direct result of his relationship with his father."

"You knew him?"

"I did, yes. When Stanley's wife died he brought me to live with him on the farm. It caused a bit of a stir in those days and still does in some quarters. We had been seeing each other for years in secret but Stanley insisted it all be brought out in the open. His father ranted and raved; it was their last fight. Stanley won."

"That would help explain his taunt about me being my da's man."

"True – he always has a go at the male of the species in that way.   For him it's a part of the test."

"Did I pass?"

"With Stanley no one passes."

"Except for you," he could not resist, "and what about marriage; he's never offered…"

Her face calm, Sarah stared at him.   He felt himself blushing.

"I'm sorry.   That was uncalled for, please forgive me." *Change the subject you fool!*   "You were saying: about Kenneth and Kevin."

"Right, all was to be kept secret but then Barney McCann let the cat out of the bag.   He and his son got drunk one night and Barney blabbed the whole story.   Kevin confronted Kenneth who went to Stanley who owned up.   As far as we know it's all still in the family.   Come to think of it, it's not a good idea to reveal all of this to a writer.   I take it I can trust you to keep mum.   You'll not – what's the word – plagiarise, that's it, any of what I've told you and put it in some story?"

"Who do you think I am?   Of course not; you can trust me." A slide off this area was imperative, so: "The other son; the one who was killed in a tractor accident.   He was…"

"Harold was our son, Stanley's and mine."

"But he was – you must have known Stanley some time before."

"I knew him well before the birth of the twins.   I was the district nurse and was as they say 'in attendance' at their birth.

All was carried out on the farm, partly to keep the secret and also because hospital births were not so common in those times. Mary, Stanley's wife died shortly after. Local gossip put her death down to problems linked to child bearing. We never bothered to contradict the rumours. Anyway, Stanley has always been above all that. Let people say what they damn well please has always been his attitude.

"She had been a school-mistress and had never taken to life on the farm; she had been sickly for years. There was the question of who would look after the children. Stanley was an only son, his parents had died, as had mine – I was an only daughter. At the time it seemed the right and reasonable thing to do and so it has proved and I have never regretted giving up my career and home, and moving here to start all over again."

"What about, what about when, when…"

"When Stanley dies, you mean."

"Well yes, what will happen then?"

"Stanley has left me the house and he will have seen I'm well provided for."

"How do you… I mean you've no…"

"Legal rights; not being married you mean." She smiled. "I guess there's nothing for it but to trust Stanley's word."

"I'm sorry, I didn't mean to…"

"You're forgiven."

"You're an extraordinary woman, Sarah Patterson." He held her gaze, then: "Just one question. A cheeky one, so you do not have to answer if you don't want to."

"Don't worry, I won't."

"Alright then; what does Kenneth have to say about all this?"

"You mean me and his father.   The house: inheritance, that sort of thing."

"That's it."

"Kenneth doesn't mind.   In many ways he's his own man and like his father he ploughs his own furrow.   Yes they had their rows, Stanley and he in the past.   I did what I could to act as go-between and as the years went by, things calmed down.   Kenneth has his faults, but then so do we all.   He never liked farming and he's gone and made his own way in the world, made his own money and built his own home.   You've seen it so you know it could not be more different.   This farmhouse means nothing to him.   No it's not Kenneth who concerns me."

"Who then?" he asked slyly, knowing the answer but wanting her to continue talking so he could snort up any grains of information in the process.

"Kevin's the one; Kevin and that father of his.   Piggy McCann has turned out to be a real scoundrel and his influence on Kevin has spread like a cancer.   Watch those two.   Piggy has convinced Kevin he's been given the wrong end of the stick, that he's the victim of an injustice, so now he's filled him with resentment and convinced him he's been ousted while Kenneth has been nurtured in his place.   Kevin believes the treatment he received and is receiving is second-rate and to be fair he has a case. Stanley would be the first to admit he's made mistakes in the past but he's done what he can to make amends and believes now the past should be buried and all forgiven and forgotten.   That's not the way Kevin sees it and behind him he has Piggy, pouring fuel on the flames."

"How do you know all this?"

"Kevin's been here; made a scene." Suddenly her eyes dropped tears and she groped for her handkerchief. "Stanley's too old to cope with all this now. He thought he had moved on, but the past has come back to haunt him and he's scared because he knows the world as it is now will be against him, knows there would be little or no sympathy for his side of things. Any road, he no longer has the stomach or the strength for all the confrontation. Kevin on the other hand, with Piggy pulling the strings, believes his time is come. He wants the farm, says it's his by right of birth and has made it clear he's prepared to contest any will that denies him what is rightfully his.

Tears were flowing freely now. She pressed the handkerchief to her eyes and sighed deeply.

"Stanley and I, we've put so much of our energy into this place. It's so peaceful here. All we wanted was to be left alone to enjoy our time together and now all we can see ahead is trouble and more trouble. What's to come of it all? It's broken Stanley's health and destroyed our peace of mind."

"Look, I'm sorry. I know the suggestion will probably offend you, but surely… Well, somebody has to say it. I mean living together as you and Stanley do is fine with me. As far as I'm concerned it's a brave and honourable set-up but you could solve the problem with Kevin if, well if, you and Stanley married. Surely that would…"

"No it wouldn't."

"Why would it not?"

"It couldn't solve anything because it's not possible."

"I don't understand."

"Because I'm married already; I was when Stanley and I first met."

He stared at her and shook his head. Sarah's tale had more twists and turns than a country lane.

In matter of fact terms she told how shortly after qualifying as a nurse she had met, fallen in love, married and set up home alongside a man she expected to be her partner for the rest of her life. In a short time he proved to be a drunken abusive womaniser she quickly lost all love and respect for, so she left him and managed to leave the town they lived in, find a new job and manage on her own. Shortly after she and Stanley met. There had been no divorce and she never wanted any contact with the man who never made any attempt to find her. Still, after all these years she had no wish to see him and wished only for their past together to be dead and buried. Under the circumstances it was impossible for Stanley and herself to marry. It was out of the question.

He left, angry and exasperated. What a mess the whole thing was. Anyway what had it all to do with him? The sooner he was away and out of it the better. *All we want is to be left here together to enjoy the peace and the quiet.* Sarah's words: Ulster's lament.

He slashed with his cane at a tall hedge plant. All he wished for now was to turn his back and rid himself of the whole sorry mess of their troubles and The Troubles. "Sod off!" he snarled and raised his cane at a cow appraising him over the hedge but for all the notice the creature took he might as well have been shouting at a cow in a field.

He moved and the cow mooed.

Opening his front door he was chilled at the sight of a suitcase standing in the hallway.   Surely not…   On top was a sheet of paper.   On tip-toe he made his approach, aware of the ridiculous nature of his behaviour.   What could it possibly achieve more than a more balletic propulsion skywards?

Not touching it, he read the typed instruction:

INSIDE YOU WILL FIND A SMALLER SUITCASE.

INSIDE THAT IS YOUR TICKET.

YOU LEAVE THE AIRPORT TOMORROW AFTERNOON.

STAY TONIGHT AT YOUR MOTHER'S HOUSE.

LEAVE AT 10 AM EXACTLY.

A CAR WILL PICK YOU UP ON YOUR WAY TO TOWN.

Kenneth: he would have a key to the bungalow!   So, TOMORROW!

Christ, he'd have to pack, get his affairs in order.   What affairs: there was only his car and a phone call would take care of that, so there was nothing to stop him just upping and going.   He clicked open the suitcase and hefted out the one inside.   It felt weighty and inside he found a pristine pair of black shoes.   As directed he retrieved the ticket and found attached to it a slip of paper.

YOU WILL BE MET AT THE AIRPORT.

THE TRAVELLERS' CHEQUES

ARE IN A POCKET IN THE SUITCASE.

They were too: four thousand pounds worth. Damian had said it would be better to have nothing to do with the money and he still thought that the best course of action. He found a pen and wrote *Kenneth Ferguson - No thanks* on the front of the envelope. He sealed it and left it propped prominently on the table in the kitchen.

He had much to do.

CHAPTER TWO

At their mother's he was met at the door by a dishevelled and unshaven Sam. This was a confrontation he had done his best to sidestep. He stepped inside, placed his suitcase at the foot of the stairs and hung up his overcoat.

Summoning a brisk no-nonsense manner he explained how he was going away and how staying the night here was more convenient for the lift he had arranged to take him to the airport in the morning. Sam showed little interest and seemed engrossed by some inner turmoil so to avoid addressing his brother's preoccupation he busied about opening curtains and windows, collecting and clattering dishes and cutlery in the sink and being, he realised, Jane-like. It needed doing: the house was a mess and smelled like it. All the while Sam sat in their father's chair, head back, eyes closed, hands, wrists and forearms resting on his belly, his thumbs not twiddling but making a steeple. He looked strangely at peace with himself in his own bubble of a world.

Then seemingly from no-where: "I've seen the light, James," his brother intoned solemnly, his eyes shut tight. "The light shed by our blessed Savour."

"Jesus Christ, Sam."

"Aye, that's the one. The son of God who became a man and suffered and died on the Cross so that sinners like me might be saved and have the gift of everlasting life."

He was serious.

"Would you like a drink Sam? What about a glass of whisky, or a beer. I know I could do with one, or both for that matter."

"I've taken the pledge.   No more alcohol will pass these lips.   You go ahead but you'll be drinking on your own."

Lord, this **was** serious. Fingers crossed he approached the cabinet where an almost full bottle of whisky lit up his evening. Thank God for small mercies.   He poured himself a large one, placed the bottle on the small fireside table between them and then cocked the glass in his brother's direction.

"Cheers Sam," then he gulped an inspirational draught.

Buddha like, Sam reacted not at all but head resting back and eyes still closed began speaking softly.

"A couple of Sundays ago, after a drinking spree the night before, I went for a walk and God directed my steps past the Gospel Hall.   I heard the congregation singing and you know what they sang?"

"Jailhouse Rock," he ventured inwardly while outwardly managing, "No I'm afraid I…"   And then Sam: mad, bad, Sam had him squirming as softly, but with feeling he crooned:

It is no secret

What God can do

What He's done for others

He'll do for you.

Stop.   Please make him stop!   But no, louder and with greater emotion:

With arms wide o-pen

He'll pardon you

It is no se-e-cret

What God can do.

A merciful silence, then: "And what did God do for me?"

"Landscape gardening," he had the wit not to say.

"He led the way into that Gospel Hall and there Tom Crooks, you remember Tom Crooks, still there after all those years, in God's name he welcomed me with open arms and made me realise that I was the prodigal son returned.   Bear with me."

Grunting, Sam propelled himself forward and reached over to a low bookcase from where he extracted a heavy black Bible. Then resting it on his knees he began clumsily to sift through the pages.

"Here we are: Ecclesiastes Three, Verse One."   Palm outwards he held up his hand.

To everything there is a season, and a time to every purpose under the heaven.   A time to be born, and a time to die; a time to plant and a time to pluck up that which is planted.

Closing the Bible, Sam hefted it then placed it carefully on the floor beside his chair.

"That was the very verse Tom Crooks was reading when I sat down in the back row of the Gospel Hall.   Don't you see; my season had come and it was my time to be born, for me to be born again. I've sat here yesterday and today thinking about it all and remember this," Sam leaned forward in his chair, "what God has done for me he could do for you too, James."

"Perhaps one day He will but for the moment let's just say my season is not yet upon me."

A vision of the young easily-led Sam formed in his head and as he looked across at his older easily-led brother he had to rein back an impulse to go over and give him a hug. He tuned in again to what Sam was saying "...make my confession and square things with my Maker, so now I must tell the truth about my crimes against men, because only the truly penitent can ever be granted the hope of everlasting life."

"You mean..."

"I've made up my mind and there's no point trying to change it." Sam inhaled deeply. "Tomorrow I'm going to the police station to give a statement confessing my part in the murder of Sean Maguire. Vengeance is mine says the Lord but my old self was deaf to that teaching. I've sat and thought and prayed for over a day now and I know for certain what I have to do. As a true born-again Christian it is my obligation to confess my sins not only to God but also to my fellow men."

Sam struggled out of his chair and standing tucked in his shirt and pulled up the waistband of his trousers.

"I'm glad ye called because I want ye to be the first to know and," he bent his arm, raised a finger and wagged it, "and no need to fret. Any part I got you to play I intend to leave out. I barged my way in and in no way were ye to blame for anything that transpired. The way I look at it, ye were only doing what ye could to help yer mess of a brother.　Any wickedness was mine and mine alone.　It's my cross and I'll bear it."

Sam held out his hand.　They shook.

"I'm off for a wash and a shave and then I'm going out to buy some groceries.　I'm on duty in a few hours.　A good auld fashioned fry-up would do us both the world of good."

Sam was as good as his word and in a short time the air was sizzling with the smell of bacon frying.　The meal was great but they ate in silence, each too preoccupied with their significant tomorrows to be capable of concocting any conversation.

"Good luck Sam," was the best he could do at their leave-taking and his brother was equally taciturn.　They shook hands, Sam wheeled round and he stood at the door and watched as the uniformed figure, his rifle hanging from his shoulder strap, ploughed down the path.　They should have embraced.　That was not their way but he regretted not making an attempt. Tomorrow Sam could be in prison while he...

Stepping back, he closed the door.

CHAPTER THREE

Blink by blink he emerged gradually from a dreamless sleep. He glanced at the clock on the mantelpiece: five past eight, he had been asleep for about two hours. Stretching his arms he sat up straight in the room's focal point - his father's chair.

On his left against the back wall the settee he, Jane and Sam would sit in, straight and well behaved in the presence of their father then nipping, scratching, punching and squealing when he was not there. Paul would be in the kitchen with their mother or perched on the wing of her chair. Above the couch *The Laughing Cavalier* surveyed the scene benignly.

"Bet I know who he is," Sam had gloated one day.

"Bet you don't," he could not resist.

"Bet I do."

"Who is he then then?"

"Frans Hals," Sam had swaggered. "I'm right da, aren't I?"

"You are spot on son," their father had twinkled. "Here's a tanner for ye. Yer big brother doesn't know it all, eh!"

Not then he didn't.

He panned round the room: the door, the sewing machine, his mother's chair, the shelf with the radio, the fire, the mantelpiece, the clock. He should have gone to visit her; perhaps he could go now as he had plenty of time. No what was the point, she would only make a scene and he could do without that, especially in a hospital where there was never any privacy. He would write her a letter when things settled down, that was the best way.

What to do?   It was too early to go to bed and anyway after his nap he did not feel in the least tired.   He could take a walk into town and clear his head.   It would be dark outside and anyway who was there to care about him and his comings and goings?

Pulling up his coat collar he flipped an old cap of Sam's on his head and pulled it down tight.   Then he had a thought and went to the suitcase, opened the smaller one, retrieved the shoes and put them on.   It would help wear them in for the journey ahead.   The wind was cold but at least it was not raining.   He set off, encountering no-one he knew and nothing of interest; just flickering from television sets in curtained front rooms.   At last free from the housing estate he set off down the road, and then turned left into the main street leading to the town centre. Apart from isolated twinges he had virtually no pain in his legs now and no need for his walking aid.   The new shoes squeaked a little but were gradually becoming more comfortable.   At this time of night there were few pedestrians and the road was almost free of traffic. Slowing his pace he commenced the gradual incline before the main shopping centre and when cresting the hill stopped for a breather and ran his eyes down the wide street.

A large car was swerving to a stop in front of McCann's pub in the centre of town.

In a trance he watched as first Damian emerged from the driver's side, then Kenneth Ferguson eased from the passenger's seat, stood up and shrugged his coat more snugly round his shoulders, before slamming shut his door.   Damian eased himself to the back door behind his, opened it and out stepped Teresa McCann.   Sliding across and through the door her husband Kevin lurched unto the pavement.   He could discern movement still inside the back of the car.   It appeared someone had been sitting on someone else's knee and they disengaged and a figure slid across the back seat and out onto the pavement.   He recognised her: it was the waitress who had been picking up the glass from the floor at Kenneth Ferguson's party: the one he still thought he knew from some place in his past.   Then all was explained.   The final passenger propelled himself across the back seat and out.   There was no mistaking that head of hair.   In a click it came to him: the woman was Paula, Snap's wife!

Damian eased shut first the driver's door, then the rear passenger's and started to follow the group into the pub.

A PRICE TO PAY

The words rang in his head and in an instant he understood. They were in it together, ganging up against him.   The whole thing was an elaborate pretence engineered to trap him in some elaborate plot of their contriving.   McCann would have been the instigator and he would have used his hold over Ferguson to recruit him to lend the scheme some weight and credibility.   Damian, he now realised would play any part McCann assigned him: all that about a rift between them had been pre-rehearsed.   And Teresa: the meeting at her home; the Slieve Donard; all of it monitored by Damian; why would she have accepted her role?   Had McCann some hold over her like he had with Ferguson?   Or did she hate him too?   Paula would have provided the link between Snap and McCann: all had their reasons to wish him harm.   Was it all because they were jealous of his success?   Did they hate him that much?   Would they be there in the morning to mock him or was their plan to send him off on their fool's errand and spin their fictional web further?   There were so many un-answered questions: who came up with the scam about the microfilm that most preposterous and paradoxically most ludicrously enticing element of the whole scheme?   Now he realised he would never know and neither knew nor cared any more to know.   He would take no further part in the plot.   The best ending was sometimes the most brutal one.   His mind made up and knowing what he must do, he swivelled round and set off back the way he had come.

Back at their mother's he went to the suitcase, replaced the shoes and packed all back as he had received it.   Then he walked the road back to the bungalow, encountering no-one on the way.   He still had the key, having intended to hand it to whoever would have picked him up for the journey to the airport.   Letting himself in he deposited the case where it had been left for him and placed the key on the floor beside it.   No note: just the money in the envelope he retrieved from the kitchen table and placed on top of the suitcase: he would simply exit and disappear precluding any opportunity for explanation.

Saying nothing would gift him the last word.

He stuffed his scant belongings into a plastic bag, had a quick scan of the scene and set off again.   No taxi: he wouldn't give Nosey the satisfaction; instead he would take the backroads, cross the fields and when away what he felt was far enough, he would thumb a lift or catch a bus heading for Belfast, the docks, a ship to the mainland and then…

Perhaps he would go to New York?

Who knows?

Who cares?

He hunched his shoulders, faced the road ahead, inhaled deeply and launched into his first step under soft rain falling.

Acknowledgements

My grateful thanks to the following works I relied on in researching my book.

T. Eagleton, *Heathcliff and the Great Hunger* (London, 1995); B. O'hEithir, *A Pocket History of Ireland* (Dublin, 1989); D.Kiberd, *Irish Literature and Irish History* from *The Oxford Illustrated History Of Ireland,* edited by R. F. Foster (London, 1989); B. Behan, *The Hostage* (London,1978); T. Hawkes, *Structuralism and Semiotics* (London,1988); A. N. Jaffares, *Anglo-Irish Literature* (London, 1992); general editor Seamus Deane, *The Field Day Anthology of Irish Writing* (Field Day Publication, 1991); J. Swift, *Gulliver's Travels* (London,1985); W. Chaigneau, *The History of Jack Connor* (1752); H. Fielding, *Joseph Andrews* (1742); T. Amory, *The Life and Opinions of John Buncle, Esq.*(London, 1756); B. Friel, *Translations* (London, 1981); V. Mercier, *The Irish Comic Tradition* (Souvenir Press Ltd,1991); S.Gupta, *Race in the Context of Joyce's Irishness and Bloom's Jewishness* (Bullan: An Irish Studies Journal, Autumn, 1994); L. Sterne, *Tristram Shandy* (London, 1978); A. Sanders, *The Short Oxford History of English Literature* (London, 1994); S. Deane, *A Short History of Irish Literature* (London, 1986); C. Johnstone, *Chrysal, or the Adventures of a Guinea* (New York and London, 1979); F. Sheridan, *Memoirs of Miss Sidney Bidulph,* (Dublin, 1761); T. Paine, *The Rights of Man* (London, 1963); H. Brooke, *The Fool of Quality; or, the History of Henry, Earl of Moreland;* (Dublin, (1765-70); O. Goldsmith, *The Vicar of Wakefield* (London, 1982); Anonymous, *The Triumph of Prudence over Passion* (Dublin, 1781); S Kilfeather, *Origins of the Female Gothic* (Bullan an Irish

Studies Journal, Autumn, 1994); R. Roche, *The Children of the Abbey* (W. Nicholson and Sons Ltd); T. Leland, *Longsword, Earl of Salisbury* (New York, 1974); S. O'Faolain, *The Irish* (London, 1947); Patricia Craig, *The Rattle of the North* (Blackstaff Press, 1992); S. Heaney, *North* (London, 1975); Dermot Bolger, *The Picador Book of Contemporary Irish Fiction* (Picador, 1993); E. Longley, *From Cathleen to Anorexia The Breakdown of Irelands* (Attic Press, 1990).

When Irish Eyes are Smiling Lyrics by Chauncey Olcott and Geo. Graff, Jr.; Music by Ernest R. Ball Copyright 1912 by M. Witmark & Sons, N.Y.

TRIO Poetry 1 Will Colhoun, Robert Johnstone, David Park (Blackstaff Press, 1980).

Made in the USA
Middletown, DE
18 September 2020